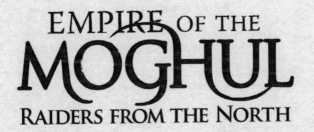

EMPIRE OF THE MOGHUL
RAIDERS FROM THE NORTH

ALEX RUTHERFORD

headline
review

First published in 2009 by HEADLINE REVIEW
An imprint of HEADLINE PUBLISHING GROUP

First published in paperback in 2010 by HEADLINE REVIEW
An imprint of HEADLINE PUBLISHING GROUP

3

Cataloguing in Publication Data is available from the British Library

ISBN 978 0 7553 4753 7 (B Format)
ISBN 978 0 7553 5654 6 (A Format)

Typeset in Bembo by Ellipsis Books Limited, Glasgow

Printed and bound in the UK by CPI Mackays, Chatham ME5 8TD

Headline's policy is to use papers that are natural, renewable
and recyclable products and made from wood grown in sustainable forests.
The logging and manufacturing processes are expected to conform to
the environmental regulations of the country of origin.

HEADLINE PUBLISHING GROUP
An Hachette UK Company
338 Euston Road
London NW1 3BH

www.headline.co.uk
www.hachette.co.uk

Sketch Map of Babur's World

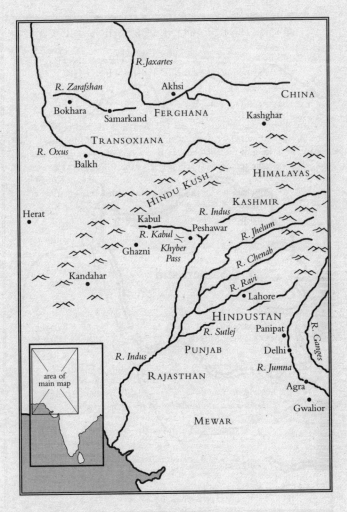

Samarkand

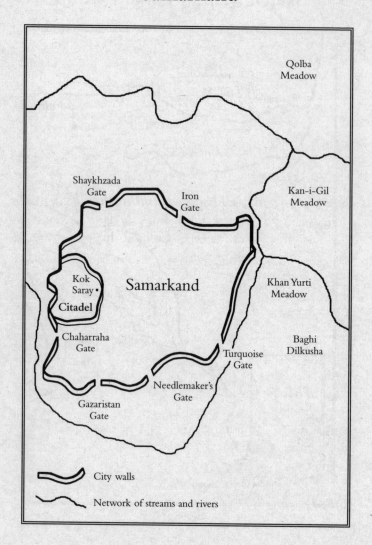

Qolba
Meadow

Kan-i-Gil
Meadow

Shaykhzada
Gate

Iron
Gate

Khan Yurti
Meadow

Kok
Saray
Citadel

Samarkand

Baghi
Dilkusha

Chaharraha
Gate

Turquoise
Gate

Needlemaker's
Gate

Gazaristan
Gate

City walls

Network of streams and rivers

Main Characters

Babur's parents, siblings, grandmother and uncle
Ahmed, King of Samarkand, Babur's uncle
Esan Dawlat, Babur's maternal grandmother
Jahangir, Babur's half-brother
Khanzada, Babur's older sister
Kutlugh Nigar, Babur's mother
Umar-Shaikh, King of Ferghana, Babur's father

Babur's wives
Ayisha, daughter of the chief of the Mangligh clan
Maham, Babur's favourite wife and mother of Humayun
Gulrukh, mother of Kamran and Askari
Bibi Mubarak, daughter of the chief of the Yusufzai clan
Dildar, mother of Hindal

Babur's sons

Humayun
Kamran
Askari
Hindal

Babur's cousins
Azar Khan, nobleman of Ferghana
Mahmud, Prince of Kunduz
Mirza Khan, chieftain of Ferghana
Tambal, nobleman of Ferghana

Babur's inner circle
Baburi, a former market boy and Babur's closest friend
Baisanghar, originally an officer of Samarkand, subsequently
    Babur's loyal commander and, even later, father-in-law
Kasim, one of Babur's political advisers, often used by him
    as an ambassador
Wazir Khan, milk-brother to Babur's father and Babur's guide
    and chief mentor in his childhood and early years as king
Abdul-Malik, a physician

Ferghana
Baba Qashqa, comptroller of the royal household
Baqi Beg, court astrologer
Fatima, chief waiting woman
Qambar-Ali, vizier
Rehana, an old woman whose grandfather rode with Timur
    to sack Delhi
Roxanna, concubine of Babur's father and mother of Jahangir
Walid Butt, Esan Dawlat's steward
Yadgar, Babur's favourite inhabitant of a Ferghana brothel
Yusuf, keeper of the treasury
Babur's tribal leaders

Ali–Dost, a chieftain from western Ferghana

Ali Gosht, Babur's master-of-horse and later chief quarter-master

Ali Mazid Beg, lord of Shahrukiyyah

Baba Yasaval, warrior from near Herat

Hussain Mazid, headman of Sayram and cousin of Ali Mazid Beg

Babur's chief enemy in Central Asia

Shaibani Khan, powerful leader of the Uzbek clans and blood enemy of Babur's people and all those descended from Timur

Persia

Shah Ismail of Persia

Mullah Husayn, Shiite mullah serving Shah Ismail

Turkey

Ali–Quli, master-gunner

Kabul

Bahlul Ayyub, grand vizier

Haydar Taqi, keeper of the Royal Seal

Muhammad–Muquim Arghun, chief of the Hazaras

Wali Gul, guardian of the Royal Treasuries

Hindustan

Buwa, mother of Sultan Ibrahim Lodi

Firoz Khan, Hindustani warlord

Gwalior royal family, owners of the Koh-i-Nur diamond, the 'Mountain of Light'

Rana Sanga, Hindu ruler of the Rajput state of Mewar

Sultan Ibrahim Lodi, ruler of the great Delhi Sultanate and
  overlord of Hindustan
Roshanna, Buwa's serving woman

Babur's ancestors

Genghis Khan
Timur, known in the West as Tamburlaine from a corruption
  of 'Timur-i-Lang', 'Timur the Lame'

Mountain of Light

I do not write this to complain; I have written the plain truth. I do not write to praise myself but to set down exactly what happened. In this history I have been determined to write truthfully about everything. As a consequence I have set down all that is good or bad I have seen of father, kinsman or stranger. Reader, pardon this . . .

Diary of Babur, Founder of the Moghul Empire

Part I

Timur's Heir

Chapter 1

Death Among the Doves

In a small dusty fortress in Central Asia in the summer of 1494, the baked-mud battlements, grey as elephant's hide in daytime, were pinkening before Babur's eyes with the sunset. Far beneath, the Jaxartes river gleamed a dull red as it flowed westward across the darkening plains. Babur shifted his weight on the stone step and returned his attention to his father, the king, who was pacing the fortress walls, hands clasped against the turquoise fastenings of his robes. His face was working excitedly as he launched into the story his twelve-year-old son had heard so many times before. But it was worth the retelling, Babur reflected. He listened carefully, alert for the new embellishments that always crept in. His lips moved with his father's when the king reached the climax – the one part that never changed, each of its grandiose phrases sacrosanct.

'And so it happened that our ancestor the great Timur – Timur the Warrior, whose name meant "Iron" and whose horses sweated blood as he galloped through the world – won a vast empire. Though he was so cruelly injured in his youth that one leg was longer than the other and he walked

3

with a limp, he conquered from Delhi to the Mediterranean, from wealthy Persia to the wildernesses along the Volga. But was that enough for Timur? Of course not! Even when many years were upon him, he was still strong and robust in body, hard like a rock, his ambition boundless. His final enterprise was ninety years ago against China. He rode out with the thunder of two hundred thousand horsemen in his ears and victory would have been his, had Allah not summoned him to rest with him in Paradise. But how did Timur, this greatest of warriors – greater even than your other ancestor Genghis Khan – do all this? I see the question in your eyes, my son, and you are right to ask it.'

The king patted Babur's head approvingly, seeing that he held his complete attention. Then he resumed, voice rising and falling with poetic fervour.

'Timur was clever and brave but, above all, he was a great leader of men. My grandfather told me that his eyes were like candles without brilliance. Once men looked into those slits of muted light they could not turn away. And as Timur gazed into their souls he spoke of glory that would echo through the centuries and stir the lifeless dust that would be all that was left of their bones on earth. He spoke of gleaming gold and shimmering gems. He spoke of fine-boned women whose black hair hung like curtains of silk such as they had seen in the slave markets of his capital of Samarkand. Above all he spoke of their birthright, their right to be the possessors of the earth. And as Timur's deep voice flowed over and around them, visions filled their minds of what was theirs for the taking until they would have followed him through the burning gates of hell.

'Not that Timur was a barbarian, my son.' The king shook his head vigorously so that the fringe he liked to leave hanging from his maroon silk turban swung from side to side. 'No. He was a cultured man. His great city of Samarkand was a place of grace and beauty, of scholarship and learning.

4

But Timur knew that a conqueror must let nothing – no one – stand in his way. Ruthlessness ruled his soul until the job was done and the more who knew it the better.' He closed his eyes, picturing the glory days of his magnificent ancestor. He had worked himself into such a lather of pride and excitement that beads of sweat were bursting out on his forehead. He took a yellow silk scarf and mopped it.

Exhilarated as usual by the images his father had conjured, Babur smiled up at him to show he shared the same joyous pride. But even as he watched, his father's face changed. The fervent light in his dark eyes faded and his expression grew despondent, even brooding. Babur's smile faltered. His father's story usually finished with this paean to Timur, but today the king continued, his tone bleak, the vibrancy gone.

'But I – descendant of the great Timur though I am – what have I? Just Ferghana, a kingdom not two hundred miles long or one hundred wide. Look at it – a place of sheep and goats grazing in valleys ringed on three sides by mountains.' He flung out an arm towards the soaring, cloud-circled peaks of Mount Beshtor. 'Meanwhile three hundred miles to the west my brother rules golden Samarkand, while south across the Hindu Kush my cousin holds wealthy Kabul. I am their poor relation to be snubbed and despised. Yet my blood – your blood – is as good as theirs.'

'Father—'

'Even so, all we princes of the house of Timur,' the king interrupted, voice trembling with passion, 'what are any of us, compared with him? We squabble like petty chieftains as we struggle each to hold on to our own little scrap of his empire. I am as guilty as any of the others.' He sounded really angry now. 'If Timur came back today he would spit in our faces for the fools we are. We are so proud to call ourselves Mirza, "Offspring of the Amir", so eager to call him ancestor, but would he be so ready to acknowledge us? Wouldn't we have to fall on our knees and beg his forgiveness for dissipating our inheritance and forgetting our greatness?'

The king's strong hands gripped Babur's shoulders so hard it hurt. 'You are old enough now to understand. That is why I am telling you this. We owe Timur a debt. He was a great man, my son. His blood is your blood. Never forget it. Be like him, if you can. Live up to your destiny and let it be greater than mine.'

'I will try, Father . . . I promise.'

For a moment, the king's eyes searched Babur's face. Then, seemingly satisfied, he grunted and turned away. Babur sat very still. His father's unexpected passion had shaken him. As he digested what he had said, he saw that the sun was almost down. Like so many other evenings, he watched the jagged landscape soften in the dying light. The cries of boys herding their sheep and goats back to their villages came out of the gathering gloom. So did a gentle, insistent cooing. His father's favourite flock of white doves were fluttering home to their cote.

Babur heard a gentle sigh escape his father's lips, as if he acknowledged that life still held pleasures as well as disappointments. He watched the king take a swig of cooling water from the leather bottle dangling at his side and, his face relaxing once more into its usual good humour, turn and hurry along the battlements towards the conical dovecote high on top of the wall and partly overhanging the dry ravine below. His gold-embroidered red velvet slippers slapped against the baked-mud floor and his arms were already outstretched, ready to take his favourite doves in his hands and caress their plump throats with the tenderness of a lover. Babur couldn't see the attraction. Stupid little birds. The best place for them was plucked and poached in a sauce of pomegranates and crushed walnuts.

Babur's mind returned to Timur and his marauding soldiers. What would it be like to feel that the whole world was

6

yours? To take a city and have its king writhe in the dust at your feet? His father was right. How different it would be from ruling just this little kingdom of Ferghana. The petty politics of his father's court bored him. The chief vizier, Qambar-Ali, stank like an old mule in his sweaty robes. With his long yellowing teeth he even looked like one. And he was always up to something, whispering in his father's ear, bloodshot eyes swivelling to see who was watching. Timur would have sliced off the ugly fool's head without a moment's reflection. Perhaps, Babur reflected, he would do it himself when he eventually became king.

Soon it would be time to pray and then to go to the women's quarters to eat. He jumped down from the step. At that moment he heard a tremendous crack, the battlements shuddered beneath his feet and a few seconds later there came a dull crash. He put out a hand to steady himself and realised he could see nothing. What was happening? Was it one of the earth tremors that sometimes shook the castle? No, the noise was somehow different. As he gasped in shock his mouth drew in choking dust and his eyes streamed involuntary tears as they attempted to clear themselves. Instinctively Babur put up his hands to cover his face and head. As he did so, he heard swift-running feet, then felt strong arms grip him and haul him backwards. 'Majesty, you are safe.'

He recognised the deep voice. It belonged to Wazir Khan, the commander of his father's bodyguard. 'What do you mean . . . ?' It was hard to talk; his mouth was dry and gritty, and his tongue felt suddenly too large for it. His words sounded thick, incomprehensible, and he tried again. 'What's happened . . . ?' he managed. 'It wasn't an earthquake, was it?'

Even as he asked the question Babur forced his watering eyes to open and saw the answer for himself. A large chunk of the battlements where the dovecote had been had gone,

7

as if a giant hand had reached out to break the rim off a pie crust. Dried and fissured by the intense summer heat it had suddenly given way. The doves were fluttering in the air like snowflakes.

Babur wrenched himself from the tall soldier's protective arms and rushed forward. His stomach seemed to fall from his chest as he realised he could not see his father. What had happened to him?

'Majesty, please come back.'

A cold sweat broke on his brow as Babur worked his way along what remained of the ruined battlements and peered down into the ravine. Through the slowly settling dust he could just make out the remains of the wall and the dovecote, pulverised on the rocks. Of his father there seemed no sign. Then Babur saw his maroon turban suspended at a jaunty angle from the branch of a bush sprouting from a fissure in the rock. He must have fallen with the dovecote. He must be buried, injured, perhaps even dead, Babur thought, with a shudder.

As he looked down, soldiers with flaming torches were running from the gate at the base of the fortress and scrambling down the rocks into the ravine.

'Hurry, you fools, hurry!' yelled Wazir Khan, who had come up beside Babur and again taken a protective hold of him. They watched in silence as, by the light of their flaring orange torches in the gathering dusk, the soldiers clawed through the rubble. One found a dead dove and tossed the limp little body impatiently aside. A kite swooped low and flew off with it.

'Father . . .' Babur could not stop the shivering that had seized his body. Down in the ravine as the men cleared the chunks of mud and stone he glimpsed what looked like a fragment of cloth. His father's robe. A little while ago it had been pale blue. Now it was stained purple with blood. A few moments more, and the soldiers pulled out his father's body.

To Babur it seemed as lifeless and broken as the dove's. The soldiers looked up at their commander high above them for a sign telling them what to do.

Wazir Khan gestured to them to carry the body into the fortress. Then he pulled Babur further back from the edge and gently turned him from the sight of the destruction below. His face was grim but also thoughtful as, for a moment, he looked down at Babur. Then he knelt and touched his forehead to the ground. 'All hail to Babur Mirza, the new King of Ferghana. May your father's soul fly like a bird to the gates of Paradise.'

Babur stared at him, trying to take in what he had just said. His father − so full of life just moments before − was dead. He would never hear his voice again or feel his warm hand on his head or be embraced in his great bear-hug. He would never again accompany him when he went hunting in the valleys of Ferghana, or sit close by him beside the campfire at night, listening as his men's singing mingled with the rising wind. He began to cry, silently at first, then aloud, convulsed by great sobs welling up from the pit of his stomach.

As he wept, doubt and uncertainty, as well as grief, engulfed him. He was king now . . . Would he live up to his father's hopes and his glorious ancestry? For some reason a leaner, older face with slanting cheekbones and cold, determined eyes 'like candles without brilliance' replaced his father's image in his mind. As it did so, he seemed to hear his father's much-repeated mantra: 'Timur's blood is my blood.' His own lips began to repeat it, softly at first but then with more conviction. He would make both Timur and his father proud. Pulling himself to his full height and wiping his tear-stained, dirty face with his sleeve, he turned. 'I must be the one to tell my mother what has happened.'

Exciting though he found Farida, his beautiful young wife, Qambar-Ali's lovemaking had been more perfunctory than usual. The vizier was preoccupied. The king's sudden and extraordinary death had left much for him to think about and little time if he wished to act. A twelve-year-old boy as king? Possibly . . . but, then again, possibly not. Splashing water hurriedly over his groin and pulling his navy brocade robes back round him, the vizier hurried from Farida's chamber without a backward glance.

As he passed through the fortress's interior passageways, lit by flickering oil lamps, he caught the sound of wailing coming from the royal harem. So, the official mourning had begun, led no doubt by Babur's mother and grandmother, formidable women, the pair of them. He would need to be wary of them. Neither would be so lost to grief that they would not be seeking to protect and promote Babur's interests.

The vizier approached the royal audience chamber to which he had summoned the other officers of state. As the two guards opened its green, leather-covered, brass-studded doors to allow him to enter, he saw that three were already there: Yusuf, the stout keeper of the treasury, the golden key of office dangling on its long chain round his jowly neck; Baqi Beg, the diminutive court astrologer, whose thin, restless fingers were twisting the beads of a rosary; and the wiry, beetle-browed Baba Qashqa, comptroller of the household. Only Wazir Khan was absent.

The ill-matched trio were sitting cross-legged on the red, richly patterned carpet beneath the empty throne. Without its occupant it looked a small, faded, insignificant thing, the gilt a little tarnished and the red velvet, gold-tasselled cushions shabby with use and age.

'Well,' said Qambar-Ali, looking round the assembled faces, 'who would have thought it?' He waited, wanting to gauge their views before he said more.

'It was the will of God.' Baqi Beg broke the silence.

'A pity you did not foretell what would happen. For once the stars kept their secrets veiled from you,' Baba Qashqa said.

The astrologer flushed angrily at the comptroller's spiteful words. 'God does not always wish a man to know his own destiny – especially a ruler who must be as a god to his people and act for them as well as himself.'

'I meant no offence, but if the king had foreseen his own death, he would not have left a twelve-year-old boy as his heir,' Baba Qashqa said slowly, and shook his head.

Qambar-Ali's pulse quickened. 'Indeed. The kingdom needs a strong, seasoned ruler to survive. Shaibani Khan and his Uzbek mongrels will be baying at our gates when he learns the news. He has sworn to build a tower from the bleeding, eyeless heads of all the princes of the House of Timur. A puny youth won't keep him out of Ferghana for long.'

The others nodded, all wearing melancholic expressions as if their only concern was the well-being of Ferghana.

'And it is not only the Uzbeks we must fear. Our late king made many enemies among his own family – his incursions westwards over the border into the lands of his brother, the King of Samarkand, will not have been forgotten.'

'Of course, the King of Samarkand is a great warrior,' Qambar-Ali said slowly. 'So is the Khan of Moghulistan.' His mind dwelled for a moment on the purple velvet bag plump with gold coins that the khan had pressed into his receptive hand during his last visit to Ferghana. He remembered his words: 'If Ferghana should need me, only send me word and I will come.' The khan would surely reward him generously for the gift of a throne.

'There is also the ruler of Kabul – he, too, is of the House of Timur, a cousin of our late king.' Baba Qashqa looked directly into the vizier's eyes. 'He would protect Ferghana . . .'

Qambar-Ali, bowing his head in courteous agreement,

11

resolved instantly that this very night he would send a messenger north-east through the mountains to the Khan of Moghulistan or the chance would be lost. 'We must be cautious and not hurry in case we stumble,' he said, with an air of deep thought. 'We need to take time to reflect and to consider the best interests of Prince Babur. The throne must be his when he comes of age. We should seek a regent from among our neighbouring rulers to keep Ferghana safe from its foes until then.' Not that Babur ever would mount the throne, he reflected inwardly. A little accident would not be long in happening. It would be so simple . . .

The four men sat up as Wazir Khan entered the chamber. He looked tired and the pink scar across his tanned face – the memento of a sword swipe a decade earlier that had also robbed him of the sight in his right eye – stood out livid and raw as if it had been received only weeks ago. 'Gentlemen, my apologies.' He touched his hand to his breast and bowed to Qambar-Ali in acknowledgement of the vizier's position as the chief among them. 'I have posted a double guard around the fort but all is quiet. The king's body is being prepared and everything is in readiness for the funeral tomorrow.'

'We are in your debt, Wazir Khan. I thank you.'

'You were speaking of appointing a regent for Ferghana?' Wazir Khan sat down beside Qambar-Ali and fixed on him his one eye with an unblinking intensity that the vizier resented.

'We were. Prince Babur is too young to bear the responsibility of government. And we face a threat from those dogs of Uzbeks.' At the mention of the Uzbeks, the vizier simulated spitting.

'It is true that the prince is young, but he is the king's only surviving son and has been reared since his earliest days to reign. It is his destiny, and what his father would have wished. Babur is brave, determined and learns fast. I should know. At the king's request, especially when it became clear that Babur would be his only heir, I spent much time instructing him in swordplay and archery, how to wield a spear and hurl a battleaxe. Babur is also astute beyond his years. Surely we five can guide him through the early days,' Wazir Khan said quietly.

'My dear Wazir Khan, if only it were that simple.' The vizier smiled. 'If these were peaceful times your plan would be suitable, but the Uzbeks' ambitions know no limits. As soon as they hear that the King of Ferghana has died leaving his kingdom to a mere boy they will be upon us, ripping out our entrails and raping our women.'

'What do you propose, Vizier?'

'We should ask one of our dead king's relations to hold the throne in trust until Prince Babur comes of age. The question is, which one . . .'

'I see. Well, I am just a simple soldier and still have much to do tonight. Your heads are wiser than mine. May God guide you to the right decision for our kingdom.' Wazir Khan rose, bowed, and walked slowly from the audience chamber. As soon as he was outside he quickened his pace, making for the royal harem across the courtyard on the far side of the fortress.

• ◆ •

Babur was sitting beside his mother, Kutlugh Nigar, letting her find comfort by running her fingers through his long dark hair. As, haltingly, he had broken the news of the tragedy, she had gone so pale he was afraid she might faint, and her eyes had stared at him blankly, like a blind woman's. As the reality penetrated, she had begun to rock back and forth and a thin, terrible wail of grief had risen from deep inside her, gathering in intensity. Though the king had had concubines, she had been his only wife and the bond between them strong.

He watched his grandmother, Esan Dawlat, pluck at the

strings of a lute. The sad notes echoed and soared around the chamber like a bird seeking sanctuary. Her white hair, thick as it had been when she was still a girl, or so she liked to boast, hung in a plait over her shoulder. Her raisin eyes were red rimmed but she had mastered herself. After all, she had told Babur, determinedly staunching her tears, she was a *khanim*, a direct descendant of Genghis Khan, the man they called the Oceanic Ruler who, two hundred years before Timur, had plundered half the known world.

As Babur watched his grandmother's face he recalled her constant arguments with his father over who had been the greater warrior – Genghis Khan or Timur. Esan Dawlat had never ceased recounting how Babur had been a large-headed baby, the labour long and agonising. Throughout it she had comforted her daughter with predictions that, like Genghis, Babur would be born clutching a blood clot – symbol of his warrior destiny – in his tiny fist. But she had been wrong. Nevertheless she would inevitably continue, 'May he still be a great ruler!'

As if she sensed his scrutiny, Esan Dawlat looked across at Babur and he saw in her eyes something he had not seen there before: uncertainty. She put the lute down. 'Khanzada, send for some iced sherbet,' she snapped, at her sixteen-year-old granddaughter.

Babur watched as his sister, tall and graceful, leaped to her feet to summon an attendant. As she reached the entrance of the room, where the light of the oil lamps was dimmest, she almost collided with Fatima, head attendant of the harem. Her broad, plain face was streaked with tears. 'Mistress,' she began, before Khanzada had a chance to say anything about cooled sherbet, 'mistress, Wazir Khan begs an audience with your august mother and grandmother.'

'Can't it wait until morning? They are grieving and need to rest.'

'He says it is urgent.' Fatima put out her hand in supplication, as if pleading his cause.

Khanzada looked at her mother and grandmother, who exchanged a glance. Then Kutlugh Nigar said, 'We will see him. Babur, leave us, please.'

'But why? I should stay.'

'Do as I say.' His mother sat up.

'No,' said Esan Dawlat, 'he is the new King of Ferghana. Anything Wazir Khan has to say affects him more than any of us. Let him stay.'

Kutlugh Nigar glanced at her son's earnest young face, the determined set of his jaw, and nodded. The three women pulled their veils across the lower part of their faces and composed themselves, the old woman standing in the middle, her daughter and granddaughter at either side. Babur rose and stepped away from them. At his grandmother's words, something within him had changed. He was apprehensive but also excited.

Wazir Khan stooped beneath the low lintel and prostrated himself before them. 'Forgive this intrusion at so late an hour, Majesties.'

'What is it?' Above her veil, Esan Dawlat's shrewd eyes scanned his face.

'It concerns His Majesty.' Wazir Khan glanced for a second at Babur in the shadows. 'It is not safe for him here. Even as we speak, men are plotting for their own gain to take the throne from him.'

'You must speak more clearly. Who is plotting?' demanded Esan Dawlat. Her colour had risen and rough red patches stood out on her high cheekbones.

'We trust you,' Kutlugh Nigar said, more gently. 'You were the king's most loyal commander. More than that, your own mother suckled my husband as a baby, making you milk-brothers, bound by ties as deep as blood. In the days ahead I look to you to honour that bond . . . to protect my son

15

as his own father would have done . . . Please, speak frankly. What have you heard?'

'Men of a dark temperament, impatient and seditious, scheme against you. The vizier and the other members of the royal council plan to offer the throne to another – they think I caught only the end of their conversation but, concealed outside, I heard it all. They claim it is for the good of the country, that your son is too young to reign and that chaos will descend on Ferghana if they do not appoint a regent from outside until he comes of age. But they have all been bought long since by our neighbouring rulers. Each will promote his own paymaster. There will be civil strife, and all of their making. Because of their greed, rivals will battle for the throne, sowing the seeds of blood feud after blood feud. And whoever emerges the victor, your son will not live long. He will always be a threat – until he is dead.'

'That is impossible. The lives of Timurid princes are inviolable under our code of honour . . .' Kutlugh Nigar's voice faltered.

'What must we do?' Esan Dawlat gripped Wazir Khan's arm. Despite her skinny frame there was a martial force about her. She had Genghis Khan's spirit as well as his blood.

'Yes, what must we do?' Babur stepped out of the shadows. His face, in the flickering light of the oil lamps burning in a niche in the wall, was set and determined.

'We must be quick. We must be decisive,' Wazir Khan said shortly. 'Tomorrow, after His Majesty your father's funeral, we must immediately declare you king, here in the royal mosque within the fortress. Once the mullah has read the sermon naming you in the sight of God as the king, anyone who challenges you will be a traitor. And we must have our supporters around us as witnesses. My guards are loyal. So, too, will be many of the nobles of Ferghana – especially if you promise to reward their loyalty.'

'Fetch me paper, ink and quill,' Esan Dawlat requested of

her granddaughter. 'We will not spend this night in mourning, lest our indolence brings even greater woes upon us. I know those we can rely on and those who are untrustworthy and deceitful. People think my old eyes and ears notice nothing but I see what goes on. I won't trust a scribe to write letters such as these, I will do it myself. Wazir Khan, you will make sure that each reaches its destination safely. If anyone dares enquire what they are, tell them they are invitations to the funeral feast. That is partly true, but they will also be invitations to the ceremony in the mosque that will serve as Babur's coronation. I am summoning every trustworthy chieftain who lives within half a day's hard ride here to Akhsi. I will ask them to make their way secretly and silently to the mosque as soon as the funeral feast has begun. Babur, sit by me and hold an oil lamp close.'

As the hours of night drew on and the fortress fell silent around them, Babur looked on as the old lady wrote and wrote, pausing only to sharpen her quill and to call for more ink. It was extraordinary, he thought, how much she knew of the blood rivalries and bitter enmities but also the complex marriage links and deep personal loyalties between the clans that went back almost to the days of Genghis Khan. For the first time he felt grateful to her for all the hours she had forced him to spend learning who among the tribal chiefs were friends, who were foes and – most important of all – why. Watching the thin set line of her mouth, he was glad that she was his ally, not his enemy.

As every note was written – the Turki script sprawling over the paper – it was folded, sealed with red wax and handed to Wazir Khan to be entrusted to one of his men. Outside, the courtyard echoed to the sound of departing hoofbeats. Only when the call to prayer rose through the early-morning mist did Esan Dawlat finally lay down her pen.

Chapter 2

First Blood

Babur watched from his horse as the green-grey jade sarcophagus containing his father's body was borne into the tomb by eight of Wazir Khan's guards. Thick sheepskins on their shoulders cushioned them against the hardness of the stone but the coffin was a mighty weight. Sweat poured down their wind-tanned faces and one man stumbled, almost losing his hold. There was a gasp from the assembled onlookers – it would be a dreadful portent if the sarcophagus should fall to the earth. Babur's stomach tightened and he glanced at the vizier a few feet away, but Qambar-Ali's tortoise face was impassive.

'Careful, man, you carry our king.' At the bite in Wazir Khan's voice, the guard steadied himself, rebracing his shoulder to the burden, and the pall-bearers shuffled slowly into the passageway sloping down to the burial chamber in the heart of the tomb.

Babur's father had long ago planned his mausoleum. Babur had been just a baby, mewling in the arms of his big-breasted wet-nurse, when the king had summoned stonemasons and craftsmen from across Ferghana and beyond. Under his personal direction they had laboured on the banks of the Jaxartes river a mile and a half or so west of the fortress of Akhsi to create a smaller version of the great Timur's resting place in Samarkand. Now the tiles on the egg-shaped dome, bright aquamarine counterpointed with rich cobalt blue, sparkled in the June sunlight. His father would have been proud, Babur thought, and at the idea a half-smile crossed his tense face.

As the sarcophagus disappeared from his view, a great wailing rose from the crowds – from courtiers and chieftains in silken robes to simple herdsmen who stank of the animals they tended. Men of whatever condition in life rent their robes and sprinkled their turbaned heads with earth in a ritual that predated even Genghis Khan. What were they really thinking? How many were genuinely grieving like himself? Babur wondered. The chieftains had come in response to Esan Dawlat's summons but, when the time came, could he rely on them?

'Beware of those who seem to have no ambition – it is unnatural,' his father had always counselled him. Babur could not help glancing at Wazir Khan but felt instantly ashamed. With his father dead, after his mother and grandmother the tall, straight-backed soldier he had known all his life was the person he trusted most in the world. But what about that grey-bearded, pockmarked chieftain over there who had ridden so hard through the night from his mountain fastness that his robes were stained with his own and his horse's sweat? Or that buck-toothed one, with his head shaved in the old Mongol fashion, who had once been banished by his father for his scheming, deceit and greed and only recently forgiven? Esan Dawlat had been forced to take risks with her invitations: she had hoped to summon allies but, even at his age, Babur knew some might easily turn out to be jackals.

But all of this must wait. First his father must be laid to rest. As Wazir Khan, head bowed, held his jewelled bridle, Babur dismounted. Brushing away a tear he took a deep breath, ready to lead his father's favourite mullah and the most important mourners down into the crypt to pay their final respects. For a fraction of a second he longed for the soft touch of his mother's hand. But Kutlugh Nigar was waiting within the harem with his sister and grandmother, as was proper. Such occasions were not for women. They had made their silent adieus from behind screens carved high in the walls as the cortège wound down out of the fortress and on towards the banks of the swift-flowing Jaxartes.

As Babur approached the mausoleum's dark mouth, he saw that Qambar-Ali was already ahead of him, his brown robes swirling around him in his eagerness to be first. 'Vizier!' Babur's young voice was stern. It sounded good.

A faint twitch of irritation flickered over Qambar-Ali's face as he paused and turned aside. 'Majesty.'

'I will lead the mourners for my father. It is fitting.' Babur stepped past, making sure he trod hard on one of the vizier's felt-booted feet. That felt good too.

'Of course, Majesty.'

Babur gestured courteously to the mullah to join him. Qambar-Ali followed them down the low, dark passageway. The other royal council members came next, as their high office decreed they should. Yusuf, as treasurer, was carrying a bowl of gleaming gold coins to be laid at the foot of the sarcophagus. Baba Qashqa was bearing the huge red leatherbound journal in which, as comptroller of the royal household, he had recorded the minutiae of royal expenditure. This, too, would be left in the tomb to show that the king had gone to the next world with his affairs in order. Baqi Beg was cradling a crystal globe, the symbol of office of the court astrologer. Later, when the funeral was over, he was thinking, he would gaze into its shining depths and proclaim in a voice laced with sorrowful regret that the stars would not accept a mere boy as king.

Courtiers flattened themselves against the damp walls of

21

the crypt while others jammed into the passageway. The heavy air reeked of men's sweat. Babur's arms were almost pinned to his sides by the crush. As the mullah began to intone, softly at first but voice then rising and soaring around the chamber, fear prickled along Babur's spine. He was in a confined place. What if an enemy should choose now to strike? In his mind's eye bright red blood spurted from his slit throat and spilled on to the jade casket with its delicate tracery of tulips and narcissi. He heard himself trying to scream but managing only a blood-choked, bubbling gasp.

Faintness and nausea gripped him. Babur closed his eyes, struggling to master himself. Despite his lack of years and hairless chin, he must be a man. In a few hours, if he played his part courageously, he would be on the throne of Ferghana. *Timur's blood is your blood.* Silently he repeated once more the words his father had spoken so often and with such pride. As they echoed around his brain images formed in his mind of great and glorious battles fought long ago and of even greater conquests to come. Resolve steeled his blood – together with an anger that men should even think to deny him what was his.

Babur felt for the jewelled dagger his mother had pushed into his purple sash before he had set out and, as his fingers curled around the hilt, his breathing steadied. He looked speculatively around him. Wazir Khan's men were in the crypt. They would surely not allow an assassin to cut down their prince. Or would they? Scanning their faces, he realised how little he knew about any of the guards. Until yesterday he had taken their allegiance to his family for granted. Today all that had changed. His grip on the dagger tightened.

He focused his attention back on the mullah who, in his deep, sonorous voice, was chanting: 'May Allah be merciful. May the soul of our king, Umar-Shaikh, even now be in the gardens of Paradise. Let we who are left weep pearl drops of sadness but let us also rejoice that our king is drinking a pure draught of the waters of perfect happiness.' He came to an end and, folding his hands, backed away from the sarcophagus up the passageway, the spectators parting with difficulty to allow him through to the outside.

Babur closed his eyes for a moment and bade a silent farewell to the father he had loved. Then, holding back tears, he followed the mullah to emerge blinking into the sunlight. A whooshing sound, like a bird in flight, so close it almost grazed his left ear, startled him and he leaped backwards. Was someone out hawking? He looked around to see who would dare seek such sport while the King of Ferghana was being laid in his tomb. But there was no bright-eyed bird with jewelled collar and silken tassels dangling from its claws and shreds of prey in its curved beak. Instead an arrow, long-shafted, with blue-black feathers, quivered in the ground at Babur's feet. A few inches more and it would have pierced his body.

Shouts of alarm rose from the crowd and people were running for cover behind bushes and trees, staring up in alarm as if expecting the late-afternoon skies to darken with a shower of missiles. Chieftains were yelling for their horses and their men and reaching for their own bows and quivers. Almost instantly Wazir Khan was by Babur's side, shielding him with his body as his gaze swept the landscape. Out on the plains there were few hiding-places but a large rock or patch of scrubby bushes would be enough for a lone archer with skill in his hands and murder in his heart. With a curt motion of his gauntleted hand, Wazir Khan despatched a detachment of mounted guards in search of the would-be assassin.

'You must return to the palace at once, Majesty.'

Babur was still staring at the arrow. 'Look,' he stooped and wrenched it from the earth, 'there's something round the shaft.' He ripped off the coarse red thread that was securing a sliver of parchment and stared at the writing on it. The language was his own tongue of Turki, but the words leaped and danced before his eyes and for a moment he struggled to take in their meaning.

Wazir Khan took the paper from him and read the message aloud: ' "The mighty Shaibani Khan, lord of the world, presents his compliments. He wishes it to be known that before three full moons have come and gone he will take possession of the shit-hole that calls itself Ferghana and piss on its throne." '

'Bastard of an Uzbek,' the soldier said contemptuously, but Babur saw anxiety in his face.

'What is it?' The court astrologer came hurrying over and twitched the paper from Wazir Khan's fingers. Baqi Beg glanced at its contents and Babur heard his sharp intake of breath. The little man began to rock back and forth on the balls of his feet, hands clenched, his reedy voice rising in a wail: 'Shaibani Khan is coming, that *alachi*, that killer . . . I see it . . . He rides a black horse that smashes men's skulls to dust beneath its hoofs.' His wail turned to a shriek: 'Shaibani Khan is coming! Death and disaster ride behind him!'

Qambar-Ali, too, appeared by Babur's side, the treasurer and the comptroller close behind. All three were shaking their heads. 'The royal council must meet tonight after the funeral feast. Shaibani Khan does not make idle threats,' the vizier said. Yusuf and Baba Qashqa nodded vigorous assent. So, too, did Baqi Beg.

Wazir Khan made no such gesture of agreement. Instead he was staring at the vizier in a way that Qambar-Ali did not seem to relish. 'Vizier, perhaps you would do well to use your undoubted authority to calm the people. My guards are at your disposal should you require them to restore order.'

'You are right, Wazir Khan, I thank you.' Qambar-Ali inclined his turbaned head and hurried off, the other royal councillors in his wake. Babur could hear Baqi Beg still muttering about the apocalypse to come and felt a surge of irritation. Once he was crowned he would have a better man than that spineless worm as his astrologer. It was a mystery why his father had put up with him – indeed why he had ever chosen him. Perhaps Baqi Beg's family had done him some service he had felt he must reward.

Now that no further attack seemed imminent, men were emerging slightly sheepishly from their hiding-places, dusting themselves down. As the name of Shaibani Khan passed from mouth to mouth, Babur could hear some beginning to lament and moan as if they thought their doom already sealed. He glanced up at the sky to find it suddenly bloated with black clouds that had sailed in unnoticed over the plains and across the sun. Drops of rain splashed on his upturned face.

'Majesty.' Wazir Khan shook him again, so roughly this time that he thought his shoulder would jump from its socket. The soldier lowered his voice to an urgent whisper: 'This message from Shaibani Khan. How can it possibly be him? How could he have learned of your father's death so soon when he and his hordes are the far side of the mountains? No, it is a device, probably planned by that traitor Qambar-Ali. Perhaps he hoped to kill you. At the very least, he wished to strike panic into the hearts of the people so that they will less readily accept a youth as their king. But we must not be deflected from our plan. Ride for the fortress – stop for nothing and no one. As soon as I can, I will follow.'

The urgency in Wazir Khan's voice burned into Babur. He shouted for his horse and leaped into the saddle. For a second Wazir Khan gripped his bridle. 'Just a few hours more, Majesty, and all will be well,' he said. Then, signalling to a detachment of guards to escort Babur, he slapped the horse's creamy rump and it shot forward.

As he galloped over the tussocky grass and the rain fell more heavily, Babur glanced back over his shoulder. He could make out Qambar-Ali moving through the agitated people, arms raised. What was he really trying to do? Calm them or spread panic? Every instinct told him Wazir Khan was right:

the malevolent hand that had guided the arrow had not been an Uzbek one.

Digging into the deep pocket of his quilted overtunic Babur found the arrow he had stuffed into it. Taking his reins between his teeth for a moment, he pulled it out, snapped it in two and tossed it contemptuously to the ground. The pieces landed in a dark mound of sheep droppings.

• ◆ •

'How goes it with my son?' Kutlugh Nigar's face was drawn, her eyes pink with crying. From deeper within the harem, Babur caught the sound of muted weeping. All the women were observing the rituals of mourning for the dead king. Their gasps of sorrow sounded strangely in unison as if no woman dared to be first to stop.

'It goes well.' He had decided not to tell his mother about the arrow – at least, not yet. It was the first time in his life that he had kept something from her but the knowledge that he could have lost his life might frighten her.

'And your father. He is at peace?'

'Yes, Mother. We prayed for him and he sleeps in Paradise.'

'Then it is time to look to the living.' She clapped her hands and her waiting woman, Fatima, stepped forward from the shadows. In her arms were what looked like robes of yellow silk embroidered with flowers in gold and silver thread and a velvet cap of the same yellow, topped with a nodding peacock feather. Kutlugh Nigar took the garments from her, handling them reverently. 'These are the coronation clothes of the kings of Ferghana. Feel them, they are yours.'

Babur reached out to touch the gleaming folds and felt a quiver of pride. A king's robes – his robes. The silk was cool beneath his fingertips.

His reverie was broken by the clatter of hoofs. From the casement, Babur glanced down into the wet courtyard. Evening was already approaching and torches were being lit in readiness for nightfall. He saw Wazir Khan and the mullah ride in, their horses snorting and steaming. Soon the rest of the mourners would return to the fortress and it would be time to enact the plan that would give him the right to wear these robes. Babur looked at his mother. Her expression was anxious but her eyes were determined. 'Quickly,' Kutlugh Nigar said. 'We have little time. The robes will be too large for you but we must do the best we can.' With Fatima's help she wrapped Babur in them, tying the sash tightly to hold the voluminous folds together, then placed the cap on his long dark hair. 'See, my son? At this moment you are a prince but by the time the moon rises you will be a king.' She held up a mirror of burnished bronze, and Babur saw the shining reflection of a stern, slightly startled young face.

'Khanzada!' his mother called. She had clearly given thought to how Babur's introduction to the trappings of kingship should be managed. His sister had been waiting and listening in the corridor for her mother's call. Now she stepped quickly into the chamber. She was carrying a long, thin object wrapped in green velvet. Carefully she laid down her burden, threw back the velvet with a somewhat exaggerated flourish and pulled a curved sword from its scabbard.

Kutlugh Nigar took it and held it out to Babur. 'The sword of justice, the symbol of Ferghana – "Alamgir".'

He recognised the hilt, cunningly ornamented with white jade to resemble an eagle and studded with gems. The bird's spread wings formed the hand-hold and the head, with its glittering ruby eyes, protruded over the top of the hilt, glaring defiance at any would-be attacker. His father had shown it to Babur several times but had never permitted him to hold it. 'It feels good to have it in my hands for the first time.' He gripped the hilt and made a few tentative passes through the air.

'It was one of your father's greatest treasures. They say that the rubies were once Timur's and that he brought them back from Delhi. It is yours as Ferghana's new king.' Kutlugh Nigar knelt to fasten the jewelled scabbard at his waist, adjusting the steel chain on which it hung.

'Where's my grandmother?' There was no sign of Esan Dawlat and Babur would have been glad of her strength at such a moment. He would also have liked her to see him – to tell him he looked every inch a king.

'She is praying. She says she will greet you when you are ruler of Ferghana.'

A servant entered and knelt. 'Wazir Khan begs leave to enter, Mistress.'

Kutlugh Nigar nodded. She and Khanzada had barely pulled their gauze veils over the lower half of their faces before he was in the room. Babur noticed that, for once, he did not prostrate himself – the business in hand was too urgent for such niceties. The tall soldier's gaze swept over Babur in his robes of state and he nodded his approval. 'Majesties, the mullah is ready and my men are prepared.. But, even as we speak, Qambar-Ali is preparing to address the mourners at the funeral feast. He will tell them that the kingdom is in peril and that the prince is too young to rule. He will urge that another prince of the House of Timur be appointed regent. Last night one of my patrols intercepted a treasonous message he sent to the Khan of Moghulistan, offering him the throne, and I have other evidence of the vizier's murderous deceit.'

'But we have time?' Kutlugh Nigar gripped Wazir Khan's arm tightly in a breach of the harem protocol.

'We have time, but the prince must come with me now, before Qambar-Ali suspects what we are about. He believes that the prince has returned to the harem to grieve with you.' He turned to Babur. 'Majesty, you must cover yourself.' He held out his dark, dust-stained riding cloak to Babur who hastily threw it around himself, his mother's deft fingers helping to fasten the metal clasps and pull the hood over the coronation cap with its waving plume.

Hand on his sword, Wazir Khan gestured to Babur to follow him out into the corridor. As he brushed past her, Khanzada touched her fingers to Babur's cheek. His sister's eyes above her veil were wide with apprehension.

Babur felt a mixture of exhilaration and nervousness. His life depended on what happened this evening. The vizier's guile was not to be underestimated. Wazir Khan, seeming to sense his anxiety, stopped for a second. 'Courage, Majesty, all will be well.'

'Courage.' Babur repeated the word to himself and ran his fingers over the hilt of his sword.

They walked swiftly through dark corridors and up winding, sharp-edged stairs, the light from oil lamps in niches casting grotesque shadows. The mosque was in the most ancient part of the fortress, hewn on the orders of Babur's ancestors from the rock of the cliff behind. The solid cave-like chambers would last for ever – unlike the fragile mud-baked battlements that had collapsed and carried his father to Paradise.

All was quiet as he followed Wazir Khan into the open and across a small courtyard to the entrance to the mosque. The rain had stopped and the moon was rising between the clouds. By its cool, inconsistent light Babur could make out six of Wazir Khan's guards stationed outside. Silently they saluted their commander.

Signing to Babur to wait, Wazir Khan stepped through the pointed archway with its verses from the Koran carved above it. A few moments later he reappeared. 'Majesty,' he called softly, 'you may enter.'

Babur peeled off his cloak and stepped inside. Torches burned on either side of the *mihrab* facing towards Mecca where the mullah was already quietly at prayer. In the shadows Babur counted the kneeling forms of some twenty or so chieftains, every man prepared, for reasons of blood loyalty and tribal allegiance, to swear fealty to him.

Conscious of eyes upon him, judging him, Babur felt the

weight of the past – all those earlier kings of Ferghana – pressing down on him so heavily that his young shoulders seemed to ache, tensing as if under a great burden. Advancing into the centre of the mosque to the space outlined in black stone where his father the king had always prayed he prostrated himself, touching his forehead to the cool floor. As outside an owl screeched across the star-lit sky, the mullah began to preach the *khutba*, the sermon that would proclaim Babur King of Ferghana before God and the world.

• ◆ •

'And so you see, Excellencies, we have little choice in the matter.' Qambar-Ali's expression was one of dignified resignation. 'Even today, at the funeral of His Sacred Majesty, the Uzbek devil Shaibani Khan – may he rot in hell – dared to threaten us. We are but a small kingdom. Many covetous eyes are upon us, not just those of the vile Uzbeks. We need a strong, experienced man from among our neighbouring rulers, not a boy of tender years like Prince Babur, to govern and protect the realm. Who that should be we do not yet know . . . Later tonight the royal council will meet to consider the matter.'

Qambar-Ali gazed down at the flagstoned floor, listening to the anxious murmurings from the chieftains seated cross-legged on cushions at the low wooden tables around him. It was a pity his archer had failed to strike Babur down.

The other officers of state, Yusuf, Baba Qashqa and Baqi Beg, also watched and waited, each allowing his mind to dwell pleasurably on a future when his candidate would be regent and he would be rewarded accordingly.

'No, by God!' The rough voice of Ali-Dost, a chieftain from the west of Ferghana, broke into Qambar-Ali's wishful thinking. Ali-Dost slammed his fist down on a wooden trestle bearing a whole roasted lamb stuffed with apricots. His hand was waving the greasy-bladed dagger with which he had been hacking off lumps of meat. 'It is true that the prince is too young to rule, but why should we have a stranger? I am of the House of Timur. My father was a blood-cousin to our dead king. I am a proven warrior – did I not kill twenty Uzbeks with my own hands last winter as the first snows fell and they raided our flocks . . .? I have as much right as any man to the regency.' Face dark red with passion and smeared with lamb fat, he glared at the assembly.

'Brothers, please.' Baqi Beg spread his hands in appeal but no one was listening to him.

Ali-Dost was heaving himself to his feet, his men clustering round him, murmuring like angry bees. In a moment chieftain after chieftain was rising, each roaring his own candidature, his own demands. Ali-Dost swung his great fist at a man he believed had insulted him and, as the man crumpled, put the tip of his dagger to his throat. Tables that, just a few minutes earlier, had been laden with dishes of buttered rice, meat and dried fruits, were pushed over as men fought to get at one another, wrestling among the cushions.

Qambar-Ali, who had withdrawn out of harm's way to the far end of the hall, was not dismayed. They were such children, these so-called warriors who would kill for a sheep – or even just a woman. This wine-fuelled brawl would soon fizzle out and only bolster his case. He watched one grizzled chief take another by the throat and shake him like a rat till his victim, over-filled with lamb, spewed it up in his face.

'Stop in the name of the King of Ferghana!'

Qambar-Ali whirled round. Wazir Khan was standing in the great doorway, his mail-clad guards at his heels. The vizier's derisive smirk was short lived as he was pushed to the floor by Wazir Khan's men rushing past to take up positions around the walls of the large chamber.

At first the noisy brawlers did not realise what was happening. Only when the guards clashed their swords on their leather shields did the heaving, flailing, swearing mass of bodies pull apart and fall silent.

'Prepare to greet your new king.' Wazir Khan's voice was stern.

'Sadly, it is Allah's will that, for the moment, we have no king,' the vizier said, hauling himself up from the ground and flicking dust from his robes.

Wazir Khan seized Qambar-Ali's thin shoulder. 'We have. The *khutba* has been read in the mosque. All of you, on your faces, now.' The men, fuddled with drink, gazed stupidly at him. His guards began moving among them, pushing them to their knees and striking those who resisted with the flat of their swords.

'All hail, Babur Mirza, rightful King of Ferghana,' Wazir Khan's voice rang out, and he prostrated himself as Babur, in his oversized yellow robes and tall, velvet cap, slowly entered the room. The chieftains who had endorsed his kingship towered behind him, eyes watchful, hands on their swords in case of trouble.

Babur doubted they felt any special allegiance to him. They had simply taken a gamble. But now they would want to make sure they had backed the winning side and could claim their reward.

To Babur the scene seemed almost comical as he surveyed the chaos – heavy-breathing men lying among strewn meat, cushions and rice, their dogs snuffling and snarling as they fought over the unexpected feast that had come their way. Qambar-Ali's expression was no more friendly than those of the drooling hounds as, slowly, he knelt before Babur and touched his forehead to the floor.

'Vizier, all of you, you may rise.' As Babur gave his first order an almost visceral thrill went through him.

Qambar-Ali scrambled up, features clearly betraying a futile attempt to master his consternation. 'We, the members of your council, are at your command, Majesty.'

'Then how do you explain this – your letter of invitation to the Khan of Moghulistan?' Babur flung out his hand and Wazir Khan handed him a leather box. Inside was a scroll which Babur extracted and held out to the vizier who did not even bother to take it.

'It was for the good of the country.' The vizier was breathing rapidly and heavily.

'It was for your own good—' Wazir Khan began, but Babur gestured to him to be quiet. This was his first test as ruler and he must prove himself worthy or next week, next month, next year, but inevitably at some time, there would be other plotters seeking to strip him of his birthright.

Qambar-Ali's face was working with agitation and Babur caught the sour odours of sweat and fear. But he felt no pity for the man who had enjoyed such favour from his father, only anger and a desire for revenge.

The treasurer, the astrologer and the comptroller of the household were bunched in a tight little gaggle, eyes and mouths round with dismay. 'Take them away,' Babur ordered the guards. 'I will deal with them later.' He glanced up to a small grille set high in the wall and thought he detected movement behind it. This was where the royal women sat and watched, modest and unseen, during feasts and festivals. He knew instinctively who was there – his mother and grandmother were watching his first acts as king and urging him on.

It was strange to think that now he had the power of life and death. Babur had seen his father send men to their death many times. In the last year or two he had even witnessed the executions – beheading, flaying, ripping apart by wild stallions. The screams and stench had caught in his throat but he had never felt it was wrong, as long as justice was done.

And he knew exactly what his mother and grandmother would expect of him now. His name meant 'Tiger' and he must act with the great cat's deadly speed. 'You plotted treason and you wished me dead, did you not?' he said coldly.

Qambar-Ali did not meet his eyes. Slowly Babur drew his sword from its scabbard. 'Guards!' He nodded at two of Wazir Khan's men, who seized the vizier and pushed him to the ground, pulling his arms tightly behind him. Then they pulled his turban from his head and ripped back his robes, exposing the nape of his neck.

'Stretch your neck, Vizier, and thank the celestial stars that I am merciful enough to give you a quick death despite your treachery.' Babur pulled himself up to his full height and swung the sword through the air in a practice stroke, just as he had in his mother's chamber a few hours earlier. God give me strength to do this, he was praying. Let the cut be clean.

The vizier twisted in the soldiers' grasp and there was venom in his eyes. Babur hesitated no longer and, sweeping the sword high, brought the blade down hard. It sliced through the vizier's thin, gristly neck as easily as if it had been a ripe melon. The head, yellow teeth bared, rolled away across the flagstones, leaking red blood like liquid rubies.

Babur allowed his gaze to pass slowly over the awed crowd. 'I may be young but I am of the blood of Timur and your rightful king. Does any man present challenge my right to rule?'

There was complete silence. Then, slowly, chanting began: 'Babur Mirza, Babur Mirza.' The sound swelled and rolled around the chamber and as if the noise was not enough, men beat their swords on their round hide shields or pounded their fists on walls and tables until the very chamber seemed to shake with their passion.

Chapter 3

Timur's Ring

As Babur entered the chamber his chiefs put their hands to their breasts and bowed their heads. Only eighteen, Babur thought, and some, as his grandmother had warned him, of doubtful loyalty. His eyes narrowed as he gauged each man. Only a month ago, while his father was still alive, his thoughts would have been very different. He would have been wondering which of these warriors might invite him to train with them in swordplay or to gallop with them in a game of polo on the banks of the Jaxartes. Not now. His childhood was over. This was no game but a council of war.

Babur sat on his velvet-draped throne and signalled that the chiefs, too, might sit. He raised a hand. 'Kasim, the letter.'

The tall, slim man in dark robes who had entered the room behind him stepped forward and, bowing low, handed him the letter that an exhausted messenger had delivered the day before. Babur's knuckles whitened as he gripped the document that had destroyed his peace of mind. Even now his mother was weeping in her apartments, head slumped on her breast, refusing to listen to words of comfort from his sister Khanzada or even the sharp common sense of her own mother, Babur's grandmother, Esan Dawlat. His mother's collapse had shaken him. Kutlugh Nigar had been so strong after his father's accident but now she was allowing despair to overwhelm her.

'Vizier, read out the letter so that every man present can hear of the perfidy of my uncle, Ahmed, King of Samarkand.'

Kasim took the letter again and slowly unfolded it. He had been a good choice as vizier, Babur thought. A poor man of no family but considerable learning – not an ambitious intriguer like his predecessor, Qambar-Ali, whose decaying head now reposed on a spike over the fortress gate.

Kasim cleared his throat. '"May the manifold blessings of God be upon my nephew in the hour of his grief. God has seen fit to spare his father, my brother, from the burden of earthly existence and to send his soul winging to the gardens of Paradise. It is we who are left who have cause to mourn, and to remember our duty to the living. The territory of Ferghana – I cannot in all conscience call such a small, impoverished pimple a 'kingdom' – is alone and unprotected. Enemies of the House of Timur are circling. My brother's son, a mere boy, has been left naked and vulnerable. I would be failing in the love I bear my family if I did not intervene for his protection. As you read these words, beloved nephew, my armies are already marching through the Turquoise Gate of Samarkand. I will annex Ferghana for its own security. Your thanks are unnecessary. I grudge neither the trouble nor the expense, and little Ferghana will at least make a pleasant hunting ground. As for you, dear nephew, soon I will enfold you in my arms and you will again know a father's love. And when you come of age, I will find you a small fief where you may live in peace and content."'

The warriors stirred uneasily, no man daring to catch another's eye. Tambal, a distant cousin of Babur's, merely grunted while Ali Mazid Beg, a burly chieftain from Shahrukiyyah in the west of Ferghana, whose lands lay directly in the path of the advancing forces of Samarkand, was poking about in his embroidered sheepskin jerkin as if suddenly afflicted with a plague of fleas. Babur sensed their anxiety. His uncle was the most powerful of all the rulers descended from Timur, and Samarkand, on the great Silk Route between China and Persia, surrounded by fertile fruit orchards and fields of wheat and cotton, the richest of all the Timurid possessions. Its very name meant Fat City while the Zarafshan river, which ran past its walls, was called Gold Bearing.

'Now you understand why I sent my swiftest riders to summon you here. We must plan our response to this despicable threat to Ferghana's independence. Young as I am, I am your rightful king. The *khutba* was read in my name and you were present. I have dealt with the internal threat from Qambar-Ali and his crew. Now I call on you to stand behind me against our external enemies, as your honour says you must.' Babur's voice was steady and clear, his words resonating pleasingly off the stone walls. With the help of Wazir Khan he had rehearsed what he would say.

Silence. Babur's optimism wavered and he felt a lurch in his guts. If necessary he would call on Wazir Khan to speak: his cool reasoning would carry weight with the chiefs, though Babur would prefer to be seen to succeed unaided by the loyal commander of his bodyguard. He must be strong . . . He persisted in as deep a voice as his years would allow: 'We must act. If we do nothing the armies of Samarkand will be outside our gates before the next full moon.'

'What does Your Majesty suggest?' Ali Mazid Beg raised his head and looked Babur straight in the eye. He had been among the most faithful of Babur's father's chieftains and Babur felt gratitude for the support he read in the man's almond-eyed gaze.

'The king's forces will ride eastward from Samarkand along the Zarafshan river. We must circle round and come at them out of the mountains from the north. They will not be expecting such an attack. We will show my uncle that Ferghana is strong enough to defend itself.' Wazir Khan had suggested the plan to him and, as he outlined it, Babur knew it was a good one.

Ali Mazid Beg nodded thoughtfully. 'You are right, Majesty. They will not look for us to come over the northern passes.'

'We may fend off your uncle. It is possible – at least, for a while. But what will we do when Shaibani Khan comes – as he will?' Tambal asked quietly. Unlike Ali Mazid Beg, his eyes slid away, unwilling to engage Babur's.

Babur sensed the unease caused by Tambal's words. The Uzbek clans had long preyed on the Timurid kingdoms, riding out from their settlements on the northern steppes to harry and raid. But recently, under their new leader, Shaibani Khan, their ambitions had been growing. They were looking for conquests and little Ferghana might indeed prove tempting. 'We will deal with the Uzbek and his scum, too, when that time comes,' Babur said.

'But we will need allies. Neither Ferghana nor any of the kingdoms of the House of Timur can stand alone. The Uzbeks will pick us off one by one, like a fox biting the heads off chickens,' Tambal continued.

'Of course we need allies but let us seek them as free men, not like fearful slaves craving a good master,' Babur insisted.

'The slave may live longer than the free man. And when the time is right he can make his bid for freedom. If we accept your uncle's protection we can piss on the Uzbeks. When Shaibani's head is lopped from his shoulders and stuffed with straw as an ornament for the harem, that will be the time for us to think once more of Ferghana's independence.'

A murmur of agreement spread round the chamber and now, finally, Tambal looked into Babur's face. His expression was grave but the slight curve of his lips betrayed satisfaction that his words had struck home.

Babur suddenly rose, glad of the little step beneath his

throne that gave his youthful frame extra height. 'Enough! We will turn back my uncle's men and then, from a position of strength, I – not you – will decide who will be Ferghana's ally.'

In turn the chieftains leaped to their feet – it was unthinkable to remain seated once their king was standing, whatever thoughts they might be harbouring. Even a warrior strong enough to rip off another's arm was steeped in court etiquette.

'We ride in four days' time. I order you to be here with all your men. Tell them to be ready for battle.' Instinctively, Babur turned and strode from the chamber followed by his vizier and Wazir Khan.

'You did well, Majesty, to allow no further debate,' Wazir Khan said, as soon as the door had closed behind them.

'I don't know. We'll have to wait four days to see who answers my call. Perhaps some of them are already sending messengers to my uncle in Samarkand. He can give them richer rewards than I.' Babur felt weary and his head ached.

'They will come, Majesty.' Kasim's quiet voice surprised Babur. The vizier seldom spoke unless spoken to first. 'The *khutba* was read in your name just four weeks ago – it would dishonour your chiefs among their people to fail you so soon and without allowing you to prove yourself in battle. And now, Majesty, if you have no orders for me, I will return to my duties.' He hurried off down the passageway.

'I hope he's right,' Babur muttered, and then, in a sudden, furious gesture, kicked the wall with his foot, not once but twice, to release his pent-up emotions. When he saw Wazir Khan's surprise he allowed himself a brief smile and, for a moment, the blackness lifted from him.

• ◆ •

As Babur approached the women's quarters, servants rushed ahead to announce the king's approach. How different it was from the days when, as a carefree boy, he had run down these corridors and burst in on his mother causing her to scold, then caress him. Now there was so much ceremony. As he entered the honeycomb of rooms he caught the flash of a dark eye and the gleam of a golden bangle on smooth, slender ankles, and breathed in the musky scent of sandalwood. He had not yet been with a woman but, young as he still was, the women were already competing to catch his eye – even Farida, the young widow of Qambar-Ali, taken into the harem by his mother out of compassion. Though she was still in mourning, he had seen her watching him. And others had put themselves in his path, their eyes bold and inviting.

His mother was lying where he had left her, but at least she was sleeping now. His sister Khanzada was sitting hunched up, knees under her chin, in a corner of the room and playing idly with her pet mongoose, pulling gently with her hennaed hands on the golden chain attached to the turquoise-studded collar around its neck. At the sight of her brother she jumped up. 'Well?' she asked eagerly, but in a low voice so she did not wake Kutlugh Nigar.

'We will see. I've given orders to march in four days. How's Mother?'

Khanzada frowned. 'She won't listen to reason. She's convinced our uncle will seize the throne and murder you. She once heard him boast that Ferghana would make a nice addition to his kingdom of Samarkand. She says he has always regarded us both acquisitively and with contempt. That's why Father used sometimes to raid his borders – from pride, to show he wasn't afraid.'

'Well I'm not afraid either. If we don't respond to this threat we'll lose face among all of Timur's descendants. I would rather die in battle than give way.' Babur's voice shook with a passion that startled him. Glancing round he saw his mother had woken. She must have heard what he had said.

Though her eyes were still red her handsome face was alight with pride. 'My son,' she said softly, and held out her hand. 'My youthful warrior.'

· ◆ ·

The stars had never seemed so bright, Babur thought, staring up from the battlements into the heavens, or so numerous. The air felt cold and pure, and as he breathed it deep into his lungs he could almost taste the approaching winter when the rivers would freeze and wolves would come howling from the mountains to haunt the villages and prey on the herdsmen's fat-tailed sheep.

In just a few hours he would be riding on his first campaign. His father's eagle-hilted sword, Alamgir, hung from his belt but his father's armour was still too wide for him. Wazir Khan had found him chain-mail, a jewelled breastplate and a plumed helmet from the royal armoury, which did not fit too badly. Which Timurid prince had they once belonged to, he wondered, running his fingers over the gems, as cold and brilliant as the stars above him, and what had been his fate?

A soft whinny came from the stables below. Wazir Khan had told him that horses always sensed a coming battle. Beyond the fortress walls, Babur could see the red glow of charcoal already starting to burn in the braziers as the encampments came to life. Shadowy figures were emerging from hide tents and stamping on the ground to drive the early-morning cold from their limbs. Servants were scurrying about with jugs of water and lighting flares of cloth dipped in pitch.

Nearly every one of his chiefs had come, Babur thought, with satisfaction. He would march with an army of four thousand. Small, perhaps, compared with the might of Samarkand, but large enough to do some damage and make a point – maybe enough to force a truce and agree a settlement. He should have paid more attention to his father's lengthy, excited accounts of military strategy. Instead he would have to rely on Wazir Khan's advice — but he would learn quickly, he promised himself. He had to.

Dawn was breaking now, a pale orange glow rising over the mountains and illuminating their jagged outline. Suddenly Babur spotted a cluster of horsemen galloping hard along the valley — latecomers, perhaps. Pleased by their sense of urgency, he ran down the steep stone steps from the battlements to the courtyard to greet them.

Steam was rising from the horses' heaving flanks as the riders surged up the castle ramp. Their leader shouted for the metal-studded gates to be opened and for permission to enter.

'Halt!' Wazir Khan's voice rang out. Hurrying to his side, Babur saw what the commander of his bodyguard was staring at through the grille of the gate. The crouching tiger on their green silken banners proclaimed the new arrivals subjects not of Ferghana but of Samarkand.

The leading horseman's mount reared as he pulled hard on the reins. 'We bring news,' he shouted hoarsely. 'Our king is dead.'

'Majesty, stay back. I will deal with this. It may be a trick,' Wazir Khan cautioned, then signalled his guards to stand aside and open the gates to allow the riders into the courtyard. Hand on the hilt of his sword, he strode forward to confront them. 'Identify yourselves.'

'I am Baisanghar, a captain of the King of Samarkand's bodyguard. These are my men.'

Baisanghar's face was streaked with sweat and dust but what struck Babur most was his utter exhaustion beneath the grime. This was no ruse. Disregarding Wazir Khan's caution, he stepped forward. 'I am Babur, King of Ferghana. What has happened to my uncle?'

'The king was on his way to Your Gracious Majesty in Ferghana to offer you his . . . protection. He and his forces had camped overnight by a fast-flowing river and were building a temporary bridge over it when Uzbeks ambushed us not two hours after dawn. In the surprise and confusion all was lost – the war elephants, camels and our baggage animals ran off in terror, trampling anyone or anything that stood in their path. Our men fought bravely but many were killed. Some tried to escape back over the half-built bridge but it collapsed under them and they were swept away. The waters of the river soon ran red with blood – Uzbek as well as ours, it's true – but we were overwhelmed.'

'And my uncle?'

'When the attack began he was in his scarlet tent on the riverbank. He managed to mount his horse and ride against the enemy but an arrow struck him in the throat and he fell to the ground where he lay, his heels drumming the earth in his agony. We managed to reach him and drag him from among the horses' hoofs. But there was nothing the doctors – the *hakims* – could do for him. They could not staunch the loss of blood. He was dead within the hour. As the news spread among our forces some of the chieftains, fearing what was to come, called off their men and turned for their home villages.' Baisanghar's voice was bitter with contempt.

'And why have you come here?'

'It was your uncle's dying wish. He believed that God was punishing him for coveting Ferghana. As his last breath bubbled through the blood in his throat he asked me to seek your forgiveness so that he may rest in tranquillity in Paradise.'

That didn't sound at all like his uncle, Babur reflected, but perhaps the proximity of death changed men.

'What proof have you of what you say?' Wazir Khan's one eye was still alive with suspicion, and Babur noticed he had not ordered his men to stand down. Even now three had their bows raised, trained on Baisanghar.

'Here is my proof.' Baisanghar thrust his hand deep inside

his hide jerkin and pulled out a small, stained pouch. Loosing the plaited thong around its neck he extracted a piece of brocade. Carefully, reverently, he unrolled it to reveal what lay inside: a heavy, blood-smeared gold ring.

Babur gasped as Baisanghar held it out. 'See,' his voice was almost a whisper, 'the ring of Timur the Great.' The snarling tiger etched into the yellow metal seemed to writhe and spit.

• ◆ •

The atmosphere at the council of war was very different this time. As Babur entered, flanked by his vizier and Wazir Khan, the chiefs were noisily debating the astonishing turn of events.

'The message is clear, Majesty.' Tambal's eyes gleamed with excitement. 'The king has named you his heir – he had no sons. Others will try to claim it, but Samarkand is yours if we move quickly.'

Babur could not resist an ironic smile. 'And the Uzbeks? A few days ago you were afraid of them. And you were right – they have just butchered my uncle, ravaged his armies and looted his baggage train. Suppose they, too, now have their eyes on Samarkand?'

'But it's almost autumn. The seasons are our friend. Every year it's the same. As winter approaches Shaibani Khan withdraws north to his lair in Turkestan and does not move again until the snows melt.'

'What do you say, Ali Mazid Beg?' But Babur already knew. The man's whole body exuded ebullience and confidence and his eyes were brilliant at the thought of the glories and booty ahead. Samarkand was rich but, more than that, it had been the centre of Timur's empire, the glorious place every Timurid prince and noble ached for. Babur felt the same longing. While still so young, fortune had handed him an opportunity that might never come again. He had no wish for a long life and a peaceful death propped on silken cushions if his last living thoughts were to be of missed chances. His road to Paradise must not be paved with regrets.

Ali Mazid Beg did not disappoint him. 'I say we should ride quickly, before the winter comes.'

'And you, Wazir Khan, what is your view?'

Babur had had no time to discuss plans with him. Would he say something to quell the excitement pumping so violently through him that his body was almost vibrating? Wazir Khan's single eye was gazing intently at him, considering. Here it comes, Babur thought, the words of cold reason to slow my pulses. He will tell me I am just a youth, that defending my kingdom is one thing but conquests are another. He will counsel me to wait, tell me prudence must be allied with courage, patience with ambition.

'Tambal is right. Having tasted blood, Shaibani and his Uzbeks should now be riding north, away from Ferghana along the Jaxartes river. I will send out scouts to make sure. But even without the Uzbek menace our armies are too few for such a venture. We need allies, paid men – mercenaries, if you will. We must persuade the mountain tribes to ride with us. If we pay they will come, and if they come we may – God willing – be victorious.'

Babur gazed at Wazir Khan as if he had never before appreciated him properly. 'You will be my commander-in-chief. Do whatever is necessary. We ride in two weeks.'

'Majesty.' Wazir Khan bowed his head.

· ◆ ·

Hoofbeats pounded the cold earth, over and over again, so that their rhythm seemed the only reality. Babur twined his fingers in his horse's mane to steady himself as he swayed with fatigue. Since leaving his fortress at Akhsi, he had ridden ahead each day with the advance guard, leaving the heavily laden pack-beasts carrying tents and cooking equipment to follow and meet up with them at nightfall. Four days ago his entire force had crossed from Ferghana into lands belonging to Samarkand but had encountered nothing more threatening than a few herdsmen.

Babur looked up. In an hour the sun would be sinking in their faces but before then their three-hundred-mile journey west between high mountain passes and across foaming rivers should be over. The domes of the city of Samarkand itself would lie before them like an offering. Perhaps even tonight he would occupy Timur's capital. Babur indulged himself by picturing the grateful populace thronging round him, overcome that a new Timurid king had come to save them.

At the thought, he kicked on his horse once more and, despite its fatigue, the animal shot forward up the slope of a hill. There in the distance, across the shining waters of the Zarafshan river, Samarkand lay silhouetted against a vibrant sky. Babur stared as if mesmerised. His breath caught in his throat. Perhaps, until this moment, he had not quite believed that Samarkand really existed. Now there was no doubt. This was no fable, no haunt of phantoms, but a place, inhabited by men of flesh and blood, that he had come to claim as his own.

Babur let out a whoop but his cry of jubilation died on his lips. To the south, several miles from the city, was an encampment among the nearly leafless tress of Samarkand's fabled orchards that, just a few weeks earlier, would have dipped under their burden of fragrant apples and golden pomegranates. Banners flew in the chill breeze and smoke spiralled from cooking fires. As he watched, Babur saw a detachment of riders gallop into this camp, swerving expertly between the tents to be greeted by the metallic blare of trumpets.

So, despite all his haste, he was not the first would-be king to reach Samarkand. Someone had forestalled him. Disappointment sharp as physical pain skewered him.

Wazir Khan was beside him, cursing vividly as he, too, stared at the scene ahead. 'I will send scouts, Majesty.'

'Is it Shaibani Khan?'

'I don't think so. The camp isn't large enough. And the city doesn't appear to be under attack or even siege, which it would surely be if Shaibani Khan were here.'

'Then who?'

'I don't know. But it isn't safe to go forward. We must retreat down this hill, make camp in its lee, where we cannot be seen, and wait for our main force to catch up tomorrow.'

Wazir Khan read the bleak disappointment on Babur's face. 'This is Qolba Hill, a place of dreams and hopes. Five years ago I was with your father, here, on this very spot, with the armies of Ferghana behind us. Like you, Majesty, he gazed on Samarkand and what he saw made him catch his breath with ambition and desire.'

'What happened?'

'The king, your uncle, was away fighting rebellious tribes to the west. It was the perfect time to attack, but God was not with us. That very night your father, who had ridden so hard that one of his best horses collapsed under him, was stricken by such a deep fever that the doctors feared for his life. We had no choice but to turn back. Your father took it hard but it was his fate.'

'Why did my uncle and my father hate each other so much? They were brothers.'

'Only half-brothers, born of different women, and rivals from the moment they were old enough to realise that each coveted the same thing – Timur's city. Your uncle Ahmed was the older by four years. He seized Samarkand and spent the rest of his life taunting your father. Yet your father had something he did not. In spite of all his women and all the potions he swallowed or rubbed into his groin, your uncle could not father a son to succeed him. And that, more than anything, he could not forgive. That was why he planned to take Ferghana from you and leave you nothing – perhaps not even your life.'

In his mind's eye Babur saw his distraught mother sobbing in anguish at the news of his uncle's advance. She had understood the depths of his enmity. But in his dying moments his uncle had relented and sent Babur Timur's ring. Surely that was a sign? He was meant to rule Samarkand and not, like his father, live out a life blighted by disappointment.

'Come, Majesty.'

Babur fought the impulse to gallop wildly on and confront these interlopers who thought they could snatch away his dreams. Sadly he turned his horse and followed Wazir Khan slowly back down through the tussocky grass of Qolba Hill.

Soon the tents were pitched but there was no hot food in case smoke rising from the cooking fires alerted those on the plains beyond. Despite their weight, Babur shivered beneath layers of pungent-smelling sheepskins as the temperature dropped. Finally he drifted off to sleep only to be shaken awake what seemed like just a few minutes later. 'Majesty, I have news.' Wazir Khan was kneeling at his side. His face was relaxed. There was even a twist of a smile. 'It seems we have interrupted an affair of the heart.'

'What do you mean?'

'Five days ago your cousin Mahmud, son of the King of Kunduz, arrived here. His goal was not to take the city but a girl. With Samarkand in confusion he planned to steal into the city and find her. She is the daughter of the grand vizier.'

'What stopped him?' Babur could hardly believe his ears. The last time he had seen Mahmud, the son of his mother's favourite sister and three years older than him, he had been a clumsy, cheerful boy with angry spots on his hairless chin and a passion for pranks that often got him into trouble. Babur had followed worshipfully where he led. The idea of a lovelorn Mahmud sighing his heart out for a girl was ridiculous.

Wazir Khan's face assumed its usual grave expression. 'Your

cousin found the city gates barred. The grand vizier is claiming the throne of Samarkand – the city and all its territories.'

'What gives him that right?'

'Nothing. He has no blood descent from Timur. But he is powerful. He controls the treasury and can bribe anyone he wishes.'

'But when he learns that I, the former king's nephew, am here he must give way. My right is greater than his, however many fistfuls of golden coins he can shower on those around him.'

The youthful indignation in Babur's voice made Wazir Khan smile again. 'He knows you are coming but has declared he will not yield the throne to a raw stripling. Neither will he give his daughter to Prince Mahmud. He plans a great match for her with another of your cousins – the son of the King of Kabul.'

'We'll see about that.' Babur jumped to his feet, so that the sheepskins tumbled around him. 'Bring my horse. I will ride to my cousin's camp.'

Dawn was rising as Babur, wrapped in a thick cloak, galloped towards his cousin's encampment, his escort close around.

'Halt.' A soldier's voice came gruffly out of the pale grey light. 'Declare yourself.'

'Babur, King of Ferghana, who wishes to greet his cousin, Prince Mahmud of Kunduz.'

A silence, then a murmuring, then a blazing torch held high, casting haloes of light. Babur shaded his eyes as soldiers encircled his small party. Then he heard a voice he recognised, deeper than he remembered but still brimming with good humour. 'You are welcome, cousin.' Mahmud, unruly black hair flowing over his shoulders and a falcon on his gloved wrist, strode towards him and threw his other arm round Babur's shoulders. 'You have interrupted my plans for an early hawking expedition but I'm still pleased to see you. Come.' He gestured towards a large square tent.

Rich carpets covered the earth and brocade hangings concealed the hide walls and ceiling. Mahmud hooded his falcon and returned it to its golden perch, then flung himself on to a pile of plump velvet cushions. Babur did likewise. 'I was sad to learn of your father's death. He was a good man and a good warrior. May peace be with him. We of course observed mourning for him in Kunduz.'

'Thank you.' Babur bowed his head.

'And now my little cousin is a king.'

'As you will be one day.'

Mahmud smiled. 'True.'

'But today your thoughts lie in a different direction?'

Mahmud's smile broadened to a grin. 'You should see her, Babur. Skin like silk, slender as a willow wand and nearly as tall as I am. I will have her, I have sworn to, and I will not break my word.'

'Where did you meet?'

'Don't worry – I didn't disguise myself as a woman and slip into the grand vizier's harem. It happened last year while she was accompanying her father on an embassy from Samarkand to Kunduz. Brigands attacked their party soon after they had crossed our northern borders. I and my troops had been sent to meet them. We were close when the attack occurred. We heard the clamour and rode to their rescue. That was when I saw her – she came out from behind the rock where she had been hiding, her veil and half her clothes torn off . . .' Mahmud paused, clearly remembering the pleasurable sight.

'The grand vizier should have been grateful to you.'

'He was – but Kunduz is not as rich as Kabul.' Mahmud shrugged. 'And you, cousin, what brings you here?'

'Beware the man who has no ambition.' His father's words flickered unbidden through Babur's mind. But wasn't it also right to be wary of the man who did? Had Mahmud really come to Samarkand at such a time merely for the sake of a girl, however desirable?

Babur decided to be frank. 'The King of Samarkand, though my father's brother, was no friend to Ferghana and meant to rob me of my throne. But as he lay dying, he ordered his men to bring me this.' Babur held out his hand. Timur's ring, cleansed now of blood, was on his index finger. It was a little too big, but he had secured it with a twist of red silk. The metal gleamed in the light from a brazier of burning charcoal and he heard Mahmud's sharp intake of breath.

'You believe you are Timur's heir?'

'His blood runs in my veins. I will have his city.'

'His blood runs in my veins also,' Mahmud said slowly. Their eyes met and suddenly there was nothing boyish about either of them. Babur felt glad of the dagger in its jewelled scabbard tucked into the mauve sash around his waist.

'Don't worry, little cousin – though perhaps I should not call you "little". I have seen kinder expressions on the faces of she-wolves whose young I've just slain.' Mahmud was grinning again. 'True, I came to Samarkand because I guessed there would be confusion in the city. But look around my camp and you will see I've brought no more than a few hundred men. I never planned to seize the city, merely to raid it, steal some of its wealth and quell this fire in my loins.' He pulled a face and gave his groin a playful rub.

'I wish you luck. May the fire soon be quenched.'

'And you, cousin, how many men have you?'

'When my main force arrives, we will be more than six thousand strong, including many archers.' In reality, Babur's army totalled some five thousand but it would do no harm to exaggerate a little.

Mahmud looked impressed. 'I didn't think Ferghana could muster so many.'

'Many are my own retainers and their men, but others are from the hill tribes.'

'Let's attack together.' Mahmud grasped Babur's wrist.

'When you have the grand vizier's head on a spear, I shall have my wife.'

'Why not?' Babur smiled back. With his superior forces there could be little danger of Mahmud outmanoeuvring him and taking the throne.

• ◆ •

Two months later the winter winds whipping around them were not as bitter as the pain Babur felt as his men plodded wearily eastwards back towards Ferghana. The horses, shaggy manes clotted with ice, were sinking into the snow to their hocks. As they snorted with the effort, their breath rose in clouds of mist. In some places the drifts were so deep that the men dismounted to relieve the animals of their weight and struggled along beside them. Much of the baggage lay scattered and abandoned on the snowy wastes behind them.

This was not how it should have been, Babur thought grimly. The ring on his finger with its piece of red silk still hung a little loose. It seemed vainglorious now, a testament to his failure and humiliation.

Wazir Khan was by his side, shrouded in a heavy wool blanket with frost mantling his beard and brows. Wise Wazir Khan who had urged him to abandon their assaults when the pale skies pregnant with snow announced that winter had come early and vengefully. But Babur had not listened – not even when Mahmud turned for home, the longing in his loins unsatisfied, or when his own paid allies, the hill tribesmen, rode away, cursing about loot promised but not provided. And now he was paying the price for his stubbornness and pride. The walls of Samarkand were unbreached and inside them the grand vizier was sitting snug with the crown that was not his and with the daughter for whom he had such great plans – her maidenhead destined for the son of the King of Kabul, not Mahmud.

'Majesty, we will return.' Wazir Khan as usual had read his

mind. His words forced through frost-bitten lips came slowly. 'This was only a raid. We saw a chance and took it, but circumstances were against us.'

'It hurts me, Wazir Khan. When I think of what might have been, I feel a pain sharp as any cut from a blade . . .'

'But it has given you your first experience of warfare. Next time we'll be better prepared and equipped, and you will know the sweetness of success.'

In spite of his misery, the words cheered Babur. He was young. He already had one kingdom. It was not weakness to recognise the inevitable – that he could not take Samarkand this winter. Weakness lay in despair, in giving up while he still had breath in his lungs and strength in his arms, and that he would never do. 'I will return,' he shouted, above the howling of the wind, and lifting his head gave the war whoop his father had taught him. The defiant sound was swallowed by the wintry storm but continued to echo in Babur's head.

Chapter 4

Into the Fat City

How lucky that a winter that had descended so cruelly early had been followed by a premature spring. From the balcony of his chamber Babur watched boys casting stones on to the frozen Jaxartes, saw the ice fissure and the waters surge up. A few unwary sheep that had wandered on to the frozen watercourse were borne away in the chill torrent. Their thin, high-pitched bleating lasted only a few seconds.

On the plains beyond the Jaxartes, his chiefs were again assembled with their men. This time he had sent his messengers even further, calling in the nomad tribes from north, south, east and west and promising them rich booty. With Shaibani Khan still in his winter quarters in the far north, this must be the moment to strike, Babur thought. Soon he would give the command to ride.

But before he embarked on his unfinished business of Samarkand he must pay his respects to his mother. He hurried to her apartments. This time, his reflection in Kutlugh Nigar's mirror of burnished brass looked very different from when he had gazed on it in the dark, uncertain hours after his father's death. A few weeks ago he had celebrated his thirteenth birthday. Hairs sprouted on his chin and he was taller and broader. His voice had deepened and Timur's ring no longer hung loose on his hand.

'You are becoming a man, my son.' There was pride in his mother's voice as she kissed him farewell. Even his grandmother seemed satisfied – and it took much to please the stern old woman, whose face was as wrinkled as a dried apricot but whose shrewd dark eyes missed nothing.

'When the city is mine I will send for you all.'

'You promise?' Khanzada thrust out her chin.

'I promise.' He bent to kiss the sister who was now, to Babur's satisfaction, a good six inches shorter than he.

As he strode away through the harem, he passed an open door. In the windowless chamber within, lit by the soft light of a row of oil lamps, a tall young woman in bodice and wide trousers of pink flowered silk was bending forward, combing her flowing hair. Babur stepped beneath the low lintel.

As soon as she saw him, she knelt before him so that her forehead touched the ground and her hair flowed round her like a pool of shining water. 'Greetings, Babur, King of Ferghana. May God smile on you.' Her voice, low but clear, held the cadences of the mountain people of the north.

'You may rise.'

She got up gracefully. Her eyes were elongated, her figure slender and her skin the colour of honey. In the corner of her chamber Babur noticed two rustic wooden chests with garments tumbling out of them.

'I was tired after my journey. I ordered my attendants to leave me . . .' She paused and Babur noticed uncertainty in her face, as if she was weighing something up. He turned to go. There was still much for him to see to before the army departed.

'I thank you, Majesty, for summoning me here.' She took a step towards him and he caught her musky scent.

'My father's concubine is, of course, welcome in my house.'

'And his son by his concubine?'

Babur felt a flash of irritation. 'Of course.' This woman, Roxanna – the daughter of some petty chief – had no right to question him so. He'd only learned of her existence a few weeks ago. For some reason his father had chosen not to bring her to his castle but had left her among her own people to be visited and tumbled when he was away on hunting trips. He had told no one of her. Neither had he revealed that eight years ago, when she could have been no more than fourteen, she had borne him a son, Jahangir.

When, in the first days after the snows had ceased to fall, Roxanna's father had arrived at the castle, no one had paid much attention to the shabby tribal chief with his straggling beard. Then he had drawn from his sheepskin robes a letter written by Babur's father acknowledging Roxanna as his concubine and her young son as his seed. It asked that if anything happened to him, they should be admitted to the protection of the royal harem.

Kutlugh Nigar had responded with barely a shrug. It had been her husband's right to take as many concubines as he wanted and, indeed, three other wives. She knew she had been his great love, his daily companion, the mother of his son and heir. No other couple on earth could have matched the depth of their physical and mental compatibility. The sole shadow in their union had been that only two of their children had survived. The unexpected existence of Roxanna and Babur's half-brother mattered not to her – or so she had insisted to Babur who, embarrassed like all young people to discuss his parents' affairs of the heart, had tried to curtail the conversation. 'Let her come with her brat,' she had concluded coldly. Later, Babur noticed that she had ordered Roxanna to be given apartments near her own. Out of sympathy for a young woman alone among strangers? No. So that she could keep an eye on her.

'You are gracious, Majesty.' Roxanna was smiling at him now. 'Your brother thanks you also.'

Half-brother only, Babur thought, and did not smile back. He hadn't seen him yet. The child was apparently ill with a fever – no doubt bitten by fleas or a sheep tick, Kutlugh Nigar had said on learning of it. 'May your son soon be blessed by the return of good health,' Babur said. Courteous words but he knew they sounded cold. He meant them to. Turning on his heel he walked swiftly away, his mind already on the great game that awaited him.

• ◆ •

This time he had nearly eight thousand men under arms Babur thought, with pride, as the ranks of his horsemen fanned west across the plains. Behind them rode his liegemen and their forces, then the motley contingents of the tribal chiefs, like the wild Chakraks, who dwelled in the high wilderness between Ferghana and Kashgar with their horses, sheep and the shaggy yaks they preferred to cattle. The baggage wagons, hauled by long-horned oxen, creaked and groaned under the weight of equipment. This time Babur had left nothing to chance. Again and again, in his councils of war, he had gone over everything he would need for a lengthy campaign, from siege engines to ladders to be placed against Samarkand's walls, to the cooking pots required to feed so many men, to the musicians who would play to lighten their spirits and give them the appetite for victory.

During the inactive winter months Babur, with Wazir Khan, had also considered how best to ensure Ferghana's safety in his absence. He had decided to leave his vizier Kasim, whose loyalty and competence were beyond question, as regent. There had been no reports of Uzbek incursions, and if any danger should threaten, Kasim would at once send word to him.

What mattered now was to anticipate every move his enemies in Samarkand might make. Babur knew that, once again, the grand vizier – now daring openly to call himself King of Samarkand – would have been warned of his coming. The city's granaries would still be well stocked with last autumn's harvest and its gates and walls manned by soldiers whose loyalty the vizier had plenty of money to buy.

After ten days' hard riding, Qolba Hill came into view. Babur did not wait for the return of the scouts Wazir Khan had sent ahead but kicked his grey horse across the emerald grasslands, still spongy with the moisture from melted snow and dotted with the yellow, pink and white of spring flowers. His horse disturbed one of the pheasants for which the area was famed – it rose into the air with a whir of wings and a cackle of alarm. Babur's heart leaped at the sight of the great domes and minarets of Samarkand outlined against the sky. Strong, high walls surrounded the city and within them Babur's sharp eyes made out a second set girdling the inner citadel built by Timur to protect his ultimate stronghold, the four-storey Kok Saray. In the years since his death it had acquired an evil reputation. Babur had grown up with stories of the torture, murder and blindings of ambitious princes and nobles invited to the Kok Saray to feast and never seen again.

He wheeled his horse to a standstill. Even from this distance he could sense the city's watchfulness, as if it was a great creature, tense and waiting. Many eyes would be looking out, trying to assess when and from which direction Babur would come and how many men he would bring. Spies would have observed every step of their three-hundred-mile journey west from Ferghana.

This time there was no sign of any other army. Babur grinned, wondering how his lovelorn cousin Mahmud was faring. Doubtless he had already found himself another woman to sate his throbbing loins – but if he still wanted her, Babur vowed, the grand vizier's daughter would be his. He would send her as a gift.

• ◆ •

'You must have patience, Majesty,' Wazir Khan said, as he had every day for the past five months.

Babur scowled into the basket of glowing charcoals Wazir Khan had lit to warm them as they squatted in the middle of a grove of trees, well beyond the camp with its prying ears and eyes. They needed the warmth. Autumn was coming and the night air was bone-numbingly chill. 'We have traitors in our midst, I am sure of it. Every time we attack a section of the walls or try to tunnel beneath, the enemy seem to know and to be ready for us.' Babur poked the charcoal with the tip of his dagger.

'Every camp has its spies, Majesty. It is inevitable. And don't we also have our own spies?'

'But they tell us nothing.'

'They will, when there is something to tell. We have held the city under siege for five months. We still have food and water but the enemy's must be running low. Soon they will have to send out foraging parties. We must set our spies to watch for them and learn their secret exits. What cannot be taken by force may be taken by stealth.'

Babur grunted. Wazir Khan, so wise and level headed – the man who since the time Babur first stood unaided had tutored him in the arts of war – was good at reminding him how much he still needed to learn. All the same, the last months had taught him much. In the scorching heat of summer, he had learned that grass growing brighter and taller than anywhere else was a sign of hidden water channels. He had learned how to drill his men and keep them active and high spirited when there was no fighting to be done. He had ordered them to play polo insolently close to Samarkand's high walls and, braving the city's best archers, had joined in, thundering over the ground to swipe his mallet at the sheep's-head ball, which – when they had finished – they had lobbed contemptuously over the battlements.

Babur knew now how to move silently through the darkness with his men and to position long ladders, the tops wrapped in sheep's wool to deaden any sound, against the high walls. He had climbed with them, only to be met by missiles, clouds of arrows and buckets of burning pitch, and forced to retreat. He had crept along dark, sandy tunnels dug by his men towards the walls, hoping to burrow beneath them but encountering foundations as unyielding as the mountains of Ferghana.

Babur had also attacked by day, his sweating men dragging up the great siege engines which had hurled massive rocks. But Samarkand's metal-bound gates and thick walls had withstood these barrages, and the pounding of his battering rams.

'I don't understand. The King of Samarkand was my uncle. I'm directly of the blood of Timur. I've sent assurances that I'll not put the city to the sword. Why don't the people open their gates to me of their own accord? Why do they prefer the rule of a usurping vizier?'

Wazir Khan's patient half-smile again told Babur that he had spoken with the ignorance of youth, not the wisdom of maturity. 'Perhaps he rules them by fear. Remember also that the people do not know you. Since Timur died, Samarkand has been besieged by many chiefs and kings hungry for glory and gold, claiming kinship with the great conqueror. Your own uncle seized the city by force. Why should the citizens look kindly on any aggressor? With the grand vizier they at least know what they have.'

The hoot of an owl made them look up at the sky, in which the stars were already fading.

'We should return, Majesty.' Wazir Khan pushed the brazier over and kicked earth over the still burning charcoal.

It wasn't only the loss of their heat that made Babur shiver. 'Wazir Khan, I'm worried. If we don't take the city soon, winter will be upon us and my armies will melt away once more. I'll be forced to return a second time to Ferghana without victory. Then what will my people say about me?'

Wazir Khan gripped his arm. 'We still have time. The sun has yet to enter the sign of the balance. God willing, Samarkand will fall.'

He was right, Babur reflected. His father had endured many setbacks but had never despaired. What was it he used to say? 'If your soldiers see you falter, then all is lost. They look to you for leadership and discipline.' Yes, it was a king's duty to be strong. He must remember that.

They mounted their horses and rode back towards the camp. As they drew nearer, Babur heard, above the rhythm of galloping hoofs, a man shouting in anger. Not another dispute between the lawless rogues who made up so much of his army? he thought wearily as the sounds grew louder and more strident and oaths split the air.

The commotion was coming from near the bathhouse tents. As he and Wazir Khan rode up, Babur saw that one of his mercenary commanders – a nomad from the wildernesses – was examining the contents of two sacks with a couple of his scar-faced warriors. Another man, a simple farmer by his clothes, was watching. 'You've no right to steal from me. How will I feed my family this winter when you've taken everything – my grain, even my sheep?' The man gestured at the small flock of shaggy, brown-fleeced animals tethered close by. He was almost weeping with anger.

There could have been something ludicrous about this thin, insignificant peasant stamping in rage and frustration before warriors who could have flattened him with a swipe of their hard fists, but his defiance was impressive, Babur thought.

'Get back to your midden and think yourself lucky you

go with your life. And when you see your wife, give her another kiss from me and tell her I enjoyed her,' grinned one of the warriors who then launched a kick at the peasant, sending him sprawling. When the man tried to get up, he kicked him again.

'What is happening here?'

Taken by surprise, the men stared up at Babur.

'Answer His Majesty,' rapped Wazir Khan. Still no answer came.

'Get up.' Babur gestured to the farmer, who rose slowly and painfully, clutching his stomach, his lined face apprehensive. If he hated the soldiers, plainly he had no faith in kings either. He backed away from the imperious youth on the horse with the jewelled bridle.

'Stay where you are.' Babur leaped down and surveyed the tableau. The two jute sacks lolled before him, their pathetic contents spilling out. Babur ripped off his leather gauntlet, plunged his hand into one and pulled out some dun garments, a wooden cup and a couple of cotton bags. Opening the bags he found only some mouldy-looking grain intermixed with dark mouse droppings. The other sack felt heavier. Inside were half a dozen skinny chickens, necks newly wrung, and a round cheese, the rind clotted with feathers and chicken blood.

Babur pushed the sacks aside but noticed the farmer gazing at them as if they represented everything he held dear in this life. 'Where did this come from?' Babur demanded. Silence. 'I said where did this come from?' The second time of asking he looked straight into the farmer's face.

'From my village, Majesty, across the Zerafshan river.'

'And all of it was taken from you?'

'Yes, Majesty.'

'By force?'

'Yes, Majesty. By these two men.'

'And your wife. They took her by force?'

The man hung his head.

Babur turned to the commander. 'I gave orders that there was to be no looting from the villagers, that we would pay our way. Timur's heir does not come to ravage poor people and spill their blood upon on the earth.'

The nomad glared at him. 'We've been here many weeks. We've taken nothing. No booty worth a fly's arse. My men are weary. They needed some sport. And all they've taken is a few paltry things from this maggot of a farmer.'

'And raped his wife.'

'They say she was not unwilling.' The chief grinned, showing gaps in his broad, tombstone teeth.

Anger surged through Babur. He would have liked to run these men through with his sword, here and now, like the animals they were, and kick their brainless heads on to the dung heap. 'Arrest the two looters, Wazir Khan. They are guilty of plunder and rape. They know the penalty. I wish it to be carried out immediately in the presence of the other members of their tribe.'

Wazir Khan raised his hand and guards stepped forward to seize the tribesmen who, instead of resisting, stood blinking stupidly as if what was happening was beyond their comprehension.

'As for you.' Babur turned to their chief who was smirking no longer. Babur noticed his fingers feeling for his dagger in the greasy swathe of brown woollen cloth wrapped round his waist, and tensed his body, ready in case the fool should lash out. 'You swore an oath of allegiance to me that on this campaign you would be bound by my laws or suffer the consequences. If you cannot control your men in future you will suffer the same fate.' Babur's voice was laden with menace. 'You will acknowledge publicly that this is justice – royal justice. I will have no blood feuds in my camp. Summon all your men here, now!'

The chief's eyes swung between Babur, Wazir Khan and

the guards gripping the arms of the two now desperate-looking looters. Babur read murder in his gaze and in his heart but, with a muttered oath, the chief slowly lowered his hand from his dagger and bowed his shaved head in submission.

Ten minutes later, the twenty other members of the small clan were gathered in a silent circle around the condemned men. At a nod from Babur the chief cleared his throat and addressed the prisoners: 'You have broken laws that I had sworn to uphold. I, as your chief, give you up to suffer justice. Your bodies will be hewn to pieces and left for dogs and carrion. Let every man here understand that it is my will that this should happen. There will be no blood feud against the executioners.'

Wazir Khan signalled a detachment of his guards to step forward. Swords drawn they advanced on the quivering prisoners and forced them to their knees. The men's screams rose in the cold early morning air as the shining blades cut into them.

Babur felt his gorge rise and breathed deeply to steady himself. This was the law. He had only done what any leader must to maintain discipline and respect. He did not allow himself to turn away until the screaming had stopped and all was quiet except for the cawing of birds of prey quick to spot a feast.

'Take your possessions and this.' Babur held out a purse of camel leather filled with silver coins to the dazed farmer who stared at it for a moment then grabbed it. Babur had already turned his back when he heard the man clear his throat and hesitantly begin to speak.

'What is it?' Babur felt wearied and disgusted – even by the farmer, so skinny and abject. Nothing that had happened had been his fault but had he been more of a man and stood up to the looters when they came to his village . . . Babur dismissed the thought as unworthy. The man was a toiler, not a warrior, and he had had the courage to come to the camp to seek justice.

'Majesty . . . there is something you should know . . . something I saw with my own eyes just three nights ago when the moon was full.'

'What? . . . speak.'

'I saw men — spies, perhaps — leave the city. I waited, hidden behind the trees, while my sheep grazed, and many hours later I watched them return. There is a passage leading into Samarkand — beside the Needlemaker's Gate. I can show it to you, Majesty.'

Babur's heart leaped. 'If you're telling the truth, you'll have more than that paltry bag of silver — you'll have your weight in gold.'

◆

'Majesty, this is insanity.'

'Perhaps.' Babur felt a visceral excitement uncurling within him. In a few hours he would be inside Samarkand.

'At least let me come with you.'

'No, Wazir Khan. Who'll pay attention to a ragged youth? But there are men in Samarkand who know you. I'm safer alone.'

For once Wazir Khan seemed nonplussed. The scar across his blind eye looked more puckered than usual. 'But you are the king,' he said stubbornly. 'What will happen to Ferghana if you do not return?'

'I will return. Now let me go.'

Babur mounted the stocky, sure-footed dark pony he had chosen and, without a backward glance, rode off into the night.

Moonlight silvered the rough track following the westward course of the stream that Babur, Wazir Khan and the farmer had ridden along the previous night. Every inch of the way seemed burned into his brain. He was riding through the Khan Yurti meadow where — as his father had so often told him — Timur had once pitched his pleasure pavilions in summer to lie beneath the silken canopies and listen to the waters, as cool and pure as those coursing through the gardens of Paradise. Now the sound of rippling water seemed to carry the great Timur's voice: 'Go forward. Dare everything.'

After an hour the stream branched and Babur followed the left-hand fork, which he knew flowed south within half a mile of the great Turquoise Gate. He must be careful. Keen eyes watching from the battlements might spy even a lone rider if he ventured too close. He would keep to the far side of the stream where he could merge into the shadows of the willow trees along its banks and move insubstantial as a ghost.

Wazir Khan was right, of course. This was insanity. If Babur wished to know the city's weak spots and the mood of its inhabitants after all these months of siege he should have sent spies into the tunnel, not gone himself – alone. But from the moment the farmer had uttered his few, hesitant words, Babur had felt the hand of destiny thrust him forward.

The sky was cloudless and clear above the drooping willow branches. Across the stream, he could make out the shadowy outline of the city. A few minutes more and the Turquoise Gate would rear like a dragon out of the darkness. One day soon, Babur promised himself, I'll ride through that gate at the head of my men, not sneak into my city like a thief in the night.

A small creature – a mouse, perhaps, or a river rat – ran beneath his pony's hoofs causing it to skitter sideways, neighing in alarm. Babur slipped down and ran his hand soothingly along the pony's soft, shaggy neck. It would be better to go forward on foot from here. Babur pulled off the bridle and the thick folded blanket on which he had been sitting, then turned the pony loose to find its own way back to the camp, as he had agreed with Wazir Khan. This time tomorrow night Wazir Khan would be waiting for him here among the willows with a fresh mount.

Another eight hundred yards of stealing southwards through the soft darkness and he could see the red pinpricks of torches burning on either side of the Needlemaker's Gate. Tall and narrow, it was one of the more modest of Samarkand's six gates. In ordinary times it was the entrance for farmers and tradespeople. Timur would seldom have passed through it. For him there were the mighty Iron Gate and the blue-tiled Turquoise Gate where, in the chambers high above the entrance arches, men would have pounded the kettle-drums and blown harsh-voiced trumpets to announce his approach.

It was time to cross the stream which was deep at this point – almost a river. Babur waded in, bracing himself against the surging waters that rose almost to his shoulders. He was nearly across when his feet slipped on the tumbled stones and he lost his footing. Cold waters closed over his head, choking him, and he felt his body being carried along. He managed to thrust an arm out of the water and winced as his hand struck what felt like the branch of a tree. Trying again he managed to grip another branch and, using both arms now, hauled himself on to the bank.

Gasping, he pushed his dripping hair out of his eyes and looked around. At least he was on the right side of the stream. Instinctively he checked for Timur's ring, which he had secured on a leather thong round his neck. As his fingers came into contact with the rich, heavy metal he grunted with relief. He crouched in silence, shivering and listening intently. Nothing. Not the crack of a twig or the soft beat of a bat's wing. He peered towards the dim outlines of the Needlemaker's Gate. Creeping forward he came to the low, tumbled walls of an old orchard where, amid the pomegranate trees, lay the entrance to the secret tunnel concealed by a heap of dead branches.

Last night there had been no guard. Babur prayed it would be the same tonight. Also that he would not encounter anyone in the tunnel. He must be quick – but, above all, careful. Suppressing the urge to dart forward towards the opening, he forced himself to find a hiding-place in the hollow of an old tree and sit still, watching and listening. You were named for the tiger, Babur told himself, so be like him tonight. Shun the open, love the shadows and master your impatience.

After a while, a young fox trotted by. Its sharp nose twitched as it caught Babur's scent but it ran lightly on. The animal's composure reassured him that no other human was close by and he uncoiled from his hiding-place. His coarse brown cotton robe and sheepskin jerkin — the garb of a humble peasant — were still sodden and cold against his skin. He shook himself like a wet dog, then rubbed himself vigorously.

Heart pounding, he approached the entrance to the tunnel and pushed aside the branches. Then he wriggled forward on his stomach and pulled the branches back into place behind him. Stretching out his hands he felt for the edge of the wooden trapdoor covering the tunnel entrance. There it was! As he gripped it some tiny creature — an ant or an earwig — ran across his fingers. Carefully, Babur raised it and felt inside. The narrow shaft was lined with bricks and wooden supports had been driven into the sides. He climbed in, and bracing his feet on two of the supports ducked his head and pulled the door back in place over him.

He was in pitch darkness and a dank, unwholesome, earthy smell filled his nostrils as if something — or someone — had died in here, which perhaps they had. Samarkand had had a glorious past but also a violent one. Who had first burrowed this passageway? he wondered. Had they been digging their way in or fleeing a terrible fate?

Cautiously Babur lowered himself to the bottom of the shaft, which he knew, from his previous night's exploration, was only about ten feet deep. But where did the tunnel lead? He felt his way forward, keeping his hands pressed to the walls on either side of him. The ground squelched beneath his feet and seemed to slope down. He slipped and slithered and was relieved when, after a few paces, he felt hard stone.

The roof was low and Babur bent his head as he moved on through the darkness. This would be no place to encounter an enemy. How could a man defend himself when he could not stand upright and had no room to swing a sword? Not that he had brought his father's eagle-hilted sword with him. That would hardly be a weapon to be found on a peasant boy if by any ill twist of fortune he was captured. But without it he felt vulnerable.

It was also getting hard to breathe, hunched as he was in the dank, fetid air. He hurried on, counting the paces – ten, twenty, thirty. He had calculated that six hundred would bring him to the city walls but he had no idea how far the tunnel extended. He tried to keep counting. Ninety, a hundred. Sweat dripped from his brow and ran into his mouth. Impatiently he flicked away the salty beads with his tongue. A hundred and fifty . . . The passageway was broadening now, wide enough for two men to pass. Babur went faster. He was almost running. Four hundred . . .

Then he stopped. What was that noise? He caught the unmistakable rumble of male voices and a raucous laugh. All of a sudden the passage ahead was lit by an orange glow. Babur could make out the rough walls and see that, a few yards ahead, it twisted sharply to the left. The voices were growing louder, echoing in the confined space. In a moment their owners would round the corner and see him. Babur turned to flee into the darkness. Almost sobbing with frustration he ran back and flattened himself in an alcove. But the voices were dying away now. If the men were guards sent to check the tunnel they had not been very thorough. He allowed himself a grim smile. Had they been Wazir Khan's men they'd be flayed alive for their negligence.

Babur waited. Darkness again and silence. He breathed more deeply and after a few moments moved on again. He had lost count of his paces now but surely he must be near the city walls. He edged round the sharp, left-hand bend and onwards. After another five minutes he could make out pale light ahead, not the orange glow of a torch but the chill radiance of the moon and stars.

He dragged the back of his hand across his sweating forehead and moved slowly forwards, back against the wall, exposing the smallest surface of his body in case a guard lurked at the far end, bow-string taut, arrow ready to sing out. But ahead was nothing but silence. The city would be sleeping. There was enough light for him to make out his damp, muddy clothes and hands. No need to fear that anyone would take him for a Timurid prince. Inside the city he could blend into the populace, just another ragged youth anxious for a piece of yesterday's bread.

The tunnel ended in a huge circular pit filled with a few inches of putrid water, like the shaft of a disused well, Babur thought. Peering up, he could see the star-pricked canopy of the night sky. Quietly he began to climb up the side of the shaft where metal spikes had been driven into the wall. How many of these tunnels were there? No wonder the enemy had seemed to know his every plan. Spies had been creeping out like rats to infest his camp and steal home with his secrets. But now, Babur thought, it's my turn. I'm the rat.

Gripping the carved stone parapet around the top of the well he heaved himself out and dropped down into the shadows. He was in a courtyard, empty but for two pale skinny dogs asleep in the moonlight. Babur saw the rhythmic motion of their ribs and heard their soft whimpers. What a way for Timur's heir to arrive in mighty Samarkand – stinking and ragged, with only mongrels for company.

And where exactly was he? Babur wished he knew. All he could do was hide and wait for people to rise and begin to move about. He needed their camouflage. Shivering, he spied a pile of woven matting against a wall. That would do.

He slid underneath it and pulled it over him, concealing himself. Samarkand, he thought. Samarkand! Then, without warning, sleep claimed his exhausted body.

◆

'This is my patch! Take your stinking carrots somewhere else.'

Babur jolted awake and peered through the matting. The place that, just a couple of hours earlier, had looked so desolate now thronged with people. In the half-light of dawn, they seemed to be setting up a market. The voice that had woken him belonged to a tall, skinny old man flapping about in dark, dusty robes. Having secured the piece of ground he wanted, he squatted and pulled some mouldy-looking onions from his pockets.

Cautiously, Babur slid out of his hiding-place. Ragged, pinched-looking people were arranging small piles of equally shrivelled vegetables on pieces of cloth – carrots that were mottled and sprouting, a few wrinkled radishes. An elderly woman, veil slipping carelessly from her furrowed face, arranged a rat with the care of an embalmer preparing a body for burial. Others, without anything to sell but clearly too poor to buy, were standing around miserably and hungrily.

These people are starving, Babur thought, in astonishment. The siege had been going on for months and he hadn't expected food stocks to be high, but this . . . A baby's thin mewling caught his attention. A young woman too emaciated to have milk in her breasts and with hopelessness in her eyes dipped a corner of her veil into a jar of water and thrust it between her child's questing lips.

'It's all right for them holed up in the citadel,' the old man said, then spat venomously, the phlegm narrowly avoiding his stack of seven onions. 'They've taken everything from us. They can last out for years, filling their bellies beneath their fine silk robes with our food. Where's the justice in that?'

'Silence, old man, you'll get us all into trouble. It will be as the grand vizier says. When the winter comes, the aggressors will leave as they did last time.'

'And then what? Pay more taxes to the vizier in gratitude! That thieving son of a whore! And they say he'd like our wives and daughters as well. His harem is twice the size of the last king's, may his soul rest in Paradise. I've heard tell he enjoys three women a night.'

'Be at peace, old man, your pockmarked wife and daughter are too ill favoured even for that randy goat,' another man jibed.

As the onion-seller's voice rose angrily in defence of the beauty of his womenfolk, Babur slipped from the square and down a side alley. Everywhere it was the same. Pale people, with hunger etched on their faces, moving slowly, wraithlike, as if every reserve of energy had been drained from them. He watched an old woman grin in toothless delight as she scooped up the body of a dead cat, holding its limp form as tenderly as if it had been a baby. He was surprised that the two dogs he had seen asleep by the well had survived so long.

The pale orange disc of the rising sun was a welcome sight – it would give him his bearings. Babur knew that if he kept his back to the sun he should come to the walls of Timur's citadel. It seemed he was right. As he hurried on he noticed the streets becoming broader, the buildings more elegant. He passed bathhouses inlaid with vibrant mosaics in floral and geometric designs, domed mosques and exquisitely carved *madrasas* where scholars studied and prayed.

Youthful pride that his ancestor had created a city so beautiful welled inside him. When he was King of Samarkand, the markets would again be full of fruit and vegetables from the gardens and orchards encircling the city. The bakeries and cookhouses – empty and forlorn now – would once more scent the air. The people, plump and prosperous, would praise his name. And, as in Timur's time, men of talent – poets, painters, scholars – would flock here from across the civilised world. Overcome by the glory of it all, Babur closed his eyes.

'Out of our way, boy.'

Something hard jabbed Babur in the small of his back. Instinctively his hand went to his waist, seeking the weapon that wasn't there. He wheeled round to see two soldiers, wearing emerald green sashes, the colour of Samarkand. There was plenty of room for them to pass but again one struck at Babur with the butt of his spear, this time catching him in the ribs and sending him spinning against the wall. Laughing, the men swaggered on.

Babur stared after them cat-like and unblinking, but they didn't look back. As soon as they had turned a corner he began to follow. From the direction they had taken, they must be making for the Kok Saray. As he tracked them, keeping a cautious distance, he began to find himself among more and more soldiers, some clearly on patrol through the quiet, cowed streets, others returning from sentry duty on the city walls. Learning by experience, he tried to keep out of their way, dodging into doorways or behind piles of refuse at their approach.

And then, looking up, he saw Timur's citadel, snug within its walls, and, at its heart, the tall façade of Timur's fortress, the mighty Kok Saray. Green silk banners fluttered from the pointed battlements. My palace, Babur thought. Unconsciously he felt for Timur's ring and clenched it in his hand.

The sound of marching feet on the stone-paved street broke his reverie. A detachment of troops was returning to the citadel. Keeping well back, Babur observed them and their weapons critically. Tall, muscular men, they showed no sign of malnutrition and carried themselves like warriors. Again, they wore the bright green sashes of Samarkand. How much was the usurping vizier paying them for their loyalty?

Suddenly a hand closed on his shoulder and Babur tensed, ready to tear himself free, but the grip was like iron. Helpless, he was swung round to face his attacker.

'Greetings. I had not looked to see you so soon in Samarkand. The siege is not yet over.'

Babur gasped. 'Baisanghar!' The last time he had seen the man had been in Ferghana when he had presented him with Timur's blood-smeared ring.

'You've been careless. I've been following you for the last thirty minutes.'

Babur's mouth was too dry for speech and he looked down. What he saw made him gasp again. Though Baisanghar was still holding him tightly with his left hand, his right arm hung stiffly by his side and ended in a raw-looking stump.

Baisanghar had followed his gaze. 'The penalty for obeying your uncle's final command and bringing you Timur's ring. I was lucky to keep my head, but the grand vizier decided he needed me to help in the defence of Samarkand.'

As he tried to calm his racing heart and looked around to assess what chance of escape there might be, Babur was dismayed to see a group of soldiers watching. They must be wondering what their commander had to say to a grimy peasant boy. If he tried to run, they would be on him in a second. 'What now?' He had found his voice.

'It is simple. If I give you up to the grand vizier, my fortune is made. I can take my ease in a luxurious palace where fountains flow with rosewater and beautiful houris fulfil my every whim.' Baisanghar's eyes searched his face. 'But life is not so simple. Your uncle was a good ruler and warranted my loyalty to his last command, whatever the price. The vizier has wounded my honour and my pride. If you will promise me his head, I will give you Samarkand.'

Babur's eyes burned. 'You have my word. The word of a king in whose veins the blood of Timur flows.'

'Majesty.' With a gesture so tiny that no one observing them would have noticed, Baisanghar lowered his head in submission.

Chapter 5

The Kok Saray

As dusk fell Babur, with Wazir Khan at his side, addressed a picked band of his men who were ready to set out on foot from their main camp, bellies full, the blades of their weapons honed and oiled, their leather-covered wooden shields strapped to their backs. First they would follow Babur's footsteps of three nights ago along the stream, but then wait in concealment for a signal to enter Samarkand through the Chaharraha Gate, the entrance to the city where Baisanghar commanded the guard and that he had sworn to open to Babur.

'My brothers-in-arms, tonight we go to meet our destiny. Let us fill our hearts with warrior spirit and summon all our reserves of courage – not only the physical bravery to fight, which I know you possess, but the resolution of mind to move quietly along the stream and wait silently in hiding for however long it takes until the signal comes for us to attack. Each of us carries the lives of his comrades in his hands. If any one of us betrays his position – whether through impatience or foolishness – he betrays us all. Young as I am, I know I can play my part. Will you swear to me that you have the will to do so, too?'

The immediate response was a chorus of 'Yes, Majesty.'

Without wasting further words, Babur gave the command for the party to set off. They did so two abreast along the stream bank into the gathering gloom. Keeping as close as they could to the water, they took advantage of every bit of protection the reeds and feathery willows fringing its banks provided. Suddenly, when they had been going a quarter of an hour or so, one of the leading men was seized by a fit of coughing. To Babur his cough was as loud as the bark of any alarmed guard dog. But no sound or movement came from the direction of Samarkand. Babur relaxed once more. Then the man coughed again, seemingly even louder, and continued to do so for what appeared an age but was perhaps just a minute. Still the only other sound was the persistent whine of the mosquitoes, which were now beginning to gorge themselves on every man's exposed flesh.

'I'll send him back, Majesty,' whispered Wazir Khan.

'Good.'

Two hours after leaving the camp, Babur recognised the point near the Needlemaker's Gate where he had scrambled off towards the tunnel to make his reconnaissance of Samarkand. Tonight, however, he and his men would continue along the stream. Flowing tranquilly in the moonlight, it would once more be Babur's ally as it meandered northwards, passing close, no more than two hundred yards, to the Chaharraha Gate.

Still taking advantage of its protecting reeds and willows, Babur and his men reached the point nearest the gate without further alarms. After a brief consultation with Wazir Khan, Babur whispered the command for the men to conceal themselves in the reeds until the moon was at its zenith – the time they had agreed with Baisanghar he would open the gate.

Babur shifted, trying to get more comfortable. It was difficult. Mosquitoes continued to plague him and he could not stop himself scratching the bites raw. Mud seeped and squelched beneath his squatting form but at least the thick reeds were good camouflage. If he'd guessed the time correctly, from what he could see of the movement of the moon and stars in the small square of sky directly above his head, it must be about ninety minutes since they had concealed themselves.

From where he was crouching, though, he couldn't see anything like enough of the landscape and sky to be certain of the moon's position. He had to know more accurately how much longer there was to wait. He raised his head cautiously, disregarding Wazir Khan's fatherly insistence that he, like the rest of the men, should keep it down and leave the calculation of time to his own more experienced observation. As he poked his head warily through the reeds for a better view, the chain-mail shirt that Wazir Khan had also insisted he wear, but which was too big for him, twisted, and a fold of the overlapping metal circles became wedged under one of his armpits, pinching him. Babur struggled impatiently, reaching inside his clothes and trying to tug the shirt down, but he only succeeded in making matters worse.

A pair of teal shot squawking out of the reeds, just in front of his face. They must have been alarmed by his contortions as he tried to rearrange his garments and equipment. He ducked down guiltily but no sooner was he back among the reeds than he heard rustling just feet away and drawing nearer. Though logic told him it could only be one of his own men, his fingers tightened instinctively on the eagle hilt of his father's sword, Alamgir. He tensed, ready to spring up and fight for his life. The noise grew louder and Wazir Khan's mud-smeared face appeared through the reeds as he wriggled towards him on his belly, propelling himself with his elbows. Babur relaxed, and as he did so it occurred to him that with his shield on his back and lying almost flat, Wazir Khan looked like an ill-proportioned tortoise.

'Majesty, it's time to move. Shall I order the signal to be given?'

Suppressing a smile, Babur nodded.

Wazir Khan slithered away again, still keeping low. Moments later, at his command, a blazing arrow arced across the cloudless sky, its fiery trail like that of a comet. As Babur rose to his feet out of the reeds his guts lurched and he found his legs were shaking with a mixture of excitement and apprehension. All around him, his men were appearing from their hiding-places.

Wazir Khan was at his side. 'Now we will know whether Baisanghar is a man of his word.'

'He is.' Babur was sure of it, but Wazir Khan had been hard to convince, worried that Babur, young and untested, had been deceived.

With Babur and Wazir Khan at their head, the warriors crept out of the reeds, formed up and made swiftly for the Chaharraha Gate over the marshy ground, their leather boots occasionally sticking in the mud and their breath coming softly. As he approached, Babur could see that the gate was smaller than the soaring Turquoise Gate or even the Needlemaker's Gate. The unadorned, stubby stone towers on either side had been built for strength, not grace, and Babur could see the heavy metal grille of the gate itself barring the narrow passage into the city. It seemed to grin with gap-toothed malevolence at him.

Eyes flicking from side to side, searching for any sign of movement, Babur realised there was nothing – not even a light in the chamber over the gate where Baisanghar should be giving the order to winch up the grille. What should he do if nothing happened? Perhaps it had all been just a trick. Or perhaps the plot had been betrayed and even now Baisanghar was being tortured in some stinking dungeon to make him scream out their plans.

Babur forced himself to think coolly. What were his options? But in his heart he knew he had only one. They must go on. Even now, triggered by the flight of the burning arrow, four hundred of his warriors would be retracing his journey of three nights ago and dropping down into the dank, narrow tunnel that had led him into the city. He could not abandon them. Whatever happened, he would lead his men in an assault on the gate.

But even as these thoughts jostled in his mind, Babur saw a figure appear on the wall to the right of the gate, holding a burning torch, which he waved slowly and deliberately from side to side. Almost at once Babur heard the raw, grating noise of a great wheel being turned. The metal grille shuddered, then slowly began to rise. He shot Wazir Khan a grin of triumph, then gave the low, whooping call that was the signal to attack. He heard it repeated ten, a hundred times as his men took it up. Soft as it was, it seemed to swell, lifting him up and impelling him forward.

His father's sword in his right hand, dagger in his left, Babur ran the short remaining distance to the gate. The grille was already a third of the way up. With his men surging round him, he flung himself beneath it, curling into a ball to roll under its sharp prongs. Uncoiling himself he leaped to his feet and peered into the darkness, every nerve tense as he listened for the air to move as an arrow took flight or a throwing axe whirled towards him. But there was only the sound of feet running down the stone stairs from the gatehouse. It was Baisanghar, face grim. 'Welcome. I have kept my word.' He knelt briefly before Babur. 'We must be quick. There are spies everywhere – even now we will be being watched and the alarm may sound at any moment. Twenty of my men are holding this gate but the rest are waiting near the Kok Saray.' He gestured up the dark lane leading into the city. 'Come.'

As Baisanghar finished speaking, ahead, high on the

battlements of the Kok Saray within the walls of the citadel, spurts of orange light were suddenly piercing the darkness – torches. The garrison had been alerted to their presence. The wailing of a horn and the harsh shouts of officers as they roused their men confirmed that they had lost the advantage of surprise. Babur did not hesitate. Raising his sword, he yelled the battle cry of his people – 'Ferghana.' Blood pounding in his ears, he charged forward.

The lane was lined with tall, thin, mud-brick houses whose doors were no doubt being barred. For a second Babur thought of the families cowering behind them, praying the storm would pass over them. They were not to know that he had ordered there was to be no looting or killing of civilians. Though his enemies would pay in full, the beginning of his reign over Samarkand would not be defiled with the blood of its innocent citizens.

'Down here, Majesty.' Baisanghar grabbed Babur's arm and jerked him towards a narrow passage winding off to the left. Thrown off balance Babur staggered and almost slipped. For a split second he glanced at Wazir Khan, close beside him. The passage was highwalled and very cramped. One man, or at very best two, could pass down it abreast – a perfect place for an ambush. Who or what might not be waiting for them down there in the murk?

'It's a short-cut through to the citadel.' Baisanghar's voice was sharp and urgent.

Babur searched the man's face. He knew that, despite his youth, his men were beginning to look to him for leadership. Now was no time to hesitate, with the shouts of their enemies growing ever closer. He trusted Baisanghar, which made his decision easy. Calling to his warriors to follow and with Wazir Khan at his side, he turned down the passage behind Baisanghar. Babur was surprised that he felt no fear now that the action was under way, only exhilaration. Would every battle feel like this? Suddenly, from away to the east, he heard a great roar. His men must be disgorging from the tunnel and racing into the heart of the city. That should keep the grand vizier's soldiers occupied.

The passage twisted sharply to the right, then ended abruptly. Looking about him in the gloom, Babur saw he was in a small square, one side of which, the one directly opposite, was bounded by what looked like the high walls of Timur's citadel. Recalling his previous visit and the plans he had studied, he realised they must be on its southern side. Yes, he was right – within the walls and just a few hundred yards onward, towards the east, he could make out the sharp-toothed battlements of the Kok Saray itself. Baisanghar had guided them well. Even better, Babur could see no defenders on the walls directly above. Presumably they were not expecting their enemy to steal up on them here.

Even so, following the example of Baisanghar and Wazir Khan, Babur quickly crossed the square and flattened himself against the citadel wall. As his men emerged from the passage, he signalled to them to do likewise. They moved quickly, obeying him without hesitation. Baisanghar gave a low call and dark-cloaked, dome-helmeted figures moved quickly from where they had been waiting, concealed behind the steaming midden that occupied the western corner of the square. Baisanghar's guards. They gathered silently round their commander.

'Majesty, the citadel wall is lowest near an old blocked-up doorway on its eastern side, just round the corner,' Baisanghar whispered. 'That is where we should climb in. My men have brought ladders and I will post archers to provide us with cover.' Babur and Wazir Khan nodded agreement. Keeping very close to the wall and with Baisanghar leading the way, the party edged towards the corner of the citadel wall. Cautiously, Baisanghar peered round, then stepping back, gestured to Babur and Wazir Khan to do the same.

A swift glance confirmed that all was quiet. The doorway

was only some thirty yards ahead. Suddenly the excitement and tension became too much for Babur. Dodging Wazir Khan's restraining arm, he ran towards the door, yelling to the others to follow him. He did not even remember to keep in the shadow of the wall and immediately he heard the swoosh of one arrow, then another, as archers arrived on the battlements above, no doubt alerted by his wild shouts. A long-shafted arrow grazed his cheek, before slamming into the ground behind him. The stinging pain didn't matter. Nothing did, except the exhilaration of this moment. He hurtled on towards the doorway. Somehow reaching it unscathed, he pressed his body against the stones with which it was blocked, hoping that the overhanging lintel would provide some cover. Glancing around he noticed a crouching tiger, the emblem of Samarkand, carved into the stone frame beside him, lips curled in a snarl, ears flat against its head.

Baisanghar's archers were now in place, firing back at the defenders on the walls above. Babur could feel warm liquid dripping down his forehead and into his eyes. Touching it with his fingers he realised it was blood, but not his own. Looking up, he saw, high above, a man with an arrow in his neck leaning over the wall. As his hand clutched at his ripped flesh, he overbalanced. Seconds later, he crashed at Babur's feet with a soft thud. Spewing blood and phlegm, he twitched convulsively for a few moments and then lay still amid an ever spreading pool of dark blood.

Baisanghar's men were throwing long wooden ladders up against the walls. They were crudely made with rough wooden rungs lashed to the uprights with strips of leather, but they were suitable for the purpose. Men were already climbing them, holding on with one hand and supporting their shields above their heads with the other to deflect the arrows being shot from above.

Babur's heart was still pounding and he wanted to be into the action quickly. He looked around for a different way up.

There was no chance of unblocking the door. At first glance, the stonework of the walls looked smooth, the joints fitting neatly. But he had not grown up amid the wild mountains and ravines of Ferghana for nothing, he told himself. He could see that there were small cracks and fissures that might provide hand- and footholds to someone as lithe and light as himself. Slinging his father's precious sword across his back, Babur took a deep breath. Glancing round, he saw Wazir Khan watching him. His expression was anxious. Babur turned quickly away and ran along the base of the wall to a point well away from the ladders, dodging an arrow as he did so.

He began to swarm up, his hands exploring the surface, seeking out protruding edges and corners where the mortar had crumbled or the mason's chisel had left its mark – anywhere he could balance a toe or the edge of a foot or thrust his fingers. He must keep his momentum going or he would fall, and his hands reached up, searching for each new hold. Timur's masons had built well – hadn't he brought them specially to Samarkand precisely because they were such good craftsmen? Too good, perhaps, Babur thought as suddenly, twenty feet above the ground, his feet were spinning in empty air and he felt his fingernails cracking as he struggled to cling on with his hands alone.

Mouth dry and dusty as the stone he was trying to hang on to, Babur flailed about, kicking out wildly to right and left as he sought a purchase for his feet but meeting only smooth stone. His protesting arms burned as they took his full weight. Then, just when he felt he must let go and tumble down, he felt his right foot nudge something soft – a tussock of coarse grass that must have seeded itself deep in one of the cracks between the stones. Gasping with relief, Babur pushed his right foot on it to test its strength and as it took some of his weight felt the pain in his arms subside.

For a moment he closed his eyes. He felt like an insect, tiny, vulnerable and exposed, but at least he could rest for a second. Opening his eyes again and looking up through his tumbled hair, he saw the top of the wall was tantalisingly near – perhaps no more than seven or eight feet above him. Cautiously, he stretched up an exploratory right hand and almost laughed out loud as it found a rough, protruding edge he could grip about two feet above his head. Then, still keeping his right foot on the clump of grass that had saved him, he bent his left leg and probed upwards with his foot. Again he found a hold – not much of one – just a narrow, diagonal crack in one of the stone blocks, but enough. With one last great effort he propelled himself upward, reaching for the top of the wall and praying he wasn't about to feel the slash of a blade across his knuckles.

Heaving himself over the low parapet on to the broad top of the wall, the stone worn smooth by the feet of many sentries, Babur looked round to find to his amazement he was among the first to reach it. He felt he had been climbing for ever, but within moments all around him many more of his men, led by Wazir Khan and grunting with the effort, were dropping from their ladders.

The defenders, it seemed, had fled. Stepping back and wiping the sweat from his face, Babur tripped over a handsome, silver-bound shield that a fleeing soldier had thrown aside. He stooped to pick it up but a noise behind him made him twist around. Less cowardly soldiers of Samarkand were rushing up a steep staircase leading from the courtyard beneath the inner side of the wall. The grand vizier's personal bodyguard, Babur guessed, noting the bright green sashes of Samarkand round their waists and the green pennants fluttering at the ends of their spears. With a yell, Babur charged towards them, knowing that Wazir Khan and his men would be with him, and found himself locked in a crowd of heaving, swearing, stabbing men. Even though the top of the wall was broad – perhaps ten feet wide – men were soon tumbling from either side of it, some wounded, some simply pushed over the parapet by stronger opponents. The stench of hot, sour sweat filled his nostrils. For ever afterwards it would be for him the scent of battle.

A giant of a man with a long black beard tinged with grey singled Babur out, a voracious sneer spreading over his fleshy face as he took in Babur's slight stature and his youth. Babur had seen just such a look on the face of a cat about to devour a mouse and the utter disrespect stung him. Wazir Khan had insisted that Babur should wear nothing to identify him as Ferghana's king but he would still prove his pedigree to this arrogant, fat pig.

'Old man, you should be at home, dribbling by the fire and calling for your servants to mop up your leaking piss.'

The stout warrior looked startled for a moment but then, as he took in what Babur had said, rage suffused his features. He advanced towards Babur, balancing his spear in his large, leathery hands. 'You cheeky little rat, I'll shut you up.' In a move so sudden that Babur hardly had time to register it, he reversed his spear and jammed the blunt end into the pit of Babur's stomach.

Babur felt his feet lift off the ground as the impact flung him backwards. As his arms flailed, he was afraid the blow would hurl him off the wall but instead he felt his head snap back as it hit the low stone parapet. For a second his world dissolved into stars, not the pure, silvery starlight he'd gazed up at earlier from the reeds but a chaos of bright, jagged shapes tinged with red which seemed to ooze blood. His mouth was full of salty fluid and instinctively he spat it out. Yet still he couldn't breathe — the blow had crushed the air out of him.

The bearded man was advancing on him again. 'That was just for starters. You'll suffer more for that sneer before you die,' he spat and simultaneously jabbed at Babur's groin with his spear. Just in time, and still struggling for breath, Babur rolled sideways and the spearhead hit the stone, striking

87

sparks. His opponent cursed. For all his weight, he was surprisingly light on his feet. Moving like a determined great bear, he lunged at Babur, who, half bent, was clutching his winded and aching belly with one hand while still holding his sword in the other. His breath was coming just a little more easily now and he took comfort from it.

'Well, rat spawn – soon you'll be on the dung heap with the rest of your kind,' the man said, repositioning his spear so that the tip was pointed directly towards Babur's face. Babur stared at it, half hypnotised by the diamond bright, coldly gleaming point. For a moment, he felt strangely paralysed, powerless to react, but as the warrior thrust his spear at him again, he knew instinctively what he must do. Summoning all his agility and his speed he flung himself to the ground and rolled not away from his assailant but towards him, underneath his jabbing spear. As his body crashed into the man's legs, he slashed at the back of one of his knees with his long-bladed dagger, severing the tendons. With a howl, his opponent collapsed sideways, and blood gushed from the wound. Babur scrambled to his feet and struck again. This time he aimed for the man's ribs, at a spot just below his left armpit that the breastplate didn't cover. He felt his blade penetrate the tough muscle and thick cartilage, then slide between the man's ribs. The giant gave what sounded like a low sigh and slumped forward. As Babur pulled out his dagger blood spurted everywhere. He gazed, fascinated, at the first man he had killed in hand-to-hand combat.

'Majesty, look out!' Wazir Khan's shout came only just in time. Turning and dropping back to his knees, Babur thrust wildly at another attacker who had been about to bring an axe biting into the back of his neck. Suddenly Babur knew fear again. What an idiot to allow himself to be taken by surprise from behind. In the nick of time, Wazir Khan kicked Babur's new assailant to the ground and, with a single, powerful sweep of his curved sword, sent his head skidding across the battlements.

Grateful for the second chance that he knew so many inexperienced warriors did not live to enjoy, Babur was already back on his feet again, dagger and sword ready, but looking around he saw that the vizier's guards had all been killed or fled. They lay in ones and twos, slumped over each other or spreadeagled on the stone in unnatural postures, their once bright sashes dark with blood. Babur caught the stench of spilled guts and slashed intestines.

'Come.' Baisanghar was beside him, blood seeping from what seemed a deep wound to his shoulder, his face taut with pain. Yet he gestured insistently to the crenellated outline of the Kok Saray just a few hundred feet away. 'That is where the grand vizier will be hiding – if I know him, he will have taken refuge in the women's quarters.'

Signalling to his men to follow, Babur stumbled after Baisanghar towards the staircase leading down from the wall. As he scrambled over fallen bodies, half slipping in the gore, one face caught his eye. It belonged to a youth perhaps no older than him. Drained of blood, his lips were drawn back over the gums in a silent scream of pain and his large, dark but unseeing eyes seemed filled with fear beneath their long lashes. Babur shivered and looked quickly away. It could easily have been himself had it not been for Wazir Khan's warning shout.

The citadel was quiet and still as Babur, Wazir Khan and their men followed Baisanghar across the courtyard. After the fight on the wall there was no reason for them to keep silent – their presence within the citadel could hardly be a secret. But Babur's men moved as quietly and stealthily as the sheep- and cattle-rustlers so many of them were. Where were the grand vizier's remaining guards and troops? Babur expected a rush of arrows at any moment, but there was nothing.

As they stole up to it, the four-storey Kok Saray was also

eerily silent, its gleaming brass doors with their dragon handles open and unguarded. Timur's fabled stronghold. What confidence it must have taken to build something so magnificent. Its very stones exuded power and authority. Babur remembered his father's sinister stories. 'All of Timur's offspring who raised their heads and sat on the throne sat there. All who lost their heads in quest of the throne lost it there. To say "They have taken the prince to the Kok Saray" meant he was already dead.'

Wazir Khan and Baisanghar were conferring. Impatient to enter, Babur joined them. 'Majesty, we must be cautious,' Wazir Khan said quickly, seeing Babur's eagerness. 'This may be a trap.' Babur nodded. He was right. Only a careless fool would rush inside. He forced himself to curb the impetuousness that had so nearly cost him dear when he had run for the blocked doorway. Nevertheless, he couldn't help constantly shifting from foot to foot while Wazir Khan ordered six of his men to take torches from the brackets where they were burning and enter cautiously to check for signs of an ambush.

After what seemed an age to Babur but was, in fact, just a few minutes, they returned, signalling that all seemed quiet. Babur's heart leaped and he stepped inside, his men clustering behind him. Beyond the brass doors they found a cavernous, vaulted entrance chamber and beyond that, straight ahead, a flight of broad, shallow steps. Slowly, warily, they began to climb, guided by flickering torchlight, eyes straining into the darkness ahead. Thirty steps brought them to the second storey. Ahead rose another flight. Babur's foot was already on its first step when he heard a shout.

'Majesty, down, get down!' Babur ducked as a spear flung out of the darkness above hurtled over his head, so close that he felt his hair stir. The next moment, two dozen more of the grand vizier's men were rushing down the stairs towards them. Babur found himself twisting and slashing. In the confusion his dagger was of more use than his sword. He darted beneath his enemies' shields, stabbing upwards with his blade, feeling warm blood spurt down his hands and arms as he found his mark. All around him his men, swearing and grunting, were pushing forward.

The grand vizier's troops began to waver, struggling to maintain the momentum of their charge down the stairs. Soon they were being pushed ever backwards. Suddenly they lost discipline and began fleeing back up, slipping and crashing on the steps in their desperate eagerness to get away and not to have to die in a lost cause. Babur's men came after them, slashing and hacking at the forms disappearing up the second flight of stairs, then retreating part-way up a third.

In the rush, Babur slipped on an uneven step and slithering sideways fell. One of his advancing men was so close behind that he couldn't stop himself stumbling over Babur and in the process standing hard on the small of his back, winding him once more. As the fight receded up the third staircase, Babur scrambled painfully to his feet. For a moment he felt sick and found it hard to focus. Putting his hand against the wall he steadied himself and forced himself to take deep breaths, though his bruised ribs and strained stomach muscles made it painful.

'Majesty.' Wazir Khan was rushing down the stairs towards him. 'Are you hurt?'

Babur shook his head. 'No, I'm fine.'

'The last of the grand vizier's men – those we did not kill – have taken refuge at the top of the building. It's nearly over.' Wazir Khan allowed himself a rare smile and touched Babur's shoulder. 'Come.'

Just then came shouts from below and the sound of many feet pounding the stone steps towards them. Babur swung round to meet the new menace. But surging up the stairs from the dark shadows, he recognised some of the men who had come through the tunnel and, at their head, Ali Mazid

Beg, the muscular chieftain from the west of Ferghana he and Wazir Khan had chosen to lead them.

'Majesty, the citadel and the fortress are ours – as is the city.' Ali Mazid Beg looked exhausted but beneath the filth and sweat his almond-eyed face beamed triumph.

'You have done well.'

'Majesty.' Though he was still out of breath, Ali Mazid Beg's voice was full of pride at what he and his troops had achieved.

'Have you or your men seen the grand vizier?'

Ali Mazid Beg shook his head regretfully.

'Then it must be as Baisanghar thought. He is hiding among his women, here in the Kok Saray, unless he has escaped from the city.'

'Where would he go, Majesty? Who would hide him?' Wazir Khan asked.

With Wazir Khan at his side Babur climbed the remaining steps to the top storey of the Kok Saray. Directly opposite the staircase, through a crowd of his jubilant warriors, he could see a pair of shining silver doors inlaid with turquoises.

'The women's quarters?' Babur asked.

Baisanghar nodded.

In his mind's eye, Babur suddenly pictured his sister Khanzada wide eyed with fear. How would he feel if she was hiding behind such a door, defenceless before warriors high on victory? He turned to the men clustered around him. 'The women are not to be touched. I come to Samarkand as its new king, not as a marauder in the night.'

He read angry disappointment on many of the men's flushed faces. They'd probably believe he'd spoken as he had because he was still a boy with an incomplete understanding of a man's needs and frustrations. But they could think what they liked. Glancing at Wazir Khan he saw approval on his commander's face and felt he'd passed yet another test.

The silver doors shuddered under the impact of a battering

ram carried up from one of the courtyards below and the turquoises shattered, bright shards falling to the floor. Yet the doors held. Beneath the shining silver, the wood must be thick and the bolts strong, Babur thought as, for the fourth time, his men hurled the metal-tipped tree trunk at them. But at last the doors' silver covering buckled and the wood beneath splintered. Two warriors used their axes to hack a hole big enough for a man to enter.

For a few seconds Babur and his men waited, fingering their weapons. He was sure that at any moment they would hear the cry of guards rushing to defend the harem or be forced back from the opening by arrows fired from within. Instead the only response was silence and the rich, heavy scent of sandalwood, which reminded him of the last time he had sat with his mother. It curled around them, mingling with the odour of their sweat.

Signalling to his men to keep silent, Babur moved towards the opening, again determined to be the first inside. 'No, Majesty.' Wazir Khan's restraining hand gripped him hard. 'Let me enter first.'

I owe him this, Babur thought. Hiding his disappointment, he watched Wazir Khan and two of his guards ease themselves cautiously through, weapons ready. A few moments later he heard Wazir Khan say, 'You may enter, Majesty.'

Babur climbed through the shattered door and stepped on to rugs of a velvet softness he had never felt before. The carpets of Ferghana were like worn blankets in comparison.

Wazir Khan signalled to him to be wary. As the rest of his men pushed through behind him, Babur moved forward, scanning the corners of the large chamber, alert for any movement. The chamber was well lit by hundreds of candles burning in mirrored niches. The amber light played over woven wall hangings depicting tulips, irises and other flowers of Samarkand, and plump cushions of velvet or shimmering satin. Six smaller silver doors, three on each side, led to what

Babur guessed were the women's private rooms. Ahead another door was covered with gold leaf into which was etched the tiger of Samarkand.

Feeling his men's eyes upon him once more, Babur cleared his throat. 'Vizier!' he shouted towards the golden door, his voice young, but firm and clear. 'You cannot save yourself but you can at least make your death quick and honourable.' He thought he detected a fumbling sound from behind the door but then all was quiet again. 'Vizier, have you no dignity or shame?' Babur persisted.

This time there was the unmistakable sound of a scuffle and voices raised in anger. Suddenly the golden door swung open to reveal two of the grand vizier's bodyguards, one with a sabre slash across his cheek, dragging their protesting master by his arms, his bright green brocade coat billowing behind him. Without ceremony they hurled him at Babur's feet, then knelt before him themselves in subjection. Other guards, following nervously, also prostrated themselves. Babur gazed at the scene with contempt. 'Baisanghar, disarm them.'

As Baisanghar's men went briskly to work, a young woman in pale blue silk darted through the golden door, deftly evaded Baisanghar's men and ran to the grand vizier. Falling to her knees beside him, she tried to put her arms round him but, with an oath, he pushed her slim form away violently. After regaining her balance, the girl looked up at Babur. He saw an oval face and eyes that, though puffy with tears, were still beautiful. 'Let my father live. He is an old man.' She spoke without fear though confronted by a crowd of battle-stained warriors from whom she must know she could expect little sympathy or even mercy.

'He has no right to live. His ambition exceeded his breeding,' Babur replied curtly. 'Where are the other women?'

The girl hesitated then said, 'In their rooms.' She gestured towards the six small doors. Babur nodded to Wazir Khan. 'Search them. Make sure no soldiers are hiding there. Then

lock the women in until we have time to deal with them.'
Wazir Khan quickly detailed groups of soldiers to break
down the doors. Almost at once Babur heard wails of dismay
and screams of protest from deep within the harem, but he
knew his orders would be obeyed. He could not prevent the
women being frightened but they would not be violated.

The vizier's daughter was still looking directly at him, a
challenging expression in her chestnut eyes. He turned away
from her accusing stare. 'Take her to her private quarters and
lock her in also.' He had no intention of sparing the vizier
but found he wanted to save the young woman from
witnessing her father's end. Before a soldier could take hold
of her, she rose of her own accord and disappeared through
one of the doors, her head held high on her slender neck,
without any final entreaty or even a backward glance. Babur
stared after her, wondering what it had cost her to show
such dignity.

'Well, vizier, it seems your daughter is braver and more
loyal than your bodyguard. You do not deserve such devotion.'
Babur realised that he felt angry for the girl about the way
her father had publicly humiliated her by pushing her away.

'You have no right to the throne of Samarkand.' The grand
vizier had dragged himself to a sitting position and was looking
at Babur with a malevolent expression on his pockmarked,
square-jawed face, seemingly unconcerned that he faced
inevitable death.

'I am of Timur's blood, the nephew of the last king. Who
has greater claim?'

The grand vizier narrowed his bloodshot eyes. 'You may
think you have taken Samarkand but you'll never hold it,' he
sneered. 'Ponder that, dregs of the mountains. Go back to
Ferghana and your life among the stinking sheep. Perhaps one
of them would make you a good wife – I've heard your
people are not particular . . .'

'Enough!' Babur was shaking with what he recognised as

adolescent fury but hoped his men would interpret as kingly rage. 'Baisanghar,' he rapped.

The captain stepped towards him. 'Majesty?'

'As well as usurping a throne, this man did you a shameful wrong because you followed your true king's last command.' Babur saw Baisanghar glance down to where his right hand should have been. 'You shall have the task of despatching this wretch to whatever awaits him in the next world. Dispose of him in the courtyard below and make his end quick out of respect for his daughter's bravery. Then hang his body in chains above the Turquoise Gate so the people can see how I have punished the man whose avarice and ambition brought them such hardship and want. His bodyguard may live, provided they swear allegiance to me as their king.'

As Baisanghar's men dragged the vizier away, Babur suddenly felt deeply weary. For a moment he closed his eyes and stooped to run his fingers over the silkily luxurious carpet that tomorrow he would order rolled up and sent to his mother as a gift. 'Samarkand,' he whispered to himself. 'It is mine.'

Chapter 6

One Hundred Days

The Turquoise Gate sparkled as the bright light reflected off the high glaze of its blue, green and gold tiles. Babur felt as if he was riding into the heart of the sun as he approached the gate to make his ceremonial entrance into Samarkand. His green silk robes flowed around him, stirring in the light breeze. Timur's golden ring, with its snarling tiger, gleamed on his finger, and the necklace of uncut emeralds around his neck rose and fell with his breathing. Conscious that thousands of eyes would be watching him, he forced himself to look stern, though he felt like throwing back his head, filling his lungs and yelling his triumph to the skies.

Behind him rode his chiefs and their men. From the motley collection of tribesmen who had ridden with him from Ferghana, Wazir Khan had fashioned, in just two days, an army to impress and awe as it processed through the city. The chambers of the Kok Saray had yielded many riches in which to dress his rough, nomadic warriors from engraved helmets and cuirasses to bright silks hoarded by the grand vizier while his people lived impoverished.

He would bring prosperity back to this great city, Babur

vowed as, to a chorus of trumpets and the echoing boom of taut-skinned kettle-drums, he passed beneath the gate above which the vizier's headless body dangled, already blackening in the sun, in its iron cage. As he moved onward he could see before him the city's blue domes and minarets. Soon he was passing one of the great markets with walled caravanserais on either side to accommodate travelling merchants. His father had spoken often of the wealthy caravan trains of Timur's day – the lines of swaying, snorting camels and fast-trotting mules carrying furs, leather and fine cloth from the west, brocades, china and pungent musk from the east, and, from distant lands across the Indus, fragrant nutmeg, cloves and cinnamon, as well as bright gems.

The crowds along the streets were restrained but not hostile. Babur could feel their curiosity as he rode into the vast Registan Square where, beneath striped green silk awnings, was a marble dais. His uncle's former counsellors and the leading nobles of Samarkand were waiting in meek lines at its foot.

He dismounted, stepped on to the dais and made his way to its centre where a gilded throne, with carved tiger feet, waited. With so many scrutinising him, he was suddenly self-conscious as he gathered his voluminous robes about him and sat down with as much dignity as he could manage. He was still so young – not quite fourteen. What would people think to see a boy seated before them? But, he told himself, Samarkand was his – by blood and conquest. He lifted his chin and stared proudly ahead.

Sitting stiffly on the splendid throne, he received the oath of allegiance from his new subjects and in turn distributed offices and more of the vizier's hoarded wealth. But as rank after rank of figures advanced to prostrate themselves before him, Babur knew there was scarcely a man among them he could trust. The thought sobered him and the grand vizier's contemptuous words thrust themselves into his mind: 'You'll never hold Samarkand.'

He would prove to the people he was fit to rule. Hadn't he already shown mercy and generosity? He had pardoned all who would submit to his authority. The women of the grand vizier's harem would, in due course, be found places in those of Babur's chiefs instead of being ravished in the first moments of victory. As for the vizier's daughter, he had already despatched her to his cousin Mahmud in Kunduz. She had shown little reluctance. Indeed, she should be pleased. Not only would she be wife to a royal prince of the House of Timur, but Mahmud had saved her only two years previously from being raped by brigands. He had been so smitten with her that he had laid siege to Samarkand for her sake.

Yes, he had acted well, Babur reflected. The people had no reason to fear him and every reason to respect him. All the same, the grand vizier had planted a malignant canker in his mind . . .

Suddenly Babur heard Wazir Khan proclaim, 'Hail, Babur, King of Samarkand!' The cry taken up by thousands of voices filled the square and roused Babur from his thoughts. He was a fool to let a dead man whose body now hung in a cage to rot torment him. As he had agreed with Wazir Khan when they had arranged the ceremony, Babur took the cry as his cue. He rose and turned slowly to face each side of the crowded square, allowing all to gaze up on their new king. Then he told the populace, 'My rule will bring peace and prosperity to all the citizens of Samarkand. As a token of this, I will remit a month of the taxes levied on the city's markets.'

The crowd roared its approval. Though his own expression remained impassive, jubilation welled inside him again. Timur had been thirty-one, more than twice his age, when he had seized Samarkand. It had been his first great conquest, the springboard to a mighty empire. And so it would be for Babur.

Tonight he would have food distributed throughout the

city to alleviate the sufferings of the siege as a further demonstration of his largesse. For himself and his men, there would be feasting and here, at least, he could already outshine Timur, whose tastes had been austere: his favourite dishes had been roasted horsemeat, boiled mutton and rice. They would eat fat sheep brought into the starving city from the meadows beyond and already turning on the spit. Partridges and pheasants were simmering in succulent sauces flavoured with pomegranates and tamarinds. Ripe melons bursting with juice sweet as honey and purple grapes with the bloom still on them were being piled on jewelled salvers. Babur's mouth watered.

The ceremonials were at an end but Babur still had something to do before the celebrations began. Slowly he stepped from the dais and remounted his horse. Signalling to Wazir Khan and his guard to follow, he trotted out of the square in the direction of the Gur Emir, the ribbed, egg-shaped, blue-tiled dome with its two slender minarets that was Timur's tomb.

At the tall, arched gatehouse of the walled complex, Babur jumped down. For reasons he could not have explained, he needed to be alone. He asked Wazir Khan and his guards to wait, then went inside. He crossed a courtyard where sparrows fluttered amid the branches of a mulberry tree, took off his embroidered boots, as custom demanded, and entered the tomb.

The contrast with the bright light outside made it hard to see and he came blinking into an octagonal chamber. The sombre richness he saw in the shafts of tawny light filtering through fretted arches high in the wall made him gasp. He ran his fingers over marble walls inlaid with green alabaster and surmounted at head level by a band of gilded tiles. Above that, the walls were embellished with carved papier-mâché painted blue and gold and set around panels in which verses from the Koran were written in exquisite calligraphy. He craned his neck to see the domed ceiling painted with gilded stars dancing riotously in their private heaven.

Directly beneath the dome a sarcophagus lay on a plain marble platform. It was at least six feet long, with a lid of green jade so dark it looked almost black – a fitting monument to Timur but not, as Babur knew, where he lay. To one side of the chamber, a sloping vaulted passage led to a lower crypt. After a few moments, Babur entered it. The passage was so narrow that his shoulders brushed the cold walls as slowly he descended – bare feet slipping on smooth stone – to emerge into a much smaller, simpler room. A small marble screen high in the wall and carved like honeycomb was the only source of light, which fell in faint shafts on to the carved white marble coffin that contained Timur's body.

When Timur had died on his march to conquer China, his attendants had perfumed and preserved his corpse with rosewater, camphor and musk before carrying it back in glory to Samarkand and laying it here. Despite the lavish funeral ceremony, it was said the great conqueror had not, at first, found peace. Night after night the sound of wild howling that rose from his tomb had terrified the citizens of Samarkand. The dead emperor seemed unable to take his eternal rest. The screeches had lasted a year until, finally, the desperate people had gone to Timur's son. They had tumbled to their knees before him, begging him to free the prisoners, especially the craftsmen, Timur had seized during his wars of conquest and brought to Samarkand to beautify his capital so that, as the released men journeyed to their earthly homes, Timur could finally make his way to his heavenly one. Seeing the frightened, harrowed faces of his subjects, Timur's son had listened. The prisoners had been sent back to their homelands and Timur had howled no more.

Tales for old women, Babur thought. But there was another story he did believe – it was said that an epitaph had been engraved on the underside of Timur's coffin lid: 'If I am roused from my grave, the earth will tremble.'

Babur approached the coffin reverently. Almost afraid, he stretched out his hand to touch the lid where, standing out boldly, was a carved inscription recounting Timur's ancestry. My ancestry, Babur thought. My blood. He lowered his head and pressed his lips to the chill stone. 'I will be worthy of you,' he whispered. It was a promise to the great Timur, and to his dead father. But, above all, it was a promise to himself.

◆

The soft morning breeze stirred the gauzy, pearl-sewn hangings of the pavilion in the Baghi Dilkusha, Timur's Garden of Heart's Delight, where – nearly two months after his triumphal entry into Samarkand – Babur was asleep. Of all the parks that Timur had built in the fields and meadows around Samarkand, this was Babur's favourite. The previous evening, with the sun already setting, on impulse he had summoned Wazir Khan and his bodyguard. They had ridden out through the Turquoise Gate and down the two-mile avenue of stately, gently swaying poplars that led eastward to the garden. Though night had been falling as they galloped in through the gateway, Babur had been able to see Timur's domed and colonnaded summer palace, gleaming like a great pearl through the dark trees and the pale outlines of the airy pavilions that surrounded it.

Babur had chosen to sleep in one of the pavilions, its graceful marble pillars inlaid with Chinese porcelain and surrounded by elms, plane trees and slender, dark green cypresses. He knew that Timur, too, had liked to sleep in his gardens. He had even ordered his throne to be placed on a platform erected above the intersection of two watercourses. The four gushing channels represented the four rivers of life and symbolised his dominion over the four quarters of the globe.

The more Babur contemplated Timur, the more breathtaking

his vision and ambitions seemed. It was easy to speak of himself as Timur's heir, but when he considered what that meant, he felt humbled and exhilarated.

Something – perhaps the cackle of a pheasant – roused him from his dreams. He sat up with a start and looked around him. The luxury – the floors inlaid with black ebony and pale ivory, the marble sculptures, the golden flasks and cups encrusted with emeralds, turquoises and rubies – was still hard to take in. He touched the rose-coloured silk, shot through with golden thread, of the mattress on which he was lying. This mattress was itself screened from his attendants by a delicately wrought silver and gilt screen set with rose quartz.

Whatever the grand vizier's crimes, at least he had preserved the treasures of Timur's summer palace. At the first sign of trouble, he had ordered all the costly carpets, hangings and vessels to be carried to Samarkand where he had secreted them in underground treasure chambers within the citadel. His officials, anxious to ingratiate themselves with their new ruler, had been quick to reveal them to Babur's men. Though some of the palace's precious inlay had been chipped away and several lesser pavilions constructed mainly of timber had been knocked down to provide fuel – probably by his own men during the siege, Babur reflected – it had not taken long to restore its beauty.

Babur grinned as he contemplated what his mother, grandmother and sister would say when, as soon as it was safe, he summoned them. His letters, scratched on the fine, thick paper for which Samarkand was famous, had not done justice to its grandeur, history or scale. After all, this was a city founded eighteen centuries previously by golden-haired, blue-eyed Alexander who, coming from the far west with his armies, had, like Timur, brushed aside all opposition. Babur had ordered Samarkand's outer walls with their thick ramparts to be measured and discovered it would take a man eleven thousand paces to walk round them. Timur had indeed protected his city well – though one of Babur's first acts had been to brick up the tunnel through which he himself had sneaked in. He did not wish others – and there were many whose eyes would be on the rich prize of Samarkand – to follow literally in his footsteps. He had also ordered a thorough search for any other tunnels.

Babur lay back on the duck-down pillows. The past weeks had been so rich in new sights and experiences that it seemed incredible so little time had passed. In his letters to his grandmother, who was interested in such things, he had tried to capture his astonishment at the sight of the round, three-storey observatory on high Kohak Hill outside the city where Timur's grandson, Ulugh Beg, had studied the solar and lunar calendars. Babur had gazed in utter amazement at Ulugh Beg's sextant, a perfect arc of marble-clad brick, nearly two hundred feet long with a radius of some 130 feet and decorated with the signs of the zodiac. Ulugh Beg had made his observations and taken his measurements using an astrolabe mounted on metal rails at either side of the sextant.

If Timur had conquered the world, his armies moving like a cloud of locusts over a green field, it was Ulugh Beg who had captured the heavens. He had composed the royal astronomical tables still used by the star-gazers of Samarkand. Babur wished he had paid more attention to his lessons but, even so, the sophistication of the observatory filled him with pride at his ancestors' achievements. Ulugh Beg's own son, concerned where his father's quest for knowledge and enlightenment might lead and encouraged by fanatical mullahs, fearful that their mysteries might be penetrated and their dogmas questioned, had had him murdered.

Babur had inspected the religious college Ulugh Beg had built. It filled one side of the Registan Square, and was decorated with turquoise and navy blue tiles, their pattern so intricate that men called it *hazarbaf*, 'thousand-weave'. The huge Bibi Khanym mosque in the heart of the city had overwhelmed him. Nothing could have been more different from the plain, austere mosque in his castle of Ferghana where, what seemed a lifetime ago, in the shafting moonlight, his chiefs had sworn their loyalty to him.

A priest told Babur how Timur's favourite wife, Bibi Khanym, the ivory-skinned Chinese princess whose luminous beauty could move the great conqueror to tears, had intended the mosque as a surprise for Timur on his return from a campaign. But the architect she had summoned from Persia to build it had, in a moment of reckless passion, seized her and left a love-bite on her neck. When Timur returned just days later and saw the blemish on his wife's otherwise flawless skin and heard her story, he had sent soldiers to seize the architect who, in terror, had flung himself from one of the sky-touching minarets he had just built. Whatever the truth of the tale, the tall, graceful portal flanked by columns more than 150 feet high, and the mosque's even higher dome – decorated with mosaics – had left Babur dumb with awe.

Babur yawned and stretched. His mother would be all pleasure and delight when she reached Samarkand, and Khanzada would be dizzy with excitement and curiosity. But he wasn't so sure about Esan Dawlat. His grandmother was hard to please. He could imagine her small dark eyes scrunching up in her wrinkled face as she shook her head and told him not to get carried away with his initial victory but to think about what came next.

Yet he had claimed his prize well, Babur thought. Fate had held it out to him in an open hand and he had grabbed it. He clapped, and instantly an attendant appeared with a ewer of warm, rose-scented water that he poured into a large silver bowl. Carrying it carefully, he approached Babur, intending to wash him with the cloth he was also holding, but Babur waved him away, still unused to having someone to do everything for him, and asked him to place the bowl

105

and cloth on the stand as his side. As he gazed at his reflection in the smooth surface of the water he felt an unexpected yearning to dip his head into the chill waters of one of Ferghana's mountain streams.

But then he caught the delicious scent of new baked bread and roasting partridges. He was a fool to feel wistful or homesick when he was in Paradise. His men, too, seemed content – which was rare, he mused, as he scrubbed his neck and shoulders. But, after all, they had the booty he'd promised. The coin-stuffed coffers of Samarkand had proved deep enough for him to be generous. He had given each of his chieftains a hundred thick gold pieces and their men had been well rewarded with silver. Neither had he forgotten to send some of the bounty back to Ferghana to his regent Kasim, to reward him and Babur's other followers and to assist him in retaining the allegiance of the fractious surrounding tribes. Many of Babur's men had acquired new wives too. As he anticipated, the young women of the grand vizier's harem had gone to them willingly enough. A victorious warrior with a bag of money was not a bad bargain.

It was time to dress. Suppressing his impatience, he allowed his attendants, swarming sycophantically round him, to clothe him in a white silk shirt, and trousers of soft deerskin. Then, from the many they held out to him, he selected a brocade tunic – brilliant green in deference to his new people, but striped with the yellow of Ferghana – with enamelled clasps. The exquisitely stitched garments, the best that Samarkand's tailors could provide, felt very different from the practical sheepskins and coarser cloth of Ferghana. An attendant wound a fringed sash round his waist, arranging the folds with mathematical precision, and another knelt to guide his feet into gold-tooled, knee-length leather boots. Then, finally, from a sandalwood casket, Babur selected some jewels. He had no interest in such things but later he would pray in public in the Bibi Khanym mosque and he must appear to his watching subjects every inch a king whose riches – and consequently his bounty – were, in a world of ever-shifting alliances and loyalties, inexhaustible.

With his mace-bearer ahead and four tall bodyguards behind, Babur walked along a marble path to where his counsellors were waiting for him in the gardens, sitting cross-legged on carpets beneath a flowered awning. Babur found these endless meetings irksome but there was much to be done. The uncertainty and strife after his uncle's death, and the siege, had done a great deal of damage. Though the fields and meadows around Samarkand were fertile enough, the farmers had been too afraid to tend them, and much of this year's harvest had been lost. Babur had ordered seed corn from his own supplies, brought from Ferghana, to be distributed among them for the next spring. Also, many of the herdsmen had fled, driving their flocks westward and away from the fighting. They would need to be coaxed back.

But at least he had good men to help him, Babur thought. Wazir Khan, of course, was chief among his *ichkis*, his inner circle of counsellors. But there was also Baisanghar, who commanded much respect among the soldiers of Samarkand. Only after the city had fallen had Babur realised just how much the weak resistance he had encountered had been due to Baisanghar's cajoling, subverting and bribing. In gratitude he had given him overall command of the defences of Samarkand.

His eyes fell on the weathered face of Ali Mazid Beg. He had been wise to make him a counsellor. It was partly a reward for past loyalty – the chief had been one of the few to support Babur unequivocally from the outset – but it was also shrewd. Ali Mazid Beg was one of the most influential tribal leaders of Ferghana. That he had remained with Babur in Samarkand had helped in persuading others – including some who Babur had feared might return at once to Ferghana – to stay.

But, of course, many had not. Loot was what they had come for, and once they had it, they were restless for their homelands. The wild, unruly Chakraks, whose reputation for fickleness and brutality was notorious even in a world where treachery and cruelty were common, had melted away to their inaccessible mountain fastnesses and more were following each day as autumn drew on.

Babur's counsellors knelt at his approach but he waved them to their feet, eager to get on with the business of the day. He had already learned that a king's duties were not concerned merely with great matters. Only yesterday he had arbitrated in a tedious dispute between two hawk-featured carpet dealers, squabbling like children over the value of a red, pink and blue rug from Tabriz in far-distant Persia. It had cost him much to keep a straight face.

'Majesty, here are today's petitions.' His chamberlain presented him with a silver dish piled with papers weighted down by a square of brass to prevent them flying away in the breeze.

Babur's heart sank as he looked at the dense scrawl covering the topmost document. Probably an argument about a sheep or a goat or grazing rights on a barren hillside. 'I'll look at them later.' He wished he could go hunting instead. He waved to his council to be seated and took his own place on an ivory-inlaid stool on a low wooden dais. It was much less comfortable than sitting cross-legged on the floor as they were.

'When will the review of the city's fortifications be complete?' he asked Baisanghar.

'Soon, Majesty. The final count has been made of the weapons in the armouries but the masons are still checking the condition of the outer walls and ramparts. They say that the earthquake two years ago left some cracks in the foundations that may need attention.'

Babur nodded. 'Any repairs must be made quickly. That

Samarkand fell so easily will not have escaped attention. Wazir Khan, have there been any signs of Shaibani Khan's men?'

'We are on constant alert against their return but the many scouts we have about our borders report no trace of Uzbek patrols. Shaibani Khan will know he has little time to mount a campaign before winter.'

'But he will come,' Babur said thoughtfully. Shaibani Khan had already killed one king of Samarkand: why should he hesitate to destroy another, especially one who was just a youth and newly on his throne?

'Yes, Majesty, I'm sure of it. We all are. But he won't be here until the spring. By then we will be prepared for him and his scum.' Wazir Khan's confidence warmed Babur.

The sudden sound of voices made them all look round. Across the gardens, with their beds of bright orange marigolds and pink roses, Babur saw a small, stooped figure following a guard towards them. He was dressed in travelling clothes and, as he came closer, he unwound the purple scarf he had wrapped around his head so that he did not breathe in the dust of the road and Babur recognised the lined face and thin white hair of his grandmother's elderly steward, Walid Butt. To Babur it seemed he looked distressed, not just by his long journey in the saddle — itself a considerable trial to a man of his age — but by the import of the message he was carrying.

For a moment, despite the late summer warmth, Babur felt a chill pass over him. Was Esan Dawlat dead? Rising to his feet, he stepped swiftly from the dais and put an arm round the old man's shoulders. 'Speak, steward. What news do you bring?'

Walid Butt hesitated, as if he was not sure how to begin. Babur wanted to shout at him to get on with it, but out of respect for a man he had known his whole life he curbed his impatience.

'Forgive me, Majesty, for appearing before you like this,

but my journey has been a hard and a hasty one.' The steward fumbled beneath his cloak for a leather bag that hung from his neck on a short strap and produced a letter impressed with the royal seal of Ferghana.

Babur grabbed it and tore it open. He recognised his grandmother's writing and breathed more easily, but his relief was short lived. Esan Dawlat's first words danced before his eyes. 'If you do not answer our call of distress, we face ruin.' He scanned the rest quickly, his shock growing as he took in what his grandmother was saying.

'What is it?' asked Wazir Khan.

'I have been betrayed. My bastard half-brother Jahangir sits on the throne of Ferghana – a child puppet put there by my cousin Tambal, who has bribed the tribal leaders with promises of reward . . . He is using Jahangir for his own advantage . . .' Babur let the letter slip from his fingers to the ground where the breeze blew it a short distance until it caught on one of the rose bushes. I have lost the throne of my homeland, he thought.

While Wazir Khan retrieved the letter and read it swiftly, another even darker concern gripped Babur. Again he took Walid Butt by the shoulder, this time so firmly that the old man, who had scarcely an ounce of flesh on his frame, winced. 'My grandmother, my mother and my sister, when did you last see them? Where are they? Are they safe?'

Walid Butt gazed sorrowfully at him. 'They and your vizier Kasim are prisoners in the castle. Your grandmother managed to smuggle this letter to me and ordered me to bring it to you. But whether they are alive or dead, I do not know. I have been travelling these past two weeks.' His voice cracked.

Suddenly realising he was hurting him, Babur relaxed his grip. 'You have done well, steward. You must eat and rest. Thank you for your service.' As Walid Butt was led away, it seemed to Babur that, if the breeze strengthened only a little, his frail form would be blown away.

Babur's mind was reeling, his initial disbelief giving way to anger. How dared Tambal take his kingdom and imprison his family . . . ? But he struggled to master himself. Everything could depend on the decisions he was about to take. He looked up to see his council watching him expectantly and took a deep breath.

'Wazir Khan, prepare my bodyguard. We will ride at once for Ferghana. Baisanghar, assemble a force. Call up my chiefs and their men – two thousand should be enough to deal with Tambal and his indisciplined tribal levies. I expect most of the citizens of Ferghana to return to my side as their rightful ruler when I arrive at Akhsi. However, leave enough troops here to defend this city should Shaibani Khan return, and follow us within the week. Also, have battering rams, siege engines and catapults made ready in case I send for them. Ali Mazid Beg, you will be regent of Samarkand in my absence. Guard it well.'

The three older men nodded. Babur turned away, already ripping off his jewelled fripperies and calling for his riding clothes and his arms.

·◆·

As he rode shoulder to shoulder with Wazir Khan, galloping over meadows still baked hard by the summer heat, Babur was in torment. Guilt, fear for his family and fury against those who thought they could supplant him with a nine year old battled inside him. What a fool he had been these last weeks, wandering around Samarkand lost in a dream, planning how to show off his fairytale city to his family.

He had neglected what was most important, arrogantly assuming that in Ferghana he would now be a hero whom no one would dare challenge. Instead Tambal and his supporters had bided their time, like wolves waiting until the shepherd's back was turned to run in among the flock. And they had surely been cunning or Kasim, his grandmother and his mother

111

would have suspected a plot and warned Babur earlier. If anything had happened to the women of his family . . . If Roxanna should use her power as mother of Ferghana's new king to rid herself of enemies and rivals . . . He could not bear to think of it.

Each night when, exhausted from long hours in the saddle, they made camp, Babur found it hard to sleep. He grudged every second that he was not riding eastward and became angry with Wazir Khan for insisting he must rest. But on the fourth night, there was no question of sleep. As he lay on the ground, his body began shaking violently and his brow was clammy with sweat. By the time dawn broke, his teeth were chattering so much that he could barely speak. When he tried to stand, his legs gave way and he fell helplessly to the ground. At once Wazir Khan was beside him, feeling his pulse and pulling back his eyelids to check his pupils. 'Majesty, you cannot ride today.'

For once, Babur lacked the strength to argue. He felt Wazir Khan cover him with thick woollen blankets, but as he tried to look up at him, the world swam before him and grew dark. Then it went black.

· ◆ ·

Water was trickling between his parched lips. Babur's tongue, half stuck to the roof of his mouth, loosened, seeking the drops eagerly. He had no idea where he was. All that mattered was getting some of that precious moisture. At last his eyes jerked open. The familiar figure of Wazir Khan was leaning over him, a long strip of cotton cloth in one hand and a water bottle in the other. When he saw that Babur was conscious, he put them down and knelt back.

Babur was still burning with thirst. 'More water,' he wanted to say, but managed only a dry-lipped croak. Wazir Khan understood. He placed the end of the cloth between Babur's lips and continued what he had been doing, unknown to

Babur, for the past hour: pouring a thin stream of water down the cloth so that it flowed a few drops at a time into Babur's mouth.

After a long while, Babur choked, spluttered and managed to sit up. Wazir Khan put the cloth and the water bottle to one side and felt his forehead. 'Your temperature is falling at last, Majesty.'

Looking around him, Babur saw they were inside a small cave with a fire at the centre. His head spun and he closed his eyes. 'How long have I been ill?'

'Four days, Majesty. It is now midday on the fifth.'

'What was it? Not poison, surely . . . ?'

Wazir Khan shook his head. 'No. Just a high fever – probably the result of a sheep-tick bite.'

Babur almost smiled – a tick bite at a time like this.

'Fetch some broth,' Wazir Khan called to one of his men. When the bowl of millet-flour soup was brought he knelt beside Babur, holding it to his lips with one hand and supporting his head with the other. The warm liquid tasted good but Babur could only manage a little before his stomach clenched and he waved the bowl aside.

'Has there been news from Samarkand? Baisanghar must be almost ready to bring the army after us.'

'No, Majesty. There has been nothing.'

'Or from Ferghana?' Silently Babur cursed the ill luck that had struck him down. By now, riding hard and light, the mountains of Ferghana should have been in sight.

Wazir Khan shook his head. 'I did not look for any news. I sent out no scouts. My concern was to keep you hidden until you had recovered. There will be many spies between here and Ferghana. If reports reached Ferghana that you were ill – or dead . . .'

He left the words unspoken but Babur understood. If the traitors pulling the strings of their little puppet king thought he was dead, his womenfolk might not see another sunrise.

113

'Thank you, Wazir Khan. As always, you think of things I fail to.' Wazir Khan's words reminded him chillingly of his predicament. Babur lay back, willing the strength to flow back into his limbs but miserably conscious of how weak he was. 'I will rest for the remainder of today, but tomorrow, we will ride.'

'Yes, Majesty, if you are able to.'

'I will be.' Babur closed his eyes again, praying that he was right.

He slept most of that day and night but woke as soon as the dim light of the following morning crept into the cave. Sitting up cautiously he found that his head was clearer and that, though he still felt a little unsteady, he could stand unaided. With one hand against the lichen-covered wall, he walked stiffly towards the cave opening and ducked outside. Wazir Khan and some of his guards were squatting around a small fire of sheep's droppings that was burning brightly. A copper kettle was suspended above it from a makeshift frame.

Wazir Khan handed him a clay cup of hot water that tasted of smoke and a piece of dry bread that he began to chew. He noticed that the horses, tethered by a clump of gorse bushes, were already saddled and loaded. Wazir Khan had, as always, done well. Within half an hour they had kicked earth over the remains of their fire, filled their leather water bottles from a stream and were mounting.

Babur pulled himself into his saddle with none of his usual spring, feeling the eyes not only of Wazir Khan but of the rest of his men upon him. For a moment he swayed, but then he kicked his horse on in the direction of the sunrise and Ferghana.

• ◆ •

Babur's heart quickened as, in the distance, he made out the Jaxartes river and his home. The robust little castle of

Akhsi, half built into the cliff above the river, was the place of his earliest and fondest memories. At this moment, the glories of Samarkand could not compete and he felt tears rising.

'Majesty, it is dangerous to go further tonight.' Wazir Khan's eyes, too, were bright with tears. 'They'll be watching for us. We should stay concealed until I've sent out scouts.'

Babur wanted to gallop to the gates and demand entry, but Wazir Khan was right. He got shakily down from his horse, feeling the feverish ache in his limbs, and listened as Wazir Khan selected his two best and swiftest horsemen to ride onwards and find out what they could.

The fortress was at least an hour's journey, perhaps more in the gathering darkness, and the scouts would need to take care not to be seen. It would be some while before they returned. Perched as Babur and his men were high on the side of a hill and reluctant to retreat back over the crest, their position was too exposed to risk a fire to warm themselves or cook over. Not that they had much to cook. In the six days since Babur's recovery, they had travelled too fast to forage or hunt. Instead they had relied mainly on the now mouldering bread, cheese, apples and dried fruit they had brought from Samarkand. Babur wrapped himself in a blanket and chewed a strip of dried melon. Its sweetness disgusted him and he spat it out, taking a long draught of water to rid himself of the cloying taste.

The scouts returned two hours before dawn, and the news was bad, as Babur had suspected it would be. The castle gates were barred and many defenders were keeping watch from the walls. According to a herdsman the scouts had surprised as he sat around his fire in a riverside pasture with his two young sons, who had been too terrified to speak anything but the truth, many of the nomadic tribal leaders had sworn to support Babur's half-brother. It didn't surprise Babur to learn that the chieftain whose men he had ordered hacked to death for stealing the peasant's goods and raping his wife outside Samarkand was among them. And of course, Jahangir's grandfather. Babur thought of the sly-faced old man who had brought Roxanna and her brat to the castle. He should never have taken them in – but what else could he have done? Jahangir was his half-brother. Blood was blood.

It was no surprise either that Yusuf, his father's stout treasurer, together with Baba Qashqa, his comptroller of the household, and Baqi Beg, his thin, fidgety astrologer, had joined his half-brother since – though Babur had allowed them to live – he had forced them to yield their profitable appointments.

His thoughts returned to his grandmother, mother and sister. The scouts had not been able to find out anything about them. He cursed his powerlessness. What could he and two dozen bodyguards do anyway? He must wait for his army to join him.

As the sun rose behind Mount Beshtor, making the ever-present snow on the summit sparkle like crystal, Babur wrapped his cloak round him, and, signalling he wished to be alone, began to tramp up the hill on which they had camped. The emerald-green grass was slippery with dew beneath his feet. It smelled fresh and sweet. But before long winter would descend and these slopes would be frozen hard and white. It was a worrying thought. How could he campaign in winter?

The wind blowing in from the east had a cold bite. Babur settled in the shelter of a slab of rock and his keen eyes scanned the landscape whose contours he knew so intimately they felt like part of him – every sweep of green meadowland, every steep-sided valley with its patches of grey scree, every jagged mountain peak, every bend in the Jaxartes. The sense of loss overwhelmed him and he bowed his head.

The sun had risen high in a bright, cloudless sky when Babur heard the distant thud of hoofbeats coming from the west. Leaping up, he turned to look behind him and, sure enough, in the distance, he could see a long line of riders coming along a valley. Narrowing his eyes, he tried to count them – perhaps two hundred, maybe more – and caught the flash of a green standard. It must be the advance guard sent by Baisanghar.

Feeling new energy surging through him, driving out the despair, he turned and ran down the hill towards the camp, slipping and rolling in his eagerness. 'Wazir Khan, the troops are coming,' he shouted, as he ran into the camp.

'You are sure they are our men?'

'I'm certain. They carry the green banners of Samarkand.'

'I will send a patrol to guide them to us, Majesty.'

Heart pounding, Babur watched the men gallop off. Now we'll flush those scum out of the castle. Tambal will repent his treachery and as for the rest . . . Babur ran to his saddlebag and unstrapped his father's sword. As he drew it from its scabbard, the rubies in the eagle hilt flashed in the sunlight. It felt good to balance it in his hand and he imagined bringing it down, in a slashing sweep, on Tambal's bare neck, as he had done on the neck of Qambar-Ali on the first day of his rule in Ferghana.

It wasn't long before the riders were in view, Baisanghar himself at their head.

Babur stepped forward. Beneath his pointed helmet, Baisanghar looked exhausted. 'When will the main army get here? Are they far away?'

Baisanghar hesitated a moment before he answered. 'There is no main army, Majesty.'

The light in Babur's eyes died. 'What do you mean?'

'Mahmud of Kunduz, your cousin, has seized Samarkand. He must have been plotting with Tambal and had his armies ready. He waited until I had ridden from the city with the advance guard, then made his attack. He was aided from within by some of the former associates of the grand vizier whom the vizier's daughter, Prince Mahmud's wife, seems to have suborned through messengers promising extravagant rewards. We had been riding for five days before men reached me with the news of Samarkand's fall. I'm sorry, Majesty. I have failed you.'

'Mahmud . . .' Babur could hardly take in what Baisanghar had said. That the cousin he'd known all his life and had thought of as a friend – the cousin to whom he'd only recently sent the gift of a bride – should betray him like this seemed impossible. 'What of Ali Mazid Beg?'

'He is dead, Majesty. His body, not the grand vizier's, now swings above the Turquoise Gate, and many others who were loyal to you are dead.'

Babur turned away, disgust at his cousin and grief for the loyal Ali Mazid Beg almost overwhelming him. At the same time, his mind was trying to grapple with something else: the sheer enormity of his loss. His reign over Samarkand had been – what? A hundred days . . . ? And now he was king of nothing, not even of Ferghana. He was still clutching his father's sword and the solid feel of the hilt in his hand comforted him. This was not to be his fate, he vowed, gripping the hilt still tighter. He would not let it be. However long it took, however much blood he spilled, he would take back what was his. Those who had injured him would pay.

Part II

King Without a Throne

Chapter 7

Hit and Run

The mixture of snow and sleet penetrated even the thick sheepskin-lined jacket in which Babur was wrapped. He shivered as, head bowed against the elements, he rode at the head of his remaining men beside a small river, the edges of which were half frozen, up a remote valley among the high mountains to the north of Ferghana.

During the first difficult days after he had discovered that he had lost not one but both of his kingdoms, Babur had wanted to stay near Akhsi in the hope of being able to stake all on getting into the fortress to free his family. But Wazir Khan had with difficulty dissuaded him, pointing out that his enemies would expect such a desperate attempt and would be on guard against it. Wazir Khan, fatherly in his comforting support, had advised, 'If you wish to save your grandmother, your mother and your sister, you must not throw your life away by taking extravagant risks but make your enemies fear you. To do this you must pressure them, attacking now here, now there, disappearing before they can concentrate their forces against you. Be elusive, ever-threatening. Your foes must never sleep soundly. And if you do this, Majesty, they will not dare to harm your family.'

At length, Babur had recognised the sense of what Wazir Khan was saying. Thinking carefully, he had suggested a plan. 'We will need a safe base where we can see out the winter and plan our first raids. I remember that, as part of the military training you gave me each summer, you once took me on an expedition to the northern mountains and we stayed in an old mud fort at the head of a valley where a vassal of Tambal commanded the small garrison. That might make a good base. It is little visited. What d'you think?'

'I remember the place. It is indeed remote and could serve our purpose well.'

And thus two weeks ago he and Wazir Khan had begun their ride towards the mountains. Only two hundred men were accompanying them. Babur had selected them carefully with Wazir Khan's help, choosing only those who were young, like himself, and without family ties, or those who, like Baisanghar, formed the trusted core of his inner circle. The rest he had despatched to their homes, telling them to await his call, which they could be sure would come. The snow had started at the beginning of the second week of their journey and had grown thicker and more persistent the higher they had climbed, hampering their progress.

'How far do you think we are now from the fort, Wazir Khan?'

'If it weren't for this foul weather, Majesty, we should be able to see it by now. But at least the defenders won't see us coming. Let's pause under cover of those trees and eat some of the dried meat we still have in our saddlebags while we send some scouts ahead.'

The snow continued to fall throughout the ninety minutes the five scouts were away, sometimes thickly, sometimes less so. When the men returned they and their mounts were crusted with snow and their leader spoke through lips that were almost blue with cold. 'The fort is only about two miles ahead, around a bend. There are no hoof- or footprints to show that the occupants have been out today, either to patrol or to man outposts. When we dismounted and crept closer, we could make out smoke rising from one part of the fort – presumably the kitchens – but, most importantly, the main gate stood open. Clearly no one is suspecting an attack in this weather.'

'Well they're going to get a nasty surprise. Wazir Khan, let us not hesitate but mount up at once and while the snow continues to fall, concealing us, let the scouts lead us quietly and quickly towards where the way bends towards the fort. Then let us gallop for the gate.'

Wazir Khan nodded, and within five minutes the column was on the move, riding in single file up the gentle slope towards the head of the valley. After about two miles, through the snowflakes, which were falling more lightly now, Babur saw the shadow of a rocky outcrop emerge. As he did so, his chief scout whispered, 'The bend is at that outcrop. The fortress is only about a thousand yards ahead. The path becomes broader now.'

'We'll make our attack from here. Tell the men to have their weapons ready but to leave saddlebags and any other unnecessary equipment here in the shadow of the outcrop so that we can gallop to the fortress as fast as the snow will allow.'

Quickly the soldiers began to prepare but before many had completed their task the snow stopped entirely and there, ahead, was the fort – a dark shape against the white of the surrounding snow.

'Mount up, those who are ready! We must attack before we are seen!' yelled Babur who, even as he spoke, had drawn Alamgir from its scabbard. He leaped into the saddle and urged his black horse into a gallop towards the fort whose gate he could see remained open. With at most ten riders immediately around him, and the rest strung out to his rear, he felt the blood pound in his ears as he bent low to his horse's neck. When he was only two hundred yards from the gate, he heard a shout from within the fort – they had been seen. The gate shuddered and juddered as men inside tried to push it closed to bar it against the sudden threat but the newly fallen snow piled against it stopped it moving far. Two men rushed out, futilely kicking at the snow and trying to force the gate over it.

'Shoot them down!' Babur shouted, but did not slacken his pace. Within seconds he saw one of the men fall, an arrow in his throat. Then he was at the gate. Slashing at the second man with Alamgir, he felt the sword bite home into soft flesh but did not pause to look where. Instead, pulling hard on the reins, he jerked his horse's head round to guide it through the still partly open gate. The black horse snorted and Babur felt one of its legs slip but it made the turn, as did the three riders immediately behind him.

But the fourth did not. Babur heard a thudding crash as horse and rider came down, blocking the entrance. He was in the fort but – for the moment at least – with only three men to assist him. Looking about, he saw men rushing out through the tall wide door to what must be the fort's main hall. Some were struggling to pull on chain-mail, others to draw their weapons.

'Come! Attack them now!' Babur kicked his horse into a gallop once more, and soon he and his three companions were among the panicking men, cutting them down. Suddenly Babur saw a tall man, who appeared to be one of their chiefs, duck back into the hall and urged his horse on after him, bending low to pass beneath the wooden lintel. Blinking in the semi-darkness, he saw that the twenty or thirty men who had emerged from the hall must have been pretty much the entire garrison. Only the officer remained within. He had run back towards a rack of weapons and grabbed a spear and shield before turning towards Babur.

'Lay down your weapons on the orders of your rightful king, I, Babur of Ferghana.'

'I will not. You are not my king. My name is Hanif Khan. I owe my loyalty to Tambal, who now controls the land. Vanquish me in combat if you can.'

Babur leaped from his horse and, with Alamgir in his hand, advanced towards Hanif Khan who – as soon as he was near enough – thrust at Babur with his spear. Babur jumped aside, but as he did so his left foot caught against the leg of one of the low tables on which lay the remains of a meal. Arms flailing, he fell on to the table, knocking over some rough wooden goblets and spilling their contents. The wrist of his sword hand caught against the lip of a large metal pot, half full of stew, knocking Alamgir from his grasp.

Hanif Khan rushed towards him, eager to take advantage of this piece of good fortune and to finish him off. Raising his spear above his head in both hands he was about to stab its point into Babur's exposed throat when Babur grabbed a large wooden platter to use as a rough shield. The spear penetrated but did not split it. Rolling to one side amid the sticky warm mess of spilled food and liquid, Babur let go of the platter and grabbed the spear shaft, twisting it as he did so and wrenching it from Hanif Khan's grasp.

Undaunted, Hanif Khan jumped back and pulled a slim dagger from his sash. Babur had no time to look for where Alamgir had fallen but hit the man hard with the spear, knocking the platter from its tip. As he did so, he felt a stinging pain across his cheek. Hanif Khan had thrown his dagger at Babur's throat but missed his mark. Now Babur thrust at him with the spear point and Hanif Khan could only half turn aside before the spear caught his right side and he fell among some rough cushions beside the table. Babur twisted out the spear and, without a moment's reflection, jabbed it hard into his opponent's neck, pinning him to the cushions, which were soon soaked with his pumping red blood.

In no time, Wazir Khan, Baisanghar and the rest of his

125

men were surrounding Babur congratulating him on his bravery. The fort was theirs. He had taken his first small step on the long road to recovering Ferghana. Going outside, Babur saw that the snow was falling again, turning scarlet where it covered the bodies of his enemies. He longed for the moment when he could thrust his spear through Tambal as he had just done through his vassal.

• ◆ •

And so it had begun. Babur had become a raider, attacking swiftly and always leaving his name scratched in blood on a paper left stuffed into the gaping mouth of one of his dead enemies. And he had done well. Gradually he had increased the size of his forces, using soft words and sweet promises as well as harsh steel and the booty from his raids to attract new supporters and win over his adversaries. Within just twenty months of his capture of the mud fort, systematically and tenaciously, small fort by small fort, village by village, he had reclaimed much of the west of Ferghana. His strategy was working. Tambal no longer dared stir very far to the north or west from Akhsi towards Babur's strongholds, and Babur had become powerful enough to feel able to issue demands to him.

The first, made six months ago and often repeated, had been for the release of his grandmother, mother and sister from imprisonment in Akhsi in return for a promise not to attack the fortress until a year had passed. Three months ago Tambal had sent messengers to Babur with oily assurances that Esan Dawlat, Kutlugh Nigar and Khanzada were all in good health and being treated with the respect due to women of the royal house. But he had not offered to let them go.

Now Babur was advancing eastwards towards the town of Gava fifty miles away, recently refortified by Tambal and garrisoned with Chakrak mercenaries. He had a particular

126

score to settle there. The Chakrak commander of its garrison had been one of the first to pledge allegiance to his half-brother Jahangir and to Tambal as regent. The town's capture would send another signal to Tambal that it was time to conciliate Babur by returning his family.

Babur and his men stopped by the bank of a small river to allow their horses to drink. As Babur was eating without relish a hunk of sour cheese, made from mare's milk, he saw one of his scouts approaching on his horse. To Babur's alarm a body was strapped limp across his saddlebow. Running towards the man, Babur shouted, 'What has happened? Who is this man?'

'He was a merchant. I found him lying half alive in a pool of blood by the side of the track with a sword slash across his stomach. I lifted him on to my horse but he died soon after. Before he did, though, he told me he had been heading for a small caravanserai about ten miles from here with three other merchants when about two hours ago they were attacked by a Chakrak raiding party. They killed his fellows and left him for dead before making off with all the goods.'

'We must find the Chakraks and avenge him if we can. Send out some of your fellow scouts.'

'Majesty, that may not be necessary. With his last breath the merchant told me that he'd overheard the Chakraks talking of making for the caravanserai to see if they could find more victims there . . .'

'In that case we make for the caravanserai.'

• ◆ •

The singing was wild and raucous – just like the Chakraks themselves. Men's voices, slurred with drink, soared to a new crescendo, belting out suggestions for obscene actions so gross and so physically impossible that, despite himself, Babur grinned. He glanced at Wazir Khan – he was smiling too.

Babur signalled to his men, who were all around him in the long grass, and, like him, lying flat on their stomachs, to keep down and wait. Then he wriggled closer to the single-storey, mud-brick caravanserai overlooking a ford across one of Ferghana's swift-flowing rivers where the revellers were letting themselves go. The jingling of bells told him dancing girls were there. So did a sudden, indignant female shriek, followed by gusts of male laughter.

It was still only mid-afternoon, but the twenty or so Chakraks were clearly already pissed as rats. They hadn't even troubled to tether their horses properly and some, with matted manes and tails so long they brushed the ground, had already trotted away. As for their booty, seized from the four merchants, they couldn't even be bothered to carry it inside. The merchants' grey pack mules, roped together and contentedly grazing, were still loaded with wicker panniers stuffed with what looked like furs and leather. All the Chakraks seemed to have taken inside were barrels of wine.

Barbarians, Babur thought. They were about to get what was coming to them and it was a nice thought. Raising his head above the long grasses, Babur looked round but could see no one. Just as he'd thought, they'd not even the wit to post a boy to keep watch over the animals or the bags. Rising to his feet, he crept towards what was more of a hole in the caravanserai's thick walls than a window, just to the right of the low entrance, and peered cautiously inside. The room was bare, except for a long wooden table pushed against the back wall, some three-legged stools and a half-broken bench. In the middle of the room a plump, snub-nosed girl, wearing a tightly belted red-flowered jacket over pale, baggy yellow trousers with bells around her ankles and her wrists, and another taller girl in blue trousers and jacket and with a tambourine in her grubby hands were whirling and gyrating, stamping their bare feet on the flagstone floor. As he watched, a couple of Chakraks, sweaty faced under their round, shaggy sheepskin hats, lunged at them unsteadily, grabbing unsuccessfully for a breast or a buttock and tumbling to the floor, amid the cheers of their companions.

In one corner, a large black kettle was suspended over a smoky fire. In another, Babur watched a Chakrak drop his trousers and begin busily defecating, his comrades seemingly oblivious to the stink. Another got to his feet and spewed an arc of yellow vomit before slumping down again, flicking a gobbet of sick from his sleeve with a long fingernail. Babur ducked away again. He had seen enough in every sense.

Keeping low to the ground again, he made his way back to Wazir Khan. 'They're ours for the taking, the drunken fools. They've even left their shields and swords piled by the door.'

Wazir Khan raised an eyebrow. 'Now, Majesty?'

'Yes!'

Babur and Wazir Khan rose to their feet, signalling to their men to do likewise. They had done this so many times before that spoken orders were no longer needed. Finger to his lips, Wazir Khan gestured to several men to work their way around the caravanserai to the back, in case there were other ways out. Then Babur yelled his battle cry: 'Ferghana!'

With Babur at their head, the men burst in. Stupid with drink and taken by surprise, the Chakraks put up little resistance. The only blade that Babur faced, as he and his men went ruthlessly to work, belonged to the snub-nosed girl. She whipped a dagger out of her bodice and made a spirited attempt to stab Babur in his arm but he turned her wrist with its jingling bells with ease and, flicking her round, put a boot to her wide rump and sent her sprawling.

In a couple of minutes it was all over and Babur's men, barely out of breath, were cleaning and sheathing their swords. Not one had been wounded – but they were hardened warriors, used to fighting better men than these drunkards. 'Take the bodies outside – let's see who we have,' Babur ordered, and hurried out himself, glad to leave the fetid, smoky room for the fresh air.

As soon as his men had hauled the dead Chakraks out by their boot-clad feet and arranged them in a line, Babur counted them. There were fifteen. Many had their throats slit, some were headless. His men had also neatly arranged the severed heads, a few with their shaggy hats still on. Babur ran his eyes over them, grunting with satisfaction when he recognised a face. He had vowed to kill every Chakrak who had betrayed him and each skirmish that brought him closer to his goal was highly satisfying.

At the sound of squealing Babur turned. Two of his warriors had each grabbed a dancing girl and were dragging them out of the caravanserai. 'Do not force them – you know my orders. If they will go with you willingly for money, well, that is another matter.' Babur turned away.

The girls were indeed willing and, after a few moments of brisk negotiation, led the warriors into an apple orchard beyond the caravanserai. Babur guessed they were the daughters of the squint-faced innkeeper who, at the first sign of trouble, had hidden himself under the table and was still there. Soon a regular procession of Babur's men were making their way to and from the orchard. From the smiles on the faces of those returning, it seemed that the women were well used to providing favours to their father's customers.

Wazir Khan was already organising the rounding up of the Chakrak ponies that had drifted off and was checking the goods the Chakraks had looted from the merchants. 'Look, Majesty,' he called to Babur, pulling out two brightly coloured rugs. From their sheen the weavers had mixed silk with the wool and the patterning was unusual – perhaps the merchants had been travelling from the east, from Kashgar, where the people were skilled in such things. With the furs and the leather, they would fetch a good price, which would help him pay his men, Babur thought, pleased.

130

It would also be a good move to give his men a feast. They had done well and he must show his appreciation. He would hold it as soon as they returned westward, back to Shahrukiyyah. There, in the fortress he had seized from Tambal's forces six months ago and made his base, they would toast the memory of Ali Mazid Beg, lord of Shahrukiyyah until his murder in Samarkand. They would also drink to his son, slain as he tried to defend the fortress against Chakrak mercenaries despatched by Tambal as soon as he had learned of Ali Mazid Beg's death.

At the memory of his loyal chief, Babur's thoughts grew sombre as they often did these days. What had he achieved in the two years since Ali Mazid Beg's corpse had been hoisted over the Turquoise Gate? Was he any closer to freeing his family or to regaining Ferghana, never mind Samarkand? How much longer could he go on as a king without a kingdom? It would take time to build an army large enough to storm Akhsi, liberate his womenfolk and regain his throne. As for Samarkand, his brief days there as ruler were just a shadowy memory. It was hard to believe they had actually happened. The grand vizier's ghost had had the last laugh after all.

The thought angered Babur. He lashed out with his foot at one of the severed heads, sending it flying across the grass. His men deserved some fun, he thought, and so did he. 'Cut branches for sticks,' he shouted. 'Let's play some polo with these vermin's heads. We'll use the trees over there for goals.'

For an hour, he lost himself in a wild game, swerving from side to side on one of the nimble Chakrak ponies and whacking with the branches stripped of their twigs at the severed heads so that they bowled and bounced through the grass. The heads were soon unrecognisable – features smashed, eyeballs tumbling out – and Babur and his sweating fellow players, as well as their mounts, were flecked with blood.

Tiring of the sport at last but having released some of his

pent-up anger and frustration, Babur halted his steaming mount. Glancing round he caught Wazir Khan watching him. For once there was no approval on his face. But Babur refused to feel ashamed. His enemies deserved everything they got, dead or alive.

'Let's go,' he ordered. 'It is a long way to Gava and we mustn't keep our hosts waiting.' Kicking his horse so sharply that it sprang straight into a gallop, Babur rode from the inn down towards the ford over the river without a backward glance at the mangled, bloody heads already being pecked at by crows and the two girls slightly bow-leggedly picking over the bodies of the Chakraks for anything Babur's men had missed which they could add to the proceeds of their whoredom.

· ◆ ·

Yellow, pink and white flowers sprinkled the bright green upland meadows when, three weeks later, Babur and his men came galloping through them towards Shahrukiyyah. The raid against Gava had been bloody but successful. Babur himself had shot down the town's commander with an arrow despatched from the saddle at a distance of three hundred yards. All the hours of practice with his small, sharply curved double bow using a bronze ring to protect his thumb as he drew back the taut string had paid off. He could empty a quiver of thirty arrows in under a minute.

After that, resistance had ceased. Pissing themselves with fear, the garrison had surrendered not only themselves but also their full war chest, whose contents now reposed in the bulging leather saddlebags of Babur and his men.

Wazir Khan would be pleased. Babur had been missing his old friend but he had injured his thigh after being thrown when his horse shied at a snake the day after the attack on the caravanserai. Babur had insisted he return to Shahrukiyyah to rejoin Baisanghar, whom he had left there in command.

Tonight they would celebrate, he would decide which of his men to honour with the *ulush*, the champion's portion awarded at feasts to the warriors who had fought bravest and best – and he would tell Wazir Khan and Baisanghar about the raid on Gava. Wazir Khan would laugh at his stories, and perhaps even the serious Baisanghar might manage a smile.

As soon as he entered the courtyard of the stone fortress, Babur jumped down from his horse and looked around for them. There was no sign of Baisanghar but Wazir Khan was in front of the stables inspecting a horse's fetlock. Babur frowned: his friend was still limping heavily as he came towards him. Then he noticed Wazir Khan's beaming face.

'Great news, Majesty! Truly momentous news.'

'What has happened?'

'A week ago a messenger came from Akhsi, from Tambal speaking, or so he says, for your half-brother Jahangir and agreeing to send your mother, your grandmother and your sister to you.'

'Did he ask anything in return?'

'Nothing explicit, Majesty. All he added were fine words about his respect for you.'

Babur's heart leaped. At last. The knowledge that his family would soon be with him again was overwhelming.

'When will they be here?'

'By sunset tomorrow, if all has gone well.'

The next evening, in the gathering dusk, Babur was on the battlements, where he had been for most of the day, straining his eyes impatiently eastward where the road wound up to a pass. At last, emerging from the gathering gloom, he spied an undulating line of camels with baskets hanging at either side of them. Behind them rode the detachment of soldiers Wazir Khan had sent, under Baisanghar, to meet and protect the women on the final stage of their journey.

Babur could not see who was riding in the baskets, but

it must be his family. Unable to contain himself any longer, and without pausing either to summon guards to accompany him or to have a mount saddled, he jumped on to a horse and urged it out over the grassy meadows towards the small caravan.

Tears were flowing down his sunburned cheeks but he didn't care. There was no one to see them and, anyway, what did it matter? They were tears of happiness, not of weakness. Dashing them from his cheeks with one hand as he clung to his horse's mane with the other, Babur urged the beast to a pace so fast he felt he was flying.

Suddenly four soldiers detached from the escort and, spears tilted, galloped towards him. Although Baisanghar had probably guessed who was riding bareback so swiftly and wildly towards them, prudent soldier that he was he must have ordered the men to confirm his identity. As the riders drew near, Babur swung his own horse round sharply to force it to a standstill. Lathered with sweat, it snorted in protest.

Babur threw back his head and yelled his ancestral cry. 'Ferghana!'

The riders, quite close enough now to recognise him, saluted and Babur cantered on to where the camels had halted. If his heart had not been so full, there would have been something comical about the sight of Esan Dawlat's head poking out of a pannier like a chicken being carried to market. She was so light that there had been no need to stuff the basket on the other side with anything heavier than cabbages and her lute which was secured to the outside of the basket with hide thongs. Kutlugh Nigar and Khanzada were riding in baskets suspended on either side of a bigger camel with a creamy, long-haired coat that spat at Babur's approach. On the camels behind, Babur recognised several of his mother's waiting women, including Fatima, and his vizier, Kasim.

The camel drivers jumped down, tapped the camels' knobbly

knees with their sticks and forced them to the ground. Remembering what was due to age, Babur ran first to his grandmother and lifting her from the basket knelt before her. He could find no words and neither, for once, could she. He felt her hand rest briefly on his head. As he rose again and looked into her small bright eyes he saw, to his relief, that her spirit seemed unquenched. She still looked what she had always been, a *khanim* – a woman of the blood of Genghis Khan.

Then he turned to his mother, lifted her to the ground and clung to her, breathing in the familiar warm scent of sandalwood. When he released her, he saw tears in her eyes. 'It is good to see you again, my son,' she said simply, and a smile lit her face that was thinner and more lined than he remembered.

Khanzada had, by now, climbed from her basket herself and she flung herself at him. Her pet mongoose, which she was holding in her left hand, squeaked in protest. Last time he had seen her she had been a skinny girl with a few spots. Now she was a woman, her body rounded, her face smooth and beautiful – but with the same grin, he was relieved to see. He hugged her then stepped back to look at her properly.

Khanzada was scrutinising him too. 'You're taller,' she said, 'and your shoulders are broader. And you look terrible. Your chin is all stubbly and your hair is wild – it's nearly as long as mine! And look at your nails – they're black.'

Behind him, Babur heard Esan Dawlat click her tongue in reproof at Khanzada's disrespectful words and he smiled. They were together again at last and everything was as it should be. Later, they would talk and he would learn all that had happened to them, but for now this was enough.

As they approached the fort, trumpets blared and drums thundered their welcome to the royal women of Ferghana, free at last and – for the moment at least – safe.

While the women settled into the chambers Babur had ordered to be prepared for them on the top floor of the fortress, he summoned the cooks to check that all was in place for the celebration he had planned. It would be a far cry from the magnificence of Samarkand, to which he had once hoped to welcome them. However, twenty lambs had been slaughtered and were already roasting over fires in the courtyard. Chickens had been plucked and drawn and were now being baked in butter with walnuts and apricots. Apples were being glazed with thick, golden honey and red pomegranates stuffed with almond paste and pistachios. He was particularly pleased as he looked at a pile of silvered almonds that his men had seized during one of their raids. Esan Dawlat loved these more than any other sweetmeats.

As the moon rose in a clear, star-lit sky and guards kept watch from the fortress walls in case of any sudden attack, the feast began. Babur and his men ate in a long, low chamber on the ground floor while, in their own apartments above, the women were served the choicest portions. As the candlelight danced and flickered, one of Babur's men began to sing in a deep, rich voice. The others kept the rhythm, striking the hilts of their daggers on the low wooden tables around which they were seated, cross-legged. They were happy, Babur thought. The release of the women had pleased them too. It had wounded their honour as well as his that they had lacked the strength to set them free.

Babur tried to eat but felt little appetite. He longed to withdraw and be private with his mother, sister and grandmother but courtesy to his followers demanded that he wait. The singing was growing louder and more strident, the warriors roaring out the exploits of their ancestors, and Babur added his own voice. But at last, as some slumped forward, overcome by strong drink, and others staggered blearily from the chamber to relieve themselves in the courtyard outside, Babur could leave them and climb the winding stone stairs to the women's chamber.

Kutlugh Nigar held out her arms to him and he came

and sat by her on the carpeted floor. From what remained on the brass dishes spread before them, he could see that they had eaten well. Yet, now that he looked at their faces again, he could see signs of strain. All three were pale and drained as if they had not felt the warmth of the sun or breathed fresh air for a long time. Someone would pay for this – in blood. But for their sakes he mastered his feelings. He must show them a calm face, whatever they told him.

For a time they were all silent. Now that the initial euphoria had passed, it was hard for anyone to know where to begin.

Finally, Esan Dawlat spoke: 'So, Babur, you took Samarkand.' Her shrewd little face cracked into a rare smile.

'Yes, but I could not keep it.' Babur bowed his head. There was something he must say. 'Grandmother, I failed you. You wrote asking my help and I could not give it. I came too late and with too few men to free you.'

'You did not fail us. And it was because of us that you lost Samarkand. You rode to our help at once. What more could you have done?'

Babur shook his head. 'My first duty was to you and Ferghana. In Samarkand I was like a child with a new toy. I thought of little else. I should have sent back Wazir Khan to ensure that you and Ferghana were safe.' He leaned against his mother and felt her fingers stroke his hair just as she had always done. It soothed him.

'Tambal kept us well informed of some things,' Kutlugh Nigar said. 'I think it amused him. We learned, of course, of your cousin Mahmud's treachery – that it was he who took Samarkand from you. He and Tambal set a trap for you, my son. They agreed that in Ferghana Tambal would depose you and put Jahangir in your place, knowing that this would bring you – and many of your troops – back to Ferghana and Mahmud would have his chance. You were such a new lord of Samarkand – they say its nobles felt no allegiance to you so it was easy for Mahmud and his young vixen of a wife, the grand vizier's daughter, to bribe them.'

Babur closed his eyes at the confirmation of his worst suspicions. What a naïve fool he had been.

'You should know, too, it was Mahmud's wife who demanded Ali Mazid Beg's death.' Esan Dawlat's voice was bitter. The chieftain's mother had been her friend and she had been fond of him. 'She said that if she could not have your head, his would have to do in the meantime – in vengeance for her father. Mahmud could not deny her. They say she is the real ruler of Samarkand, greedier and more vindictive even than her father was.'

Babur blinked in surprise. He had not thought the slender young woman who had begged bravely for the grand vizier's life could be so cold blooded and ruthless. One day she would answer for her spite but that could wait. Now there were other things he must know, and come to terms with.

Gently he took his mother's hand between his own. 'Tell me about yourselves. How did they treat you during your imprisonment?'

'We were closely confined with just a few attendants but we were afforded the dignity due to our rank and lineage. Tambal did not threaten or insult us,' his mother said, 'and recently – presumably when he heard of your successes – he gave us more spacious apartments.'

'And he would not allow Roxanna to take our jewels, though they say she screamed and raged and even though she shares his bed,' Esan Dawlat added, with contempt.

'And my half-brother, Jahangir? What's been his role in all this?' Babur had often thought about the boy who had supplanted him and whom he had never even seen. When Babur had last been at Akhsi, preparing for his attempt on Samarkand, the brat had been sick.

'He is a pawn and often ill. Tambal has only a few spoonfuls of royal blood in his veins so he could never claim the throne himself – the other chiefs wouldn't let him. But as Jahangir's regent he has the power he craves,' Esan Dawlat said shortly. 'Now he fears you. Why else should he release us if not to appease you?'

Babur thought back to his own early days as king, remembering how Tambal had tried to sow doubt among the other leaders. All the time he had had his own ambitions. What an opportunist the man was – too astute to join in with Qambar-Ali's schemes and patient enough to wait for his moment. Was that why he had encouraged Babur twice to attack Samarkand? He could still recall the shining eagerness in Tambal's eyes when Baisanghar had brought Timur's ring. He also remembered how quickly after the capture of Samarkand Tambal had returned to Ferghana.

'The worst thing for us was not knowing for so many months what had happened to you. Fatima – you know what a gossip she is – brought us a tale – no more than a rumour but enough to frighten us – that you had fallen ill and died on the road back to Ferghana.' His mother's voice trembled. 'But then we began to hear stories that you were alive and hiding in the hills. We didn't know whether it was true until Tambal himself came to us in a rage ... He told us you were attacking villages, destroying, pillaging and slaughtering, giving no quarter.'

'So it is true, is it, Babur, what Tambal said? That you have become a common bandit and cattle-rustler?' Esan Dawlat looked thoroughly approving.

Babur nodded and after a moment grinned at his grandmother. Sometimes he had worried what she and his mother would think of him, whether they would understand how a prince could embrace, indeed relish, the life of a mountain brigand.

'Tell us about it, Babur.'

As the sputtering tallow candles burned low, Babur tried to conjure for them what his life had been. The excitement

139

as, with his band of two or three hundred adventurers, he had swooped down from the hills. The exhilaration of night-time hit and run raids on forts held by Tambal's forces and the elation of vanishing into the night, the dripping heads of his victims lashed to his saddle. The night-long carousing when his head spun from drinking *kvass*, fermented mare's milk, prepared by one of his men according to an old Mongol recipe. The only thing he left out was the wild polo games played with Chakrak heads – though he might tell Khanzada later.

Khanzada's eyes were shining as he talked, her fists clenching and unclenching as if she saw herself there, fighting side by side with him. Esan Dawlat was also rapt, but he noticed his mother frown as he described times when he'd been just a heartbeat from death.

'But I only attacked those who had betrayed me. And I never forgot you. Your freedom – not my throne – was what I wanted most.' Glancing round, Babur saw that a shaft of pale, grey light was already seeping through the narrow slit of window. It was almost day.

'You have achieved it. But what is past is past. Now we must look to the future.' Esan Dawlat's tone was brisk and the look in her eyes as they rested on him made him feel uncomfortably like a child about to be quizzed by his teacher. 'What have you learned, Babur?' She leaned towards him and grasped his wrist. 'What have your "throneless days" as you call them taught you?'

It was a good question. What had he learned during these desperate, dangerous times?

'The importance of trustworthy friends and allies,' he said at last, 'and the ability to reward them well. Also the need for a clear objective, a single-minded strategy, and the determination to let nothing stand in the way of it.'

Esan Dawlat nodded. 'Of course. And what else?'

'I've learned that a ruler cannot always be merciful but

140

needs to be stern – sometimes even harsh – to earn respect. Otherwise he may seem weak, more eager to be loved than to lead, and hence prey to any smooth-tongued schemer. I've learned that to win loyalty you must inspire not only admiration and gratitude but also a little fear. I should have had Baqi Beg, Baba Qashqa and Yusuf executed when I first came to rule Ferghana, rather than merely depriving them of their positions, and leaving them living and festering with resentment. Also, I should have made an example of some of the grand vizier's supporters on capturing Samarkand.

'Above all, I have appreciated the duty never to forget my destiny. It's only now after everything that's happened to me – to us – that I'm finally beginning to understand the man that Timur really was. How alone he must have felt sometimes . . . how difficult he must have found it to make his decisions work. After all, across the long years he alone always had to take responsibility for them . . . I've learned the courage to command too . . . No matter how many good counsellors, like Wazir Khan, I have, only I can decide my fate.'

Babur raised his face to his grandmother's. 'I will be like Timur, I swear it . . .'

'Fine words, indeed,' said Esan Dawlat. 'Now, let's get down to business. A new day dawns.'

Chapter 8

The Bridegroom

Esan Dawlat looked satisfied as with her thin, veiny little hand she smoothed the parchment on which Babur's scribe had sketched an outline of Ferghana. The drawing was crude, depicting the Jaxartes flowing on a straight east-west axis instead of showing how its cold waters curled through wide valleys and down rolling hills as they flowed from the snow-tipped mountains in the north-east. But that was irrelevant. What mattered were the pleasing numbers of towns and villages, marked with dots of vermilion ink, that Babur now controlled.

Two years of confinement had not dulled his grandmother's knowledge of the political alliances of the nobles of Ferghana, their weaknesses and ambitions. Esan Dawlat still knew all there was to know about the complex blood lines and loyalties. But, above all, she seemed able to see into men's minds, to understand their foibles, vanities and weaknesses and how best to exploit them. With her guidance, Babur had developed skills in persuasion, not to say manipulation, that he'd not known he possessed, coaxing several important chieftains to his cause. Others, sensing how the balance of advantage was

143

shifting, had followed, calculating that even if Babur could not reward them immediately, the time would come when he could and richly.

With his burgeoning political acumen and his increasing armies, Babur had been pushing steadily eastwards. Over the last six months, the fortresses of Sokh, Kassan and Karnon had all fallen to him, the latter two without a fight, and at last he was closing in on Akhsi. It wouldn't be long before he could depose Jahangir and once again call himself King of Ferghana, he was sure of it. But he must curb his impatience until winter was over, he told himself, biting his lip as he considered the map. Little moved on the frozen landscape – only the odd fox or deer darting hither and thither in search of food and kites hovering in the icy skies as they kept watch for an unwary mouse. It was no time for campaigning, with icicles hanging from the battlements and the air so cold it hurt a man to breathe.

'Babur, pay attention. There is something I need to discuss with you. Your mother and I are agreed that it is time you were married. You are seventeen years old. But, more important than that, the right match will strengthen your position.'

Esan Dawlat was looking at him triumphantly. 'It has all been arranged – in principle, at least. Your mother and I started to plan while we were captive. As soon as we were freed, I began to sound out potential alliances for you, and two days ago a messenger brought me good news. The offer of marriage that, above all, I hoped would prosper has been accepted. If you are content – and I can't think of a reason in the world why you shouldn't be delighted – you may ride to claim your bride as soon as the snows begin to melt.'

Babur stared at her, open mouthed, unable to think of any response – not even to ask who the girl was that his masterful grandmother had so thoughtfully obtained for him.

• ◆ •

The air was still cold, but the patches of bright green beyond the walls of Shahrukiyyah were growing bigger as winter retreated. The excitement in the women's quarters was unbearable – Khanzada in particular could talk of nothing but his coming marriage, Babur thought moodily, as he walked across the courtyard from the stables where he had been inspecting his horses. Their winter feed had left them thin and irritable. The hoofmarks where they'd kicked at the wooden slats penning them in showed their impatience to be galloping over the hills again. Babur sympathised. He felt exactly the same.

In fact, he felt more than impatient. He was angry. Members of royal houses married for political, not personal, reasons and alliances were important – he had known that since boyhood. Even as a baby, potential betrothals had been spoken of for him, some even formalised. But with his father's death and the ebb and flow of his fortunes, they had fallen away. Since then, he had assumed that when the time came to take a wife he would settle matters for himself. Instead, his grandmother and mother were treating him like a callow youth, not a king, arranging things slyly between themselves and presenting him with a *fait accompli*. Esan Dawlat seemed to expect to be congratulated whereas, much as he loved and respected her, he felt like wringing her neck.

But seeing his mother's quiet joy, after all she had been through, and listening to her explain that her marriage with his father had been arranged solely for political reasons but had turned into a perfect union, Babur couldn't see how he could protest. And at heart he knew he shouldn't. The two women were right: he needed the extra support a strong alliance sealed by marriage would bring. The pair had, as all his advisers insisted, chosen and negotiated well, even if they had taken his name in vain in the process. Wazir Khan's smile and lack of surprise when Babur told him what was planned betrayed more than a hint that he, at least, had been consulted at an early stage.

In just a few days, he would have to set out for the province of Zaamin, seven days' ride to the south-west on the southern borders of Ferghana, where the marriage was to take place. The bride they had found for him was Ayisha, eldest daughter of Ibrahim Saru, the leader of the Mangligh clan and ruler of Zaamin. Ayisha was two years his senior. What would she look like? Would she have the fine-boned grace of the grand vizier's daughter, or had they found him a foul-breathed camel? Babur shrugged. The important thing was that Ibrahim Saru was a powerful chieftain who, until this moment, had shrewdly taken no side. From now on his troops – especially his renowned crossbowmen – would be at Babur's command in his campaign to revive his fortunes. In view of that, as Esan Dawlat kept telling him, it mattered little what the girl looked like. His young blood would allow him to fulfil his nocturnal duties more than satisfactorily and, of course, he could take more wives or concubines later.

As Babur entered his mother's apartments, there was no sign of either Kutlugh Nigar or Esan Dawlat but Khanzada was on her knees, picking through some trinkets she had tipped from a little wooden casket on to the floor. 'Shall I give these to Ayisha? Do you think she'd like them?' She held out a pair of long filigree earrings, the fine gold wire studded with tiny red rubies and, at the bottom, a row of pearls that trembled.

'As you wish.' Babur shrugged. His own gifts to his bride – rolls of flowered silk, sacks of spices, a set of heavy gold necklets and armlets that had belonged to the royal house of Ferghana for centuries – had been selected by his mother and grandmother and sent to Zaamin three weeks ago under escort. To his prospective father-in-law he had sent gold coins, a fine stud ram and a pair of perfectly matched black stallions with white fetlocks that had cost him a pang to part with.

The bride price Babur had paid was all he could afford in his current circumstances. It wasn't much for a chieftain of Ibrahim Saru's standing. Babur wondered again why he had agreed to the marriage. He must believe that Babur would not be long without a throne. Doubtless he would like to see his daughter a queen and to be grandfather to Babur's heirs. And who could blame him? Ambition was a fine thing.

'Or perhaps these?' Khanzada's dark hair tumbled around her as she continued to search through her jewels.

Suddenly Babur was ashamed of himself. Khanzada had had little to enjoy in recent times, it should please him to see her so happy for him – and so generous and open hearted. Also, she was older than Ayisha – they should be thinking about a husband for her. When he was again King of Ferghana he would arrange a good match for her, he promised himself, and consult her about it more than he had been consulted about his own marriage.

Two weeks later, Babur watched as, wrapped in fur-lined cloaks against the still biting winds, Esan Dawlat, Kutlugh Nigar and Khanzada climbed into a high-wheeled, covered bullock cart. It was well lined with cushions and sheepskins, while crimson leather hangings screened them from public view. The horns of the four white bullocks pulling it had been gilded, and the yokes above their broad, muscular necks were painted blue and gold.

Babur mounted his favourite horse, a dark-maned chestnut, which, sensing the excitement, skittered and pranced. It felt good to be in the saddle again and Babur gave the horse an affectionate slap on its shining neck. He had ordered Baisanghar to remain at Shahrukiyyah with a strong garrison while he took Wazir Khan and an escort of five hundred well-armed men with him. News of the wedding would have spread and eyes – some hostile – would be observing their progress as they passed southwards towards Zaamin. But with a force of that size and teams of scouts and outriders, Babur was satisfied there was little risk of an ambush.

Wazir Khan had been exchanging some final words with Baisanghar on the wall above the gatehouse. Now he began to make his way down the steep, uneven stairs to the courtyard, where a groom was struggling to keep hold of his horse as it stamped and snorted with pent-up energy. With what difficulty Wazir Khan was moving compared to even a year ago, Babur thought. He would take that limp to the grave.

At last, with the bullock cart trundling behind, Babur and Wazir Khan rode slowly down the castle ramp and out into the meadow beyond, where the escort was already waiting with the supply wagons drawn by mules carrying the tents, food and the equipment they would need to make camp. And, of course, the chests of wedding clothes and yet further gifts for his new wife's family, including a yellow-eyed hawk for his father-in-law.

As the procession wound its way slowly south, it was some time before the farewell salute of the drums on the battlements of Shahrukiyyah finally faded to be replaced by the creaking of wood, the rumble of wheels, the jingling of harnesses, the grunting of pack animals and a new rhythm of many hoofs thudding on soft spring turf.

Every day, the cordon of warriors posted by Wazir Khan around the convoy kept careful watch, but nothing stirred in the quiet valleys and meadows except flocks of sheep, the ewes swollen bellied with the lambs that would soon be born. Sometimes, restless at the slow pace and nervous at what lay ahead, Babur galloped off with a small escort.

He enjoyed the sting of the wind on his face. He hadn't felt this free since before his father had died. At this moment, the loss of Samarkand, the betrayal in Ferghana didn't seem to matter so much. The burden of his responsibilities – his obligations to others, duties to be fulfilled and ambitions to be achieved – which at times oppressed him – seemed to roll away. It was like the coming of spring when, after months of being enveloped in heavy sheepskins, he could shrug them off and feel the warm sun on his back. Crouching low over his horse's neck, Babur allowed his mind to go blank, blotting out all the things that – at this moment – he just didn't want to think about.

On the afternoon of the sixth day, when Babur was again riding sedately beside the bullock cart and they were approaching the lower slopes of a hill, a line of dark-robed riders appeared on the skyline. At once Wazir Khan raised his leather-gauntleted hand to signal a halt.

'What do you think, Wazir Khan? Is it them? The Manglighs?' Babur squinted, but couldn't make out any distinguishing features – no banners no flags. The riders were sitting very still, just watching.

'Probably, Majesty. We must be approaching the borders of their territories. But we should see what our advance guard report.'

'Yes. Also, send out further scouts and draw the convoy into a defensive position.'

Babur watched the dozen warriors picked out by Wazir Khan gallop off, swords at their sides, battleaxes strapped to their saddlebags but within easy reach, and left arms thrust through the leather straps of their round shields that, till now, had been tied to their backs. The last two were also carrying spears. It was as well to be prepared. Realising that the women must be wondering what was going on, Babur trotted over to the bullock cart and, leaning from his horse, thrust his head inside the leather curtains. 'There are riders ahead, probably Ibrahim Saru's men but we must be certain. We are waiting for our scouts to return but in the meantime we are making ready to defend ourselves.'

His mother and Khanzada were dozing but Esan Dawlat, bright eyed and alert, nodded. 'It is well. Take no chances.'

In a matter of minutes, Wazir Khan had sent archers to

conceal themselves behind trees and rocks, had the supply wagons drawn in a circle around the bullock cart and had positioned the remainder of the troops in a defensive perimeter around them. But, as they waited, time seemed to pass so slowly. Babur strained his ears, trying to catch any sound borne on the wind. There was nothing until a discordant jangling of bells announced the arrival of a herd of shaggy goats on the hillside above them. The boy driving them took one horrified look at what he had stumbled on and, waving his staff, hastily kicked and drove his goats out of sight again.

At last Babur's men came galloping back. Behind them were the dark-clad riders, faces swathed against the wind. All must be well. As the riders came closer, Babur saw on one of their pennants the red hawk that was the symbol of the Manglighs. He rode a few paces forward, then reined in his chestnut and waited for the strangers to approach.

'Greetings, Babur of Ferghana.' The leading rider bent forward in his saddle by way of salute. As the powerfully built man unwound his black face-cloth, Babur saw his thick dark beard, wide cheekbones and above them a pair of penetrating, very long dark eyes, strangely flecked with amber. He looked about forty. 'I am Ibrahim Saru, chieftain of the Manglighs. I bid you and your family welcome. Today you are my guests and tomorrow, Babur, you will become my son.' Though he spoke Turki, the language of Babur's people, his accent made the words sound strange. The Manglighs had originally come from Persia – perhaps Persian was still their native tongue.

Babur returned the bow. 'Thank you. You honour us.'

'Our encampment is two hours south from here. We have been waiting and watching for you. I came in person because I wished to be the first to greet you.'

Babur bowed again and kicking his horse followed Ibrahim Saru slowly up the hill.

• ◆ •

The round tent in which he had spent the night was quite well furnished, Babur thought critically, his gaze wandering over the red and blue woven hangings that covered the ten-foot-high walls of stitched, cured hides. Candles burned in brass holders cast to resemble coiled snakes, their bases set with chunks of gold-speckled lapis-lazuli. The soft dark blue cushions on which Babur was resting his head were embroidered with thick gold thread that tickled the back of his neck, and his mattress was a sumptuous bag of what felt like duck down, covered in a thick, slippery brocade. The tent floor was spread with furs.

It was crude, of course, compared with Samarkand, but Ibrahim Saru had gone to great trouble to set up such an elaborate camp to which to welcome his guests. The night before, as they had ridden in, the lines of tents – pennants in the yellow of Ferghana flying from those set up for Babur's men and, in their centre, his own much larger ceremonial tent – had been an impressive sight. No doubt exactly as Ibrahim Saru had intended.

From the light creeping in through the entrance flaps, closed with engraved metal clasps, Babur guessed it must be well past dawn. He thought back to last night's feast of buttered rice, lamb, root vegetables and heady liquor in Ibrahim Saru's tented audience chamber with its elaborate awnings and carpeted walkway leading to the entrance. Babur would much rather have spent the evening with Esan Dawlat, Kutlugh Nigar and his sister in the women's tents but, of course, that had been impossible. Instead he had politely watched the antics of jugglers, fire-eaters and supple-limbed acrobats, and the gyrations of a troupe of plump dancing girls whose eyes had looked boldly into his as they shook their full breasts and hips. Later, he had sat smiling as his own and Ibrahim's men had danced and sung together, pledging each other's health as the brothers-in-arms they were soon to be, until eventually, fuddled with wine, they had slumped to the floor to sleep.

Babur, who could usually drink as much as any man, had drunk little, hoping that Ibrahim Saru would talk to him of their coming alliance. There was much to discuss. With his father-in-law's help, he could storm Akhsi and regain his throne in weeks, not months, he was sure. Then there was the small matter of throwing his cousin Mahmud out of Samarkand. But Ibrahim Saru had made only polite small-talk and Babur deciding it would be discourteous to talk of war on such an occasion had reluctantly curbed his tongue.

Throwing back the fur coverlet, beneath which he had slept only fitfully, Babur got up. At this thought of what lay ahead he allowed himself a quick sigh. He felt impatient with himself as well as with his situation. At this moment he'd have given anything to be leading his men into combat rather than having to marry an unknown young woman. But he was a king, a conqueror, a warrior, and he was also now a man. How often during his wild days had he not lain at night on hard ground beneath cold skies thinking of the soft, warm bodies of women?

Why had he not summoned one to him? He couldn't say for certain. Perhaps it was the prudishness of an only son who lacked a father. Perhaps a disinclination to father a child in his circumstances? Perhaps a consciousness of his dignity preventing him associating with the available women or a wish not to let such women get close to him – other princes before him had been ruled and ruined by unsuitable women. But tonight he would finally discover how it felt to hold and possess a woman. He should be glad.

Babur clapped his hands for the four attendants his father-in-law had pressed on him as a courtesy. This was his wedding day and he must observe the proprieties. He could already hear them murmuring outside the tent, and at his signal they entered, throwing back the tent flaps and letting the sunlight stream in.

Babur's wedding clothes – trousers of soft doeskin, a tunic

of yellow silk, belted with the heavy gold chain his father had worn on his wedding day, and a long coat of bronze brocade – had been unpacked the night before and were draped over a dome-lidded chest. A high, dark blue velvet cap, sewn with tiny pearls by Khanzada and with a crest of eagles' feathers was on a nearby stool.

Two hours later, after bathing in water heated over hot stones in the bath tent and allowing his attendants to rub his body down with bundles of fresh herbs, brush and perfume his long hair and dress him in his finery, Babur was ready. As he stepped into the sunshine, the eagle feathers in his cap sent long shadows dancing over the ground as he moved.

Suddenly shrill cries rose from the other side of the encampment. 'From the women's quarters, Majesty,' said an attendant, seeing Babur's puzzlement. 'They are bidding farewell to the bride, just as in a few hours she must bid farewell to her virginity.' The women's voices gathered intensity, becoming almost a screech. It wasn't a pleasant sound – not at all like the joyous singing heard in the villages of Ferghana when a marriage was taking place. It was more like a lament.

Babur was glad to see a finely dressed Wazir Khan duck out of the low entrance to his tent pitched beside Babur's. 'Greetings, Majesty, on your wedding day.' Wazir Khan's one-eyed gaze was warm and Babur felt grateful he would be at his side. 'Have you eaten, Majesty?'

'I'm not hungry. I've just drunk some water.'

Babur saw understanding in Wazir Khan's expression.

'Our guard will soon be here to escort you to the wedding tent.'

'Wazir Khan . . .' Babur wasn't sure what he wanted to say and before he could even think, the sound of drums and trumpets filled the air, drowning the women's eerie wailing, and he saw Wazir Khan's men approaching in a double line, wearing the bright yellow of Ferghana and preceded by his own musicians. A groom was leading Babur's chestnut horse, splendidly caparisoned with a yellow saddlecloth, yellow ribbons woven into its mane and tail and a bridle set with yellow tiger's eyes.

Babur climbed into the saddle and allowed his men to lead him to the same tented chamber in the centre of the camp where, last night, he had feasted and where Ibrahim Saru and his daughter now awaited him. As Babur dismounted, the black-clad Mangligh guards outside the tent saluted him. Slowly, and in a blare of trumpets, he made his way to where Ibrahim Saru, dressed in dark purple velvet, was waiting to greet him.

To one side, separated off by a three-foot-high latticed wooden screen, were the ladies of Ibrahim Saru's court. The lower halves of their faces were veiled but above the filmy gauze, their dark eyes, elongated and thickly lashed, were examining him with frank curiosity. In their centre, in places of honour, he saw his grandmother, mother and sister. Esan Dawlat was sitting very erect, a blue shawl embroidered with gold stars clasped tight round her head and shoulders. Kutlugh Nigar, in a loose yellow silk tunic and with several long strands of pearls hanging round her neck, was looking proudly at him while Khanzada's eyes – far rounder than those of the Mangligh women – were shining.

In the centre of the vast tent, seated on a golden cushion on a maroon-carpeted dais his bride was waiting. A brazier of charcoals scented with incense was burning in front of her so she was concealed not only by the heavy cream veils, falling from beneath a cap of golden cloth, but by wisps of smoke spiralling into the air, drawn upwards by the open flap in the roof. As Babur walked up to her, Ayisha remained motionless, betraying no awareness that Babur, so soon to be her husband, was standing before her. He wished he could see her expression.

The trumpets faded, and for a moment there was complete silence.

'Ayisha!' At her father's voice, the girl rose. She was tall but whether fat or thin, gracefully proportioned or clumsily built, Babur couldn't tell, though he caught a brief glimpse of long feet elaborately hennaed in diamond patterns.

'Come.' Ibrahim Saru motioned to Babur to step on to the dais and face his bride. Next, he gestured to his daughter to give him her right hand from beneath her veils. Taking it, he placed it in Babur's right hand. Ayisha's hand was cool and dry.

A tall, black-clad, white-bearded mullah stepped forward and in a deep, resonant voice half sang, half spoke what Babur assumed must be prayers or benedictions. Though he listened carefully, he couldn't recognise the tongue in which the man was speaking. It must be Persian. As the priest finally came to an end and stepped back, prayer book clasped to his chest, Ibrahim Saru flung a fistful of grain over the young couple. A chorus of roaring male voices rose, filling the tent, and fistful after stinging fistful of grain was suddenly flying through the air. The Mangligh women began to ululate, high and piercing, like a flock of birds in flight.

Ayisha turned to Babur. He smiled and hoped for some sign from her, but after a moment she pulled her hand from his and stepped down from the dais. At once the Mangligh women rose from behind their screen and surging forward swooped on Ayisha. To Babur's astonishment, shrieking with merriment, they began pulling her cream veils from her, spinning her round and round and ripping at the fragile cloth.

What were his family and his chiefs making of all this? Babur saw Wazir Khan standing near the entrance to the tent, his expression as nonplussed as Babur knew his own must be. Still seated decorously behind the screen, Khanzada had allowed her jaw to drop in frank amazement while Esan Dawlat and Kutlugh Nigar were gazing fixedly ahead, as if too well bred to notice such bizarre happenings.

Ayisha was still half cocooned as musicians, with long brass pipes, cymbals, bells and taut-skinned drums, suddenly struck up. The women stepped back from her and began to sing, clap and stamp, beating out the rhythm with their hands and feet. Babur realised that the men had drawn right back against the walls of the tent and that the women had formed a human barrier around the bride so that she was visible only to him and to her father. Now Ayisha started to dance, sinuously twisting and turning until the last of her draperies, except the veil concealing the lower half of her face, fell away.

Babur saw a pair of coal-dark eyes flicker over him. Her hair, instead of hanging free, was plaited and coiled round her small head. Her long body, in dark purple trousers gathered at the ankles, a tight-fitting bodice that left her midriff bare and a long, filmy coat that fastened at her breast, looked slim and muscular. A dark gem – an amethyst perhaps – sparkled in her navel.

'Take her. She is yours.' Ibrahim Saru shoved Babur towards her. 'The wedding couch waits – go. Enjoy her, then the feast . . .'

Seeing his startled expression, his father-in-law laughed. 'Don't the princes of Ferghana have fire in their loins?'

Babur flushed and took Ayisha's hand. Ibrahim Saru flung a cloak around his daughter, clapped twice and the musicians rose. Still playing their wild music, they formed up into two rows.

'They will play you to your marriage bed. My nobles and I will follow you.' Ibrahim Saru was beaming broadly.

Babur's head throbbed as the caterwauling musicians led the wedding procession out of Ibrahim Saru's magnificent tent into the sunlight. The wedding tent, pitched close to the women's quarters, was gaudy with flags and pennants in the yellow of Ferghana and the black and red of Zaamin. Not a pleasant combination, Babur thought.

The musicians fanned out, taking up positions at either side of the entrance. Attendants in red and black knelt and touched their foreheads to the ground as Babur led Ayisha inside. The large tent was sumptuously carpeted but barer than Babur had expected. At its centre was a thick mattress covered with a pale, flowered silk sheet that glimmered in the light shed by two huge candelabra on either side. Over the mattress was a rectangular wooden frame hung with curtains lined with squirrel fur which could be pulled all the way round to screen the bed. And that was all. No chests, mirrors or stools.

Babur barely had time to take it in before giggling women were leading Ayisha to the mattress and drawing the curtains around her so that she was hidden from view. A moment later and male attendants were pulling at his clothes. Babur fought the impulse to lash out at the eager, questing fingers lifting his cap from his head, untying his coat and tunic, unfastening his trousers and drawing off first one boot, then the other. In a few moments he was naked. The attendants draped a silk robe round him, then began to call out. Babur couldn't understand what they were saying but guessed they must be speaking to the women who hastily came out from behind the curtains and, eyes averted, hurried from the tent. The male attendants followed, closing the tent flaps tightly behind them.

He and Ayisha were alone. For a moment he hesitated. Then, letting the robe drop to the floor, he approached the mattress and pulled apart the curtains. Ayisha was lying naked, her hair still tightly bound but the soft curves of her body fully open to his view. Her slender arms and long, slim legs were decorated with the same elaborately hennaed patterns Babur had glimpsed on her feet. Her nipples had been painted crimson and ringed with circles of henna. She was eyeing his own nakedness with what seemed to Babur unnerving coolness. What was she thinking? His scars at least showed he was no mere boy but a warrior who had shed blood.

Babur lowered himself beside her and lay so that their bodies were close but not quite touching. After a moment – saying nothing because he was unsure what to say – he placed a gentle, exploratory hand on the warm flesh of her waist and, when she did not react, moved it down to caress the soft curve of her hip. Still getting no response, he tentatively slipped it towards the dark triangle between her thighs.

Suddenly Babur felt that his young blood could be contained no longer. The tension of the day seemed to explode inside him, translating into a fierce physical desire that must be satisfied. He pulled himself on top of her and, with eager hands, grabbed clumsily at the soft flesh of her breasts. He tried to enter her but found he couldn't. Beneath him her body was rigid and unyielding. Raising his head, he looked into her eyes, wanting her help, but found no warmth there, no willingness to respond to his silent plea or play any more than a passive role – only, or so it seemed to him, contempt for his inexperienced fumblings.

Goaded, he tried again and, pushing hard, finally succeeded in penetrating her. He could feel her tightness as he began to thrust and then, as she gave a single sharp cry, that entry was becoming easier. Panting, he pushed deeper and deeper, oblivious to everything until, at last, he collapsed, spent and sweating, on her supine body.

With his blood still roaring through his veins, it took Babur a moment to recover himself, to remember where he was and what had just happened. When he did, he pulled himself away from Ayisha, unwilling to meet her eyes. When, finally, he did look at her, she had not moved and her expression remained distant, inscrutable and unsmiling. He might have got himself a wife, but this was not how he had imagined it would be. Babur sat up and turned his back on her, barely noticing the small pool of blood that had seeped from beneath her to stain the sheet, which would in due course be exhibited to the general view to prove she had been a virgin on her wedding day and was now no longer.

Chapter 9

Baburi

The hunting around Shahrukiyyah was good. Deer and fat squealing boar abounded in the dense forests while the coppices and pasture provided pheasants, hares and foxes enough for excellent sport. Babur narrowed his eyes as he pulled back his bow-string, then smiled as he watched his arrow cut through the air and hit its mark – the white throat of a young buck that staggered, then fell. Since his return from his marriage in Zaamin two months ago, he'd been spending a lot of time out hunting.

Now, with dusk falling, Babur turned his horse for home, his hawk again quiescent beneath its gilded leather hood, the deer slung from poles and rabbits and pheasants dangling limply from his huntsmen's saddles. He felt a dark mood envelop him. Never before had he quarrelled with his grandmother, but Esan Dawlat's interference was growing intolerable. She was actually keeping count of his couplings with Ayisha and complaining constantly. 'At first you went to her twice a week. Now it is only every seven days – sometimes longer . . . You are insulting her. Remember your duty to Ferghana,' she had snapped this morning, oblivious both to his embarrassment and his anger. 'You know no fear as a warrior, so why hide from a woman . . . ?'

Stung, he had yelled back, 'You are not my commander, nor I your stud stallion required to service to order your choice of mare.'

He had not objected to the marriage, and understood the reasons for it, but he had not sought it either, and the cold disdain of his bride – apparent even on their wedding night – had persisted and hardened. She rarely spoke to him and, when she did, it was only to reply monosyllabically to his questions or requests. He had never seen her smile – not once. A smile might have softened her and, in turn, softened his feelings towards her. Instead, lying with her seemed almost like sleeping with a warm corpse – no response, no passion, no engagement, just those unblinking dark eyes seemingly focused on the middle distance as he spent himself in her unresisting body.

What was in Ayisha's mind? Why wouldn't she respond to him either physically or mentally he wondered, yet again, as he rode along a track green with the tender shoots of spring. Was the fault his or hers? Surely it was hers. What was wrong with her? At her request, she and her Mangligh attendants had their own chambers away from the rest of the women's. Whenever he approached he could hear them speaking their strange language and sometimes laughing, but as he entered they would at once fall quiet. Ayisha would salute him with a formal bow of her head, then wait in silence, expressionless eyes downcast, for his bidding, like a slave rather than a wife. Except that a slave was humble and Ayisha was not.

It seemed to Babur that she wore her pride like a weapon against him. Her detachment goaded him. Sometimes when he made love to her, he became rough in spite of himself, trying with his sheer physicality to force a reaction from her – anything. But there was nothing, and although she did not resist, he was left feeling like a ravisher, a forcer of women, instead of her lawful husband. At other times he had tried to be gentle, caressing the soft lines of her body, cupping her breasts, kissing her nipples and her small rounded belly – just as he had treated the pliant women of his adolescent dreams – but unlike them Ayisha had not responded, remaining rigidly indifferent.

When, blushing and stammering, he had asked Khanzada – who had been so eager for the companionship a royal sister-in-law would provide and so generous with her carefully chosen presents – whether Ayisha had ever confided anything about him or his behaviour, she shook her head. She told him that immediately after the marriage she had often visited Ayisha but had found only the most formal and aloof welcome, no willingness to empathise or to unbend and share confidences – so she had ceased her unreciprocated visits. It was, Khanzada said, as if Ayisha wished she were somewhere else, and in her mind pretended she was.

Babur was still caught up in his thoughts as he and his men galloped into the jumble of mud-brick houses, wooden shacks and round hide tents that clustered beneath the walls of Shahrukiyyah. The poorly clothed inhabitants were squatting over smoking fires to cook their evening meals while their children played barefoot in the sloping alleyways, jumping over the little rivulets that carried sewage and other refuse down the hill. As they approached the stone gatehouse with its iron-bound doors, a small child – no more than two or three years old – suddenly ran out in front of Babur. His horse reared, neighing in alarm.

Pulling hard on the reins, Babur turned the chestnut so that its flailing hoofs missed the child, who was now standing wide eyed, wailing and immobile with fear. A rider behind Babur was not so quick to react and it seemed he would ride the child down. But there was a shout and a youth dived forward, seizing the child, pulling it to the ground and shielding it with his body. The rider, cursing volubly as he fought to control his black horse, managed to jump over them but one of his horse's rear hoofs caught the youth hard on the back of the head.

Babur dismounted and knelt by the unconscious young man whose arms were still round the child – a little girl, Babur could now see. She was whimpering, a thin trail of snot running down her upper lip. As one of his men lifted her out of the way, Babur turned the youth on to his back. He was about the same age as himself, Babur thought, with an aquiline nose, high cheekbones and a stubbly chin. He probed his head, with the expertise gleaned from many battles, and found beneath the dark hair a place that was spongy and sticky with blood. The youth, whose breathing was shallow, seemed deeply unconscious. He had taken a hard blow, risking his life for the little girl. It would be a shame if he didn't live to know he'd saved her.

'Bring him up to the castle. Let's see what our *hakims* can do for him.' Babur remounted and, feeling even more sombre than before, continued towards the castle gates.

• ◆ •

That night, Babur knew he should go to Ayisha. It would please his grandmother and his mother and perhaps, once she was pregnant, Ayisha herself might find some contentment. More importantly, the prospect of a grandchild might prompt Ibrahim Saru to honour his promise of crossbowmen to help Babur retake his birthplace, Akhsi. It was full spring now and high time for Babur to be moving against his half-brother Jahangir. Instead, each time he sent a messenger to Zaamin asking for news of when the crossbowmen would arrive, the reply was the same: soon they would come, soon . . .

After he had bathed, Babur set out dutifully for his wife's quarters, but when he saw the green, leather-lined double doors ahead, he stopped. No. As he had shouted at Esan Dawlat, he wasn't a stud beast required to perform to order. He was a man who knew his own mind and would do as he pleased. Turning on his heel, he walked quickly away.

• ◆ •

At least Babur's pessimism about the youth proved misplaced. Six hours later, a servant brought word that he had recovered consciousness. That should have been the end of it. But for some reason Babur was curious to know more and, on the second day after the accident, ordered the youth, if he was well enough, to be carried to him on a litter.

The young man was very pale but saluted Babur from his supine position, touching his hand to his chest and inclining his head – a gesture that clearly hurt because he winced.

'You were brave to save the child like that. I'm glad God has been compassionate to you, preserving your own life. What is your name?'

'Baburi, Majesty.'

Babur looked down at him in frank surprise. Baburi was an unusual name, but also so similar to his own. 'Where are you from? What is your tribe?'

'My father was a warrior of the Barin people and served your father, but he died when I was a baby. I have no memory of him. My mother took me to Samarkand but she died of smallpox when I was seven. I've fended for myself ever since.'

'What are you? A soldier?'

'No, Majesty.' Baburi raised his eyes to Babur's. They were a dark blue, almost indigo. 'Till recently I was a market boy. I hawked cabbages on the streets of Samarkand.'

'How did you come to be in Shahrukiyyah?'

'When you captured Samarkand, Majesty, I got a job as a water-carrier with one of your chiefs. He has since gone home to Ferghana but I decided to stay.' Baburi spoke directly, with a simple dignity.

'But I have not seen you before?'

'That isn't surprising. I work in the kitchens now, skinning animals and pulling the guts out of chickens. It isn't glorious but it's a job.' A half-smile curled his lips. 'It could be worse.'

He's laughing at me, Babur thought, astonished. I amuse him. 'I'm sure it could be worse – sometimes we must accept what fate doles out, even disembowelling chickens. But now perhaps fate has something different in store. Your bravery suggests you could be a soldier.'

'I'd like that . . . After all, I've proved I've got a good thick skull to take a blow . . . And it would be preferable to the kitchens – even if occasionally I have to spill human guts or even lose some of my own.' Still the youth smiled.

'Very well. As soon as you are recovered, you shall join my cavalry.'

Babur had expected rapturous gratitude but the youth's smile disappeared. His expression changed to one of discomfort and his pale face flushed. 'What is the matter?'

'I can scarcely ride, Majesty.'

Babur bit his lip at his own stupidity. In a society of nomads where only the poorest were ignorant of horses, it was a shaming thing to have to confess. How could a poor market boy have learned to be a good enough horseman to join the cavalry?

Anxious to spare Baburi further embarrassment, he said quickly, 'You have already shown you have no fear of horses. Tell the master-of-horse to arrange your training as a cavalryman as soon as you're fit.'

•◆•

'So, we are agreed. If no Mangligh crossbowmen have come from Zaamin by the time of the new moon after next, we will march on Akhsi anyway.' Babur gazed at his counsellors, seated cross-legged in a half-circle round him.

There was still no news of the Mangligh reinforcements

164

and Babur had had enough. The lands he had seized were still securely in his hands, the forts he had taken well garrisoned under chieftains he could trust, but he could not afford to wait much longer. He must regain Akhsi and quickly. Then he could truly call himself Ferghana's king and plan for a greater future.

'In the meantime, Majesty, we must continue to drill our troops. We have enough siege engines and enough catapults but many of the men are still undisciplined. Under fire they may forget what we have tried to hammer into their heads. And we must also build up our supplies. Though we do not want a long siege, it may come to it,' said Wazir Khan.

'You're right. And when we march out, we must send raiding parties ahead to seize flocks before they are taken to feed the garrison of Akhsi. Baisanghar, I look to you to have men ready for such a task – men we can trust. There is to be no killing or looting of my people. We will pay for what we take. I am a king returning to his own, not an Uzbek bandit out on a raid.'

Babur rose, pleased that he had taken control and that the waiting would soon be over. Feeling restless, he hurried out into the courtyard and ordered his favourite horse to be saddled. Taken by surprise, the grooms rushed to obey while his bodyguards, shouting for their own mounts, added to the confusion. They were getting sloppy and lax. He noticed the broad-shouldered, slim-waisted figure of Baburi, broom in his hands, coming from the stables and summoned him with a wave.

'Majesty?' Today Baburi seemed unwilling to look Babur in the eye.

'How is your riding?'

Silence.

'I gave orders that you were to train for the cavalry.'

Still silence.

'And I am not used to being disobeyed.' Babur was perplexed.

The youth had seemed so eager yet he had done nothing. He had wanted to help Baburi and had thought he detected a spark in him, but he must have been wrong. Baburi was as dull as the cabbages he had once peddled. Disappointed, Babur turned away. As he did so he noticed a bruise on the side of Baburi's high-cheekboned face. 'Wait. What is that mark?'

'Your master-of-horse hit me.'

'Why?'

Now, at last, Baburi looked at him. 'Because I said that I wanted to ride, to be a cavalryman. He said I was fit only for shovelling horse shit.'

'Did you mention that it was my personal wish?'

'Perhaps not in so many words. I thought he would have heard. And he gave me no chance to explain before he hit me. Afterwards, it was all I could do to restrain myself from thumping him. It didn't seem the time for explanations . . . or for pleading. If you were serious, I knew it would get sorted out sometime. If not, the stables were better than the kitchen.'

Babur turned to one of his guards. 'Fetch Ali Gosht.'

A few moments later, the man was kneeling before him. He was of the Saghrichi tribe, descended, like Babur himself, from Genghis Khan, and famous for his skill with horses. It was said he could break a stallion in two days. Ali Gosht was loyal and conscientious, if quick tempered and conscious of the dignity of his hard-won position. Babur suspected Baburi had not chosen the time or manner of his approach with particular care. No doubt Ali Gosht had assumed that Baburi was being presumptuous – a trait for which the Barin clan had no mean reputation. It was his own fault, Babur thought, for not making his orders clear.

'I intend this man to be a member of my cavalry. We will start his training now. Fetch a horse from the royal stables.'

'Yes, Majesty.'

Twenty minutes later Babur, with Baburi clinging to his mount – a quiet mare – rode out of Shahrukiyyah, the usual escort of guards close behind. It was a warm afternoon and bees hummed in the patches of thick white clover that covered the meadows and sweetened the air. Babur reined in and turned in his saddle to watch Baburi's progress. He was sitting a little straighter now, no longer clutching the horse's mane. 'Grip with your knees. Keep your ankles in, your heels down and your feet in the stirrups.'

Baburi nodded, with a frown of concentration. He had natural grace in the saddle and would make a good rider, Babur thought. What had his life been like till now? It was hard for Babur to imagine. Images came into his head of the scrawny old man with his mildewed onions in the square in Samarkand where Babur had hidden after creeping into the city through the tunnel. Perhaps Baburi had been somewhere in the square that morning.

'Come on,' Babur shouted. 'Hurry up.'

'I will – if I can persuade the horse to agree, Majesty.'

. ◆ .

A few days later, Babur was handing his horse to his groom outside the stables, when he saw Baburi inside, bending down with his back towards him to groom his horse's legs. Babur walked over to him quietly and extended his hand to tap his shoulder to ask him how he was progressing. As he did so, his wrist was gripped and twisted. Baburi had whipped around and grabbed him. As soon as he saw who it was, he let go and dropped to his knees. 'Forgive me, Majesty, I didn't realise it was you.'

'Of course you did not, but even so why did you react like that?'

'Instinct. When you live on the streets as a child and you sense someone sneaking up behind you, you must act quickly to protect what you've got – whether food or a coin or indeed your freedom. There were plenty of men ready to abduct children to sell them into slavery or worse.'

'Was there no one to look out for you?'

'Not after my mother died. Sometimes people were kind but usually because they wanted something – even if it was only gratitude or flattery or to have you do their bidding. Those you were most likely to be able to rely on – for information on the back way into a bakery to steal a loaf or a good place to sleep in winter – were your fellow street children and even they looked after themselves first.'

'Was it really like that? Are people so selfish?'

'Perhaps I exaggerate. I made some good friends,' Baburi said, then added, with a wry smile, 'Is it so different at court? How many can you rely on unquestioningly among your counsellors? Who doesn't put his own interest before yours, seeking some advantage for himself, some honour or reward to raise himself above his peers? How many of your fellow rulers – relatives or not – wouldn't sneak into your territory to plunder it when your attention is distracted, like I did into bakeries when the owner was serving someone else?'

Babur suddenly scowled, reminded so forcibly of the actions of his half-brother Jahangir and his cousins Tambal and Mahmud. 'I still prefer life in the castle to that on the streets – and so do you, or you wouldn't be here.'

'At least I have a choice. You are a chieftain or nothing. You can never live an obscure, quiet life. Someone will see you as a threat and kill you. I'm free to choose my fate, so my options are more numerous if less exalted. Yes, I do prefer it here, but I shan't get too comfortable.'

'Quite right. My father used to say it was possible to be too clever for one's own good and that, I think, applies to paupers as well as princes.' With that Babur turned away, satisfied to have had the last word.

• ◆ •

As he had done a dozen times before over recent weeks, Babur tied the length of coarse blue cloth round his waist.

His black trousers were ragged at the hem and the leather jerkin he pulled on over the dun tunic was shiny and worn.

'Take care, Majesty.' Wazir Khan looked worried.

Babur guessed he disapproved of these night–time excursions and, even more, of his growing closeness with Baburi, his companion in them. But for Babur his adventures were becoming addictive insight into the lives of his people. 'I will.' He smiled at his old friend as he slipped from the chamber and hurried down a narrow back staircase to a small courtyard at the back of the fort where, as they had agreed, Baburi was waiting for him in the darkness.

Silently, they made for a side gate where Wazir Khan's guards, knowing who they were, let them pass without challenge. Several hundred yards beyond the castle, grazing contentedly, were the two ponies Babur had ordered to be saddled and tethered there.

They untied them, jumped on to their backs and, with a click of their tongues and a drumming of their feet on the ponies' well–fed sides, cantered into the darkness. It was extraordinary, Babur thought, how in just a few short weeks Baburi was becoming like the full blood–brother he had never had. He was teaching him to fight with a sword, to wrestle, even to fire arrows from the saddle – as Wazir Khan had once taught him. Baburi had indeed proved a natural horseman and, made wiser by a few bruising falls, could now almost keep pace with Babur.

Baburi, in turn, was teaching him the songs and dances of the people – and even the concealment skills and deftness required of the sneak thief. It had been Baburi, too, who had taught him how to dress as a peasant for their nocturnal ramblings. When they rode out into the night, they bargained in the villages and settlements for goods in the bazaars and sat hunched round communal fires sipping smoky tea while the elders told their stories.

Sometimes Babur heard them inveigh against himself and

the other warlords who made the lives of ordinary men so precarious. At first such comments had angered him, but now he listened, trying to understand what was in the hearts and minds of his people. However, both he and Baburi laughed at the outrageous rumours circulating about the peccadilloes of those in the fortress. Kasim – Babur's quiet, unassuming vizier – was said to have a male member of which a stallion would be proud but to be able to enjoy sex only when dressed as a woman and shackled to his bed.

But tonight there was an even more potent attraction than a discussion of Kasim's appetites. In Dzhizak, the village they were making for, was a brothel they had visited several times already – a broken-down wooden shack where the women danced in the firelight, flaunting their wares, and the men could take their pick. At the thought of the luscious breasts and wide hips of one of them, Yadgar, Babur's pulse quickened. In daytime his thoughts were on preparing for his coming campaign, but when night fell he could scarcely contain his eagerness to gallop through the soft darkness to her.

Yadgar's warm, available body and hot, questing mouth had revealed a new world and taught him many techniques and sensations. She was so different from Ayisha who, in all their couplings, had never caressed him. Her hands were always clenched by her sides, her lips cold and shut against him. Perhaps if he had been a more experienced lover on his wedding night, things might have been different . . . But that was in the past. When he was again King of Ferghana he would make Yadgar his concubine. He would enjoy enhancing her lush beauty with bright gems and watching the shimmer of golden chains against her amber skin, the lustre of pearls rising and falling on the soft cushion of her breasts, moist with the sweat of their lovemaking. The thought made him kick his pony on urgently.

Soon they reached the willow grove that marked the outskirts of Dzhizak and called out to the night-watchman that they were travellers in need of refreshment. After he had examined their faces by the light of his guttering torch he grunted and let them continue. They dismounted and led their ponies past the low, mud-brick houses and down the narrow alley to the bazaar, where the thin yellow light from the merchants' oil lamps barely illuminated the piles of gritty, poor-quality rice and mouldering root vegetables. The ground was speckled with sheep and goat droppings and a sprinkling of chicken turds deposited by a few scrawny hens.

The brothel lay on the far side. Yes, Yadgar was there. Babur could see her warming her hands over the dung fire. So was Baburi's usual choice – a wild mountain girl, boyish and slim, with red glints in her hair and an impudent little face.

As soon as she saw them, Yadgar came running, the cheap bells on her sturdy ankles jingling as she leaped at Babur, flinging her arms round his neck as her mouth sought his. She pressed herself close, laughing as she felt his instant response. Taking him by the hand she led him inside the brothel where, in a wooden cubicle barely large enough for the mattress on the floor, she shrugged off her clothes and went expertly to work with her hands and lips, before spreading her thighs to allow him to enter her warm, moist body.

The pale pink dawn was rising as Babur and Baburi, sated and happy and more than a little drunk from the strong spirits served in the brothel, came back within sight of Shahrukiyyah. They had spoken little on the return ride except to trade a few frank comments about their women and to boast of the frequency and inventiveness of their own performances. Inside the castle, Babur returned to his apartments, waving away the attendants who always seemed to materialise out of nowhere so that he could savour a few last moments of freedom and irresponsibility.

As the doors of his chamber closed behind him, he was

already tugging off his clothes. He was unprepared for a sharp blow to his left ear. He turned to see Esan Dawlat, hand still raised, eyes blazing. Never had she come to his apartments like this. Two of her elderly waiting women were standing behind her, eyes downcast but half-smiles on their lips.

'If you are sure you and your market boy have quite finished your whoring, we have matters to discuss,' his grandmother snapped. 'A messenger arrived during the night from Samarkand with a letter. It is from the chamberlain of your cousin Mahmud.' She flourished a bit of paper in his face.

'What does my cousin say? Does he want to make me a present of the kingdom he stole?' Babur rubbed his ear. He wasn't surprised Esan Dawlat knew he had been with a woman. She always knew everything. But he felt embarrassed she was seeing him in peasant garb, fresh from Yadgar's embraces and probably still smelling of her.

'Your cousin says nothing – and never will again unless you count the boom of a drum. Shaibani Khan has taken Samarkand and had Mahmud flayed alive. His skin has been made into a drum to be beaten above the Turquoise Gate every time Shaibani Khan enters and leaves the city.' Esan Dawlat's shrewd old eyes were pinpoints of anger at the outrage inflicted by an Uzbek barbarian on a Timurid prince.

'Listen.' Squinting, she began to read: '"The Uzbeks fell on us like an army of ants devouring everything in their path. They overwhelmed the city's defences by sheer weight of numbers and have butchered hundreds of our citizens. Bodies are piled in the marketplaces and rot in the wells. I and a few members of the court have survived in hiding thus far but we are in terrible peril . . . They have left us few places to conceal ourselves. May God show us the mercy that, in his infinite wisdom, he has denied to others."'

Babur felt instantly sober. While he had been cavorting, a thunderbolt had struck. 'I will summon my council and decide what to do. But we must have more information. The news in that letter must already be old. I will send scouts westward . . .'

Esan Dawlat nodded. It seemed there was nothing further she wished to say to him. A flick of her fingers brought her serving women to her side and she was heading for the door of his chamber. Babur himself opened it for her and watched her resolute figure walk briskly down the dimly lit passage back to the women's quarters, her servants bobbing behind her.

He washed quickly, still in shock at the tidings from Samarkand. Despite everything, he would not have wished such a fate on Mahmud, and the thought of Shaibani Khan's men defiling Timur's exquisite city and murdering its people hurt. If he'd wanted revenge on his cousin or Samarkand's fickle citizens, he would never have resorted to such obscene butchery . . .

Three quarters of an hour later, dressed once more as befitted a king, Babur looked at his counsellors, many recently roused from sleep for this early-morning meeting. On his finger was Timur's ring – a mark of the gravity of the situation. 'You have heard the news, of course?'

His counsellors nodded.

'I fear it is true, but in case it is a trick to distract us from attacking Akhsi, Baisanghar, I want you to send scouting parties west towards Samarkand to see what they can learn. I want regular reports of whatever they find – even if all seems peaceful I want to know. When they reach the city, I want a full account of it. If the Uzbeks are indeed there I need to know whether it seems Shaibani Khan plans to hold the city or whether this was just a raid. Go now.'

Baisanghar rose.

Babur turned to his scribe. 'I must despatch a letter.' The man smoothed a piece of paper on his writing block, then dipped his pen into the onyx jar dangling from his neck on a thong that held the thick black ink he mixed each morning.

'My beloved father-in-law,' Babur began. Then running quickly through the flowery courtesies – enquiries after Ibrahim Saru's health and hopes for his unbounded prosperity, all as necessary as they were insincere, he cut to the chase: 'In your beneficence, you promised me crossbowmen to help me regain my throne and make your daughter a ruling queen. My heart grieves that, despite my many entreaties, those troops have not yet come. Those around me begin to whisper that perhaps you are not a man of honour. I refuse to entertain such thoughts. But if you cannot assure me now that your men are on the road to Shahrukiyyah, I shall be forced to assume that you have, indeed, broken our agreement.'

He scratched his signature and ordered the scribe to affix his seal. This was Ibrahim Saru's last chance. It was intolerable that an uncouth tribal leader should toy with him.

For the next hour Babur and his counsellors, grim-faced and earnest, debated, but without more information their discussion was sterile. All they had were questions that could not yet be answered. Frustrated, Babur dismissed the council but asked Wazir Khan to remain.

'Majesty?'

'If Shaibani Khan has taken Samarkand, I've been trying to work out what I would do next if I were him and I keep reaching the same answer. I would send my forces east to destroy us here before moving on to Akhsi and crushing Jahangir and Tambal. Shaibani Khan has sworn to obliterate the descendants of Timur. He would enjoy boasting that he had wiped out the last two remnants of the male line of Ferghana.'

For once Wazir Khan had no words of comfort. For a while they sat in silence, each locked in his own thoughts.

But at least they didn't have to wait long for more news. By sunset, further reports were reaching Shahrukiyyah of a momentous catastrophe to the west. A band of agitated

174

merchants who had been camped on the hills beyond Samarkand brought tales of a clash between horsemen outside the city walls. They had not waited for the outcome but, gathering their pack animals, had fled eastward. Other travellers brought stories heard along the road that Shaibani Khan and his hordes had swooped down from the north and fallen on Samarkand.

That night Babur couldn't sleep, the still, warm air — oppressive and heavy — adding to his restlessness. Yesterday he would have sent for Baburi to amuse him with his stories or to gallop with him to the brothel and Yadgar, but not now. He sat alone by the window, gazing out. The heavy ring glinted on his finger. What would Timur have done? Would he have been prepared to wait passively to see what fate dished out to him? No. He would have found a way to take the initiative, to turn circumstances to his advantage.

Babur continued to sit, jaw in hand, as one by one the candles sputtered out and he was left in the darkness. Again and again, he kept turning everything over in his mind. As a thin line of golden light appeared on the eastern horizon, a glimmer of hope began to shine in the dark corners of his mind. Suddenly he knew what he would do. It was a huge risk, and it would cut him to the heart, but it was the only chance he had . . .

As soon as it was full daylight, he summoned his council. 'Shaibani Khan is a threat to the entire House of Timur. If he wipes me out he will turn next on my half-brother Jahangir. It will be only a matter of time. He wants all the Timurid lands and he will have them — unless we put aside our own quarrels. That is why I intend to offer Jahangir and Tambal an alliance. If they and the clans loyal to them will help me push the Uzbeks out of Samarkand, I will relinquish Ferghana to them . . .'

Wazir Khan's sharp intake of breath told Babur how much he had shocked him. 'But, Majesty—'

'It is the only way. Kasim, you will be my ambassador.'

Babur looked sternly at his council, feeling a new steeliness within him. 'For the moment, until we have an answer from Akhsi, you will say nothing of this to anyone. Those are my orders.'

As Babur rose, he saw how troubled Wazir Khan looked. In former days he would have talked through his plans with his old friend to try to convince him. But no one could help him now. This was his destiny, his choice. If his boldness worked, he would again be in golden Samarkand. He had never ceased to think of it as his rightful property or to mourn its loss, this place his father had ached to possess and to which mountainous little Ferghana, with its unruly chiefs and bleating sheep, had always been a poor second. If he was to succeed where his father had not, ambition, not sentiment, must be his watchword.

• ◆ •

The following days brought further trickles, then a stream, and finally a flood of refugees to the settlements around Shahrukiyyah. Babur sent men to question them and learned that most were from villages near Samarkand. Ominously, few were from the city itself and there was no sign of Mahmud's chamberlain who had written in such despair. Neither was there any news of Mahmud's wife, the grand vizier's daughter . . .

From the battlements, Babur watched the drab procession of travel-stained, weary people, who had simply grabbed what they could and fled for their lives – old men and snotty-nosed infants loaded onto carts, some of which had been hauled the one hundred and fifty miles by hand, desperate-looking mothers clutching babies to their skinny breasts. All hungry mouths – a burden not a help. Babur ordered distributions from his granaries and those of the other fortresses he held, but even those supplies would not last for long.

He had hoped that some of the soldiers of Samarkand

might have managed to flee the Uzbeks and would make their way eastwards, but the reports arriving from Baisanghar's scouts blasted any such idea. It was clear there had been great slaughter as the Uzbeks had hacked and hewn their way to victory. The meadows around Samarkand were strewn with the bloated corpses of its soldiers. Few had escaped. Only an army of ghosts would march to Babur's assistance.

Everything now depended on Jahangir and Tambal. Should he have ridden to them himself under a flag of truce? he wondered. Would Kasim convince Jahangir and Tambal that their best – perhaps only – chance of survival lay in accepting his offer of a peace settlement and an alliance against Shaibani Khan or would they be blinded to the threat of Shaibani Khan by their suspicion of his own motives?

He was with his mother and grandmother when he heard that Kasim had returned. Without explanation, and avoiding Esan Dawlat's sharp eyes, he hurried to his chambers where he had ordered his ambassador to be brought. Kasim was his usual quiet, self-possessed self, betraying not a hint of excitement or agitation about the news he was carrying.

'Well?' It was all Babur could do not to grab him by the shoulders.

'I bring an answer, Majesty. They accept your terms.' Now, at last, Kasim allowed himself a faint smile. 'See, Majesty.' From a dark-red camelskin bag, fastened with plugs of ivory, he extracted a letter.

Babur scanned it and his heart beat faster. Yes! Passing over the empty courtesies he found what he was looking for. He read the words to himself several times, savouring them. 'What you propose, my brother, is the only way to save us all from the Uzbek menace. By the time you receive this, my troops will already be preparing to march to Shahrukiyyah. I am sending you four thousand cavalry and a thousand archers, all that I can spare.' It was signed by Jahangir and stamped with the royal seal of Ferghana.

177

It cost Babur a pang to run his fingers over the thick wax – the right to affix the royal seal was his: by blood and birth he was King of Ferghana. But he had made his choice and must abide by it. He must also trust Jahangir and his controller, Tambal, to keep their word. If they betrayed him now, they would all be ruined.

Chapter 10

An Ancient Foe

Babur turned to look at the lines of riders strung out behind him, their brilliant yellow banners proclaiming them all warriors of Ferghana. Tribal and dynastic feuds forgotten, they were riding against an ancient enemy. Three hours earlier, in their apartments in the fortress, Esan Dawlat and Kutlugh Nigar had given him their blessing and his mother had pressed her lips to the eagle hilt of his father's sword, Alamgir, hanging from his metal-studded belt. He was surprised that they had not objected to his bargain with his half-brother – Esan Dawlat had actually commended his vision and daring. Only Khanzada had seemed shaken at the thought that she might never again see her childhood home of Akhsi.

As for Ayisha, he had gone to her last night for one final, brief encounter. If he did not return, he might at least be leaving an heir inside her, he had thought, thrusting energetically but joylessly, his eyes fixed on the wall rather than on her expressionless, half-averted face. As soon as he had reached his shuddering climax, Ayisha had done what she now always did – rolled away from him and pulled the coverlet over her nakedness. He had not looked at her as he dressed hurriedly and left her chamber immediately without either speaking a single word of comfort or farewell. They would never be other than emotional strangers.

At least her father had come to his senses. Towards the rear of the long column, beyond the yellow pennants of Ferghana, were the ranks of mounted Mangligh crossbowmen in black and red. They had arrived at Shahrukiyyah within days of Ibrahim Saru getting wind of the alliance between Babur and Jahangir against Shaibani Khan.

Wazir Khan and Baisanghar were riding by his side and somewhere among the ranks of his cavalry would be Baburi. He had not spoken more than a word or two to his friend since the news of the fall of Samarkand and missed his light-hearted company. But companionship – friendship – was perhaps not for kings, whose minds must be fixed on greater things, Babur reflected.

They were travelling quickly, galloping over ground baked hard by the heat of summer. They were also travelling light. Babur had decided there was no time to transport cumbersome siege engines. He was staking everything on a swift surprise attack. Till now Samarkand had always been in the hands of one Timurid ruler or another. The citizens of Samarkand – those left alive – should be desperate to rid themselves of a cruel, alien predator like Shaibani Khan. When they saw his forces approach, he hoped they would rise against their oppressors.

What really counted, though, were Shaibani Khan's plans. With autumn almost upon him, did he intend to winter in Samarkand? Babur frowned as he rode, his chestnut's hoofs beating a rhythmic tattoo, trying to put himself inside the mind of his enemy. What did he really want? To rape and loot Samarkand and then return with his pack of marauders back to the northern steppes to enjoy his booty, or did he have grander ambitions? Was his attack on Samarkand simply a sustained raid or had he come to stay to establish a dynasty and empire of his own?

If the stories Babur had heard in his boyhood were true, Shaibani Khan bore Samarkand a grudge. He recalled his father's tales of how, as a boy, Shaibani Khan had been captured during a raid by the King of Samarkand's forces on an Uzbek settlement. His father and brothers had been killed but, at scarcely more than ten, he had been dragged at a camel's tail, a leather thong round his neck, as a slave to Samarkand. Quick witted and clever, he had survived the harsh conditions in the blacksmiths' workshops, where the symbol of the slave had been burned into his left cheek, and had come to the attention of a courtier in the Kok Saray.

The nobleman had had him educated and given him a good position as a scribe, but had also forced him to share his bed. One night the young Shaibani Khan had slit his master's throat. Dipping his finger in the murdered man's blood, he had written his final missive as a scribe; a message scrawled on the wall, calling down a curse on the city. He had vanished back to his own people. Reunited with his clan, he had risen to become overlord of all the Uzbeks and still nursed a brooding hatred for the royal House of Timur. He was now a man of some thirty-five summers and in his prime, a formidable enemy who cast a dark shadow before him and left death in his wake. Defeating such a man would not be easy . . .

Guile rather than force might be the answer. Within some four days, if they could keep up their pace, they would be within striking distance of Samarkand. To retain any advantage of surprise, he would have to attack at once. But perhaps it would be better to make Shaibani Khan uncertain of his intentions – or, best of all, to mislead him. If he could convince him he was trying to break out of Ferghana – to bypass Samarkand and travel west – he might draw his enemy away from the city.

That evening, as Babur sat at a campfire with Wazir Khan and Baisanghar, he stared into the flames, still seeking inspiration. The ground where they had made camp was sandy. Suddenly he rose, picked up a stick and traced the outline of Samarkand – the five-mile girdle of walls pierced by the six gates, the surrounding patchwork of meadows, orchards and gardens, the tracery of streams and rivers on the eastern and northern sides. 'What if we sent a detachment of our men along the far side of the Ab-i-Siyah river, parallel with the northern walls of Samarkand . . . They would be visible to those guarding the Iron and the Shaykhzada gates but still too far off for the Uzbeks to gauge their strength accurately. We might make them think it was our entire army . . .'

'And then, Majesty?' Baisanghar asked.

'If we are lucky, the Uzbeks will ride out in pursuit – and we will have our chance. If we conceal the remainder of our men in the scrubland that borders the Kan-i-Gil meadow, east of the Iron Gate, we'll be able to see what is happening and – if God is with us and the Uzbeks are indeed deceived – attack the eastern walls of the city by the Turquoise Gate.'

Wazir Khan was staring thoughtfully at the map in the sand, through which a line of long-bodied ants, disciplined as soldiers, was tramping, some carrying leaf shreds, to their nest. 'The detachment that tries to lure the Uzbeks out of the city must be our best and fastest horsemen. They must be able to outride their pursuers, circle round and rejoin the main force to help in the attack on the city.'

'Yes.' Baisanghar nodded vigorously. 'They would need to work their way south and east like this . . .' With his left hand, he picked up the stick Babur had thrown down and scratched arrows in the sand, sweeping past the Chaharraha Gate round the southern walls and up past the Needlemaker's Gate towards the Turquoise Gate. In so doing he disturbed and killed some of the marching ants, but the remainder re-formed and continued as though nothing had happened.

'But it would be risky, Majesty.' Baisanghar looked anxious. 'We have little knowledge of how many Uzbeks are in the city or of their defences. Even if we succeed in tempting some out of the city, the defenders may still be too many for us to overwhelm. Perhaps we should first try to send in spies.'

'As I was once a spy?' Babur thought of how he had crept like a sewer rat into the city. 'No, we don't have time. If we are to trick the Uzbeks we must be quick and take the risk.'

Babur was certain he was right, but if his plan failed, what would the consequences be? That was something he refused to contemplate. There was an ancient proverb in Ferghana: 'Who dares not take his chance will regret it until old age.'

Better to have no old age than to spend his life in regret.

• ◆ •

Three days later – they had covered the one hundred and fifty miles even faster than Babur had hoped – Samarkand lay just beyond the next rows of hills that were now scorched brown by the heat of summer but in a few weeks would begin to be silvered with frost. For the past three hours, on Babur's express orders, his men had ridden at no faster than a trot and in silence. Scouts despatched to scour the landscape for potential ambushes had returned at regular intervals to report that they had seen nothing, heard nothing, to alarm them.

Nevertheless, Babur would take no chances. The Uzbeks were formidable fighters, with the guile of foxes desperate for fresh meat. And that was how they killed – as indiscriminately as a fox in a hen house that slaughters every bird but steals off with only one between its jaws.

As purple dusk softened the landscape, the silent lines of riders at last approached Qolba Hill – the highest of the final range before Samarkand, from which Babur had first glimpsed the city more than five years earlier. This time, instead of heading for the summit, he called a halt, summoned Wazir Khan, Baisanghar and his other chieftains, then gave his final orders. 'Using Qolba Hill to give us cover, we will ride westward and camp under cover of the trees bordering the Qolba meadow where we will make our final preparations. We will light no fires for fear of giving away our position. Just before the sun rises tomorrow, Baisanghar, you will be our decoy. Take three hundred of our best horsemen, ride down to the banks of the Ab-i-Siyah, then head west. Make sure you are seen from the city walls. The morning mists will make it difficult for the guards to estimate your numbers accurately. Take no risks. Don't ford the river until you are beyond the Shaykhzada Gate. I depend on you to rejoin us and help in the assault on the city walls by the Turquoise Gate no more than four hours after we part.

'Wazir Khan, as soon as we see that the Uzbeks have taken the bait and are riding in pursuit of Baisanghar, we will attack the walls from the east. Once we are inside, my orders are to kill every Uzbek we find – give no quarter as they gave none to our people – but treat the citizens of Samarkand and their property with respect. They are my subjects.'

'Yes, Majesty.' His commanders nodded, each man seeming wrapped in his thoughts, perhaps wondering whether he would live to see another dawn. Shaibani Khan had never been defeated on the battlefield. But this was a trial of wits as well as weapons, and the thought gave Babur renewed courage.

◆

It was half an hour since Baisanghar and his men had departed. Babur rested his back against a well-grown apple tree whose branches sagged with fruit, their ripe scent making him think for a moment of Yadgar. Dawn mists softened the outlines of trees and bushes. The poles for the scaling ladders had been cut and the ladders fashioned wide enough for three men to climb abreast. They would be carried to the attack between pairs of horses. Wazir Khan was kneeling in silent prayer, every few moments bending forward to touch his forehead to the ground.

Perhaps he, too, should be praying, Babur wondered. Instead he allowed himself a few moments' quiet contemplation, but then returned to thoughts of action. His scouts had reported no sign of any large Uzbek encampment outside the city walls. Perhaps that meant some of Shaibani Khan's forces had already moved on. The temptation – now that Samarkand had fallen – to pillage the surrounding villages and settlements would be great for some of his ill-disciplined troops. With luck, it would not have entered Shaibani Khan's arrogant head that anyone would dare attack him and he would have been content to let them go.

Suddenly, Babur thought he heard something and it jerked him from his reflections. Leaping to his feet, and half-skidding on rotting windfall apples, he peered through the trees. In the distance, above the mist shrouding the river, he could make out the familiar walls of Samarkand and – here and there – pinpricks of light on the battlements.

Then, as he strained his eyes and ears, he heard it again: the deep, rhythmic throbbing of a drum, then more drums. Suddenly the battlements were alive with moving dots as figures ran hither and thither. Baisanghar and his men must have been spotted, as intended, as they circled westward. Would Shaibani Khan take the bait?

'Tell your men to be ready to ride but no man is to move until I give the order,' Babur said in a low voice to his commanders, who had gathered around him, listening, like him, to the drums.

The thudding had settled into a heavy, ominous rhythm. Babur hoped it wasn't Mahmud Khan's flayed skin he could hear being beaten. As the minutes passed, the uncertainty was growing intolerable. Under cover of the mist, Babur moved forward to get a better view and concealed himself in a coppice nearer the walls. As far as he could tell from his new vantage point, the Iron Gate and, beyond it, the Shaykhzada Gate – closest to where Baisanghar and his men, Baburi among them, had passed – were still shut. But then, when Babur thought he could stand the suspense no longer, the portcullis over the Iron Gate began to rise. As soon as it was high enough, a stream of horsemen, two abreast, cantered out and, wheeling north-westwards, broke into a gallop. On and on the column came – at least four hundred warriors, he thought, in near ecstasy. When, finally, the last riders had disappeared wraithlike into the mist there was a pause. Babur expected the Iron Gate to be lowered but instead a single man rode slowly out. A few paces beyond the gate, he reined in his horse and turned his head from left to right. He appeared to be snuffing the air, as hunting dogs did before they gave chase. For a moment, the lone rider seemed to be looking across the low-lying fields and meadows through the mist straight at him, though he knew that was impossible.

Babur had little doubt as to who it was – Shaibani Khan himself. What would the Uzbek leader do? Finally the rider raised his hand. As yet more warriors surged through the Iron Gate behind him, he kicked his horse and, calling to his men with a harsh cry that, though faint by the time it reached him, Babur could still hear, disappeared north-west. After another couple of minutes, all the riders had gone and the portcullis was being slowly lowered back into place.

Curbing his impatience, Babur returned to the main body of his troops and signalled yet again to his men to stay quiet and still. If they moved into the open too quickly, sounds of alarm from the city might yet reach Shaibani Khan and bring him back. Wazir Khan was using the time to tighten his horse's girths and check his weapons – sword, dagger and throwing axe. Grateful for his old mentor's calmness and commonsense, Babur did the same. On his shoulder was his leather quiver and it gave him confidence to run his fingers over the sharp tips of his long, newly fletched arrows. He took his curved bow from its case and tried the tautness of the string, grunting with satisfaction at the tension in the oiled sinew. It felt as tightly strung as he did.

Finally the moment came. All was quiet again on the battlements, and Shaibani Khan's force must now be well beyond earshot.

'We ride!' shouted Babur, his voice raw with excitement. Leaping on to his horse he rode clear of the trees and waited as his men formed up. His bodyguard, under Wazir Khan, was immediately behind him, then the pairs of riders bringing the ladders, the rest of the cavalry and finally Ibrahim Saru's mounted crossbowmen.

Babur dug in his heels and his horse leaped forward. They tore south across the meadows through the dispersing mists, the city walls on their right as they made for the Turquoise Gate. They were on the far side of the river that flowed past the walls but this time they had no need to ford it. A wide, strong bridge of wooden planks – newly built, no doubt, by the Uzbeks – stood three hundred yards upstream from the Turquoise Gate.

Babur and his men thundered over it and made straight for the gate. As shouts of alarm rang out from the battlements, the Mangligh crossbowmen sent up volley after volley of bolts. Within minutes the ladders were against the walls at their lowest point, on either side of the Turquoise Gate. Looking up as he began to climb, Babur was astonished to see not a single defender.

It was a matter of moments to scale the ladder and climb the last few feet by grabbing on to the stonework. There was hardly room to move, let alone draw a sword, as his warriors swarmed around him. But of Uzbek defenders – apart from those lying dead with Mangligh bolts sticking into them like a porcupine's quills – there remained no sign.

Then a volley of arrows from a strong point about a hundred yards away revealed that not all the Uzbek defenders had fled. A black-feathered arrow struck Babur's domed helmet a glancing blow. Another embedded itself deep in the thigh of a man behind him. A third penetrated the cheek of a soldier who was clambering from a ladder over the battlements on to the wall. Blood pouring out of his mouth, he lost his grip and, falling backwards from the wall, took the man climbing below with him in his death fall to the rocky ground beneath.

Babur raised his shield to protect himself from the next volley and, yelling for his men to follow, charged towards the strong point. Two more arrows thudded into his shield but the thick hide and wood did its work. However, behind Babur a young soldier fell, an arrow in his neck. Then Babur was in the strong point, which had no door. He slashed at the first man he encountered before he could drop his bow and pull out his sword. A second had his fingers on his sword hilt but Babur gave him a slashing cut across the wrist, almost severing his hand. The man turned and ran out of the opposite doorway and along the walls towards the gatehouse of the Turquoise Gate another fifty yards away.

The other occupants of the strong point tried to follow, but Babur and his men killed two as they tried to extricate themselves from the close-quarters mêlée. His archers brought down two more as they rushed for the gatehouse, although one succeeded in half staggering, half crawling into its protective embrace.

'Majesty, we've put them to flight!'

Babur turned to see Wazir Khan, breathing heavily but triumphant, dagger in one hand and bloodied sword in the other. 'Not quite. Post guards to hold this section of the walls and the gate. You are to stay here in command. Meanwhile

I and the rest of the men will try to get into the gatehouse to open the gate to the rest of our troops.'

Wazir Khan looked abashed but Babur was not going to risk his increasingly lame counsellor in street fighting when a man's ability to run fast might make the difference between life and death.

Shield in front of his head and running bent double, Babur covered the fifty yards to the gatehouse. Inside, he found that the only Uzbek left was the man who had almost lost his hand. He had collapsed against the wall, breathing heavily and cursing in his pain as his lifeblood pumped from his wound on to the stone floor. The clatter of feet from the stairs leading down to the gate told Babur where the rest of the defenders had gone. He and his men followed cautiously, fearing an attack as they emerged from the staircase, but none came.

'Smash the lock and open the gate,' Babur yelled.

Axes ready, two of his bodyguard ran to carry out the order. There was the sound of metal against metal as they slammed their axes into the lock and a final crash showed they had succeeded. Soon, the ancient, iron-studded gate was swinging open to admit the remainder of Babur's troops, including the Mangligh crossbowmen.

With Alamgir in his hand, Babur glanced about. It was very quiet. Where were the Uzbeks hiding? Babur put caution aside and advanced up the wide street, yelling, 'Ferghana! Ferghana!'

His shouts echoed in the silence. There was no volley of arrows or even an answering cry of Uzbek defiance. Then, to Babur's astonishment, doors and shutters began to open. He darted for cover and again reached for his bow and an arrow, but the heads poking out were not those of Uzbek warriors. They belonged to the ordinary people of Samarkand – merchants, shopkeepers, innkeepers – who, recognising Babur, were calling out blessings upon him and his men, thanking them for their liberation. Soon they were pouring from their houses, almost insane in their joy and jubilation

'Quick! This way!' a man was calling. 'I saw one of those Uzbeks run up here.' He pointed to a narrow alleyway where tell-tale drops of blood were already congealing in the dust. Before Babur could order his men to investigate, two ordinary citizens – one burly enough to be a butcher and the other a smaller, wiry man with a wart on the side of his nose – disappeared in that direction. Within moments they had reappeared, dragging a young Uzbek by the legs so that his head banged along the ground. A Mangligh bolt was protruding from his chest, and as he struggled for breath, he begged for mercy. Before Babur could say anything, the burly man drew his knife and cut the boy's throat from ear to ear, beaming as the warm blood splashed his boots.

All around, citizens were arming themselves with anything they could find – stones, pitchforks, blacksmith's tools . . . A light in their eyes reminded Babur of wild dogs as they ran with him and his troops through the streets, searching for Uzbeks and continuing to stab and club any they found long after they were dead, so great was their hatred, so bad had been the treatment they had received.

But apart from those injured on the walls who had not been able to get far, there were few – and still no resistance. The Uzbeks must be fleeing before them. Reaching the Registan Square, Babur called a halt. Maybe the Uzbeks were convinced he had attacked with a much greater force than he had or perhaps this was a trap and they were waiting in ambush a little way ahead. Babur consulted briefly with his commanders, then ordered detachments of soldiers to advance cautiously into the west, north and east of the city.

By now it was mid-morning and beneath a streaked and brilliant sky more and more people were surging into the square. They were carrying food – bread, fruit, even skins of wine – which they thrust on Babur's men. A babble of excited voices was rising all around him. This was chaos – what if the Uzbeks were regrouping and about to counter-attack? Babur's men could not fight amid this throng.

Babur ordered his guards to push back the jubilant people. Making barriers of their spears, his warriors advanced, shoulder to shoulder, and slowly succeeded in driving the crowds back, clearing the entries and exits to the square. That was better. 'I want all of these buildings searched, and men posted at every high vantage-point around the square,' Babur ordered. Even now Uzbek archers might be concealed among all the blue-tiled domes and minarets of the palaces, mosques and *madrasas* bounding the square, just waiting their chance.

'Majesty . . .' A young soldier, broad face beaded with sweat, was at Babur's elbow. He sounded as if he had been running hard.

'What is it?'

'The main body of Uzbeks are fleeing the city northwards through the Shaykhzada Gate in the hope of rejoining Shaibani Khan – our archers are firing at them as they go. However, the local people have trapped some in the gatehouse of the Iron Gate.'

'Excellent. We must clear the city of the last of our enemies and man the walls before Shaibani Khan can return.' Babur called for his horse and, bodyguard behind him, set out towards the Iron Gate. The fabulous blue dome of Timur's mosque caught the light, but beyond it smoke was rising and Babur heard screams. As he approached the Iron Gate he saw that flames were pushing through the roof of the gatehouse and that the screams were coming from Uzbeks trapped inside. Drawing nearer, he saw a man try to escape by climbing through a window only to be pushed back into the flames by some citizens of Samarkand, who immediately closed the shutters and barred them from the outside. Another Uzbek, his clothes on fire, plunged from the top floor and crashed to the ground where the crowd immediately surrounded his body, stabbing frenziedly at him to ensure he was dead. Soon the cheering people were flourishing his bloody head as a trophy.

At Babur's arrival, one of the citizens – his face smoke-blackened – rushed towards him and, recognising the royal standard of Ferghana held by one of Babur's guards, fell to his knees. 'Majesty, we have trapped them and are burning them. They are suffering like they made us suffer. None will die an easy death, I promise.' His shining eyes contained only blood-lust as he looked to Babur for congratulation, but the sweet stench of burning flesh sickened Babur and he simply nodded and waved the man away.

He turned his back on the flaming gatehouse where, already, the agonised cries of the Uzbeks were growing less frequent and rode back slowly towards the Registan Square. Samarkand, it seemed, was his again but he could scarcely believe how quickly and easily it had fallen.

There was a clattering of hoofs ahead and a familiar figure came into view. It was Baisanghar, and among the riders accompanying him, he glimpsed Baburi.

'Hail, Babur, King of Samarkand!' Baisanghar shouted, and behind him the other men took up the cry. Babur raised a hand and rode slowly past, still coming to terms with what had happened. He should be ecstatic, but instead he felt a strange detachment. Suddenly, more than anything, he wanted space and time to think.

• ◆ •

That night in the Kok Saray, Babur ordered pen and paper to be brought to him. When his servant asked whether he also wished for a scribe, he shook his head. He had decided something. He was nineteen, a fully grown man, and he had achieved momentous things. From now on he would keep a diary in which he would speak from the heart. He alone would know what was written there.

192

He dipped his pen into the ink, thought for a moment then began to write: slowly at first but then more fluidly as his emotions welled up inside him:

For generations Samarkand belonged to the House of Timur. Then the Uzbeks – the alien foe from outside our civilised world on the fringes of mankind – seized and ravaged it. Now the city that slipped from our hands has by God's grace been given back. Golden Samarkand is mine again.

With a deep sigh, he put down his pen and snuffed out his candle. He lay down and, moments later, was asleep.

Chapter 11

Bitter Almonds

The first frosts had made the delicate outlines of Samarkand's egg-shaped domes, slender minarets and tiled gateways look as if they had been covered with silver leaf. Now, as bitter winds howled through the leafless orchards and the snow tumbled in earnest, the city seemed to Babur like a bride beneath her veils – her grace shrouded from the eyes of men but not entirely concealed.

His favourite chestnut horse was snorting clouds of misty breath and lifting its hoofs high out of the soft snow. Wolfskin cap on his head, fur-lined robes wrapped tightly round him, and feet in sheepskin boots, Babur was returning from his inspection around the exterior of the city walls. His bodyguards were close behind him. Wazir Khan, ill these past two weeks with a fever, was, for once, not with him, but Baburi was, his face protected from the scouring cold by a swathe of brilliant green cloth.

It was too cold to talk, even if they could have heard each other's words through the wind and the scarves that muffled their heads. Babur's lips were so numb he would have struggled to utter a word but as they rode towards the

Turquoise Gate, hung with icicles, he forgot how chilled he was. The exhilaration of success pumped an inner warmth through him, like a draught of strong spirit.

Yet as he and his men trotted in through the gateway and headed westward towards the citadel, he felt the stirrings of an anxiety that had seldom left him during the three months since he'd taken Samarkand. For the present, winter's frozen grip offered protection against attack, but what would happen when the snows melted? Although Shaibani Khan had not immediately laid siege to the city, preferring to return to his northern fortresses to overwinter, he would surely not just accept the loss of Samarkand, and Babur had known from the outset that, given his limited resources, it might be harder to hold the city against Shaibani Khan than to take it from him. Immediately after its capture, he had set his men to strengthen the fortifications by building extra watch-towers and raising the wall itself in places until the frost had virtually ended their work.

Riding into the courtyard of the Kok Saray, Babur wondered whether to go and see his grandmother, mother and sister in the luxurious apartments they'd occupied since arriving in Samarkand soon after his victory. Instead he decided to visit Wazir Khan. He must be improving by now . . . Jumping down from his horse and slapping his hands against his sides to warm himself, he strode to the low, stone-built house where Wazir Khan lodged. He missed him and was impatient for his recovery.

Stamping the snow from his boots and pulling off his cap – the long hairs of the wolfskin spiky with ice – Babur went inside. On ducking through the low doorway into Wazir Khan's chamber, he saw his old friend lying on his back in his bed, an arm flung across his face as if asleep. Coming nearer, he was shocked by how violently Wazir Khan was shaking despite the goatskin coverlets the *hakim* had piled on him and the fire in the hearth. Yesterday he had been shivering only a little.

'How is he?'

The *hakim* was stirring some concoction in a copper pot over the fire. 'He is worse, Majesty. I am brewing an elixir of wine, herbs and cinnamon to try to drive the fever from him.' The man's tone was sombre, his face preoccupied – very different from his respectful jollity at their previous meetings.

A knot tightened in Babur's stomach as, for the first time, he considered the possibility that Wazir Khan might die. 'You must save him.'

'I will try, Majesty, but decisions about life and death are for God alone. All I know is that if he does not improve soon, he will be beyond any powers I have . . .' The *hakim* turned back to his pot and began stirring vigorously again.

Babur went to Wazir Khan and gently moved his arm from his face, which was covered with a film of sweat. Wazir Khan stirred and, for a moment, his one eye opened. 'Majesty . . .' His usually strong, deep voice was a thin, painful croak.

'Don't try to speak. You must save your strength.' Carefully, Babur took hold of Wazir Khan's shoulders, trying to still the shaking, willing some of his own strength to flow into his sick friend. Through the thick fabric of his robe, he could feel the hectic heat of Wazir Khan's body.

The *hakim* approached with a clay cup.

'Let me.' Babur took the cup and raising Wazir Khan's head with one hand, held it to his lips with the other. Wazir Khan tried to drink, but the warm red liquid ran down his stubbly chin. Cursing his own clumsiness, Babur tried again, recalling how, in the dank cave, Wazir Khan had once nursed him through a fever, painstakingly and devotedly trickling drops of water down a strip of cloth into his dry mouth. He raised Wazir Khan's head higher – that was better. Wazir Khan managed to swallow a little of the *hakim*'s brew, then a little more. When he had finished, Babur laid his head back on the pillow.

'I will send word if there is any change in his condition, Majesty.'

'I will stay.' Wazir Khan had no one closer to watch over him. It was many years since the smallpox had taken his wife and son, and nearly a decade since his daughter had died in childbirth. Babur gathered up a couple of brocade bolsters, shoved them against the wall next to Wazir Khan's bed and flung himself down on them. If these were to be Wazir Khan's last hours on earth, he would be with him.

As night drew on, Babur watched, and sometimes helped, as the *hakim* hovered around the bed, checking Wazir Khan's pulse, rolling back an eyelid to peer into his eye and placing a hand on his forehead to gauge his temperature. Sometimes Wazir Khan lay quietly, though still shaking and shuddering. At other times, he would shout out. Most of his words were incomprehensible but Babur caught something among the ramblings . . .

'Doves . . . doves with ruby-red blood on their feathers . . . See how they fall, Majesty . . .'

He must be re-living that day on the battlements of Akhsi when Babur's father and his dovecote had tumbled to oblivion. After all this time Babur could still feel Wazir Khan's iron-strong hands dragging him back from the edge of the ravine where his father's broken body had lain . . . He owed so much to Wazir Khan, who had been as a father to him since that time, yet there was nothing he could do to save him.

As Wazir Khan fell silent again, Babur shut his eyes. How would he manage without him?

• ◆ •

'Majesty . . . Majesty . . . Wake up!'

Babur sat up with a start. The room was in almost total darkness except for a flicker of light from an oil lamp the *hakim* was holding high in his right hand.

Blinking, Babur stumbled to his feet. He didn't want to

look at the bed because of what he might see. Instead he fixed his eyes on the *hakim*'s face. 'What is it?'

'God has spoken, Majesty.' The doctor moved over to the bed and allowed the small halo of light from his lamp to fall on Wazir Khan.

He was sitting up against the pillows. He was no longer shivering, his one eye was bright and clear and there was a half-smile on his wasted face. The fever had gone. For a moment Babur couldn't take in what he was seeing, but then he rushed to the bed and threw his arms round Wazir Khan in a gesture of overwhelming relief and affection.

'Majesty, please, my patient is weak . . .' the *hakim* protested but Babur barely heard him, conscious only of the profoundest gratitude. Wazir Khan had been spared . . .

Leaving him to rest, Babur went outside. The cold air stung his bare face but he didn't care. Released from the sickroom, worries over, he felt his own youth and strength surge up inside him and, with it, the need for young, carefree company. Though dawn was still only a pale sliver on the eastern horizon, he asked for Baburi.

A few minutes later he appeared, bleary eyed and fastening his sheepskin jerkin. Babur could see his warm breath rising in white spirals as he looked around him, clearly puzzled to have been summoned so early. 'Come on – we're going for a ride,' Babur called to him.

'What? . . .'

'You heard me – get a move on . . .'

Ten minutes later, they were galloping out of the Turquoise Gate, the hoofprints of their horses pockmarking the fresh snow as sunlight began to warm the landscape. It was good to be young and alive, whatever was to come.

◆

At first it was hard to be certain. At this time of the year, the pale, almost colourless light played tricks on men's eyes.

Babur stared hard towards Qolba Hill. As he watched, he thought he saw more of them – yes: he was right – the distant black shapes of horsemen.

Wazir Khan was also gazing fixedly at the hill.

'Uzbeks . . . ?'

'I fear so, Majesty. Probably scouts.'

Babur turned away. Over the past three weeks rumours – at first vague and insubstantial, then more detailed – had begun reaching Samarkand. The two facts on which all seemed agreed were that Shaibani Khan was in Bokhara, to the west of Samarkand, recruiting mercenaries, and that he was summoning those Uzbek fighters who had wintered with their clans and promising them a rich prize.

On Babur's orders the armourers of Samarkand, who had laboured hard through the winter, had redoubled their efforts and were working night and day, the sound of clashing metal filling the air as they forged sharp-edged blades and spears in their furnaces and tempered them on their anvils. He would have enough weapons and he had done what he could to improve the fortifications, but what about men?

He frowned. At the last count he had seven thousand, including the Mangligh crossbowmen who had remained in the city through the winter. Since he had learned that the Uzbeks might be on the move, he had despatched messengers to other chieftains in the region – even to Jahangir and Tambal in Akhsi whose troops had returned after Babur had taken Samarkand – asking their help against the common enemy. So far none had answered.

'I'm not surprised the Uzbeks are coming, Wazir Khan. I knew it was only a matter of time. While you were ill, Baburi and I sometimes talked about it . . .'

'And what did the market boy say?'

The unaccustomed sharpness in Wazir Khan's tone startled Babur. 'Market boy he may have been, but he still talks sense . . . and he knows Samarkand and its people . . .'

'He should remember who he is and you should remember who you are, Majesty . . . You are the king . . . It doesn't look good to be seen to consult an upstart like him rather than older, wiser and better-born men . . . I'm only saying what your father would, if God had spared him . . .'

Babur glared at Wazir Khan. Perhaps his grandmother had been getting at him – Esan Dawlat never hid her contempt for Baburi or her disapproval of Babur's association with him. Then he remembered how much he owed Wazir Khan and how ill he had recently been. 'I will never forget I am king and of Timur's blood. I enjoy Baburi's company . . . but I ask his advice because it is sound. Like you, he doesn't tell me what he believes I wish to hear – but says what is in his mind. That doesn't mean I always agree with him . . . I take my own decisions . . .'

'As your oldest adviser I had to say something. Baburi may be shrewd, but he's pleased with himself and hot tempered, too. If you're not careful, your friendship with him will make others who feel overlooked jealous and resentful . . . Sometimes, I confess, even I've not felt immune from this . . .'

Seeing how troubled Wazir Khan looked, Babur touched his shoulder gently. 'You are my greatest support, valued above all my other *ichkis*, and I know you only speak for my own good. I will be careful . . . Now, summon the council. They need to know what we've seen on the hill . . .'

As Wazir Khan walked quickly away despite his limp, Babur stared towards Qolba Hill again, but the black shapes had vanished. Was Wazir Khan right to warn him about Baburi or was it just that Wazir Khan couldn't understand his need for company of his own age? Events had already shown him that a king's life could be as precarious as a market boy's. If he was going to prosper and triumph, as Timur had done, he needed help wherever he could find it. For the present, survival was what mattered and Baburi knew all about that . . .

201

Babur hurried to his audience chamber where he saw on a low table inlaid with shimmering mother-of-pearl the plan of the regions around Samarkand he had ordered to be prepared. Half an hour later, his counsellors were clustered round him.

'There's no point waiting meekly within the walls. With the men we have it won't be easy to repel Shaibani Khan's attacks or to withstand a long siege. We'll stand a far better chance of success if we take the fight to him in the early spring before he has had time to gather all his forces. Even though we'll still be outnumbered, we can strike fast and hard when he least expects it. If, as I believe he will, he advances against us direct from Bokhara, his swiftest route is along this river flowing eastwards towards Samarkand.' Babur traced the almost straight path with the tip of his gold-hilted dagger. 'But before he reaches Samarkand, he will need to rendezvous with his other troops before moving against us in force . . . This will be our moment to attack.'

His counsellors murmured agreement except for Baisanghar who was looking anxious.

'What is it, Baisanghar . . . ?'

'Shaibani Khan is not predictable. That is one of the few things we have learned about him – to our cost. I remember how his barbarians descended out of nowhere to kill your uncle and massacre our men . . .'

'That is why I am sending spies to Bokhara. I won't be lured out of Samarkand by tricks – as we ourselves tempted Shaibani Khan. But as soon as I've proof that he is moving against us, I'll lead our troops westward and surprise him. If he does advance along the river, I propose we lie in wait here.' Babur drove the tip of his dagger into the map at a place three days' ride from Samarkand where the river narrowed as it passed through low, stony hills.

• ◆ •

Ten days later Babur was riding at the head of his men towards the very place he had described at the council meeting. A week ago his scouts had confirmed that Shaibani Khan's men were indeed on the move, with great numbers of horsemen, heading for the river. Babur had ordered his armies out from Samarkand, leaving a garrison of just sufficient size to defend it if it came under surprise attack. He and his troops had kept themselves at a distance from the river while scouts had tracked the Uzbeks' progress towards and along it. That morning they had reported that the Uzbeks had already broken camp and, if they kept up their normal pace, they would reach the narrows about midday.

Babur had given his orders to Wazir Khan, Baisanghar and Ali Gosht, his master-of-horse. Babur and the advance guard, galloping fast in spearhead formation, would slam from the flank into the centre of the Uzbek line of march and punch through, slaughtering as many Uzbeks and causing as much chaos as possible, before regrouping and attacking again from the other side. As soon as they had seen him drive through the Uzbeks, his main forces should advance swiftly under the command of Wazir Khan to attack the front of the column while another detachment under Baisanghar swept round to encircle the Uzbek rear. Ali Gosht should hold the small remainder of the troops in reserve.

Now Babur saw before him the low ridge that overlooked the river. Soon his chestnut horse was at its top and with the men of his advance guard around him he looked down on a long, wide column of Uzbek riders, kicking up clouds of dust along the riverbank, seemingly oblivious to his presence. This was his moment. He ordered the charge down the gentle incline towards his enemy, about twelve hundred yards away. Almost as soon as he had kicked his horse forward he saw, for the first time, an Uzbek riding at a little distance from the main column, perhaps as a lookout. Simultaneously the man saw him and raised a trumpet, sounding a warning to the main body before himself galloping for its protection.

On hearing the trumpet, the Uzbek column slowed and the riders turned their horses to face the threat. Some had time to grab their bows and unleash a shower of hissing arrows, and several of Babur's advance guard crashed to the ground before they could reach the Uzbeks. The rest, led by Babur, hurtled onwards, hitting the enemy column at full gallop and slashing around them. The Uzbek lines seemed to buckle and waver and Babur thought victory was surely his.

But then they began to enfold Babur's men rather than to scatter before them. Babur saw his young standard bearer tumble from his horse in front of him, his head pulped by one blow from a metal-studded Uzbek flail. Pulling his horse's head hard round, Babur avoided the youth's body and succeeded in skewering his killer with his spear but then more Uzbeks were hacking at him. Discarding his spear, Babur fought back with Alamgir. The sheer weight and numbers of the Uzbek onslaught around him was forcing him away from his bodyguard and he realised he was all but surrounded. If he were not to die he had to break through. Extending Alamgir before him in his right hand and bending low to his horse's neck, he made for the only gap he could see in the Uzbeks around him.

Moments later, he was in open ground, gasping for breath. Blood was trickling into his right eye from a wound in his temple. An Uzbek warrior had nearly succeeded in driving a spear through his head. Only Babur's swift, sideways dodge had prevented it and even so the sharp point had caught him. Attempting to brush away the blood and with his vision blurred, he tried to make out which way to ride to get back to his main force.

After a minute or so his vision began clearing though blood was still oozing from his wound. Hastily Babur cut a strip of cloth from his horse's saddle blanket with his dagger and tied it round his head. Peering round, he realised that his initial attack had failed and that his terrified horse had carried him off at a tangent into a no man's land between the Uzbeks and his own remaining forces. He was in imminent danger again. Kicking his chestnut, he galloped quickly back towards his own lines, expecting at any moment to feel the bite of an arrow or a spear. It did not come.

There was no time to discuss fresh tactics with his commanders when Babur regained his lines near where Ali Gosht was sitting on his grey horse overlooking the action, holding his force in reserve as ordered. Even as he reined in his nearly spent mount, Babur heard a great roar and a clashing of swords on shields behind him. A few seconds more and the Uzbeks would be on them. 'I will take command here,' Babur yelled to Ali Gosht. 'Send riders along the lines to Wazir Khan and Baisanghar. They are to forget all previous orders. As soon as the Uzbeks are in range our archers are to fire. Then, at my command, our entire force will charge.'

Sword raised, Babur turned his sweat-streaked horse to face the Uzbeks, who had, in fact, slowed and were now advancing at a canter. In their centre, between two tall purple standards, he made out a rider who could only be Shaibani Khan. He was too far away for Babur to see his features but there was something in his arrogant bearing, his stillness, that drew the eye, just as it had when he had led the sortie out of Samarkand six months previously. As Babur watched, Shaibani Khan slowly raised his left hand as if in salutation and the war-cry of his warriors rose with it – a sound to chill the blood.

Babur's men yelled their own defiance, but they had barely filled their lungs when, with a wave of his sword, Shaibani Khan signalled the attack and the thunder of Uzbek hoofs drowned all other sounds as they accelerated into a gallop. Around him, Babur's men struggled to hold their horses in check with one hand while with the other they held up their shields against the volleys of arrows falling from the skies. Babur's archers were firing back and many of their missiles were finding their mark, but the dark, fast-approaching wave of Uzbeks did not falter even when riders slipped from the saddle to be crushed beneath the hoofs of those galloping behind.

The Uzbeks were close enough now. 'For Samarkand!' Babur yelled, and charged, followed by his men. Seconds later, the two lines crashed into each other. The shouts and screams of men and the whinnying of horses mingled with the clash of metal. It was hard – in fact, impossible in the press and confusion of battle – to tell what was happening, but it seemed to Babur as he cut and slashed that his men were gaining ground. Energy flowed through him as he lunged at a tall, mail-clad Uzbek who, instead of trying to fight him, backed his rearing horse away. The Uzbeks easily outnumbered his forces but all round, they seemed to be giving ground, wheeling off to left and right as Babur and his men pushed determinedly forward.

But he needed to see what was happening. Spurring his horse, Babur shot through a gap that had suddenly opened ahead of him. Yelling to those men who were still by his side to follow, he made for a low, scrub-covered hillock, which – so far as he could see – was unoccupied and would be a good vantage-point. There, he looked down on the battle. A pattern began to emerge from among the wheeling, fighting riders. Suddenly everything was obvious, and Babur swore in anguish. He knew what the Uzbeks were about. It was the ancient Mongol tactic of the *tulughma*. He had read of it but never witnessed it till now.

As they seemed to part before the onslaught of Babur's men, Shaibani Khan's troops were in fact forming into two units, one on the right, one on the left. In a moment they would sweep round to cut off Babur's right and left wings, leaving the centre of his lines isolated and unprotected. Uzbeks would then detach from the two units to encircle and smash the centre. Afterwards they would rejoin their comrades to share in the destruction of Babur's left and right wings. The men under Wazir Khan would be funnelled towards the river and trapped on its steep, sandy banks while Baisanghar's men would be completely surrounded unless they could break out quickly.

The harsh blasts of a horn from somewhere behind Babur rose above the sounds of battle. A formation of Uzbek warriors was galloping from behind a hill some quarter of a mile away where they must have been waiting, concealed. As they came nearer, their black hide shields with silver bosses told Babur who they were: Shaibani's crack troops, warriors of his own clan, blood of his blood. They were heading for Baisanghar's men, no doubt intending to block off their last chance of retreat.

Suddenly Babur realised that Baisanghar wouldn't be able to see them because of a fold in the land. But he himself was closer to Baisanghar than the riders. Swiftly he picked one of his men whose horse still looked fresh. 'Warn Baisanghar – tell him to get his men away and retreat towards Samarkand as best he can. Do you understand?' The youth galloped away down the hillock. Babur waited until it seemed certain his messenger would beat the swooping line of Uzbeks, then, yelling to the others to keep close, he charged towards the riverbank where Wazir Khan's men were fighting for their lives.

Circling round to where the lines of attacking Uzbeks looked thinnest, Babur managed to hack his way through, but of the twenty or so men who had ridden with him, only a dozen made it. The situation seemed hopeless. Wazir Khan's men were indeed being pushed right back to the river by Uzbeks, some continuously firing arrows from the saddle while others, wielding curved swords, plunged into the disorganised and heaving mass of men and horses struggling to stay upright as the sandy banks gave way under them. Babur couldn't pick out Wazir Khan.

Suddenly, Babur felt his horse shudder beneath him. With a scream of pain, the beautiful chestnut, hit almost simultaneously in its neck and throat by two arrows and already twitching in its death throes as scarlet blood pumped from a severed artery, went crashing to the ground. Babur jumped clear, only just avoiding being pinned to the earth by the thrashing animal. As he scrambled unsteadily to his feet, he still had his sword, Alamgir, in his hand but had lost his dagger and shield. Disoriented and dodging flailing hoofs and slashing blades, he looked around for another horse.

'Majesty.' It was Baburi, his face blood encrusted, eyes desperate. Leaning forward in the saddle, he pulled Babur up behind him on his grey horse.

'To the river!' Babur shouted. Their only hope was to get away with as many men as possible and leave the fight for another day. Waving his sword above his head, he looked round for his other commanders, yelling to them to get their men over the river. He still couldn't see Wazir Khan.

The river was in full spate with the meltwater from the mountain snows. It was freezing as they plunged in and the currents were strong. Baburi's horse struggled beneath their double weight as it tried to swim. It would never make it with two of them. Thrusting Alamgir into its scabbard, Babur slid off, avoiding Baburi's attempt to keep him aboard. But as he struck out for the opposite bank, no more than twenty yards away, the powerful current grabbed him and carried him downstream.

'Majesty . . .' Babur recognised Wazir Khan's voice, but with cold water flowing about his ears and threatening to suck him under, he was in no position to look round. Then he felt something thin and hard knock against him in the water. Instinctively he grabbed it. It felt like the shaft of a spear. As the current whirled him against an outcrop of sharp rocks on the far side of the river, he jammed the end of the shaft into a narrow crevice. It bowed but held. Kicking hard against the current, Babur hauled himself along it to reach the rocks and with scratched and bloodied hands heaved himself, gasping, out of the water.

Arrows were falling all around him. Across the river, Uzbek archers lined the banks, jeering at their retreating opponents, some even finding time between shots to gesture obscenely. As he dodged behind a rock for cover, Babur saw Wazir Khan. He was still in the water. His black horse had been hit in the flanks and rump by several arrows and its eyes were rolling in terror and pain. Wazir Khan was urging it on but was still only halfway across. Had he tossed Babur the spear that had saved him? Forgetting his own danger, Babur rose from behind his rock and yelled Wazir Khan's name. The old soldier looked up.

Then Babur saw an archer on the far bank take deliberate aim and draw back his bow-string. The black-feathered arrow swooped through the air like a hawk on its prey. For some reason, Wazir Khan turned and, as he did so, the arrow embedded itself in his exposed throat with such force that the tip came through the back of his neck. Slowly, he slid sideways from his horse into the roaring, swift-flowing waters. Babur's desperate, despairing shouts pursued him as the blood-flecked river bore his body away.

Babur felt as dazed as he had on the day when he had seen his father fall from the walls of Akhsi. He sank to the ground and closed his eyes.

'Majesty, we must get away . . .' It was Baburi's voice. When Babur didn't respond, Baburi shook him, then yanked him roughly to his feet. 'Come on . . . don't be an idiot . . .'

'Wazir Khan . . . I must send a search-party downstream . . . He may be washed up alive.'

'He is dead . . . Let the dead care for themselves. You can't do anything for him except save yourself . . . That's what he would have wanted. You know that . . . Come on . . .'

'The granaries are almost empty, Majesty.' Babur's vizier, Kasim, meticulous as ever, was consulting the red leatherbound book in which, since the siege had begun, he had recorded the state of Samarkand's provisions.

'How many days' supplies are left?'

'Five days' worth. A week at most.'

There was no point cutting the ration again. Even now it was only three cups of grain for soldiers, two for male civilians and one for each woman and child. The people were already devouring anything they could find, from crows they shot with catapults to the carcasses of asses and dogs that had died of hunger or been killed for their meat. In the royal stables, all pack animals had long since been slaughtered for meat for the garrison. His men were already feeding their precious riding mounts on leaves from the trees and sawdust soaked in water, and their condition was growing daily more wretched. Soon they would have to start killing them. Once the horses were gone, they would not even be able to send out raiding parties to run the Uzbek blockade around the city walls and forage for provisions.

Every day for the past three months Babur had wondered whether Shaibani Khan would attack. But why should he? He must know it was only a matter of time before Babur would be forced to surrender. And he seemed to take a perverse pleasure in the city's suffering, feasting his men before the walls and burning food pillaged from the surrounding villages before the besiegeds' eyes as if to say, 'I have so much I can waste it — you, however, have nothing.'

Worse, three weeks ago he had captured six deserters from Babur's forces who had slipped over the city walls and had ordered them to be boiled alive in oil in great copper cauldrons set up in full view of the city walls. At least their shrieks had put paid to any further desertions.

Babur dismissed Kasim, descended to the courtyard and called for a horse and escort. The loss of Wazir Khan still hurt – he missed him not only as a loyal friend but as a wise counsellor, especially in these bleak times. But Baburi, as usual these days, was among those riding with him, his high cheekbones even more pronounced through hunger. He was a good gauge of what was going on and prepared to speak frankly.

How different Samarkand seemed compared with those days of celebration when Babur, hung with emeralds, had sat on the dais beneath silken awnings, to be hailed in the Registan Square. Even Samarkand's fabulously tiled and sparkling buildings seemed diminished.

The thoroughfare Babur was riding along was deep with stinking refuse that no one had the energy to move unless to sift through it in the hope of finding something to eat. Baburi had reported that some desperate citizens were even sieving dung, searching for seeds to cook. Others were boiling any leaves or grasses they could find. Wherever he looked, Babur saw pinched faces and dull, sunken eyes. Where once people had cheered him, now they turned away.

'Baburi, what's in their minds?'

'Little but how to appease their hunger, but those few times they do think of anything else, it is to fear what Shaibani Khan will do if he takes the city which they think is near. The Uzbeks killed and raped and destroyed last time when they had no cause. This time Shaibani Khan will recall how the citizens welcomed you, how they fell on his men, and he will want revenge.'

'I'm going to Timur's tomb . . .' Babur announced suddenly. Baburi looked surprised but said nothing.

Riding into the courtyard before the entrance gate to the tomb, Babur jumped down from his horse and gestured to Baburi to accompany him. Waving aside the tomb attendants, he led the way swiftly across the inner courtyard and down to the crypt where Timur lay.

211

Babur pressed his hands to the cold stone. 'This is where Timur lies. When I first came to this place I promised that I would be worthy of him. The moment has come for me to fulfil that pledge. I'm going to lead out my men in one last stand before the city walls. Future generations will not be able to say that I yielded Timur's city to a barbarian without a fight . . .'

'It will be a better death than waiting till we are so weak we can no longer grip a sword . . .'

Babur nodded and, as he had once before, lowered his head to kiss the cold coffin.

But as they rode back towards the Kok Saray, Babur sensed a change. There seemed to be more people on the streets and they were talking animatedly, as if they had news to discuss. Many were heading in the same direction as himself, surging about him. Soon his guards had to form a barrier around him and push the people back with the shafts of their spears to let him through.

One of his soldiers came galloping towards him at full tilt. 'Majesty,' he shouted, as soon as he was in earshot, 'a messenger has come from Shaibani Khan.'

Ten minutes later Babur was back in the Kok Saray, hurrying into his audience chamber where his counsellors were waiting.

The Uzbek ambassador was a tall, stout man in a black turban and a dark purple tunic. A battleaxe was slung across his back, a scimitar hung at his side and a silver-hilted dagger was tucked into his orange sash. He touched his hand to his breast as Babur entered.

'What is your message?'

'My lord offers you a solution to your predicament.'

'And what is it?'

'He is prepared to forgive your theft of the city. If you will restore his rightful property to him, you, your family and your troops may leave. He offers you safe passage back to Ferghana or, if you prefer, to the west or south. He gives you his word on the Holy Book that he will not attack you.'

'And what of the city and its people? Will he make more drums from human skin, as he did with my cousin, Prince Mahmud?'

'My lord says that the citizens must pay for their insult to him – but in taxes not in blood. Again, he gives you his word on the Holy Book.'

'Are there any conditions?'

'None, except that you leave Samarkand before the next new moon, two weeks from now.' The ambassador folded his hands on his ample stomach.

'Tell Shaibani Khan I will consider his offer and send my reply before noon tomorrow.'

'And in the meantime I have brought you a present from my lord.' The ambassador snapped his fingers and one of his attendants, who had been standing discreetly to one side, approached with a large basket. Removing the conical lid, he tipped the contents on to the rugs beneath the dais – melons from the orchards outside Samarkand, honey-ripe and golden, their mouth-watering fragrance filling the chamber. 'I have brought two mule loads. They are waiting by the Turquoise Gate. My lord hopes you will find the fruit most delicious.'

'You may tell your master we have no need of such things. The gardens inside Samarkand's walls drip with ripe fruit. We will feed these to our mules . . .' Babur rose, and as he swept past the ambassador made sure he kicked one of the melons aside. It rolled across the chamber and hit a stone door frame, so that its golden pulp oozed out.

• ◆ •

'Can we trust him?' Babur's eyes searched the faces of his counsellors as, that night, they convened in the candle-lit audience chamber. He had needed time to think on his own before summoning them.

'He's a barbarian and the enemy of our blood, but he has given his word,' said Baisanghar.

'The word of a cattle thief . . .' Babur replied grimly.

'But he'll lose face if he goes back on a promise so publicly given on the Holy Book.'

'But why has he made this offer? He vastly outnumbers us and knows the city is starving. Why not wait? Shaibani Khan doesn't lack patience.'

'I think I may know the answer, Majesty.' Baburi stepped forward from where he had been standing, on guard, to one side of Babur's dais.

'Speak.' Babur gestured to him to join the circle of men seated around him, ignoring the surprise of some that their king had invited a common soldier into their midst.

'There are rumours in the bazaars – from those who spoke to the ambassador's attendants today – that Shaibani Khan faces a challenge from within the Uzbek clans. They say that a nephew, far away on the steppes, is raising an army against him. Shaibani Khan wants to ride north and smash the rebellion before it grows. If he doesn't go soon, the weather will be his enemy and he will have to leave it unchecked until next spring . . .'

If that was true, Babur thought, Shaibani Khan had no time to waste on sieges. He would want to reoccupy the city, garrison it and be on his way. It probably also meant he would keep his word not to attack them. He would not want to expend men and resources – or risk stirring up the other Timurid chieftains and rulers of the region – by harassing Babur's retreating forces.

'I have decided.' Babur stood up. 'I will accept the Uzbek terms – provided that our men are allowed to depart fully armed.' Then he added, with as much certainty as he could muster, 'The people will be saved and, *inshallah* – God willing – we shall return.'

Next morning, Babur watched from the walls of the Kok Saray as Kasim, his ambassador, accompanied by two soldiers carrying the green standards of Samarkand, rode slowly through the Turquoise Gate towards Shaibani Khan's camp.

Despite his fine words to his people, this was surrender – something he'd never done before, never believed he would do. The knowledge sickened him. Yet he had known from the beginning of the campaign that the odds were stacked against him. In the end he had had no real choice other than to agree to Shaibani Khan's terms. It had clearly been the right thing to do for the sake of the citizens of Samarkand but the thought of retreat – of ceding the city to a hated foe – left a bitter taste in his mouth, like almonds left too long on the tree. Even so, this way he, too, would be free and have the opportunity to re-build his fortunes and those of his family, provided he retained his self-belief and determination which he knew he would. He was still a young man and had not been born or brought up to fail but to achieve great things. He would fulfil his destiny.

. ◆ .

Babur mounted his horse and, without a backward glance at the tall Kok Saray, rode out. His bodyguard, Baburi among them, was behind him and at the back, well protected by cavalrymen and screened by leather curtains, his mother, sister and grandmother were with their attendants in a bullock cart.

His wife and her women were in another cart, escorted by the Mangligh crossbowmen who would now return to Zaamin. Ayisha had asked Babur whether she might go with them to visit her father and he had agreed. As far as he was concerned, it was the only bright spot in one of the darkest moments of his life.

The rest of Babur's forces were already riding northwards through the city towards the Shaykhzada Gate through which, Shaibani Khan had decreed, Babur must make his exit. In just a few hours' time, Shaibani Khan himself, flanked by his dark-robed Uzbek warriors, would ride in through the glorious Turquoise Gate.

The city was sullen and still. The windows and doors of the houses were mostly shuttered and barred as Babur and his party passed by, though occasionally a citizen would stick out his head and spit audibly. Babur didn't blame them. He would have liked to declare that he would be back, that this was just a temporary setback in what would be a golden future for Samarkand under a Timurid ruler, not a vile Uzbek, but why should they believe him? However straight his back as he rode, however stern his countenance, their eyes could not penetrate his body and see the steely determination in his heart to succeed.

It was midday and the sun was beating down. They would not ride far today, Babur thought. They would circle to the east and make camp on the far side of Qolba Hill. At least from there he would not have to gaze on Samarkand. Tomorrow he and his counsellors would consider where best to go. Esan Dawlat was urging him to seek out her people far to the east beyond Ferghana. Perhaps she was right, though Babur's instincts were to retreat to the mountains to some quiet hideaway not so far away and bide his time . . .

Ahead, he could see the high curved arch of the Shaykhzada Gate. As he approached, Baisanghar rode towards him. He looked gaunt and drawn. Of course, this was his city – he had been born here: surrendering it to the Uzbeks must hurt him deeply. His sense of loss would be no less than Babur's.

'The men are drawn up in the meadows beyond the gate, Majesty, but there is more. Shaibani Khan's ambassador requests a further audience of you.'

'Very well. Bring him before me once I have rejoined my men.'

Babur's forces – no more than two thousand now – were a wretched, ragged bunch compared to the army with which he had taken Samarkand. Death, wounds, desertions, starvation

216

and the disease it had brought in its wake, had taken their toll. And there were no bright pennants in yellow or green proclaiming them warriors of Ferghana or Samarkand. They were neither any more.

The men were silent as Babur rode towards them. How many, now that they were clear of the city, would slip back to their tribal lands or go in search of other rulers able to reward them better?

He watched as the stout Uzbek ambassador approached on horseback over the parched ground. What did he want? To gloat on behalf of his master?

'Well?'

'To mark the new understanding between you and my lord, he has come to a joyous decision. He will take Her Royal Highness, your sister, as a wife.'

'What?' Babur's hand reached instinctively for his sword. For a second he thought of the ambassador's head bouncing away, spurting blood as the melon he had kicked had leaked its juice.

'I said that my lord, Shaibani Khan, has decided to marry your sister, Khanzada . . . He will take her now . . .'

'Majesty . . .' Babur heard Baisanghar call in alarm.

Babur looked up to see lines of dark-clad Uzbek riders, bows at the ready, come sweeping round from the direction of the Iron Gate. In a moment, Babur and his men were surrounded on three sides. On the fourth they were hemmed in by the stout city walls. An ambush . . .

'So, this is how Shaibani Khan keeps his word . . .' Babur sprang from his horse, pulled the ambassador from his and had his dagger to the man's throat. The Uzbek was strong and tried to pull away but Babur allowed his blade to pierce the man's skin. As a bead of dark red blood welled up, the man ceased his struggling.

'My lord has not broken his word,' the ambassador gasped. 'He promised you safe passage and you will have it. All he seeks is a wife.'

217

'I'll see my sister dead before I give her into the hands of savages,' Babur yelled, and released the man, who tumbled to the ground.

'It will not only be your sister who dies.' The ambassador held the end of his turban to his neck to staunch the wound. 'If you reject my lord's offer he will take it as an insult and you will all die – you, your family and your pitiful army. And he will destroy the city and rebuild it over the citizens' bleached bones. It is your choice . . .'

Babur looked at the Uzbek arrows trained on him and his men. He also looked at the pale faces of Baisanghar and Baburi who, the moment Babur had attacked the ambassador, had rushed forward, swords drawn. The anger and powerlessness he felt were written on their faces. Again, he had no choice. It would have been one thing to lead out his men in one last glorious sally, quite another to submit them to pointless butchery, like animals in the hunt when beaters drive them into a circle to be shot down at will.

Scanning the Uzbek lines, Babur looked for the commanding figure of Shaibani Khan, wild thoughts of offering him single combat running through his mind. But, of course, the Uzbek leader was not there: he would be preparing to ride back into Samarkand. A meeting with a throneless king would be beneath him.

Babur walked towards the bullock cart, two hundred yards away, where his unsuspecting sister was sitting with their mother and grandmother. He hesitated, then pulled back the leather curtains that concealed them. They looked up at him with alarm. Then, as they heard what he had to say, they cried out in disbelief. Tears welling in his eyes, he turned away, but Khanzada's pleas not to abandon her to the desires of a wild Uzbek and the cries of Kutlugh Nigar to spare her daughter followed him. 'I will come for you, Khanzada. I promise you . . . I will come . . .' Babur shouted.

But Khanzada was past hearing.

Chapter 12

The Old Lady with
the Golden Elephant

On a February evening Babur gave the logs burning in the large, open fireplace a poke with a stick to coax more warmth from them. Although his face and the front of his body were warm from the direct heat, his back felt chill, despite his thick brown wool cloak, as cold winds billowed the hangings from the small, unglazed but roughly shuttered windows of the mud-brick house. At least these draughts would carry some of the woodsmoke out through the chimney. It was so thick and acrid that Babur's eyes stung and watered.

He reflected that these were by no means the only tears he had shed since the late autumn day when, with the snows whirling round them, his party of at most two hundred had breasted the broad pass and descended to the small settlement of Sayram. In truth, it was little more than a walled village of shepherds with two or three inns to house occasional travellers. But it had two attractions for Babur. Its muscular headman, Hussain Mazid, was a cousin of Ali Mazid Beg, murdered by Mahmud at Samarkand, and utterly loyal to

Babur. The other advantage was the settlement's remoteness. Though it lay on a minor trade route from Kashgar, it was as many miles distant from the forces of Shaibani Khan as it was from the outposts of Ferghana.

Babur knew he had been right not to accept Jahangir's offer of sanctuary made in the aftermath of his expulsion from Samarkand. In the first place he had doubted its sincerity and in the second he had not wished to put himself in the power of his half-brother and his puppet-master, Tambal. Neither did he wish to play the poor relation, accepted on sufferance as he had once tolerated Jahangir and his scheming mother, Roxanna.

Babur's refusal had meant that he couldn't entrust his womenfolk to Jahangir either. Without his own presence, they would once more have been little better than hostages. In any case, both Kutlugh Nigar and Esan Dawlat had refused outright even to contemplate such a prospect. They had preferred to share the danger and deprivation of his wanderings.

At least now they had a roof over their heads and privacy in the small room they shared in this draughty building. But Babur wept to see them take turns to use the only fine-toothed ivory comb they had left to remove the white eggs of lice from their unfurled long hair. Neither had uttered a complaint about that or the bedbugs, which, breeding deep in crevasses in the wall, infested bed linen and garments whatever precautions were taken. Nor had they complained about the cold or the limited food – gristly horsemeat and turnips served daily from a large fat-encrusted cauldron in the kitchen. Esan Dawlat had compared it to the food of her revered ancestor, Genghis Khan.

In his despair, Babur had expected his mother and grandmother to blame him for surrendering Khanzada to Shaibani Khan but, as usual, Esan Dawlat had surprised him. Late one morning she had found him still in his sleeping

220

quarters, silently sobbing, curled into a foetus position with his head turned to the mud wall. 'What is it, Babur, that makes you so forget your position and your manhood?' she had asked. When he had not replied, she had asked again, more gently, 'Come now, what is it?'

He had uncoiled himself and faced her, eyes red rimmed with tears. 'Don't you know? Can't you guess? I'm despondent that I've lost Samarkand once more but, above all, I feel such terrible, terrible guilt about meekly yielding Khanzada to Shaibani Khan. I feel dishonour that I failed in my duty as the head of our family, and as a man, to protect my only sister, whom I love so much. I feel a desperate impotence that I'm in such a diminished position that I can still do nothing to recover her.'

Esan Dawlat had taken his large hand in her small ones. Then she had reminded him of the fate of Genghis Khan's first wife. 'Long before he became the Great Oceanic Ruler, he married a young Qongarit woman, a sturdy beauty named Borte, and, with the support of her clan, attempted to increase his power through a conflict with a neighbouring clan, the Markit. However, he was inexperienced and the Markit were cunning. In a surprise raid on his camp, the Markit carried off Borte and killed or scattered most of Genghis's followers. He fled alone into the Kentei mountains where the Markit were unable to find him, so well did the mountains protect him. For the rest of his life, Genghis Khan prayed every day to the deity of the mountain, and every day offered him a sacrifice.

'Only a year later, with the help of forces recruited by the Qongarit, he defeated the Markit and recovered Borte. When, several months afterwards, she gave birth to her first child, Jorchi, no one dared question his paternity. He grew up to become one of Genghis Khan's greatest generals.

'Both you and Khanzada have Genghis Khan and Borte's blood in your veins. You have the courage never to despair

221

but to confront harsh fate and come through to eventual victory.' Esan Dawlat had gripped his hand firmly. 'Strengthen your will, difficult as it may be. Steel yourself to look only forward, not back.'

Even now, despite his grandmother's words, the thought of Shaibani Khan's rough hands on his sister's soft flesh exploring the most intimate parts of her body came into his mind, provoking nausea and revulsion. Clenching his fists, he summoned all his mental strength to push the images away. Then he prayed that his sister would retain the will to live – as Borte had done – and submit to Shaibani Khan. Her resistance could only lead to her death. He would fight for both of them to crush Shaibani Khan and rescue her and the family honour.

Although it was approaching midnight and all in the hall around him were asleep, as the occasional stertorous snore testified, Babur was too disturbed by his recollections, too full of powerless, restless anger at what had happened and, above all, too worried about what lay ahead for himself and his family to attempt to sleep. Instead, blood pumping furiously but futilely, he pulled his cloak about him and stepped over the recumbent bodies of some of his retainers into the cold of the night to compose his thoughts, cool his mind and slow his pulse.

Outside, the sky was a mass of stars and the snow that had fallen earlier had frozen into grains of ice, which the biting wind was blowing in flurries across the compound. Babur made his way to the mud walls surrounding the village. He climbed up the rough steps on to them and looked out over the shadowy white landscape. Above the pass, the mountain peaks glistened silver as the moonlight struck them. The pure beauty of the scene took his breath away.

Suddenly, from the direction of the animal pens, he heard an isolated cry, then another shout followed by uproar. A minute or so later a dark animal shape shot across the snow directly below him and off across the frozen ground out into the darkness. As it went, pursued by unavailing arrows fired by the men who had been guarding the animal pens and had come running after it, Babur saw that it was a long, lean grey wolf, with something in its mouth – probably a chicken.

'Did you get him . . .' Babur called to one of the guards as he ran close by beneath the walls.

'No, Majesty. That is a cunning wolf that has been harassing our animals for the last few nights. At first he found a way into the horses' enclosure and tried to attack one of last year's foals. It had been sick and we were nursing it. The horses beat him off with their hoofs. Last evening, he got into the sheep pen and by the time we drove him off he had bitten one of the smaller ewes so badly we had to kill it – in fact, Majesty, it was in your stew this evening as a change from the horsemeat. But tonight the wolf got into one of the hen houses and took one before the cackling of the rest disturbed us. He's been rewarded for his persistence.'

Babur peered out into the dark again, towards where the victorious wolf had vanished. Perhaps it had a message for him. Face reality, persist as Genghis Khan – and Timur – had done. Try a different approach to your goal. Never give up until you have your reward. The wolf had been rebuffed in his attempts on both the sheep and horse folds but had succeeded in his attack on the hens. Perhaps he himself should concentrate less on Samarkand and Ferghana for a while and consider whether there were other places where he might establish himself as a ruler before expanding his empire. His hero Timur after all had rampaged from China to India and Turkey.

As Babur descended from the walls and retraced his steps to the house, he passed the low, single-storey hut where the women servants lived. For the first time in a long while, he found himself repeating out loud his father's mantra: 'Timur's blood is my blood.' For what remained of the night he, for once, slept deeply and well.

• ◆ •

'The grey is faster than the roan . . . anyone can see that.'

'You're wrong, Baburi. When the snows melt and we can ride again I'll prove it to you.' Babur held his hands to the fire.

Hearing the door open and feeling a chill blast of air, Babur looked round to see Hussain Mazid approaching, his height and bulk almost comically accentuated by the small hunched form of an old woman, wrapped in a dark green quilted jacket, by his side. Despite her apparent age and fragility, she was keeping up pretty well with Hussain Mazid with the aid of a stick.

The ill-assorted couple stopped before Babur and made the customary salutations.

'This is Rehana, Majesty,' Hussain Mazid explained, seeing Babur's surprise. 'She was my wet-nurse when I was young and she still serves the family. This morning she came to me early. She said that, woken by the disturbance following the wolf's raid on the animal pens last night, she heard you talking to yourself about Timur as you passed the kitchen of the women servants' quarters where she was boiling some tea. She reminded me – as I well knew from her tales in my childhood – that her grandfather had ridden with Timur in his raid on Delhi and had often spoken to her of it. She asked whether you too might wish to hear his stories. I told her you wouldn't want to be bothered with an old soldier's tales second-hand from an old woman. But she insisted, so I have brought her to you.'

At this, Rehana looked up at Babur and he was touched by the pride in her eyes.

'I would be glad to hear of my ancestor's deeds. Make

Rehana comfortable by the fire and have one of the servants bring us tea.'

Slowly Rehana eased her old bones on to a stool.

'Do begin.'

Rehana seemed suddenly shy, as if uncertain where to start now that her request to speak of a revered relation in such exalted company had been granted. She stammered, then fell silent.

'What was your grandfather's name?' Babur prompted her gently.

'Tariq.'

'What was his position in Timur's army?'

'He was a horse archer – one of the best.'

'And where did he first see Timur?'

'In Samarkand in the summer of 1398, just as the preparations for his attack on Hindustan – Northern India – were getting under way. His father – a veteran of one of Timur's previous campaigns – had brought him to join up, and he was among the recruits Timur reviewed in the Garden of Heart's Delight just beyond the walls of Samarkand.'

'What did he remember of how Timur looked then?'

'He was nearly sixty – only twenty years younger than I am now,' said Rehana, with the pride that old people have in reaching a good age. She paused as if expecting congratulation.

Babur did not disappoint her. 'I would never have thought you had seen so many seasons.'

She smiled. 'But my grandfather said Timur was tall and still unbowed, with thick white hair. His brow was broad, his voice deep and his shoulders wide. When he walked he had a pronounced limp from a serious injury to his right leg when, as a youth, he had been thrown from his horse. It had left that leg much shorter than the other . . .' Rehana was in full stride now, timidity gone, rocking a little as she spoke. Babur guessed she had told this tale many times before in her long life.

'Mounting his gilded throne, Timur addressed his men. "We prepare to go across the Hindu Kush, down through the passes, across the Indus to Hindustan's rich capital of Delhi. Not even Alexander reached that city. Or Genghis Khan who only got as far as the Indus. The prize is great. Hindustan is full of riches – gold, emeralds and rubies. It has the only mine in the known world for the bright diamond. But its inhabitants do not deserve such jewels. Although some of the rulers follow our God, most of the people are cowardly infidels, worshipping idols of distorted half-human, half-animal deities. God will take any who die fighting them straight to Paradise. He will grant us great victories over them and their rulers who weakly tolerate unbelief among their subjects. We will take immense booty."

'Soon afterwards the army departed. A thick pall of dust hung over the parched grasslands outside Samarkand as ninety thousand men – mostly on horseback – manoeuvred into formation and moved off. Within three days they had passed Shakhrish, the Green City, Timur's birthplace, and descended the strongly garrisoned defile known as the Iron Gates out on to the scrubby red desert plain, the Kizl Kum.

'On and on they marched, across the Oxus, past Balkh and Andarab, all the time still within the boundaries of Timur's empire. And then Timur took an advance party of thirty thousand – my grandfather among them – up through the Khawak Pass on to the roof of the world and into the Hindu Kush. There, they encountered early winter and conditions unknown to plainsmen. Their horses slipped on the ice. Some fell with their riders to their death. Others broke legs and were fit only for the cooking pot.

'Timur ordered the men to rest by day and travel by night when the ice was frozen solid and less slippery than during daytime when it had a coating of meltwater. Soon they reached an escarpment that was impossible to descend without ropes.

Now – my grandfather told me – Timur had to be lowered on a litter by his men a hundred feet down a rocky cliff since he could not make the climb down himself. The cold had reopened the old scar on his right leg and he dared not trust the limb with his full weight. And all the time they were fighting off ambushes by the local tribe, the infidel Kafirs. The snow was often stained bright red with blood . . .

'But after many struggles they reached Kabul. My grandfather told me it was a fine city, overlooked by a hilltop fort, and at a point where great trade routes meet. Smaller and less grand than Samarkand, of course, but very splendid nonetheless.'

'Indeed, I believe it still is,' Babur murmured to Baburi. 'One of my father's cousins rules it.'

'You have relatives on every throne, just as I have friends behind every market stall in Samarkand . . .'

'Ignore us, Rehana, and continue.'

'By September, Timur had crossed the Indus using a bridge made of boats lashed together and was just five hundred miles from Delhi. Everywhere his troops took prisoners, destined for the slave markets of Samarkand on their return but for the present forced to serve them as they marched. My grandfather had five. His particular favourite was a small, dark-eyed orphan called Ravi.

'In December, Timur's advance patrols sighted the great domes and minarets within Delhi's walls. But the Sultan of Delhi had a strong army, including a hundred and fifty of his most feared weapon – the armoured elephants with their shining coats of overlapping steel plates and curved scimitars attached to their long ivory tusks.

'Timur wanted to avoid a costly and uncertain assault on the walls and provoked the sultan's cavalry to make a sally against him. But before long the sultan's troops, amid heavy fighting, retreated back into the city through the same gate out of which they had charged.'

Rehana paused. 'Here I come to a melancholy part of the story. The prisoners had let out a huge cheer of support for the sultan's men, hoping to be freed if the sultan were victorious. Timur had heard this and feared that their ardour might lead them – they numbered nearly a hundred thousand – to rebel when the next battle took place.

'Determined and unsentimental, he ordered that all the prisoners should be killed. What is more, each man should execute his own captives.

'Men wept as they killed in cold blood. Even women prisoners who had become loving concubines were slain, and some say Timur made the women of his harem kill captives who had served them. My grandfather killed his adult prisoners but could not kill Ravi. He ordered him to run and hide among some dunes. However, when he returned later, he found Ravi's body half concealed by a scrubby bush under which he must have been trying to hide, his head cleft almost in two. I always remember my grandfather saying that it looked like a ripe melon cut in half on a market stall in Samarkand and that the carnage all around looked and smelled as if he were among the butchers' stalls there.

'Timur hoped that the killings would provoke the Sultan of Delhi into another attack and he prepared for battle. To guard against the much-feared elephants, he ordered his soldiers – whether cavalry or infantry, officers or men – in front of their lines to dig deep trenches and pile the earth they dug out into ramparts. Next, he had the blacksmiths stoke their fires to their whitest heat and beat out three-pronged, sharp-tipped iron stakes to strew where the elephants were most likely to charge. He had buffaloes roped together by the head and feet with leather strips, then tied up behind the stakes and in front of the trenches. He ordered camels to be loaded with wood and dried grass, lashed together and held in reserve. Finally, he told the archers to fire only at the elephants' drivers who sat exposed on the beasts' necks just behind their ears. With them dead, the elephants would run out of control.

'In the middle of December – I remember my grandfather said the skies were grey and the weather cool – the sultan's men indeed sallied out once more, just as Timur had hoped, the great brass kettle-drums on the beasts' backs sounding and the very ground seeming to shake under their huge feet.

'But then my grandfather saw the wisdom of Timur's plan. The elephants never reached their lines. Stumbling on the pointed iron tripods, they came almost to a halt among the bullocks. Then Timur unleashed his masterstroke. He set fire to the wood and dry grass on the camels' backs, then drove them towards the elephants. The great beasts panicked and fled, throwing the soldiers from their backs as they did so and trampling others in their fear, crushing their heads beneath their feet. Victory was Timur's. Delhi was his.

'Although Timur's official command was that no man should enter Delhi without permission, it was one of the few of his orders not strictly enforced. Our soldiers were everywhere, looking for booty – for women too, I dare say. My grandfather was among them, drinking spirits from a tavern abandoned by its owner, when rumours spread of a rising by the local inhabitants who had already killed several of our men . . .

'Half drunk, the soldiers rushed out into the streets. In their dizzy heads they saw enemies everywhere and killed anyone who crossed their path. Soon they were setting fire to shops and houses just to see the flames rip through them.

'As the drink drained from my grandfather, he grew ashamed and entered a tall, narrow house. Here he found a small boy, about the age of Ravi, hiding in a marble bath. The reminder of Ravi and his cleft head sobered him further. He gestured to the boy to conceal himself instead in a large chest in the corner of the room and told him not to come out until it was safe.'

Rehana fumbled in the inside pocket of her quilted coat and drew out a small object wrapped in a fragment of gold-embroidered purple silk. As she removed the cloth, Babur saw a very small golden elephant with rubies for eyes. She held it out to him. 'The boy gave him this and my grandfather passed it to me as he had no other surviving grandchildren – the others had died from the smallpox that broke out just after my birth.

'Before he left, my grandfather wrote a notice in our language of Turki to say that the house had been searched and contained nothing of value. Knowing he was one of the few of our soldiers who could read, he also drew a picture showing a man barred from entry. He pinned both to the door.

'After two days Timur stopped the massacres and burnings. My grandfather's note and drawing must have been good because when he returned that way he found the house intact and the boy sitting on the front step . . .

'My grandfather – like all the other soldiers – acquired much treasure.' Rehana's eyes closed in near ecstasy. 'In the sultan's palace they found subterranean vaults filled with gems – smooth, lustrous pearls, scarlet rubies, sapphires blue as the sky, glittering diamonds from the mines in the south – and piles of silver and gold coins, all exactly as Timur had promised. My grandfather was given his share. In addition, he took ornate armour and two white parrots he found in a cage in a deserted house.

'Suddenly, after just three weeks in Delhi, Timur gave the order to leave. Slowly his armies made their way back north and east, sometimes travelling only four miles a day, so burdened were they with their riches. Long before they reached Samarkand, my grandfather had gambled away his booty, except this golden elephant and the white parrots.

'But his eyes always lit up when he spoke of Hindustan – India. His tales were seldom of battles and even less of his own doings. Much more often he spoke of the well-watered green fields where many fat cattle and sheep grazed, of beautiful sandstone and marble buildings and of Hindustan's great wealth in gems. Above all, he said that the wonders of that land were beyond description. They must be seen to be believed . . .'

Rehana had finished, and a smile illuminated her lined face.

'You have brought one of Timur's greatest triumphs to life for me.' Babur had been transported by the pictures she had painted. 'What you have told us of Timur's methods and of Hindustan is so remarkable that I will ask one of the scribes to write it down, not only so that others can be reminded of his great deeds but so that I can consult it again. Thank you.'

Rehana rose and, with the aid of her stick, made her way out of the room. To Babur it seemed that her step was a little lighter.

'Majesty.' Hussain Mazid had spoken. 'Why didn't Timur absorb Hindustan into his empire?'

'I don't know. My father was fond of quoting some lines of a poem about Timur's raid. I can't remember the words precisely but it was something like "Nothing stirred, not even a bird, within Delhi for two months after its sack", and that Timur's route through Hindustan was "lined with a multitude of corpses which infected the air". Poets exaggerate but perhaps even Timur felt it would be too difficult to rule a place where he had wrought so much destruction . . . Perhaps he was also conscious that he was growing old and still had much to do – more conquests to make, more booty to win. After all, he stayed in Samarkand only four months after his return from Delhi, then moved west to the shores of the Mediterranean Sea to capture Aleppo and Damascus and – at the battle of Ankara – to take prisoner the great emperor of the Ottoman Turks, Bayazid the Thunderbolt. He imprisoned him in a cage that accompanied the court on its travels. They say he cried like a baby behind his bars . . . And of course, Timur died on the road to China . . . Hindustan was just one of his campaigns . . .'

'Rehana is certainly right about Hindustan's fine jewels. Sometimes traders used to bring them to Samarkand to sell and they were of great lustre,' said Baburi. 'I often wondered what it would be like to see that country.'

'Perhaps you will,' Babur said thoughtfully. 'Last night on the battlements I pondered whether I should consider beginning my empire somewhere other than in Samarkand. Rehana bringing me her ancestor's story of Timur's conquest of Hindustan seems almost like an omen.'

• ◆ •

'Come on,' Babur yelled. The barely thawed ground beneath his naked soles was stony and the hill was steep but he drove his aching body on. Baburi was quick – Babur could hear his steady panting just a couple of yards behind – but he was quicker and the knowledge pleased him . . . With the coming of spring, the desire for action stirred within him once more, and with it the determination to be ready, to harden his body for the challenges ahead. Every day for the past two weeks he had gone running through these remote hills and valleys and dived naked into the chill rivers with only Baburi for company. There was little danger of meeting anything more hostile than a herd of mangy goats.

In his mind he felt more than prepared. His struggle with Shaibani Khan was not over – and never could be until he had fulfilled his promise to Khanzada to rescue her. After that, who knew? Samarkand held a special place in his heart but he was unable to get out of his thoughts the rich and exotic world beyond the jagged, snowy summits of the Hindu Kush. If Timur had gone there, why shouldn't he?

Chapter 13

On the Run

A fter a day's hunting Babur was riding slowly back towards Sayram. Around him in the fields the country people, their womenfolk in bright garments of red, green and blue, were stooping to prepare the ground for the planting of the season's corn. Suddenly Babur spotted three riders raising golden dust as they galloped towards him from the settlement with the late-afternoon sun behind them. As they approached, he recognised two members of his bodyguard. The third was a stranger. When the three pulled up, he jumped from his horse and flung himself on to the dry ground before Babur.

'Rise. Who are you?'

'A messenger from your half-brother Jahangir. I give thanks to God that I have found you at last. I have searched for many days. You were hard to find.'

'Deliberately so. These are troubled times. What message do you bring from Jahangir? I did not think to hear from him – at least, not while fortune's hand is against me.'

'It has turned against my master too. Shaibani Khan is invading Ferghana from the west. King Jahangir beseeches you to come immediately with whatever forces you can muster.'

233

'Why should I? He did not send the men I asked for to help me defend Samarkand.'

'I know nothing of that, Majesty. What I do know is that the people of Ferghana are in great fear and need your help.'

Babur did not reply immediately. Then he said, 'That is a good reason but I must think about my answer. Meanwhile we must return to the settlement. There you may wash and eat.'

Two hours later, Babur made his way to the rooms occupied by his mother and grandmother. As he approached he could hear Esan Dawlat's lute. When he entered she put it down and his mother laid aside her embroidery. 'You have heard about the message from Jahangir?' he said.

'Of course. How will you respond?'

'I have thought hard over the last hour. I have no love for Jahangir, who has usurped my rightful throne, and even less for Tambal. However, as a man of honour I can respond in only one way. I must help defend Ferghana against the barbarous Uzbeks – the blood-enemies of our people. I love my birthplace. It is where my father lies in his tomb. I have many fond memories of a happy childhood there with both of you, and with him while he lived. I cannot stand by while my homeland is violated and subjugated. I and what men I can muster ride for Akhsi immediately.'

'Neither your mother nor I would expect any less of you,' said Esan Dawlat.

• ◆ •

Purple rainclouds ringed Mount Beshtor's spiky crown – a sight Babur had often seen in his youth. A storm was blowing in from the east and in an hour or less would burst over them. They should find shelter, Babur thought. Anyway, they had been almost ten hours in the saddle. It was time they rested. He pulled his feet from the stirrups and let his legs hang loose, feeling his stiff thighs and calves relax. His black stallion moved restlessly beneath him and he patted its sweating neck.

'We will make camp over there.' He pointed to a clump of red-barked spiraea trees about two hundred yards away that would give them cover from the rain and from spying eyes. When he was young, Wazir Khan had given him a handle for his riding whip cunningly carved from spiraea to resemble a fox with open jaws and lolling tongue. But this was no time for nostalgic thoughts of the past and the dead. The strong supple wood of the spiraea was good for making arrows and they would need plenty of those in the days ahead. 'Baisanghar, post sentries on that hill over there.'

Babur dismounted and tethered his stallion to a tree. They had left Sayram in such haste that there had been no time to bring tents. No matter. He drew his maroon riding cloak tight round him and sat down, his back against a rock, as some of his men went deeper into the trees with their bows to hunt pheasants and pigeons while others gathered wood for a fire.

He had never thought his return to Ferghana would be like this.

'Majesty?'

Babur looked up to see Baburi.

'You look sad.'

'I am, Baburi. In two days' time, perhaps sooner, we'll be at Akhsi. But we may be too late.'

'We came as fast as we could . . .'

'True. But this is my homeland. Samarkand so dazzled me that I forgot that. If I'd been less recklessly ambitious I might still be its king. And Shaibani Khan wouldn't have got his filthy hands on my sister . . .'

'Nobody's safe from the Uzbeks. Shaibani Khan will be your enemy until you – or someone else – slices off his bastard head . . .'

Babur nodded. Baburi was probably right. Things might

not have been so different. The guilt and melancholy that had descended as the familiar, rugged outlines of Mount Beshtor had emerged on the horizon lifted a little.

It was beginning to rain. Babur stood up and lifted his face to it, feeling the drops run down his cheeks. If this continued there would be no fire tonight. Instead of spitted game, they would eat stale bread and the sweet dried apricots they had carried in their saddlebags from Sayram and sleep on the damp ground, their stomachs growling. But at least he would soon see his birthplace again and, few as his forces were, have the chance to strike at Shaibani Khan.

· ◆ ·

Babur's scouts saw it first – smoke rising from the settlement of Tikand, about forty miles from Akhsi. He remembered the village well, especially his hunting trips there with his father when he had galloped his fat little pony after deer across its meadows of white clover or run with the village boys to flush plump pheasants from beds of *mirtimuri* melons. Tikand had been a pleasant, prosperous place, its fertile soil irrigated by a network of canals.

But this was a very different Tikand. Soon Babur himself could see smoke pouring into the sky, acrid and black. This was no dung fire lit to brew tea or cook the midday meal. The whole settlement must be burning.

As he and his men advanced, weapons ready, nothing stirred, not even a songbird. Ahead, a canal gleamed in the sunlight but around it the neat orchards of pear, apple and almond trees were a wasteland. Their trunks had been hacked and burned. The melon patches, too, had been laid waste.

But there was worse. One tree had been left standing – a handsome apple that should soon have been pink and white with blossom in promise of a fine harvest of fruit. But it was already laden. From its sturdy branches dangled the bodies of five boys, their rough-cut hair, coarse-woven tunics and leggings exactly like those of the laughing, swearing, smooth-skinned urchins with whom he had once chased pheasants. Except that their faces were swollen and purple, their eyes bursting from their sockets, and their necks had bled where the coarse ropes had bitten into their young flesh. Flies buzzed round the congealing blood. Babur rode up to touch the cheek of one boy as his body swayed slowly to and fro. His skin was still slightly warm.

'Cut them down.'

'Majesty, over here.' Baisanghar was pointing at a nearby well, dug to hold water from the canal.

Dismounting, Babur peered down at a mangled heap of bodies, male and female. From what he could see, all had been decapitated. Fifty feet away, arranged in a neat pile like a display of melons on a market stall, were the heads. The uppermost belonged to an old man with a flowing white beard. Probably a grandfather if not a great-grandfather. His severed penis was protruding bloodily from between his lips and his testicles occupied his eye sockets.

Babur and his men rode on in silence towards the centre of Tikand. The Uzbek raiders had left a smoking shell, the barns and houses burned down. Corpses lay everywhere, some stripped and arranged in obscene postures to make it appear as if, in their death agony, they had been copulating. The Uzbeks must have been moving too quickly to carry away the animals, so instead they had mutilated them, slashing their tendons. Babur set his men to cut the throats of any that still lived.

Half an hour later, as they were finishing their grim task, one of his scouts – a soldier whose people inhabited the lower slopes of the nearby mountain of Bara Koh and who knew the terrain well – came galloping in, his face eager.

'What is it?'

'We've picked up the Uzbeks' trail. From the fresh droppings their horses left, they are no more than two hours ahead, and from their tracks they are heavily laden and moving slowly. They seem to be heading for Akhsi.'

'Good. We ride.'

Flanked by Baisanghar and Baburi, Babur set off after the scouts. If he and his men could overtake the Uzbek raiding party he would make them pay – drop for drop of blood, scream for scream – for what they had done here. Those boys, hanged as casually as a farmer kills crows, would be avenged.

But some fifteen miles from Tikand, they lost the trail as they crossed an area of stony, scrubby ground. Perhaps the Uzbeks had turned aside to raid some other village, but there was nowhere of any size between Tikand and Akhsi. Babur decided to pause. If the Uzbeks had discovered they were being followed, he and his men might be riding into a trap. He sent two scouts ahead and another four to circle back, two to the left and two to the right, to check that the Uzbeks were not about to fall on them from the rear.

Babur and his men waited in silence, eyes and ears alert, hands tight on their reins, ready to take off in a moment if necessary. It was some time before one of the advance scouts returned.

'Majesty. We've found them. They've ridden into the forest.'

As their horses picked their way along the narrow trail the Uzbeks must have taken, Babur wondered why they should have entered the dense, dark woods. It wasn't the fastest route to Akhsi. Then he remembered. Long ago, on one of those hunting expeditions that were now a distant memory, his father had shown him the famous Mirror Rock in some low hills to the north of the forest. The great boulder had amazed him. Nearly thirty feet long, and in some places as high as a man, its grey surface was threaded with so many thick veins of rock crystal that, when the rays of the midday sun fell on it, it shone like a mirror, reflecting darts of bright light. It was supposed to have mystical powers . . . a warrior who honed the blade of his dagger on one of its sharp edges would never fall in battle. Perhaps the Uzbeks – now that their murdering was done – wished to see it and test its powers.

Half an hour later, Babur and his men emerged into open pasture where they could again see the tracks of horses heading north. Drawing Baisanghar and Baburi to his side, Babur told them of Mirror Rock. 'If that is where the Uzbeks have gone, we may catch them off-guard. They will not expect to have been followed. But we must be cautious . . . If I remember correctly, the rock is only three miles from here. Tell the men to keep silent and have their weapons ready . . .'

The Uzbeks were shouting and laughing, their voices rising from over the brow of a low hill as Babur and his men approached. He signalled his men to dismount and, leaving half a dozen soldiers to guard the horses, led the rest on foot up the slope of the hill from behind which the raucous noises were coming. Keeping very low, they peered down.

It was nearly midday and the sunlight reflecting off Mirror Rock was so dazzling that Babur had to shut his eyes. Even so, hot white spots danced beneath his eyelids. He had forgotten the rock's brilliance. Shading his eyes with his hand, he looked again. The Uzbeks were lolling on the ground beneath the rock. Wineskins – some empty, some still full – lay around them. So did their weapons. There were no more than about fifty men. Their horses, laden with spoils from Tikand, were tethered beneath a clump of trees to the right-hand side of the rock.

Sudden high-pitched screams somewhere over to his left made Babur swing round. Two Uzbeks were dragging a half-naked woman by her arms to the foot of the rock. A chorus of further cries – high and piercing – rose from behind the

239

rock where the Uzbeks must have left their female captives, to be brought out and enjoyed at their leisure.

The Uzbeks stripped the screaming, writhing woman of her robe, exposing her soft, pale body. Then, while one knelt and pinioned her wrists, two others each held one of her spreadeagled legs and a fourth, grinning, began to loosen his belt. Thoughts of Khanzada flashed through Babur's brain. He leaped to his feet and loosed his first arrow. The man was still fumbling beneath his tunic as the tip pierced his throat. With a ludicrous expression on his face he tumbled backwards, hand clutching his genitals.

Babur's second arrow penetrated the left eye of the Uzbek holding the woman's wrists who, on seeing what had happened to his comrade, had stupidly looked directly up the hill towards where Babur was silhouetted against the skyline.

With a cry of 'For Ferghana!' Babur raced down the hill, his men around him, their minds set on bloody revenge for the inhabitants of Tikand.

· ◆ ·

'We've left them a feast.' Baburi looked back at the circle of dark-winged birds wheeling in the air currents above Mirror Rock.

'It would have been better if there'd been more,' Babur muttered. Wiping out this raiding party was just a fleabite. Shaibani Khan, his power and strength, lay ahead. Still, he had left a message: his name scrawled in blood on a scrap of paper shoved between the teeth of an Uzbek. Shaibani Khan would soon know who had done this.

'But we didn't lose a single man and we've taken all their horses and the food they stole.'

Babur glanced at the lines of riderless horses at the rear of the column. The seven women his men had found – the youngest no more than twelve – were wrapped in cloaks and riding in two donkey carts that the Uzbeks had taken

240

from Tikand to carry their booty. Before he went much further, he must get rid of them. There was a small settlement east of here where, for the present at least, the women would be safe. He would send them there with an escort.

Babur rode on in silence, ignoring Baburi's attempts to talk. What would he find as he neared Akhsi? Would other chieftains rally to Jahangir? Would they reach him before Shaibani Khan's troops arrived before the gates? More than ever he missed Wazir Khan's wisdom. He, too, had been born and bred in Ferghana. He would have understood Babur's torment.

With darkness falling, they camped on the banks of a stream flowing from the Jaxartes. With Akhsi so close now – barely two hours' ride away – Babur had to curb the desire to ride on. It was too dangerous to blunder about in the dark. Uzbek patrols might be anywhere.

He sat on the edge of the stream, watching the water ripple past. He had been foolish. Rather than hacking those Uzbeks to pieces at Mirror Rock, he should have questioned them, found out where Shaibani Khan was, the size of his force. Instead, bent on revenge, he had been intent only on their death. He still had much to learn . . .

'Majesty. We found this shepherd nearby with his flock. You must hear his story.'

Babur looked round to see Baisanghar and behind him, between two soldiers, a man of about forty with a weathered face. He looked nervous but that was hardly surprising. He hadn't expected to be grabbed and hauled into Babur's camp.

'Repeat what you told my men. No one will harm you.'

Baisanghar gripped the man's shoulders and turned him to face Babur.

The shepherd cleared his throat. 'Shaibani Khan captured Akhsi five days ago.' His eyes flickered anxiously over Babur's face. 'They say he tricked King Jahangir. He told him he didn't want Ferghana, only tribute. If the king would acknowledge him publicly as his overlord and pay him what he asked he'd take his army back to Samarkand . . .'

'Go on.' Babur felt suddenly cold.

'I wasn't there, of course. So I can only tell you what I heard . . . They say the ceremony was held on the banks of the Jaxartes below the fortress. Beneath a pavilion of red silk, the king knelt to Shaibani Khan, who was seated on a divan covered with gold cloth, and called him "Master". As he waited, head bowed, Shaibani Khan rose and drew his great curved sword. Smiling, he advanced on the king. "Now that you are my vassal I can do what I like with you," he said, and hacked off his head. As he did so, Shaibani Khan's warriors fell on the king's courtiers who were standing at either side and murdered them too.'

'Tambal? Was he killed? And what of Baqi Beg, Yusuf and the others?'

'All dead. I also heard – from two stable-boys who escaped from Akhsi – that when Shaibani Khan entered the fortress he had the women of the harem paraded before him. Some he gave to his men, others he took for himself. Last of all he summoned Roxanna, the king's mother. They say he held up her son's severed head before her and, as she wept, wailed and cursed him, he ordered her throat to be cut – "to silence her whining", he said.'

Babur's head was reeling. His informant hadn't seen any of these things for himself and perhaps the details were wrong, but Babur didn't doubt the essence of the story – that Shaibani Khan had tricked and killed Jahangir and Tambal and had taken Ferghana for himself. Neither did he doubt Roxanna's fate and for a moment felt a fleeting pity for his father's concubine.

At dawn, after a restless night, Babur untethered his horse and rode alone towards a steep ridge from which he knew he could see Akhsi. His stallion was sweating as they breasted the summit. Far below, with the Jaxartes curling past, he saw the fortress built by his ancestors, their stronghold for so long.

A banner was streaming proudly above the gate. From this distance Babur couldn't distinguish the colour but he knew it wasn't the bright yellow of Ferghana. It was the black of Shaibani Khan, who had stolen his ancestral lands just as he had seized Samarkand. Babur couldn't hold back the tears that ran down his face or control the sobs that shook him. But it didn't matter. Up here on the mountain ridge there was no one to see, only the hawks circling high above.

. ◆ .

'It is the only way.' Esan Dawlat's voice was insistent. 'He will kill you just as he murdered Jahangir and your cousin, Mahmud Khan. He has sworn to exterminate every prince of Timur's house and, I tell you, he means to keep his oath.'

'I won't run from him. I'm no coward . . .'

'Then you are a fool instead. He commands armies of thousands. Over the summer, since he captured Samarkand and then Ferghana, the tribes of the northern steppes have rallied to his banner. His strength increases daily while yours diminishes.' Esan Dawlat spat into the fire – something which Babur had never seen her do before. 'What support do you have?' she continued. 'Fifty? A hundred? The rest have slunk back to their villages. You don't even have a wife . . . or an heir.'

Esan Dawlat blamed him for that, but he was glad Ayisha had gone for good. The blunt message that had arrived from Ibrahim Saru that he had never intended to give his daughter to a landless pauper and that the marriage was dissolved had afforded Babur as much satisfaction as it had angered his grandmother. According to the messenger who had delivered the letter – and returned the wedding jewellery Babur had given her – the talk was that Ayisha was shortly to marry a man of her own tribe to whom she had been promised before Babur's offer of marriage. At least Babur thought he might now understand the reason for her coldness towards him, but as far as he was concerned Ayisha could lie in another man's bed – any man who could thaw her was welcome.

'I have no time for a wife,' he said bluntly. 'It is my destiny to be a king and I must strike back . . .'

'If you truly believe in your destiny you will listen. Even now, Shaibani Khan is searching for you. He knows it was you who ambushed his men at Mirror Rock, and by now he will know, too, that you have returned here to Sayram. Many will be willing to take his gold for betraying you.'

'I made a promise to Khanzada . . .'

'Which you cannot honour if he cuts your head off your shoulders. And will it ease her suffering when Shaibani Khan tells her you are dead?' Her face softened when she saw the bitterness in his eyes. 'You are still so young. You must learn to be patient. When you live as long as I, you learn that circumstances change. Sometimes the bravest thing – and the hardest – is to wait.'

Kutlugh Nigar nodded. Since Khanzada had been taken she had became so silent it was hard to coax a word from her. 'Your grandmother is right. You have no chance if you stay here. He will murder us all. I do not care for myself, but you must survive . . . Remember whose blood flows in your veins. Don't let Shaibani Khan wipe you out like some petty bandit.'

Kutlugh Nigar wrapped her thick dark blue shawl round herself more tightly and held her hands over the brazier in the hearth. Winter would soon be upon them again, as the winds blowing around Sayram's mud-brick houses and penetrating the wooden shutters were warning them.

Babur kissed her thin cheek. 'I will think over what you have both said.'

Esan Dawlat picked up her lute. It was battered and some of the mother-of-pearl, inlaid to resemble clusters of narcissi, had fallen out, but as she plucked the strings the soft, sweet notes carried Babur back to the days of his boyhood in Akhsi.

Going outside, he walked across the courtyard, climbed on to the village wall and stared out into the gathering dusk. He would make his own decisions, but he knew his grandmother and mother were right. His priority must be to stay alive.

'Majesty.' He heard Baburi's voice from below him. A trio of plump pigeons dangled by their feet from his belt – he must have been hunting. He climbed the short flight of steps on to the wall and stood in silence at Babur's side.

'Do you ever doubt your destiny, Baburi?'

'Market boys don't have destinies. They're a luxury, for kings.'

'All my life I've been told that I was put on this earth to achieve something. What if it isn't true . . . ?'

'What do you want me to tell you? That you are heir to Genghis Khan and Timur? That life should be good to you as of right?'

Baburi's tone was impatient; rough, even. Babur had never heard him speak like that before. 'I have been unlucky.'

'No you haven't. You were fortunate in your birth. You had everything. You weren't an orphan. You didn't have to fight for scraps like me.' Suddenly anger blazed in Baburi's indigo eyes. 'I've watched you since we rode back here from Akhsi, drowning in self-pity, hardly speaking to those around you. You've changed. You weren't like this when we went riding together or when you had Yadgar in your arms. That was living and you've forgotten what it was like. If this is how you behave in adversity, perhaps you don't deserve this "great destiny" – whatever it might be – that you seem to carry around like a burden on your back.'

Before he knew it, Babur had taken a swing at Baburi and the two had tumbled from the walls on to the hard mud below. Babur was the heavier and had Baburi pinned under him but, quick as an eel, Baburi twisted to one side and, with the fingers of one hand poking into one of Babur's eyes, caught him a hard blow with the other on the side of his head. Grunting with pain, Babur rolled off him, sprang to his feet and leaped on him again, winding him. Seizing Baburi's head he began banging it hard against the ground, but a second later felt Baburi's boot in his groin. In agony, he let go of Baburi and rolled aside.

The two of them – hair dusty and tousled – looked at one another. Baburi's nose was bleeding and Babur felt blood running down his own face from a cut above his ear, while his left eye, where Baburi had jabbed it, was already hard to keep open.

'You'd make a good street-fighter,' Baburi said. 'You'll never starve – destiny or no destiny.'

As men, alerted by the sound of their fight, came running along the walls above them, led by an amazed-looking Baisanghar, the two of them started to laugh.

· ◆ ·

The air was so cold it stung Babur's eyes. Every two or three steps his feet, in their hide boots, slipped on the ice. Yet this steep pass, leading south out of Ferghana, was the only viable escape route from Shaibani Khan whose patrols had been hunting Babur and his men like foxes, flushing them from place to place and laying everywhere waste.

The absence of horses or ponies made Babur feel vulnerable, even high on this icy mountain where they would meet no one. He and his people had always been horsemen but for the moment they must rely on the endurance of their own bodies. During the first few days of the journey up the lower slopes, Esan Dawlat and Kutlugh Nigar had ridden on the backs of one of the four donkeys Babur had brought with him to help carry their possessions. But as the ascent got steeper and the weather worsened, Babur had had to order the animals killed for food.

Thereafter, it had sometimes been possible for Esan Dawlat and Kutlugh Nigar to be carried in baskets on the backs of his strongest men. But for the rest of the time, they and their two serving women, like the forty or so men who remained with Babur, had had to walk, feeling their way upwards through the frozen rocks with their wooden staves. Kutlugh Nigar had surprised her son with her agility and balance, refusing help in favour of her own weaker mother. Babur could see her now, ahead of him, so muffled in sheepskins that almost nothing of her was visible, pulling herself up the rocks quicker than some of his men. She was faring much better than Kasim, who had fallen repeatedly and was clearly exhausted.

All that the party had to shelter them were four felt tents and some fleeces rolled together round poles that three men – one behind another with the pole resting on their shoulders – could just about carry. Babur had taken his turn, his back bending as his feet fought for purchase.

After another day, they should be over the pass. In the valleys below there would be villages to provide them with shelter and later with horses. That night, lying beneath the fleeces, Babur took comfort from that thought, as he did from the companionable warmth of the bodies of Baburi and his men pressed tightly around him.

◆

Caught urinating on the ice of a frozen stream, the boy gawped in amazement two days later at the unkempt party stumbling towards him from the direction of the pass. Then he turned and fled, slipping and slithering to the village a few hundred yards further downhill.

'Shall I send men ahead, Majesty?' Baisanghar asked.

Babur nodded. Though he was numb with cold, relief and pride began to pump through him, reviving him. He had done it. He had brought his family and his men safely through the mountains. That they were a ragged few, rather than the armies he had once commanded, didn't matter for the present.

A few minutes later, Baisanghar's soldiers returned with what looked – beneath the layers of thick quilted coats and the dark woollen cloth wound round his head – like an elderly man. They must have told him who Babur was for he fell at his feet, touching his forehead to the cold snow.

'There's no need for that.' It was a long time since Babur had received such obeisance. He took the man by the shoulders and helped him gently to his feet. 'We are weary and have come far. And we have women with us. Will you give us shelter?'

'Few cross the mountains so late in the year,' the man said. 'I am the headman here. You are welcome in our village.'

That night, Babur sat cross-legged by the fire in the headman's simple, mud-walled house. The lower floor was a single room with bolsters of wool to sleep on – Esan Dawlat, Kutlugh Nigar and the headman's wife were sharing a small room above, reached by a flight of wooden stairs outside. Baburi was next to him, and both were examining the black marks and blisters on their feet left by frostbite.

'Sometimes I thought I'd never walk again – even if we survived.' Baburi winced as he touched a tender spot.

'We were lucky. We could easily have lost our way or fallen down a ravine.'

'Was it luck or that mighty "destiny" of yours?' Baburi smiled.

Babur also smiled but made no reply.

◆

Despite the early-morning mist, Babur saw the hare as it jumped out from behind a low bush then froze, ears erect, to snuff the air. He was downwind of it – the hare couldn't know he was there. Carefully he put an arrow to his bowstring and pulled it back, eyes never leaving the animal that, satisfied it was safe, was enjoying a brisk scratch.

Suddenly behind Babur came the sound of running feet and the hare took off. Cursing, he turned to see one of his men, agitated and panting. 'Majesty, an ambassador has come from Kabul. He has been seeking you for the past two months, ever since the snows began to melt. He is waiting in the headman's house.'

Irritation forgotten, Babur secured his quiver, slung his bow over his shoulder and ran down the track towards the village. The message must be from his father's cousin, the King of Kabul . . . but the two men had been estranged and there had been little contact between them that Babur could recall.

The ambassador, wearing a peacock blue robe, was more grandly dressed than anyone Babur had seen in a long time. Feathers, held by a jewelled clasp, waved from the crest of his dark blue turban and his two attendants were clad in blue trimmed with gold. They must have changed while they were waiting for his men to find him. Babur smiled inwardly. No one would ride about the mountains in such garb . . . All the same, he was conscious for the first time in many months of his own appearance – his long hair, simple yellow wool tunic and buckskin trousers.

But the ambassador didn't seem perturbed. Relief that his search was over was written in his features as Babur strode towards him.

The ambassador bowed low. 'Greetings, Majesty.'

'You are welcome. They tell me you come from Kabul. What do you want of me?'

'Majesty, I bring news that is sad but also glorious. The king, your father's cousin, Ulughbeg Mirza, died during the winter leaving no heir. His last surviving son had already died of a fever two months before. My message from the

Royal Council of Kabul is this. The throne can be yours if you will come. The council believes the inhabitants will welcome another ruler from Timur's illustrious stock, particularly one proven in battle and still young. With the council's support, which they pledge you on the Holy Book, you will have no rivals.'

Babur could not hide his surprise. Never in his wildest and most desperate moments had he thought of the kingdom of Kabul. It was so far away – more than five hundred miles. To reach it he must cross the broad Oxus and the twisting, knife-sharp passes of the Hindu Kush. Even then it would be a gamble. By the time he arrived much might have changed. The members of the royal council who, for whatever reason, seemed so generously disposed towards him might have been toppled or bribed to support another candidate.

Yet he couldn't stay here, hunting rabbits and hares, as another year passed him by and also, Babur thought, with growing elation and excitement, Kabul was far from the rapacious Shaibani Khan. It was also rich and powerful. Soldiers would flock to him again. There, he could rebuild his power and plan his next move.

'Thank you,' he said, to the messenger. 'I will give you my answer in a short while.' But he already knew. He was going to Kabul.

Chapter 14

A Sign of Fortune

'You followed me far from your homes, braving danger and hardship out of loyalty to me and your hatred of our blood enemy, the barbarous Uzbeks. I led you over high mountains and through icy passes. Our bodies warmed each other in our tents at night as the winds tried to blow us to oblivion. We shared our meagre food equally. Never in the nine years since I became a king have I felt so proud. You may be few in number but you have the tiger's spirit.' Babur's green eyes glinted as he looked round the circle of faces before him. His men were so few that he knew each by name, his clan, where he had earned his scars. He had spoken only the truth. He was proud of his ragged little army.

'Soon I will be able to reward your devotion. My father's cousin, the King of Kabul, has died. Respecting both my royal lineage and the reputation I have – with your help – built as a courageous, undaunted leader, the people of Kabul have chosen me as their new ruler, if I will come. And I will – even if I have to go alone. But I know that you will trust me once more and come with me. But, more than this, will you send word to your villages so that others may join us to share in our good fortune and fulfil the destiny that is the birthright of us all?' Babur raised his arms as if he was already celebrating a great triumph.

From all around a mighty cheer arose. Who would have thought that just a few dozen voices could raise such a sound? Babur glanced at Baburi, Baisanghar and Kasim beside him, roaring with the rest. A fresh energy was rising inside him . . .

• ◆ •

A month later Babur was in his tent, the flaps thrown open to the sun and the fresh, warm breeze. Word of his changed fortunes had carried swiftly, as he had hoped. The ragged party he had led from Ferghana now numbered more than four thousand warriors from Mongol nomads whose chiefs tied the *tugh*, or yak-tail standard, to the tails of their horses in battle, to Timurid chiefs displaced by Shaibani Khan. He wasn't naïve enough to believe that many felt any great loyalty to him or his cause: they were with him for reward. But their readiness to undertake such a long, hazardous journey showed a pleasing confidence that he would succeed. His reputation had spoken for him.

Babur had already put the gold the ambassador had brought from the royal council in Kabul to good use, buying weapons, strong horses, herds of fat sheep and tents of supple hides lined with felt that kept out the draughts. He and his army had crossed the smooth, broad Oxus with ease, loading horses, pack-mules, camels and baggage carts on to the flat-ended, shallow-draughted boats that the skilful rivermen had, over two days and nights, ferried to and fro, digging their long wooden poles into the sandy riverbed to propel their craft. Some of these boatmen — impressed by the size of Babur's army — had thrown aside their poles and joined him.

His advance south-west had begun to feel like a triumphal procession but he must not became complacent. Though

Shaibani Khan and his forces were far behind, Babur knew from the accounts he had studied of Timur's expeditions and from the stories of the old woman, Rehana, that many dangers lurked among the frozen peaks of the Hindu Kush, which lay between him and Kabul. He was glad he had left his mother and grandmother, with soldiers to protect them, behind the sturdy walls of the fortress of Kishm, given to him by one of his new allies. Once he had taken Kabul he would send for them, but until then they would be safe. He wished the same was true of Khanzada, whose anguished face he often saw in his dreams.

'Majesty.' A bodyguard entered his tent. 'Your council is waiting.'

It felt odd to have a council of advisers again. They were assembled beneath the spreading branches of a plane tree – Kasim in a long green quilted robe, Baisanghar and Baburi in new tunics of fine-woven wool, but also Hussain Mazid, who had come from Sayram with fifty men, and three others. Two were Mongol chieftains with round hats of black sheepskin, their broad faces shiny with battle scars. The third was a distant cousin of Babur's, Mirza Khan, a fleshy, middle-aged man with a cast in his left eye, who had been pushed out of his own lands by the Uzbeks' advance and had brought Babur three hundred well-equipped cavalrymen, extra horses and wagonloads of grain. Babur had no very high opinion of his brains or his valour – his status and wealth had won him his place.

Signalling to his council to sit on the carpets laid on the ground, he went straight to the point: 'We still have nearly two hundred miles to go to reach Kabul. Between us and the city lies the Hindu Kush. None of us has ever seen those mountains, let alone crossed them. We know them only in our imaginations but they will be formidable, even in summer . . . The question is, do we cross them or do we seek another way . . . ?'

'What alternative is there?' asked Mirza Khan.

'We could avoid the worst of the mountains by circling round, along the river valleys, as the ambassador did when he came seeking me . . .'

'But that would take a long time – perhaps too long,' said Baburi. 'Delay could be a much greater risk to us than the mountains . . .'

Baisanghar nodded. 'I agree. We should cross the mountains. But to do so we'll need guides, men who know the passes and can lead us over them by the best and safest route. Men we can trust . . .'

The Mongol chiefs were looking impassive as though a journey over the roof of the world was nothing to them. Babur had the feeling that if they believed the booty would be great enough, they'd follow him into the furnaces of hell – but if disappointed in their hopes of bounty would leave him there . . .

Babur looked around at his council once more. There seemed no point in deliberating any longer. He had gone over it again and again in his mind and each time his conclusion had been the same. If he wanted Kabul he must be quick.

'Very well. I have decided. We go over the Hindu Kush. As we near the mountains, we'll look for men to guide us – but if we cannot find them we go anyway . . . We will ride out in thirty-six hours. Use that time to check your men's equipment and provisions, and the condition of your animals. Baisanghar, I rely on you to tell the other chieftains. And we take only our horses and pack-mules, no livestock, not even into the foothills.'

‹ ◆ ›

The rows of ragged, jagged peaks were getting closer. Sometimes Babur imagined he could feel their frozen breath on his face. The lower slopes rose in dark green ripples but, high above, the icy tips gleamed diamond bright. Some called these mountains the Stony Girdles of the Earth, but to Babur they were more like towers of crystal. Old Rehana's tales of Timur being hoisted down a cliff face, of his frozen, starving warriors, of terrified horses slipping and sliding on the ice and of attacks by wild Kafirs were still vivid in his mind. Bringing his own family and his few men through the southern mountains out of Ferghana safely eight months previously had been nothing compared with leading an entire army and all its equipment across these high peaks, which – so the legends said – touched the skies.

'What are you thinking?' Baburi was beside him on a bay mare that kept tossing her head to rid herself of a buzzing horsefly.

'What Rehana told us of how Timur brought his army over the Hindu Kush to Delhi . . .'

Baburi shrugged. 'They were vivid stories, romantic and much embroidered. To her every word was true but I wasn't sure how much of it was real. Take that story of her grandfather saving the boy who gave him the golden elephant – I bet he looted it, and made up the rescue to compensate for having abandoned the other boy. Anyway, soon we'll see for ourselves what it's like up there. At least we have a man to guide us.'

'I hope he was telling the truth when he said he knew the mountains.'

'Your promise to throw him down a crevasse if he'd lied seemed effective.'

'I meant it.'

Babur looked over his shoulder at his bodyguard and, beyond, the long lines of riders advancing across a dry landscape that shimmered in the August heat. Sweat dripped from his forehead and was running down between his shoulder-blades. He drank some water from the leather water-bottle dangling from his saddle. It was strange to think they'd soon enter a world of snow and ice.

'What's Kabul like?' Baburi took a swipe at the horsefly with one of his gauntlets and grunted in satisfaction to see it fall lifeless to the hard-baked ground.

'My father never went there but he said he'd heard it was a strange place caught between two worlds – one hot, the other cold. Within a day's ride of Kabul is a place where the snow never falls, but two hours in another direction takes you to where the snow never melts . . .'

'I wonder about the girls . . .'

'Whether they're hot or cold? If we're lucky we'll find out.'

◆

The air was thin. Babur was finding it hard to breathe and his heart was beating faster than normal. The horses, too, were feeling the strain, snorting with effort as they climbed. With frozen fingers, Babur yanked the fur-lined hood of his cloak further over his head. An hour ago, the sky had been clear but suddenly, without warning, snow had begun to fall. Now thick, white flakes whirled dizzily round them. Looking back, Babur could barely make out the dark shapes of men and beasts plodding in a long line behind, a few men still riding but many more, like him, leading their animals up the steep, icy slopes, heads bowed against the storm. His own horse, a grey with a dark mane and tail, was whinnying in discomfort and protest as Babur tugged at its bridle.

He was well accustomed to bitter winters, but the suddenness of this summer blizzard, carried on a freezing, scouring wind, seemed a warning. Through the crazily dancing snowflakes he imagined he could see the shadowy figures of Timur's warriors battling their way upwards. The thought that they had endured and survived gave him strength.

'Majesty,' Babur recognised Baisanghar's voice close by him, 'the guide says it is too dangerous to go on when we cannot see in front of our noses. He knows of a *khawal* – a cave in the rocks — a few hundred yards further on. He urges you to take refuge there until the storm passes and he will show the rest of us how best to protect ourselves and the animals.'

Babur shook his head. 'If the guide says we should stop, we will stop,' he said, 'but I won't skulk in a cave while my men face discomfort and hardship outside. What does he say we must do?'

'Dig, Majesty. We cannot pitch our tents in these winds so we must burrow holes for ourselves and make windbreaks of snow to protect our animals and wait for the blizzard to ease . . .'

'Very well. Give me a shovel . . .'

Early the next morning, Babur woke in his snowhole. A layer of snow was covering his body but he was surprised by how well he had slept in his cocoon of blankets. Crawling out and dusting the snow off, he saw to his relief that all was again calm. The white landscape glittered beneath a bright, clear blue sky.

'Majesty.' It was the guide, a tall sturdy man of about thirty-five, well bundled against the cold. His son — a boy of fourteen or fifteen — was beside him, arms crossed and mittened hands tucked beneath his armpits for added warmth.

'Can we go on?'

'Yes, but we must be especially careful now. The snow conceals many dangers that before would have been obvious.'

The man was right. The thick crusting of snow made the landscape appear softer and more benign but it had formed bridges over crevasses. As the party set off, Babur watched how the guide, walking cautiously ahead, now and then thrust his long stick into apparently solid ground that at once collapsed to reveal a deep ravine from which there could be no rescue. When Babur asked how he had acquired his knowledge, the man said that for centuries his family had guided travellers over these mountains. Was it fanciful to wonder whether one of his ancestors had been with Timur's army?

Soon there was no time or energy for idle speculation. As they inched higher on to a curving saddle of land between two peaks, the snow was growing deeper so that the horses were sinking to their stirrups, even their girths . . .

'Majesty . . . I must have snow-tramplers.' The guide was immersed almost to his waist in the soft, dense mass.

'What . . . ?'

'Snow-tramplers . . . We're past the area where we must worry about ravines. Now I need fifteen to twenty strong men. The lead man must force a channel through the snow so that those behind can beat the snow down further and create a path for the rest of the men and animals following behind. It is the only way we will ever reach the pass . . .'

An hour later, Babur's lungs were burning and his legs felt ready to buckle beneath him. Yet he, above all others, must show stamina and fortitude. He had insisted on taking his turn as lead man and where others had cleared perhaps eight to ten yards before giving up exhausted, he was determined to manage double that . . . Sweat poured off him, despite the cold, but every step brought grim satisfaction that not even Nature herself could stand in his way.

By mid-afternoon they were finally clear of the snowfields and on higher, firmer ground. Unlike Timur, he and his men had been fortunate. The snows had not returned and they were now making steady progress through this hostile but still beautiful world. Babur had always thought of ice as white, but here, on the ceiling of the world, it shone azure and turquoise in the warm sunlight.

'How much longer to the pass?'

The guide thought for a moment. 'If we continue at this pace we should reach the Hupian Pass before nightfall tomorrow, Majesty.'

Babur clapped his hands, frozen despite the woollen cloth he had bound tightly around them and his fur-lined gauntlets, and winced at what felt like the pricking of red-hot needles as his blood flowed again into his blue fingers. 'You've done well. I thought we'd lose many of our animals.'

'That is why I am bringing you to the Hupian Pass. It is not as high as some of the others, like the Khawak, and the way up is not so hazardous – though everywhere in these mountains has its dangers . . . You must always beware—' The man was still speaking when a grinding, crunching sound split the cold air. Looking up, Babur saw a network of cracks shoot across the smooth surface of a cliff of ice high above them. With a groan that was almost human, a rectangular blue-green slab sheared off and came smashing down on to the end of the long line of men and animals.

At the same time, there was a roar so loud that Babur thought his eardrums would burst. Instinctively he put his hands over them. As he did so something hit him hard in the chest and something else sliced against the side of his head. All around, the air was full of missiles. As his horse neighed in panic, Babur flung himself to the ground and, gripping its halter, crawled beneath its belly.

As suddenly as it had begun, the avalanche was over. The surrounding peaks were silent once more though from all around came the sounds of frightened beasts and men. Babur's head throbbed and his breastbone felt tender as cautiously he climbed out from beneath his horse, which was still skittering about but seemed unhurt.

'Majesty, are you all right?' It was Baburi, cradling his left arm with his right hand, a livid bruise already welling on one side of his face.

Babur nodded. His thick garments had protected him. But the guide was splayed face down at his feet. The man's shaggy wolfskin cap had not saved him from the hunk of ice that had smashed into the back of his head with such force that his brains and blood now spattered the snowy ground.

Babur thought of the man's warning, 'You must always beware . . .' Those had been his last words on earth. Above them, the cliff of ice gleamed like a mirror in the sunshine yet at any moment it might shed another deadly load. He must get his men out of here.

'Gather up the injured,' he said softly. 'We must move as quickly as we can. Pass the order down the line . . .'

He looked again at the crumpled figure at his feet. There was no sign of the man's son and no time to look for him. 'Help me, Baburi . . .'

The guide had been a big man and it was hard to sling his body over Babur's horse but it felt wrong to leave him there. He deserved a better resting-place and Babur intended to find him one – perhaps on the pass where his spirit would rest happy.

They hurried on as fast as they could, feet slipping and scrabbling on the icy ground, until they reached a plateau. They should be safe there from any further falls of ice and snow, Babur thought, and ordered a halt so he could take stock. The casualties were not as bad as he had feared – eighteen men killed, nearly double that number injured, though most not badly, with six horses and three mules killed or too badly injured to go on. Babur's men had already slit their throats and were preparing them for the cooking pot. It could have been far worse . . .

'Majesty . . . ?' A young voice interrupted his thoughts. It was the guide's son. His eyes were red but his voice was steady. 'I know the way forward. I will be your guide now. It is what my father would have wished . . .'

'I thank you, and I am sorry for your loss.' Babur nodded. He would be sure to reward him well at journey's end.

Led by the youth, they breasted the Hupian Pass just after dawn. Low on the southern horizon, a single brilliant star was still shining.

Babur stared at it. 'Which is that? I've never seen it before.'

Baburi shrugged, but Baisanghar knew. 'It is Canopus, Majesty. It doesn't shine in our northern skies in Samarkand

260

and Ferghana, but I read of it in Samarkand, in the books of Timur's grandson, Ulugh Beg the astronomer. There is a famous verse:

How far do you shine, Canopus, and where do you rise?
You bear a sign of fortune in your eye to all upon whom it falls.

. ◆ .

Before Babur's eyes, the star vanished in the paling sky but the message was good. A sign of fortune was exactly what he needed and he felt his spirits rise. He became even more cheerful when, eight hours later, snow and ice yielded to pastures. For the first time in three days they could pitch their tents, take off some layers of clothing and ease off their boots.

But Babur was horrified as, with Baisanghar and Baburi, he inspected the condition of some of the men. Despite his orders, many had been ill prepared for the mountains. The Mongols, faces burned by the sun, looked healthy enough, but Mirza Khan's soldiers were in poor condition. The hands and feet of at least a dozen were black and swollen with frostbite.

Babur had seen such severe frostbite before. There was only one remedy if the men were to live. Soon fires were burning and swords were being sharpened on stones. With no strong spirits to deaden their pain, all that could be done for the men whose fingers and toes or hands and feet were to be amputated was to place a folded cloth between their teeth to stop them biting off their tongues.

Mirza Khan's cup-bearer – a slim, handsome youth of sixteen whose right hand was black, swollen to the size of a small melon and oozing yellow pus from beneath the nails – was struggling unsuccessfully to hold back tears as he watched a soldier test the sharpness of his blade.

261

'Courage.' Babur knelt beside him. 'It will be over quickly and at least you will live . . . Keep your eyes on mine and don't look down.' Babur gripped him by the shoulders while another man held the frostbitten arm tight above the elbow and a second man held his feet.

'Now – quickly!' Babur ordered. The boy's eyes, wide with fright, stayed fixed on his face. As the sword sliced down on his wrist his body arced in pain but though he bit hard on the rag between his teeth he didn't utter a sound. Still gripping the boy, Babur moved aside to allow another soldier to kneel down and cauterise the bleeding stump with a blade red hot from the fire. This time, though muffled by the rag, the boy did cry out but struggled to control himself.

Mirza Khan was watching, curious but detached. He had come through the mountains unscathed – he still even looked plump – but he didn't seem to care a fart for his men. Babur wanted to smash his face. 'What is this youth's name?' he asked.

'Sayyidim.'

'I would like to take him into my service.'

'As you wish.' Mirza Khan shrugged as if to say 'What use is a one-handed cup-bearer to me?'

Babur stood up and watched as the boy's arm was wrapped in strips of cloth torn from a cloak. 'Take him to my tent and bring him some broth,' he ordered. 'He's shown courage.'

The Aq Saray Meadow, the meeting-place on the borders of the kingdom of Kabul that the ambassador had appointed, was pleasant enough, with its lush, sweet grass. So was Babur's camp, the neat lines of tents radiating out from his own in the centre. It was encouraging that his army had encountered no hostility from the people in the villages on the mountainsides and in the valleys they'd passed through on their journey south-west, only curiosity that they had dared to come over the mountains.

It was September now. The harvest was gathered and the granaries were full so the villagers were more than willing to sell them food. It was good to sit around a fire at night to eat fat, juicy lamb, then ripe apples and plums, new picked from the orchards and sweetened with honey from the hives. Blackbirds, thrushes and doves fluttered in the branches and at night Babur heard the call of the nightingale. This was a prosperous, abundant land and when he was king in Kabul he'd keep it so.

But his first priority was to enforce discipline in his camp. Though he had forbidden looting, six men had disobeyed him, raiding a farm and killing two peasants who had tried to defend their livestock. Babur had had the culprits found and flogged to death, watching stony faced as the sentence was carried out in front of the murdered peasants' family. Then he had ordered the men's flayed bodies, more pulp than substance, to be thrown into a common grave dug on scrubland. It would be good when messengers arrived from Kabul. The longer he was kept waiting, the more chance there was for mischief in his army.

On the third day, as he was sitting outside his tent, watching Baburi fletch arrows, Babur saw a small party of horsemen galloping through the meadow towards them.

'What d'you think? Is it the ambassador?' Babur narrowed his eyes. The figures were too far off to distinguish properly but that so few men should ride into his camp suggested they must be friends. As they came closer, Babur saw the peacock blue of the ambassador's tunic and the sun flashing on the jewelled pin securing the tall feathers to his cap.

'Greetings, Majesty. I rejoice to see you have made a safe journey and that you have gathered so many warriors to your cause. The royal council salutes you.'

Babur nodded. 'When may I enter the city?'

The ambassador's hazel eyes flickered. 'There is a problem, Majesty. A usurper – Muhammad-Muquim Arghun – has seized Kabul and the citadel above it. The council escaped to Karabagh, outside the city, with a few loyal troops but could do nothing to take back Kabul.'

'Who is this man?'

'A chieftain of the Hazara tribe. He forced his way into the city with his troops.'

'Has he declared himself king? Has the *khutba* been read in his name?'

'No, Majesty, not yet. There are many rivalries between the tribes.'

'How many soldiers has he?'

'Perhaps a thousand, Majesty, maybe a few more, or maybe a few less.'

'I have four thousand men eager for a fight. Tell your council that. No – take me to Karabagh. I did not bring my army across the Hindu Kush so that others might profit.'

'Yes, Majesty.' The ambassador knelt before him and touched his forehead to the ground. It was the first time, Babur reflected, that he had treated him as his king.

·◆·

'W-w-we advise you to w-w-wait,' said Bahlul Ayyub, his stammer exacerbated by his anxiety. The grave old man stroked his long, silken beard. His age and status as grand vizier of Kabul demanded respect, if not his views, Babur thought impatiently, even though the other equally venerable members of the council, Wali Gul, guardian of the Royal Treasuries, and Haydar Taqi, keeper of the Royal Seal, were nodding their agreement.

'What benefit is there in delay? It will only encourage the Hazara upstart and make him believe I am afraid of him. I have the authority of the royal council. I have royal blood. I have an army. What more do I need?'

'W-w-we fear for the c-c-citizens of Kabul. Muhammad-Muquim Arghun has taken some of the principal citizens hostage – members of our families among them – and holds them in the c–c–citadel.'

'If he hurts them, he will pay. I shall make that clear to him. I shall also make clear that I am no bandit come to challenge him but the new King of Kabul come to take possession of his own.'

The three old men looked at each other. His words had struck home, Babur thought. Perhaps they had forgotten who they were dealing with: a man who – though fate had robbed him – had by his ingenuity and daring already been a king.

'W-w-we are yours to command, Majesty. That is understood.'

◆

The thick mud walls around the city of Kabul glowed apricot in the ripe autumn sun. Behind the encircling walls, Babur could see a jumble of houses, palaces, caravanserais and mosques. This was no Samarkand but he would use its wealth to create a place of beauty and magnificence. And Kabul was rich, an important trading post well placed on the caravan routes to and from China, Turkey, Hindustan and Persia. The royal councillors had told him with pride that caravans of as many as twenty thousand horses, camels and other pack animals passed through, bringing cloth, gems, sugar and spices.

Above the city to the north, on a spur of barren rock, was the citadel, its plain walls pierced by small apertures. Babur knew that many eyes – including those of Muhammad-Muquim Arghun – would be watching, which was as he intended. He had ordered his men to arm themselves as heavily and obviously as possible. Swords, spears and axes glinted. Bows hung from their shoulders and their quivers were full. He wished his enemy to be in no doubt about his overwhelming strength.

His men spread out behind him in battle formation, Babur

advanced slowly past the walls of the city towards the citadel, then halted. Ordering his men to stay ready for battle in case of any sudden sortie from the city or the citadel, he called Kasim to his side. 'You will once more be my ambassador. Take an escort and ride up to the citadel with my ultimatum to Muhammad-Muquim Arghun. If he frees his hostages unharmed and withdraws from the fortress and the city by sunset he may depart free and unmolested. If he refuses, I will give him no quarter.'

Babur watched Kasim gallop up towards the citadel with four of his soldiers. Ambassadors were always vulnerable but Kasim had proved his courage before in such a situation and Babur was confident he would not be put to the test this time . . . Muhammad-Muquim Arghun would not dare to harm him. Meanwhile, other things must be done. He summoned Baisanghar. 'I want the people in the city to know what I've said. I have ordered the scribes to make copies of my message. Tell your best archers to tie them to arrows and shoot them into the city where people can find them and read my words.'

Now he must wait. A pity there were so many flies. They were making his grey restive and it was flicking its dark tail from side to side. He slid from his saddle, hobbled the horse so that it could graze but not wander far, and sat cross-legged on the stony ground. High above, a flock of cranes flew over, the birds of heaven. A sign that God was with him.

'What do you think he'll do?' Baburi flung himself down beside him, still holding his horse's reins.

'That Hazara bandit? He's no Shaibani Khan. I doubt he has any support among the people – he should be grateful I'm prepared to let him go.'

'You've altered. D'you remember that fight we had when I accused you of self-pity?'

'What you said was right. I was feeling sorry for myself. You convinced me to keep my belief – that anything could

266

happen . . . Surviving on the streets has made you wiser than I. Perhaps princes should be turned out of doors to fend for themselves when they are young . . .'

'Perhaps – though I wouldn't recommend the food . . . or the dirty old men who try to get you into an alley.'

Babur laughed.

The sun was barely a spear's height above the western horizon and the time was nearly up when Kasim returned. He looked pleased. 'The Hazaras argued among themselves, even coming to blows – but Muhammad-Muquim Arghun accepts your terms. He is preparing to lead his men out of the citadel and head north. He is also ordering his troops in the city to join him. He asks that you remain here two hours but then Kabul, and the hostages, are yours . . .'

'He is more afraid of me than I thought. You have done well.'

As the news spread among Babur's troops, a great roar went up as men beat their swords against their shields and there was other noise as well. Though faint and far off, it was unmistakable – voices rising clamorously within the city. The citizens must have learned what had happened.

Babur mounted again and rode slowly out before his men. 'Just the sight of us was enough to make this upstart piss himself. In a short while, he and his men will slink away like beaten dogs that dare not bark, let alone bite. Let them hear our scorn and laughter as they depart into the fading light, their swords still bright and unbloodied, their honour tarnished.'

That night, dressed in robes of purple and gold – the colours of the King of Kabul – the nobles of the royal council and his commanders with him, Babur entered Kabul's main mosque. The prayer place marked for the king – just in front of the *mihrab*, which indicated the direction of Mecca – was where Timur must have knelt when he had prayed here on his way to Hindustan, Babur thought, as he knelt and touched his forehead to the cool stone. When he heard the royal mullah read the sermon, the *khutba*, in his name – the sacred moment that made him king – he felt a swell of hope and pride. He was no longer a wanderer without a home.

As the mullah moved on to a new prayer, Babur listened carefully:

It is you, God, who bestows kingdoms on whom you
   will,
And you take them from whom you will.
You raise up those whom you will,
And you cast down those whom you will.
You are the fount of goodness,
For you are almighty.

God was indeed all-powerful and he had been good to Babur.

Part III

Governing by the Sword

Chapter 15

Lord of the Bow

Luckily the city's coffers had proved even fuller than Babur had hoped. As Wali Gul had promised, the Hazaras had never found the royal treasure vaults concealed beneath the stables in the citadel. 'If they'd only shovelled away the horse shit, Majesty, they might have found them, but the Hazaras are too proud for such work.' The old man had chortled as his servants brushed away the foot-deep layer of steaming dung and straw to reveal a trapdoor and steps leading down to eight subterranean chambers. Behind the thick, iron-bound oak doors there had been enough gold and silver for Babur to reward his men well, recruit more troops and beautify his new kingdom.

He rolled up the large plan he had been studying. On it, laid out on a grid of squares, was the design for the great domed mosque he had commissioned for the central square of Kabul using some of this wealth. Even though he had been invited to Kabul and its wide territories by its leaders and welcomed by the people, his new subjects – Aymaqs, Pashais, Tajiks and Barakis on the plains and, in the mountains, Hazaras and Negudaris, and the citizens of Kabul itself –

271

were even more prone to jealousies and blood feuds than the tribes of Ferghana. It would do no harm to remind them – Sunni Muslims like himself – that it was by God's will that he ruled.

Also, it would feel good to leave his permanent mark on the city – a monument to remind future generations of his rule, something he'd never had the chance to create in Samarkand. He'd never been there long enough – and, anyway, how could he have embellished a place already made so beautiful by Timur? At least in Kabul he could fashion a capital worthy of a prince of Timur's line – a place where scholars and craftsmen would gather.

Now, though, he had unpleasant business to attend to. A month ago, Baisanghar had brought him reports that Ali Gosht – Babur's master-of-horse whom he had promoted to chief quartermaster – had been taking bribes to favour certain horse dealers and forage suppliers in Kabul. This was against Babur's express orders. He'd repeatedly promised the local people that he'd deal fairly with them but now, thanks to Ali Gosht's greed, they would be justified in murmuring against a king who had broken his word so lightly . . .

Babur had wanted more evidence – he had known Ali Gosht all his life, in fact the man had taught him to ride and play polo – but Baisanghar had brought him further proof and now he must act. He made his way to the arched audience hall where his council were standing at either side of the gilded throne in order of precedence, the most senior members closest to him. Seating himself, Babur nodded to Baisanghar. 'Bring in the quartermaster.'

He watched, expressionless, as Ali Gosht, his familiar bandy-legged gait even more pronounced because of the heavy irons dragging at his legs, shuffled towards him. Outwardly he looked defiant but Babur knew he was anxious. His battle scars were more than usually livid on his taut face and his eyes moved nervously from one counsellor to the next as he approached the throne. He didn't look at Babur, and before the guards behind him could jab at him with the butts of their spears he fell to his knees.

'You know what you are accused of . . .'

'Majesty, I—'

'Just answer me.'

'Yes, Majesty.'

'And is it true?'

'It is the way things have always been done . . .'

'But I gave you specific orders to treat the dealers and merchants fairly. You disobeyed me . . .'

Ali Gosht raised his head and licked dry lips. 'You know the tradition among our people, Majesty, from the days of Genghis Khan. The highest officials of the court should not be punished until their ninth transgression.'

'And you have transgressed at least a dozen times . . . I have all the details.'

His quartermaster crumpled even lower on the hard stone floor. Babur looked at his bowed head – the neck thick and muscular but so vulnerable to the executioner's sword. Ali Gosht must know these might be his last minutes on earth. What was going through his mind?

In the long, deep silence it seemed to Babur that all around him his counsellors were holding their breath.

'You are dismissed from my service. If you are found in Kabul after sunset tonight you will die. Take him away.'

'You should have had him executed,' said Baburi later, as they rode out of the citadel to go hawking. Babur's bird, secured to his gloved wrist by a golden chain, was turning its head restlessly beneath its tufted yellow leather hood, sensing that soon it would soar skywards.

'You say that because you didn't like Ali Gosht . . . because he clouted you . . .'

'He also told me I was only good for shovelling horse shit . . . No, of course I didn't like him. You know I despised the old goat. He was an arrogant, conceited bully who fawned to his superiors but liked swinging his fists at those in his power. But that's not why I spoke as I did. Your own men, and the people of Kabul, will think you sentimental and weak.'

Babur leaned from his saddle and gripped Baburi's wrist. 'Anyone who thinks that is wrong. It took more courage to allow him to live. It would have been far easier to order his execution. When I was only twelve, I personally hacked off the head of my father's treacherous vizier, Qambar-Ali. But Ali Gosht was loyal to me when I was a wanderer without a throne in need of friends and he had little to gain from his loyalty to me. Nevertheless, in future any man who disobeys my orders – whoever he may be – will die.'

• ◆ •

Though it was early spring, the cold northerly wind the people of Kabul called the *parwan* still flecked with white the dark green waters of the lake beneath the citadel and ruffled the feathers of the ducks sheltering among the reeds. But the snows were gone, the pastures and meadows bursting into new life. Vermilion tulips dotted the foothills, and in the forests strutting snow-cocks called in search of mates. Peasants wrapped warmly against the winds were busily tending the rows of vines that, in a few months, would yield the sweet, golden *ab-angur* grapes for the wine the courtiers relished in summer, chilling it with ice carried in chunks from the mountains and stored in ice-houses.

Babur stretched beneath the wolfskin coverlet he still needed for warmth at night, though the Negudari girl – skin the golden tawny of the honey gathered in the mountains from which she came – with whom he'd shared his bed until dawn had been more than enough to heat his blood. Later he might go hunting with Baburi. Though there was little game, the wild mountain sheep migrating between their winter and summer pastures and the occasional wild ass provided surprisingly good sport.

Or perhaps he would visit the garden he had ordered to be laid out in the clover meadows on a hillside above Kabul. Already workmen were clearing the ground and digging channels through the cold earth for the intersecting watercourses, the central pool and the fountains the nearby river would feed. Soon riders would bring the sour-cherry saplings he had ordered from the east of his kingdom to be planted among the oranges, lemons, pomegranates and apples. In this fertile earth they would grow quickly. By the time his mother and grandmother joined him, there might be something to see.

Babur flung back the wolfskin, stood up and stretched. Sunlight was pouring through the carved fretwork of the sandalwood doors on the eastern side of his chamber, which gave on to a stone balcony projecting over the courtyard below. For centuries the kings of Kabul had stood here on great occasions to show themselves to their people. It felt good to have earned that right.

• ◆ •

'What are you doing? This is the third time I've found you scribbling away.' Baburi's shadow fell across the paper on which Babur was writing.

'It's a diary. When I took Samarkand from Shaibani Khan, I decided to record what happened in my life . . . but when I lost the city . . . when I was forced to flee for my life, I put it aside . . .'

'Why did you stop? It might have comforted you . . .'

Babur put down his pen. 'Some things were too painful to dwell on – the loss of my sister, Wazir Khan's death . . . And when I was a fugitive, what could I write about except failure, the struggle to survive and how a half-bowl of millet-flour soup tasted when I was starving? There would have been no comfort in writing about such things . . . only shame . . . only the self-pity you once derided me for . . .'

'And now?'

'I am a king again . . . I suppose I feel worthy to record my memoirs . . . But there's something else. Do you remember how, as we came over the Hindu Kush, we saw the Canopus star shining so pure and bright? At that moment, I vowed that if Kabul became mine, never, ever would I lose the initiative again. Never again would I let myself be pushed around by marauders like Shaibani Khan, ambitious relations or mutinous subjects. I would control my own destiny. I can achieve that, I feel it with every breath I take . . .'

'And is that what you are writing about?'

'In a way . . . I want my future sons, and their sons after them, to know everything that happened to me – to know my achievements, my strengths – but I also want them to understand my mistakes . . . my failings . . . my thoughts . . . the choices I had to make to survive . . . From now on, I intend to record everything that happens – good or bad – frankly and honestly . . .'

'Including the number of times you had that Negudari girl the other night?'

'Even that . . . A man can be proud of many things . . .' Babur grinned, but then his expression sobered. He couldn't push from his mind his discussion with his grand vizier earlier that day. 'Bahlul Ayyub requested an audience with me this morning.'

'That waffling old woman, wh-wh-what did he w-want?' Baburi was no respecter of age or status and was fond of parodying the grand vizier's high, quavering voice and fluttering hands.

'He brought bad news, though it was not unexpected. The Hazaras are raiding caravans on the roads to and from Kabul – despite my orders that they must not be molested – and are refusing to pay the fine of horses and sheep I imposed

276

on them . . . The messenger Wali Gul sent to Muhammad-Muquim Arghun to demand payment was returned this morning . . . without his ears to signify the Hazaras' deafness to my commands . . .'

'Then Muhammad-Muquim Arghun is even more stupid than he looks . . .'

'His insolence is certainly greater than his brains and the Hazaras are a lawless breed. If I don't bring them to heel quickly, the other clans will grow rebellious. I have already decided what to do . . . As punishment for the messenger's ears, the life of every captured Hazara warrior will be forfeit. I'll build pyramids of their heads higher than anything Timur created . . .'

'Let me go – send me out with a force. I'll flush the bastards from their mountain hideaways and remove their heads from their shoulders . . .'

Babur looked at his friend. There was no doubting his seriousness: his voice shook with passion and there was an eager light in his eyes. He was a good, brave soldier but he had never been in command.

'You're sure you can lead?'

'Of course. You're not the only one to have faith in himself . . .'

Babur pondered. Others would grumble and wonder why he had chosen Baburi above them. Even Baisanghar would probably look askance. But why not follow his instincts and give Baburi the chance he was obviously aching for?

'All right. You go.'

'And your orders are no quarter?'

'No quarter to Muhammad-Muquim Arghun and his men, but spare the women and children.'

'I won't disappoint you.' Baburi's high cheekbones lent his face a predatory, wolfish look.

After he had gone, Babur thought for a moment, then took up his pen again to finish what he had been writing when Baburi had interrupted him: 'This kingdom is to be governed by the sword and not the pen.'

• ◆ •

Seven hog deer were already suspended from the huntsmen's poles but this *nilgai* was a bonus. Babur had read of the antelope's strange blue-grey coat, its black mane and the long, thick, silky hairs covering its throat but had never before seen one. The creatures concealed in the dense oak and olive forests in the east of his kingdom – gaudy parrots, shrieking mynah birds, peacocks and monkeys – astonished him. He was glad he had chosen this place for the royal hunt to celebrate Baburi's crushing of the Hazaras. Five days ago, Baburi had returned to Kabul at the head of his men to fling the mangled head of Muhammad-Muquim Arghun at Babur's feet. Now he, too, was watching the *nilgai*.

'Yours,' Babur whispered. It was only right.

Baburi fixed his indigo eyes on the *nilgai*, nosing among the juniper bushes, as he fitted his arrow to his bow-string and stretched the tight sinew till the double curved bow looked ready to snap.

Babur watched the white-feathered arrow embed itself in the soft throat of the unsuspecting deer, which, with scarcely a sound or a flicker of its long-lashed eyes, collapsed sideways to the ground. For a moment Babur saw not a stricken beast but Wazir Khan, an Uzbek arrow through his throat, sliding from his horse into a fast-flowing river and looked away. Memories and emotions came when they were least expected. He should know that by now. 'Well done. You're a good shot.'

'For a market boy . . .'

The feast that night was the most lavish Babur had given since celebrating the taking of Kabul. In the orange light of torches, he sat on a pinewood dais in the courtyard of the modest fort he was occupying on this hunting trip, Baburi next to him. Soon Babur would order the *ulush* – the 'champion's portion' – of the first sheep to be served to Baburi. He would toast him in the strong, full-bodied red wine of Kabul and award him the title of *Qor Begi*, Lord of the Bow, for his skill in battle.

But later, as he drank from his double-handled goblet, carved from ox horn and mounted in silver, and listened to his men roar out their songs of valour in the field and greater valour in bed, he felt dissatisfaction seep through him with the wine just when other rulers would have been content. After all, Baburi had quelled the Hazaras and cemented their heads into enough festering pyramids to strike fear into passers-by and serve as a warning for the future. Kabul – his haven and the balm to his dignity – was secure. He was enjoying planting his gardens and planning new buildings for his capital. Why wasn't it enough? Because ambition still gnawed at his soul, sucking out the happiness.

Taking another deep draught of wine, Babur continued to brood. In a few days his grandmother and mother would arrive from Kishm. His mother would be all pleasure at their reunion but he knew that in her heart would be the unspoken question of when he would be able to redeem his promise to rescue his sister. In Esan Dawlat's sharp eyes he sensed he would see the same question that troubled him: what to do next? What new conquest? Where and when? Neither Timur nor her revered Genghis Khan had ever rested in one place long, satisfied with what they had, as she would no doubt remind him . . .

'You look like a man whose favourite horse has gone lame just before the big race.' Baburi's lean face was flushed with wine and round his neck hung the gold chain Babur had given him for his cunning and bravery against the Hazaras.

'I was thinking . . . Ten years ago, when I least expected, I became a king. But what I always expected – even before then – was that destiny held something special for me . . .' He ignored Baburi's usual sceptical glance. How could he possibly understand what it had been like growing up in a court where the father you loved talked only of the greatness that might have been and the greatness that might yet be . . .

'The truth is I'm restless – unsatisfied. Kabul is all very well but I want more. Every day when I open my diary to write in it, I wonder what the future pages will say . . . Will they describe great glories, great victories, or will they be blank . . . ? I must not relax but hold firm to my destiny. I can't allow the pages of my life to turn with nothing memorable inscribed upon them.'

'So what are you thinking of doing . . . ? Attacking Shaibani Khan?'

'As soon as my armies are stronger. But not yet. I'd be a fool to take him on so soon . . .'

'What else, then?'

Babur took another long drink and felt the wine flow through his body, freeing his tongue and his imagination. Suddenly an idea that had long been at the back of his mind crystallised. 'Hindustan . . . that's where I'd like to go. Do you remember Rehana's story? If I captured treasure, as Timur did, no one, not Shaibani Khan or even the Shah of Persia, could stand in my way.' He swayed on his seat. Baburi's hand was on his shoulder, steadying him, but he shook it off. In his mind he saw a little golden elephant with ruby eyes . . .

'You should follow your instincts.'

Babur peered at him blearily. 'What . . . ?'

'I said follow your instincts . . . see where your so-called destiny that you love so much leads you . . .'

Though Baburi's voice seemed to come from far away and was half drowned in the drunken hubbub around them, the message penetrated Babur's mind with complete clarity, sobering him in spite of the wine . . . Yes, he would muster a force and raid south along the Kabul river towards Hindustan.

He would gaze on the broad Indus, contemplate the prospect of awesome riches beyond and perhaps even seize some.

• ◆ •

At Babur's request, the court astrologers consulted the planets. Night after night they studied their charts and scrutinised the infinitely complex web of stars lighting the dark skies over Kabul. January, when the sun was in the sign of Aquarius, would be an auspicious time for him to launch his campaign, they pronounced at last, stroking their beards. Babur wasn't sure he believed their predictions, but his men would. It was good for them to believe the stars blessed their journey into an unknown world. At least the astrologers' advice gave him time to prepare: he could spend the next few months building up his forces and considering his strategy.

• ◆ •

As the last of the autumn fruit was being gathered from the orchards around Kabul, Babur's mother and grandmother arrived from Kishm. He hadn't wanted to send for them too soon – the Hazara rising had made him cautious – but his heart swelled with pride to hear the trumpets sound and the drums over the gatehouse thud as they and their escort entered the citadel. Kutlugh Nigar had noticeably lost weight and looked tired and frail after the long journey – Babur saw how heavily she leaned on Fatima's arm – but Esan Dawlat seemed vigorous as ever.

As soon as they were alone she took Babur's face between her hands and stared at him. 'You've become a man,' she nodded approvingly, releasing him. 'Look, daughter, your son has changed these past months – see how he has broadened.' She slapped his chest and poked at one of his upper arms as if inspecting a prize animal. 'Muscles like iron.'

Kutlugh Nigar gazed at him but said nothing. She had grown so silent – so different from the mentally strong woman who had determinedly guided his steps to the throne of Ferghana in the uncertain hours after his father's death – so less physically strong than when she'd purposefully swarmed up the mountains not two years previously.

'I've something to tell you both. When January comes I'm leaving Kabul to lead my army south towards Hindustan to try my fortune there. Baisanghar will be regent in my absence . . .'

As his words sank in, Esan Dawlat nodded her approval, but something stirred in Kutlugh Nigar. She rose from the gold brocade bolster against which she had been reclining and, shaking her head from side to side, seemed to be struggling to find words. It shocked Babur to see tears begin coursing down her cheeks – tears that she made no effort to brush away. Before his eyes her whole body began to shake and her hands to twist in her long dark hair, now streaked with white.

'Daughter . . .' Esan Dawlat's voice was stiff with disapproval.

Babur took his mother in his arms, trying to soothe her as if she were a small child and he the parent. 'What is it?'

'Khanzada – have you forgotten your promise, Babur? You promised you would rescue her. Why are you wasting time riding south . . .'

It hurt as much as if she'd struck him. He flushed as the familiar mix of shame, frustration and grief washed through him. 'She is always in my mind. I will keep that promise. But now is not the time. I must have more men, more money, before I can challenge Shaibani Khan. This raid may give me those things. But I swear to you that as soon as I can I will find Khanzada . . .'

At length his mother's sobbing quietened and her body stilled. Babur kissed the top of her head, but the turmoil she had provoked inside him would take a long time to die away . . .

In the weeks that followed, he tried to lose himself in the

282

preparations for the Hindustan campaign. He would take the same route – south-east along the Kabul river and down through the Khyber Pass – that Timur had used a century earlier.

In the brief time before the snows arrived, whitening the grassy meadows and softening the landscape so that it was hard to see where the mountains ended and the pale skies began, Baisanghar and Baburi trained the men – their own forces and new recruits from the local tribes. The tribesmen weren't bad . . . Babur watched them learn to fire from the saddle at straw targets and spear melons and sheep's heads on the ground as they thundered past . . . but who knew what awaited them?

On many a night Babur listened to travelling merchants regaling open-mouthed and credulous listeners with tales of exotic creatures – even monsters – lurking in Hindustan's forests of banyan trees, whose aerial roots would twist round the throat of an unwary traveller and squeeze the breath from him, of naked holy men, yogis, followers of their idolatrous religion with white ash on their faces who lived in dark caves and never cut their hair or beards. Childish nonsense, most of it . . . but he intended to be prepared.

It was a relief when January finally arrived. Though the snow still lay thick, the worst of the winter storms were over and they could ride.

Six days' steady advance – the pace set by the drummers' rhythmic beating – brought Babur and his two thousand men to the approaches to the Khyber Pass. But on the seventh day, with the sun at its height, leaching all colour from the increasingly barren landscape, Babur thought he detected a movement among some rocks on a low hill just ahead to the right. Signalling a halt he stared up.

'What is it?' As Baburi spoke a shower of scree skittered down the hillside.

'I don't know. I've posted men in a protective cordon all

round the column. How could ambushers have slipped through? Let's climb up and take a look . . .'

Babur jumped from his horse. 'Some of you, draw your bows and keep us covered,' he called to his bodyguards. 'The rest, come with us.'

A few minutes later, Babur looked around the bare, stony summit in disappointment. Nothing. Whatever it was, animal or human, must already have made off. Then from over the far edge he heard pebbles falling. Running across he saw a man in brown tunic and baggy trousers slithering frantically down a patch of scree to make his escape. Reaching for his bow, Babur took careful aim and sent an arrow hissing after him. The man screamed but disappeared into some rocky ground at the bottom of the hill.

With Baburi and his guards close behind, Babur leaped and skidded down the stony hillside after his quarry. Reaching the bottom he glimpsed the man half running, half staggering among the rocks, the arrow protruding from the muscle of his right arm, just below his shoulder. Summoning a burst of speed, Babur caught up with him and flung himself at him, bringing him down among the pebbles. Soon his bodyguard had caught up and pinioned the man.

Babur stood up, brushing the dust from his clothes. 'Who are you?'

'Pikhi, headman of the Gagianis . . .' the man gasped.

'What were you doing?'

Pikhi's eyes – elongated like a mountain cat's – flickered, but if he had thought of lying, he seemed to realise the futility. 'Watching your progress towards the pass.'

'And why would you do that?'

'There are Pathan tribes in the pass who will reward me and my people well for information about opportunities for plunder. Last year's harvest was bad and the winter has been hard . . . My people have never been rich but this year we will starve unless I seek booty.'

'I am a king leading an army . . . not a fat merchant with a camel train.'

'Shall I slit his throat?' Baburi drew his dagger, ready to inflict the habitual punishment on spies.

'No . . . I may have a better idea.'

Babur turned back to Pikhi, who seemed to have composed himself to meet his end as befitted a headman. 'You know these mountains well, and you want to live?'

'Yes to both, of course − after all I got through your cordon easily enough, didn't I?'

'In return for your life, you will send messengers to your allies in the pass telling them that I, Babur of Kabul, am passing through. Any tribe that attacks me will be annihilated . . . And you will be our guide. At the first sign of trouble, you die. Is that clear?'

Sparing Pikhi had been a wise move. In three long marches he had brought them through the barren, snow-dusted Khyber Pass with its jagged grey defiles. As they descended to the mud-brick settlement of Jam, the air was already warmer and three more days brought them to the Indus. Babur gazed at the broad river, so high with meltwater it was almost overflowing its banks. It formed the barrier between his world and the hot, mysterious lands of Hindustan . . .

'This is the Indus, then?' Baburi was beside him on a stocky gelding that, eager for a drink, was tossing its head impatiently.

'Yes.' As Babur stared at the swirling, eddying waters, some of his elation died. 'We can't cross here. Most of our animals and baggage would never make it . . . we'd lose everything. Send Pikhi to me. I must give our men at least some chance of booty.'

Ten minutes later the man was before him, brown felt cap in his hands.

'We cannot ford the river here. I must wait for the waters to fall or find a place where it will be safe to swim our animals across.'

Pikhi shrugged. 'The river is very high this year – it may be weeks before the flow reduces. Until then there is nowhere else to cross.'

'What about boats? Why are there no fishermen?'

'There were, Majesty, but hearing of your approach through the pass they fled in their boats . . .'

Babur swore. 'Where else can we raid on this side of the river while we wait for the waters to drop?'

'Two days' march from here is Kohat, a wealthy place with ample herds and grain.' Pikhi was looking sly. 'The inhabitants' clan is the blood enemy of mine. Last summer they raided my village in the mountains, killing our men, stealing our women and driving off our livestock. Any harm I can bring on them gives me only joy.'

'Lead us there and you'll have your freedom.'

• ◆ •

For the tenth time, Babur cursed himself for a fool. It was only late April but the heat was beyond anything he and his men had ever known, the air was moist with the promise of rains that, according to the local people, would soon begin to fall. They were all sweating beneath their armour.

True, the last weeks, raiding west through the hill country of the Afghan tribes and storming their fortified stone retreats – the *sangars* they built high in the mountains as carefully as an eagle constructs its nest – had been successful. The erection of a few towers of lopped-off heads had discouraged most opposition and at least ten chieftains had sworn their allegiance, crawling before Babur on all fours with grass between their teeth as was their custom. It meant, 'I am your cow. Do with me as you will.'

Yet all he had captured were sheep, cattle, sugar, aromatic

roots and countless bales of cloth. His men appeared satisfied but to Babur it seemed hardly worth the effort of bringing a couple of thousand men and countless pack-animals from Kabul. To his disappointment the Indus had not subsided until the time had passed when he could have crossed it and penetrated Hindustan. Subduing the peoples in the mountains and plains along its northern borders had been a poor substitute. Nevertheless, the expedition had achieved one purpose, Babur reflected, wiping sweat yet again from his forehead before it ran into his eyes. It had been useful in schooling his troops – and himself – for a greater enterprise.

Now he and his long line of men, the pack-ponies, donkeys and camels bringing up the rear, were curving north-westward along the Ghazni river towards the Sawaran Pass that would lead them back through the mountains. With God's help they should soon see Kabul again and feel the cool air from the high northern mountains on their chapped, sunburned skin. There, he could plan afresh.

'What is that?' Baburi's keen eyes had spotted something on the horizon. With the great orange sun setting right in their faces it was hard to see, but Babur looped his reins over the front of his saddle and shaded his face with both hands. He could see something too – a metallic sheen straight ahead, probably an effect of the light. But as they drew nearer he saw it was a great expanse of water that seemed to hang between earth and sky.

The surface of the water glowed with a reddish light that seemed to flash on and off. The reflection of the setting sun, perhaps? No . . . Babur heard Baburi gasp beside him as he, too, stared at the extraordinary sight. Thousand upon thousand of long-legged, red-feathered birds were beating their wings as they rose in flight, their bodies a streak of blood across the livid sky, terrible and beautiful at the same time.

Despite the heat, Babur shivered with excitement . . . These southern lands had not finished with him yet. Like the birds, he was leaving but, also like them, he would return and men would gasp at the spectacle.

Chapter 16

A Fortunate Birth

The summer heat had scorched the grass in the meadows beneath the citadel of Kabul to a golden brown and the ground beneath his weary horse's hoofs was baked hard. The level of the lake had fallen, leaving a crust of cracked mud streaked with dried green slime around the edge; the water smelled fetid. After an absence of nearly five months, though, his first thoughts were of his mother and grandmother, and the stories he wanted to tell them of his expedition to the borders of Hindustan. Ordering his commanders to pitch camp, unload the lines of pack-animals and post guards around the piles of plunder until it could be distributed, Babur cantered up the ramp into the citadel.

As he emerged through the shadowy gatehouse into the bright courtyard, the drummers on the battlements beat out the customary welcome to the returning king. Babur eased his feet out of the stirrups and grunted in satisfaction. It was good to be back. Then he saw Baisanghar hurrying to greet him. His face told Babur immediately that something was wrong. 'What is it, Baisanghar? What's happened?'

'Majesty, your mother is ill. She has what the people here

289

call the spotted fever, brought by merchants from the east. It caused an epidemic in the town, which spread here to the citadel to the women's quarters. The *hakim* has bled her but without result. Now he is treating her with the juice of watermelons to cool her blood, but he fears for her life . . . Two of her attendants have already died, one only a few hours ago.'

'When did the sickness start?'

'Nearly a week ago. She speaks of you constantly. I sent scouts to watch for your return but I had no idea from which direction you'd come – or when. God has been good to bring you home . . .'

A chilling numbness crept through Babur that seemed to paralyse his body and brain. Dazed, he slid from his horse, handed his reins to a groom and walked slowly across the courtyard and up the steps to the women's quarters. As he approached the tall silver-lined double doors, inlaid with dark blue lapis-lazuli, that led into his mother's apartments, his whole body was trembling and he felt sick.

Scenes from his boyhood flickered through his brain. Khanzada slapping him for tormenting her mongoose and Kutlugh Nigar reproving her. His mother setting the feathered velvet cap of Ferghana on his head and placing his father's sword, Alamgir, in his hand on the night the *khutba* was read in his name. But, above all, he saw the agony on her face when he had told her that Khanzada was to be given to Shaibani Khan. That had sapped the life from her long before the sickness had struck . . . Babur bowed his head in anguish.

As attendants swung the doors open, the close, heavy air of the sick chamber – sweat mingled with sandalwood and camphor – hit him. He caught the sad, sweet notes of a lute. As he entered he saw Esan Dawlat sitting by her daughter's bedside, her head bent low over her instrument. 'Grandmother . . .'

She looked up at his voice but completed the refrain she had been playing before handing the lute to a subdued, pinched-looking Fatima sitting just behind her. 'Music seems to soothe her. I was afraid you would be too late. The *hakim* says the crisis is near . . .'

Babur could see his mother lying with her eyes closed. Her face and what he could see of her neck were covered with raised angry red spots. There were even some swelling her eyelids. He stepped towards her, but Esan Dawlat waved him back. 'The fever is deadly – especially to the young.' Babur stared at her. He took another step forward but, with a speed almost unbelievable in a woman of her age, Esan Dawlat sprang up, rushed towards him and gripped his arms. 'The *hakim* is doing all he can, and so am I. We can only wait and hope. Will it help if you catch it too? The best thing you can do for your mother, and for me, is to survive.'

'But is there nothing I can do?'

'There is one thing. When your mother is conscious she says little. But in her delirium she says much. Again and again she has asked God why she has no grandchildren, why you have no heirs. Let me tell her you will marry again, that there will be children she can hold on her knee when she recovers. All she feels in her soul is despair, leaving her no strength to fight. I must give her something to hope for . . .'

'Tell her I will do anything she asks. Tell her she must recover so she can dance at my wedding feast and that there will be many grandchildren . . . Tell her I need her . . .'

Esan Dawlat scrutinised his face, then – satisfied – released him. 'Now go. I will send you word of her condition.'

Fighting back tears, Babur made his way to his own apartments. Esan Dawlat and his mother were right – he must face his responsibilities. Now that he was settled in Kabul it was high time to take another wife: his people would expect heirs and, of course, marriages cemented alliances. But that was irrelevant – if it would help his mother recover he'd take ten brides, twenty . . .

The next days passed slowly as Babur waited for news.

The reports were always the same – 'no change'. He had much to occupy him in the aftermath of his expedition. The tribal chieftains who had ridden with him were anxious for their share of the booty and he put Baburi in charge of working out the allocations. The court scribes were soon recording how many sheep and goats, how many bales of woollen cloth, how many sacks of grain were being doled out.

Babur also had his own men to think of. They must be rewarded with increases in ranks and titles, as well as shares of the plunder. He'd make Baburi his new quartermaster – the post had remained vacant since Ali Gosht's dismissal. That should tickle both that prickly pride of his and his sense of humour. But what could he do for Baisanghar, loyal for so long and who had governed Kabul well in his absence? If he had daughters or nieces it would be no shame for Babur to find a wife from among them. Baisanghar came from an ancient family in Samarkand and, if Babur ever returned there, it would please the citizens. The more he pondered the idea, the more pleased he became with it . . . He'd seldom heard Baisanghar speak of his family and certainly none had travelled with him from Samarkand, yet that didn't mean he had none. So why not ask him? Summoning Baisanghar to his private apartments, he went straight to the point. 'I owe you a great deal. From the moment you clapped me on the shoulder in Samarkand you've kept faith with me . . .'

'I have always kept faith with the House of Timur, Majesty, and always will.'

'That is why I have something to ask you. My mother wishes me to marry again soon. I have sworn to do so – even if she doesn't live to see it – and it would do me honour, Baisanghar, if I could take a woman of your house. That is all I wanted to say . . .'

Baisanghar looked stunned. It was the first time Babur had seen the cool-headed, unemotional, slightly humourless commander – a man who, despite the loss of his right hand, could hack his way with his left through a parcel of assailants and barely blink – at a loss.

'I have a daughter, Majesty, but I have seen nothing of her these last ten years. My wife died giving birth to her. After Shaibani Khan killed your uncle and Samarkand's future seemed so uncertain, I sent her to my cousin in Herat for safety. She is seventeen years old.'

'What is her name?'

'Maham, Majesty.'

'Will you send for her? Will you give her to me?'

'I will, Majesty.'

'I cannot make her my only wife. To build the alliances I need, I must marry others, but I will always treat her well, Baisanghar. I give you my word.'

• ◆ •

'Majesty, wake up.' At the feel of a hand on his shoulder, Babur reached instinctively for the dagger that he kept beneath his pillow but then he realised a female voice had roused him. Shading his eyes against the light of the candle the woman was holding, he saw Fatima's plain, round face.

This was an extraordinary breach of court etiquette – and of security. Then his heart almost stopped beating. Fatima must have come from his mother's chamber. He leaped from his bed, oblivious to his nakedness. 'What has happened? How is my mother . . . ?'

Fatima was crying but they were tears of joy, not grief. 'The crisis is finally over – the *hakim* says she will live.'

Babur closed his eyes for a moment, thanking God. Then, noticing Fatima's blushing confusion and that she was averting her eyes, he reached hastily for his robe. He ran along the narrow stone passageway, pushed the doorkeepers aside and burst through the silver doors into his mother's chamber. The grey-haired *hakim* clicked his tongue disapprovingly but

Babur didn't care. Esan Dawlat was wiping her daughter's face with a damp cloth and as she turned to greet him, he saw the relief in her eyes.

Then Babur looked at his mother. Her once smooth skin was cratered and puckered with circular red scars but her eyes were bright, and brighter still as they rested on him. She opened her arms and, flinging himself to the floor beside her, Babur let her embrace him, feeling the years roll back and deep relief flood through him.

◆

The cloud of dust billowing on the western horizon was huge as was to be expected with a caravan of more than five thousand camels and two thousand mules. Maham would be somewhere amid that great trudging throng. Though he had sent an escort to protect her on the journey eastward from Herat, he had decided that, for even greater safety, the party should join the caravan.

His bride should be here before nightfall. Her apartments, spread with rich carpets, hung with silks and scented with the finest rosewater and sandalwood, were prepared, together with his wedding gifts – not the heavy gold neck- and armlets he had once given Ayisha and that she had returned, but delicately worked chains and bracelets bright with gems, the choicest in his treasure houses. What would be going through Maham's mind? he wondered. Joy at being reunited with the father she had not seen for so many years? Apprehension about the husband she would shortly have . . . ?

Babur was again watching from the battlements as, just before sunset, with the sky glowing amber, the wedding party passed through the gates of Kabul's citadel into the courtyard. He saw Baisanghar eagerly approach the enclosed bullock cart in which his daughter and her women were travelling. He wished he, too, could see her, but he would have to wait for the wedding ceremony . . .

It took place a week later on a day deemed especially blessed by the court astrologers. He and Maham sat side by side beneath a velvet canopy while mullahs recited prayers for their happiness. She was concealed beneath layers of embroidered silk veils, the colour of blue duck eggs, flowing from beneath a cap of golden filigree worked with precious gems that trembled and sparkled when she moved her head – a gift from Kutlugh Nigar. As Babur took her hand to lead her to the wedding feast he sensed no hesitation, no reluctance, but a responsive tremor that sent erotic anticipation creeping through him.

That night, in the bridal chamber, he watched her attendants undress her. Baisanghar, reticent and unassuming as ever, had never told him his daughter was so beautiful – but as he hadn't seen her since she was a child how could he have known? Her oval face was dominated by huge chestnut eyes and her dark hair reached almost to the curve of her buttocks. Her body was small but rounded. As Babur took in the high, round breasts with their pearlescent sheen, the tapering waist, the delicate curve of her hips, he felt a possessive passion, a desire to protect at all costs. The thought that anyone might hurt her made him so angry that he had to remind himself it hadn't happened, would never happen – that he was there to look after her . . .

The following days seemed to pass as if time no longer existed. His couplings with Ayisha had blunted physical need but nothing more. Even his frolics with women like Yadgar, when he and Baburi had roamed the bazaars and brothels of Ferghana, had been no more than the taste of a good meal or the joy of the hunt – just a passing pleasure.

His grandmother had no need to urge him to Maham's bed, as she had once driven him to Ayisha's. However many times they made love, just to look at her with her hair tumbling over her breasts was enough to arouse him afresh, to pull her gently to him, run his hands over the silken curve

295

of her hips, feel her body's ready response and hear the quickening of her breathing, which told him she was as ready for passion as he was.

. ◆ .

'How is the bridegroom? I am surprised you don't need the *hakim*'s services — I've heard he has a good ointment for treating the burning and chafed private parts of newlyweds . . .'

'The bridegroom is well . . .'

'Is that all you have to say . . . ?' Baburi raised an eyebrow.

'Yes.' Even now, a month after his marriage, Babur felt reluctant to talk of his feelings for Maham, even to Baburi with whom he shared nearly everything. Instead he turned the subject to something else that was preoccupying him. 'I must take another wife, from among the nobility of Kabul. The citizens expect it and it will help bind them to me.'

'Who have you chosen?'

'I haven't. I've allowed my mother and grandmother to pick for me. They're been summoning suitable candidates to the royal women's apartments . . .'

'And looking them over on your behalf?'

'Exactly. And now they've decided. Last night my grandmother told me the name of the girl . . . But what about you, Baburi? Isn't it time you took a wife? Don't you want sons?'

'Since I was eight years old I've been alone . . . The thought of ties, of family, doesn't attract me. I like variety in my bed and the freedom it brings.'

'You can have as many wives as you want. You're a poor man no longer . . .'

'You don't understand. Family, heirs, dynasty — they are a natural part of your world. You see yourself as part of a story that began long ago and will continue long after you're dead but in which your role will always be remembered. I don't care whether people remember me. Why should they?'

'Surely every man wants to leave his mark on the world and be spoken of by his descendants with pride . . . that's not just something for kings . . .'

'Isn't it? People like me fade quickly out of history. We don't matter. Let me ask you something . . . What have you written about me in that diary of yours . . . ? Have you even mentioned me recently?' Baburi's dark blue eyes flickered.

Suddenly Babur realised that this was not about fame, glory and kingly destiny. It was simpler than that. Baburi was jealous. He was used to being Babur's closest companion, his confidant, the one person from whom Babur kept nothing. Babur's passion for Maham had changed that. If he was honest, he had hardly given Baburi a thought these past weeks, and Baburi − grown man, tried and tested warrior though he was − was hurt. Something of the vulnerable market boy, fighting for scraps and confronting life with his fists, still lurked beneath the swaggering, cocksure exterior.

Long ago Wazir Khan had warned him against his growing intimacy with Baburi and had admitted his own jealousy, his own sense of exclusion. Babur found himself repeating almost the same words he had used to salve Wazir Khan's wounded pride. 'You are among the foremost of my *ichkis*, my closest, most trusted adviser and my friend. Never forget that.' He touched Baburi's shoulder.

Baburi looked at his hand but didn't twist aside. It was like taming a stallion, Babur thought. Something of the wildness always remained, despite the passing of the years. But a softening in Baburi's expression told Babur that his words had found their mark. 'So, tell me about this next bride of yours. Who is she?' Baburi said, after a moment.

'Bahlul Ayyub's granddaughter, Gulrukh. She is nineteen and, my grandmother informs me, strong enough to bear me many sons.'

'So that old fool of a grand vizier will be your father-in-law.'

'Yes.'

'So he'll have even more op-op-opportunity to p-p-prose on and you'll have even less excuse not to l-l-listen.'

'He comes from an ancient family. His ancestor was grand vizier when Timur's army passed through.'

'That explains why Timur didn't stay long. What does she look like?'

Babur shrugged. 'Gulrukh? I've not seen her. When the time comes I'll do my duty by her, but Maham will always have first place among my wives . . .'

On a cold March evening in 1508, Babur was on the citadel's battlements. His breath rose in frosty spirals and he pulled his fur-lined robes tightly round him. The skies above Kabul – as so often at this season – were clear and the stars shone with such brilliance it almost hurt to look at them. An hour ago, he had been standing in this exact spot with his astrologer gazing skywards with him. 'If the child is born tonight, while we are in Pisces, it will bring good fortune on your house,' the old man had said, mottled hands shaking with cold as they clutched his bundle of charts.

Babur had dismissed him and all of his attendants – even Baburi. Until he knew what had happened he wanted to be alone. At least up here he was unable to hear Maham's agonised screams . . . She had been in labour now for fifteen hours. It had taken every ounce of his self-control not to rush to her bedside but it was no fit place for a man. His grandmother had shouted at him to go away and leave matters to the women. He had caught only a glimpse of Maham's face, contorted with pain, running with sweat, her lip bleeding where she had bitten it, before the great doors had been closed firmly in his face.

'It doesn't matter whether it's a boy or a girl – but let Maham live,' he found himself praying. 'And if any must die let it be the child, not her . . .' The *hakims* had been warning for days that the child was large – perhaps too large for Maham's slight frame.

Gulrukh, too, was pregnant. Her child would not come for another five months yet already she had swelled up like a watermelon and looked healthy and well. But pregnancy had only made Maham ill. She had found it difficult to eat and instead of blooming like Gulrukh, her face had grown pinched. Circles dark as bruises were etched in the delicate skin beneath her long-lashed eyes.

Baisanghar, too, had been watching Maham anxiously. She was his only surviving child. These would be difficult hours for him . . .

'Majesty . . . come quickly . . .' The woman, one of Maham's attendants, was panting and finding it hard to summon enough breath to speak. She put an arm against the stone door frame through which she'd emerged to steady herself. Babur felt as if he was viewing the scene from far away . . . 'You have a son, Majesty . . .'

'What did you say . . . ?'

'Her Majesty, your wife, has borne you a son . . . She ordered me to find you – to tell you all is well . . .'

'And my wife . . . how is she?'

'She is exhausted but she is asking for you.' For the first time the woman looked at him, and, perhaps because she saw an anxious father rather than a king, she shed her nervousness and smiled. 'All is well, Majesty, truly, and you can go to her.'

She disappeared back down the twisting staircase towards the women's quarters, but he didn't follow her immediately. For just a few moments he raised his face to the cold, pure sky above, seeking Canopus, the sign of fortune. It had surely guided his steps from the moment he saw it beaming, beaconlike, beyond the snowy passes of the Hindu Kush. There it was now, shining brightly. Babur gave silent thanks.

· ◆ ·

As the mullahs in their black robes and high white turbans finished chanting their prayers, Babur showered tiny silver and gold coins from a jade saucer over the head of his five-day-old son, lying naked on a blue velvet cushion in Baisanghar's arms.

'You are my first-born, my beloved son. I name you Humayun, Fortunate One. May your life be fortunate and may you bring honour and glory to our house.' The tenderness he felt as he looked into his son's wrinkled little face was like nothing he'd ever known. He'd wanted a son – many sons – to carry the blood line down through the generations, but he had never thought of what fatherhood would mean to him. It was good he had no formal speeches to make – he might not be able to hold his voice steady or keep back the tears welling in his eyes.

Humayun's voice rose in a thin wail as Babur handed the empty saucer to Baburi at his side. Lifting the child from the cushion, he held him high so that all his courtiers, all his chiefs, could see him and acknowledge their new prince.

Maham, though still weak, his mother and grandmother would be watching through the carved marble grille high in the wall to the right of the royal dais in Babur's audience hall. They would have seen him acknowledging the traditional gifts – silver coins signifying good luck, silks, horses and hunting dogs from the wealthier nobles, sheep and goats brought by the tribal leaders.

The feasting and celebrations would last late into the night, long after Humayun had been returned to the care of Maham and his wet-nurse, a bright-eyed young woman who had recently weaned her own son. To be wet-nurse to a Timurid prince was a great honour and the position was eagerly sought. She would guard her new charge well.

Gusts of male laughter roused him from his thoughts. Back on the blue cushion that Baisanghar was still holding, a vigorously wriggling Humayun had unleashed an arc of yellow urine.

'So may he piss on all our enemies!' Babur shouted, amid the general mirth, but he had something else to say. He had not planned to do it now, in this way, but something – a new resolve – was driving him on. He signalled for silence.

'You have come here today to honour my son, to honour my house – the House of Timur. The time has come for me to claim Timur's title of Padishah, Lord of the World. I, with my son Humayun and my sons yet to be born, will prove myself worthy of it, and all who support me will share the glory.'

Chapter 17

Daughter of Genghis

Six months later Babur sat, face impassive, on his gilded throne, his courtiers erect and motionless around him, as Baburi lowered the sack to the ground before him.

'Show them.'

Taking his dagger from his blue sash, Baburi slit the sack to reveal the contents: two heads, blood encrusted and mottled purple-black with weeping putrescence. The stench of decay – sweet and rotten to the point of nausea – filled the room. The ragged flesh where a blade had roughly hacked through the base of the neck suggested that death had not come easily to the two men. The once handsome features of Sayyidim, the young cup-bearer whom Babur had helped hold down while his frost-bitten hand had been amputated, were only just recognisable in his bloated face. His bursting lips were pulled back to reveal gums suppurating pus above still perfect white teeth. As for the other head, Babur had not even recognised the man – one of Baisanghar's lieutenants – but his death, like Sayyidim's, would be avenged.

The dead men's task had been to take a letter from Babur to the King of Khorasan, his distant relation, at his court in

Herat. Merchants arriving with the biggest caravan to reach Kabul that season had reported that, beyond the Hindu Kush, Shaibani Khan was on the move again at the head of a vast army. Some said his target was wealthy Khorasan, west of Kabul, others that it was Kabul itself. Babur's letter to the king had been a warning but also a suggestion for their alliance. Except that the letter had never arrived . . .

Baburi had come upon the messengers' fate by chance during a routine raid against a clan of sheep-rustling Kafirs. While searching the mud-brick huts of their remote village he had found the messengers' heads in a large clay pot under a buzzing cloud of green-black flies. The heads of their ten-man military escort were nearby. From the account Baburi choked out of the headman, the Kafirs had tortured them for no reason other than sadistic pleasure. Some had had their tongues cut out, but even more appalling was what had they done to one messenger who had been slashed in the abdomen during the fight in which they were captured. The Kafirs had put their hands into the wound and pulled out part of his intestine and, as he screamed out, tied it to a post and then made the man dance around it, unravelling his intestines as he went until at last death had mercifully ended his sufferings.

Baburi, resisting the temptation for instant vengeance, had bound the headman's ankles to his wrists behind his back and rounded up all the other Kafirs he could find to bring back to the citadel in Kabul. The convoy had arrived just a few hours earlier and in the dungeons beneath the citadel it hadn't taken long to force from them a confession of who had bribed them to carry out such a barbarous act.

Babur addressed his courtiers in a flat, dispassionate voice. 'I asked you to assemble here before me to hear proof of an act of treason. These heads belong to my messengers to the King of Khorasan. They were murdered on the orders of a man of my blood, a man I trusted . . . Bring him in.'

A gasp went up as Mirza Khan was led into the room

surrounded by guards. In deference to his rank as a descendant of Timur he was not bound. There was nothing humble or fearful in his demeanour or his clothes: a heavy enamelled chain hung round his neck and his tunic of purple silk was secured about his stout body with a yellow sash woven with pearls. His expression was insolent.

Glancing briefly at the two rotting heads as if they were no more than a speck of dirt on his red riding boots Mirza Khan touched his hand to his breast but said nothing.

'The men who murdered my messengers – Kafirs from the mountains – have confessed to their crime. They name you as the instigator . . .'

'Any one of us, never mind villains, will say anything under torture . . .'

'Sometimes even the truth . . . They say you paid them to seize the messengers – one of them once your own cup-bearer – as they entered the Shibartu Pass and to steal the letter they were carrying to the King of Khorasan. You also told them they could do as they liked with the prisoners, provided their disposal was permanent. In their stupidity they kept their heads as proof of this . . .'

Mirza Khan shrugged. 'Kafirs are known for their lies and deceit . . .'

'My quartermaster found this among their miserable possessions.' An attendant passed Babur a shabby little bag of flowered silk. Untying the cord at its neck, Babur pulled out a small plug of ivory with a piece of onyx set into its base. 'Your seal, Mirza Khan. The craftsmen who inscribed your name did a good job – see how clearly your name and titles stand out. You were a fool to send a token like that to your hirelings, but I always knew you had manure for brains . . .'

It was good to see Mirza Khan's fear beginning to show. Sweat was running down his face into his perfumed beard and dark stains were spreading visibly into the purple silk beneath his armpits.

305

'What I don't understand is why you did it.'

Mirza Khan dabbed at his face briefly with a lilac handkerchief but remained silent.

'If you don't speak I'll have you tortured.'

'You can't – I'm of Timur's house, your own cousin.'

'I can and I will. You forfeited your rights when you betrayed me.' Babur's cold words seemed to crush the insolence from Mirza Khan. The screws were twisting now.

'Majesty . . .' It was the first time Mirza Khan had addressed him so. 'I had no choice – I was forced to act as I did . . .'

'A man always has a choice. For whom were you acting?'

Mirza Khan suddenly began to retch. A thin trail of yellowish vomit spewed from the corner of his mouth, staining the purple silk of his tunic. He wiped it away, raised his head and looked piteously at Babur. 'Remember, we share the same blood . . .'

'I do remember, and I am ashamed of it. Once more, who is your paymaster?'

Mirza Khan looked as if he was about to vomit again, but he swallowed hard and mumbled something.

'Speak up.'

'Shaibani Khan.'

Babur stared. Then he jumped down from his dais and advanced on Mirza Khan, shook him by his shoulders and yelled into his face, 'You have betrayed me to Shaibani Khan, that Uzbek barbarian – the enemy of all our house?'

'He promised to return my lands that he had captured. He promised me honour again instead of being a hanger-on at your court. I warned him you were proposing an alliance with Khorasan. He wished to stop it. He plans to attack Khorasan and then you, Majesty. Let me be your spy now, Majesty . . . Shaibani Khan trusts me. I will send him whatever messages you wish . . . perhaps we can lure him into a trap.'

To Babur, the man's oily wheedling was as repulsive as the sour stench of vomit on his breath. He let go of him and stepped back. 'Take this traitor and throw him head first from the battlements. If that fails to kill him, throw him down again. Then take his body to the dunghill in the marketplace so the mongrels that scavenge there can devour it.'

'Majesty, please . . .' Warm, yellow urine was seeping down on to the soft red leather of Mirza Khan's boots, slowly forming a small pool on the stone floor. Suddenly he vomited again, and a new smell told Babur that Mirza Khan had also lost control of his bowels.

'Take him!' Babur shouted to the guards. 'See that my orders are carried out at once.'

An hour later, Babur rode out to observe the execution of the Kafirs. So brutal had been their treatment of his men that he had ordered them to suffer a long-established punishment for the worst of traitors. They were to be impaled on sharpened stakes beneath the city walls. Their cries would not reach as far as the citadel. He was glad. Their agonised shrieking was not for the ears of Maham, Kutlugh Nigar or his grandmother although, now he thought about it, Esan Dawlat could probably have observed the whole process without flinching – as he would.

His contempt for Mirza Khan, his anger with the Kafirs for their mindless bestiality, banished any pity. He watched as the condemned men were roughly stripped of their clothes and dragged to where the stakes waited. The executioners, wearing black leather aprons over their tunics – red as the blood that would soon soak them – seized and impaled the prisoners one by one. Some had the sharp stakes driven up through their anuses. Others were spitted sideways to roars of encouragement from the townspeople. Not that Babur could condemn them – he felt nothing but satisfaction every time a sharpened stake penetrated the soft flesh of a writhing body and the warm blood spurted. He would have liked to give Mirza Khan the same treatment – only his royal birth had saved him.

That night Babur found it hard to lift his mood. Even the sight of Humayun and his new brother Kamran, with his mop of dark hair, soft as a dandelion seed head – born two months ago to Gulrukh and already gripping Babur's thumb hard – failed to cheer him. Neither could the feel and scent of Maham's warm, willing body stifle his forebodings. The storm was coming whether he was ready or not. The decisions he must soon take would be the difference between glorious victory and immortal fame or defeat and obscure death not only for him but for all of his family . . .

•◆•

A month later, the precariousness of existence was brought home to Babur in a way he had not anticipated. Esan Dawlat's body on the bier seemed as small as a child's. The delicate tang of the camphor water in which her women had washed her rose from her simple cotton shroud. As he looked down on his grandmother's body, Babur didn't conceal his tears. Somehow he had always taken her strength and determination for granted. The idea that she could die suddenly in her sleep, without uttering a final word – a command, a piece of shrewd advice – was absurd. But as he thought back over the past months, he realised now that there had been signs – vagueness, and an uncertainty and a tendency to fuss that she had never shown before. Her memory had sometimes seemed confused – she would speak to Babur with perfect clarity about his boyhood but if he asked her what she'd been doing yesterday her face would cloud.

Life without her seemed unthinkable. In their most desperate days, she had been the lynchpin of the family, the voice of reason and common sense but, above all, of courage. Soon he must face the biggest challenge of his life without her. He recollected some of her words to him in his youth: 'Have no fear of your ambitions. Stare them in the face, fulfil them. Remember, nothing is impossible . . .'

At a signal from Babur, three of his grandmother's favourite attendants – dressed, like him, in the black robes of mourning – bent down and, with Babur, each took a corner of the bier. Hoisting it on to their shoulders, they carried it slowly down the dark, winding stone staircase from her apartments – the sound of sobbing, led by Kutlugh Nigar, rising behind them – across the sunlit courtyard and laid it on the flat, horse-drawn wagon draped with bright crimson cloth. It was the red that Esan Dawlat had always claimed was the colour of the ancestor she revered: Genghis Khan.

Followed by his mullahs, courtiers and commanders, Babur walked behind the cart as it carried Esan Dawlat on her final journey. With his mother's consent he had decided to bury her in his hillside garden among the fruit, flowers and tumbling watercourses. When she had been laid to rest in the dark, fertile earth and the final prayers for the repose of her soul in Paradise had been intoned, he turned to the mourners. 'She was a true daughter of Genghis. Her bravery never failed her. She believed to despair was a sin. I will never forget her and one day, when I have overcome my enemies, I will return to this spot to tell her what I have done and to ask her blessing.'

· ◆ ·

At least Esan Dawlat had died without knowing the terrible calamity that had befallen their royal relations in Herat, Babur thought, a few weeks later, as he tried to take in what Baisanghar was telling him.

'It is true, Majesty. Herat has fallen to the Uzbeks. Shaibani Khan swept down around the slopes of Mount Mukhtar with thirty thousand warriors. The royal family fled into the Ala Qorghan fortress but the reinforcements summoned by the king were cut down before they could reach them.'

'What happened to the family?'

Baisanghar bit his lip. 'Shaibani Khan laid siege to the fortress and tunnelled under the walls from the horse market adjoining it, causing part of them to collapse. The Uzbeks surged in. They killed every male member of the royal family down to the smallest son. Shaibani Khan himself seized the child's ankles and smashed his head against the stone side of one of the royal tombs, spilling his brains, then tossed him aside on to the corpses of his family. He ordered the fortress to be burned down with the bodies still inside . . .'

'And what of the women?'

'They say those found hiding in the Ala Qorghan fortress – whether young virgins or bent grandmothers – were forced to strip and dance naked before their drunken conquerors at the victory feast, that the Uzbek chiefs fought among themselves over who was to have the most beautiful, and that some could not wait for the feast to end before publicly sating their lust.'

Babur's hands were clenched so tightly that his knuckles seemed ready to burst through the skin. 'What about Herat?'

A look of anguish crossed Baisanghar's usually calm face. 'The Uzbeks sacked it. Ordinary men were slaughtered, their wives raped and their children sold into slavery. My cousin, who cared for Maham, was slain. Shaibani Khan has also turned on the city's teachers and writers. The caravan that arrived here today brought a few lucky survivors from the *madrasas* of Herat. One – a poet – says all the manuscripts in the libraries were ripped up and Shaibani Khan ordered some of the scraps to be rammed down the throat of a scholar he caught until he choked while continually asking him, "How does it feel to live on a diet of poetry?"'

Though repelled by Baisanghar's report, Babur wasn't surprised. From the moment he'd learned his messengers had been intercepted he'd known it couldn't be long. What would have happened if his warning had reached his relatives in Herat? Their cultured, exquisite world of airy palaces, ancient mosques and *madrasas*, tucked away to the west, had been ripped apart by a whirlwind. Babur's father had sometimes talked of these distant relations, so far away he had never visited them. He had mocked their love of luxury and their obsession with beauty, their lack of manly aggression and fighting skills, and had derided their effete, cultured court where a writer was more prized than a warrior and poets eulogised not victory in battle but the succulence of a well-roasted goose or the joy of drinking the wine they called 'the water of life'.

But had they really been so foolish? Babur wondered. They had preserved their charmed existence until now. It was a shock to realise that with Samarkand, Ferghana, Kunduz and Khorasan all beneath the Uzbek yoke, he was now the only Timurid ruler left alive. It was a great responsibility, a sacred trust. Whatever the condition of his army, whatever the state of his supplies, before long he must march out against Shaibani Khan to defend what was left of Timur's world or die in the attempt.

The reports of the Uzbek mistreatment of the royal family, particularly of the women — probably true though they had a certain formulaic quality — yet again concentrated his thoughts painfully on Khanzada. Was she still alive? He had long comforted himself that she was more useful to the Uzbek as a live bargaining counter than dead. That was the argument he advanced time and again to put heart into his mother. With her own mother dead, now more than ever Kutlugh Nigar needed to believe that she would see Khanzada again. He could never share with her his darker thoughts — that Shaibani Khan's desire to avenge the abuses he had suffered as a boy in Samarkand was unabated, that he seemed to glory in humilating others and might particularly relish debasing a Timurid princess.

'Majesty . . .' Baisanghar's anxious voice interrupted his bleak thoughts.

Babur drew himself up. 'I'm not going to wait for Shaibani Khan to bring his army to Kabul. In a week's time we ride against him with whatever forces we can muster. How many troops do we have already?'

'About eight thousand.'

It was nothing compared with the size of the Uzbek horde but what had Esan Dawlat always said?: 'Never despair while you still breathe.'

'I must bring forward the plans I have long been forming to oppose Shaibani Khan once more. Send messengers at once – tonight – to all the tribes, even the Kafirs. Tell them that any who come will be free of all levies on grain and livestock for five years and that I will pay them well. Tell them what has happened in Herat and remind them that Shaibani Khan is the enemy of us all. He destroys anyone who is not an Uzbek . . .'

That night, with only Baburi for company, Babur climbed up to the battlements. It was one of his favourite places and usually brought him peace. In the meadows below, cooking fires glowed red in the darkness as shepherds and travelling merchants prepared their evening meal. Babur could hear voices calling and laughing, the bleating of sheep and the coughing of camels. Beyond, Kabul lay quiet within its girdle of walls. What was going through the citizens' minds? The caravan trains pouring into the city from the west must be bringing as many rumours as trade goods. The people must know of the catastrophe that had overtaken Khorasan and that Shaibani Khan would soon be moving in their direction.

Baburi, too, was sombre.

'What are you thinking?' Babur was curious.

'I was wondering where we'll both be a month, maybe a year from now . . .'

'You mean you're wondering whether we'll still be alive?'

'Partly, but also what will have happened.'

'Are you afraid?'

'I'm not sure – that's another thing I was thinking about . . . Are you?'

It was Babur's turn to ponder. 'No, I'm not afraid. I'm anxious but that's not the same thing. I'm worried what will happen to my family. The world I was born into – the world my father and his father knew – is changing. These past years, since I lost Ferghana, I have been a wanderer. Even here, though I am a king again, all I have, all I am, is trembling in the balance. If I cannot defeat Shaibani Khan, everything I've ever done will have been pointless and everything I want preserved will be swept away . . .'

'You're worried no one will remember you?'

'No, it's more than that. I worry that I won't deserve to be remembered . . .'

It was so dark now that Babur couldn't see Baburi's face but he felt him gently lay a hand on his shoulder – a rare gesture that did something to lessen his sense of an awesome burden. Baburi was reminding him that in the coming conflict he wouldn't be alone . . .

· ◆ ·

Babur brushed the sweat from his face and slipped his feet out of the stirrups to stretch his legs. They'd been riding for six long days now, their pace inevitably slowed by the cumbersome baggage train carrying their equipment. Soon, though, they should be approaching the Shibartu Pass that would take them westward over the mountains towards Khorasan. Once across the pass, they would enter territories where they might encounter Uzbek raiding parties . . . but he must be patient. There was no way he could tackle Shaibani Khan head-on in a pitched battle. He must build confidence among his troops and win new allies by successes gained using the tactics of his adolescent days as a hit-and-run raider from the hills. He must ambush enemy columns and disappear before they could concentrate their forces against him. He must capture isolated fortresses and use the booty and weapons within to win more adherents until

313

gradually he became strong enough to take on large formations of Shaibani Khan's men.

Reining in his grey horse, Babur called a halt. They would camp for the night on this steep, grassy hillside, with a commanding view that ensured their safety from ambush. He summoned his military council. They were an ill-assorted group – many just tribal leaders in lambskin jackets whose rule over a mud-brick settlement or two entitled them to sit alongside seasoned commanders like Baisanghar. With fewer than ten thousand troops he needed every man willing to ride with him, even unruly tribesmen. And he needed them to believe in him, despite the odds they were facing.

'In a few days we'll be over the pass. With luck, those Uzbek devils won't be expecting us. That's our strength. They'll think we're meekly awaiting our fate in Kabul, like lambs in the butcher's pen. Until our scouts and spies can tell us more, it's too risky to advance to Herat itself. But we are warriors of the hills and mountains, we have the cunning of the wolf who doesn't rush blindly among the herds of deer but waits, hidden, knowing that if he is patient he can sink his fangs into the flanks of a straggler and taste blood . . . The wolf's way must be ours. So, tell your men to keep their weapons sharpened and oiled and to stay alert.'

The nodding of heads and exchange of glances showed him his words had met their mark. 'And remember the words of the Holy Book:"With God's help, many a small force has defeated a large one."'

• ◆ •

'About four hundred Uzbeks, Majesty, just three or four miles away on the far banks of a river. It looked like they were preparing to ford, spreading the baggage more equally between the horses and pack-animals to swim them over . . . If we're quick we can attack while they're still crossing . . .' The scout

314

was breathing hard and the coat of his chestnut gelding was damp with sweat.

Babur grinned at Baburi and Baisanghar. At last, after two weeks of edging westward, of keeping beneath the cover of the dense forests that clothed the hills, there was a chance of action. The Uzbeks would be preoccupied, securing their shields to their backs and wrapping their bows and quivers to keep them dry. And their other weapons – swords, daggers and throwing axes – would be useless to them in the water.

'Baisanghar, assemble the advance guard.' With Baisanghar's advice, Babur had selected five hundred of his best warriors and divided them into groups of fifty, each under its own commander. They would be more than enough to deal with an Uzbek raiding party. The rest of the army and the baggage could stay where it was unless reinforcements were needed.

Ten minutes later, with the scout on a fresh horse beside him, Babur set out with the vanguard along a sheep track leading through softly rolling, clover-clad hills towards the river. Luckily it had rained in the night and the spongy ground would make it harder for listening ears to detect the thud of galloping hoofs. Even so, it was good the scout was taking them to a point a few hundred yards upstream from the Uzbeks where a sharp ox-bow bend beyond a plantation of willows should conceal their approach.

Babur glanced down at the steel breastplate expertly made for him in the foundries of Kabul. His coat of light chain-mail fitted well and his sword Alamgir was at his side. He was ready. The emotions surging up inside him made him want to yell his head off, though he knew he couldn't . . . not yet anyway . . .

Two miles further on and the track was broadening out – Babur's men could ride six abreast now – but there was less cover. Babur frowned, conferred briefly with the scout, then raised his hand to halt his men and summoned the youth he had recently chosen as his *qorchi*, his squire.

'Ride quickly down the column. Tell my commanders to keep their men at a trot, bows and quivers ready and their mouths shut. When we're almost at the bend in the river we'll halt and I'll send the scout ahead. If he reports that the Uzbeks are not yet across, we charge. Do you understand?' The boy nodded and cantered off.

Babur's heart beat to a thunderous rhythm as they set off again. His senses felt unnaturally acute – he noticed the spiky black hairs on the body of a caterpillar wriggling along a blade of grass and the soft, purple-pink breast of a wood pigeon startled from the tree where it had been resting. The smell of sweat – his own and his horse's and from the men and animals around him – seemed to rise in a pungent elemental cloud, the essence of life itself. Perhaps a man never felt so alive as when he was about to be in the presence of death.

'Majesty, you should halt here while I reconnoitre,' said the scout.

Two hundred yards ahead, Babur caught the gleam of water through the trailing feathery branches of some fine old willows. 'Very well. Be quick.'

'Yes, Maj—' The scout got no further as a black-feathered Uzbek arrow pierced his cheek and a second tore into his throat. A third thudded harmlessly into the ground. As the blood bubbled out, the man's eyes glazed and he tumbled from his horse, one foot still caught in his stirrup.

As cries to take cover rose around him, Babur flung himself low over his horse's neck expecting at any moment to feel the cold tip of an arrow embed itself in his flesh. Gripping his reins in his left hand, with his right he reached round to grab his metal-bound leather shield and hold it over his head for protection. But no more arrows came. Babur cautiously raised himself. To his left, through the swaying golden willows – the direction from which the arrows had come – he saw a trio of Uzbek horsemen making off along the bank towards the point at which the river took its sharp turn.

Perhaps they were scouts spying out the land while the others were still crossing. He mustn't give them time to get back and raise the alarm. Kicking his horse, Babur threw back his head and yelled the order to charge.

The willow branches whipped his face as he burst through and he tasted blood from a cut in his lip. Reaching the wide bank, he saw the Uzbeks disappearing round the bend and cursed. Taking an arrow from his quiver and pulling his bow off his shoulder, he dropped his reins. Half standing in his stirrups and holding his horse steady with his knees, he fitted the arrow to the string and pulled it back. It sped straight and fast, embedding itself in the rump of one of the Uzbek horses. Babur heard its whinny of pain and watched it skitter sideways into the river, taking its rider with it. Baburi had also fired but the other two Uzbeks had vanished.

As Babur and his close-packed riders thundered round the sharp curve, turf flying up, his heart leaped. The two surviving Uzbek riders were yelling and gesticulating but few of their comrades had noticed. A small group, still on the far bank, had seen that something was wrong and were running for their weapons but most were in the water, concentrating on getting themselves and their animals across the fast-flowing river.

Only a handful of sodden, shivering men had already reached the bank. Babur and his troops fired a first volley of arrows from the saddle, felling many. Then Babur gave the order to dismount and to maintain a steady fire of arrows from the cover of trees and rocks. Even on the far bank some Uzbeks were falling to the ground while in the blood-flecked river the bodies of dead and dying men and animals were forming a solid, tangled mass that even the current could barely shift.

'Majesty!' Baburi's clear voice rang out above the screams and groans.

317

Babur glanced round just in time to see one of the two mounted Uzbeks, whose existence he'd completely forgotten, galloping towards him. Something bright gleamed in his hand – an axe. The man threw back his arm and sent it whirling towards Babur with such force that he could almost hear the air whisper as it parted. Babur leaped sideways as the axe flew past his right ear to stick in the mud behind him.

Grunting he turned, yanked it out and weighed it in his hand – it felt good, well balanced. The Uzbek was only a few yards away now, curved sword in hand and determination on his face beneath his pointed steel helmet as he bent low in the saddle. Baburi rushed forward.

'No – I want him,' Babur yelled. Dropping his bow he stood, the axe in his right hand, waiting, judging the moment. With the man just a few paces from him, Babur threw it. The shaft – not the blade – smashed into the warrior's face, pulping his nose, but he was still in the saddle. Babur felt the hot breath of the man's snorting horse as the Uzbek bore down on him. Throwing himself forward, Babur grabbed the rider's left leg just above the knee. The rings of his chain-mail tore the flesh of Babur's fingers but it only made him hold on tighter and pull harder. The Uzbek, blood streaming from his shattered nose, fell sprawling on the ground but rolled clear of his horse's thrashing hoofs and sprang up.

He and Babur faced one another, balancing on the balls of their feet like wrestlers, watching for the chance to make the first move. If the blood-smeared Uzbek felt any pain he wasn't showing it. His cold eyes were narrowed, weighing up his opponent. Babur was wearing nothing to denote him as a king – the Uzbek was just sizing him up warrior to warrior.

Dagger in his left hand now and Alamgir in the right, Babur darted forward in a feint, then jumped back nimbly as the Uzbek lunged. Circling his opponent, Babur tried the same trick a second, then a third time. Each time the Uzbek reacted, slashing with his sword only to have Babur skip teasingly away. Muscles tensed, Babur jumped forward for the fourth time. The Uzbek hesitated, convinced that Babur was still playing with him – that he wouldn't follow through. But this time, instead of leaping away, Babur lashed at the man's exposed throat with his sword and kicked his right foot hard into his groin. The Uzbek slid to his knees, hands between his thighs, blood pouring from his throat.

But as Babur stepped forward to finish him off, his right foot slipped on the sticky clay of the riverbank and he crashed down, dropping his dagger and trapping his sword beneath him. The wounded Uzbek saw his chance of reprieve. Pulling himself upright, he recovered his sword and lunged forward. Babur raised his left arm to protect himself and immediately felt a stinging pain. Glancing down, he saw blood pouring from a deep cut in his lower forearm and running down so that his left hand was scarlet and dripping.

Instinctively, he struggled to his feet and, as he did so, twisted away from the Uzbek who, weak from his own wound, reacted slowly. Freeing Alamgir, Babur drove the sword with all his force through the man's throat and out through the back of his neck. Blood from a severed artery spurted over Babur, mingling with his own.

Looking around, Babur saw the fight was over. The Uzbeks were either dead or had fled. Holding his left hand high above his head to lessen the blood flow, with his right he untied a cotton cloth from round his neck and handed it to Baburi. Then lowering his left arm, which he already felt to be stiffening, he extended it towards him. 'Bind it tightly . . . We may need to fight again today . . .'

The euphoria was already leaving him – but why? Perhaps because to Shaibani Khan the death of upwards of three hundred of his men would be no more than a mosquito bite in the night . . . Babur would still have to ride a long, hard road before this was over . . .

319

Chapter 18

The Wine Cup

Babur breathed in the familiar smells – the acrid smoky scent rising from the twigs and animal dung of campfires, the aroma of fat lamb roasting on spits and of flat bread baking on hot stones. All around him, in the gathering darkness, his men were cleaning and oiling their weapons, laughing, cooking, pissing, enjoying the rest after the weeks of skirmishing. It was good to know that his force had swelled to at least sixteen thousand. Every day men driven out by the Uzbeks were joining him.

But they couldn't stay much longer in these sweet grasslands, deep in the mountains of Gharjistan, twelve days' ride east of Herat. According to reports picked up by Babur's scouts, Shaibani Khan had quit the city some weeks ago. The accounts were vague and the exact timing of his departure was unclear but all seemed to suggest that he had ridden out through the Qipchaq Gate at the head of a large force and had appeared to be heading north-west. Could it be a device to tempt Babur on to Herat, apparently left only lightly garrisoned? Or was Shaibani Khan planning to sweep north-east to outflank Babur? The Uzbek leader would know by now that Babur had led an army westward from Kabul. He'd also know that if he could take Babur's force by surprise he'd crush it easily. Or perhaps he was bypassing Babur. Perhaps even now he was leading his Uzbek barbarians through the mountains north towards Babur's capital, Kabul.

Babur stared deep into the glowing charcoal in the metal brazier outside his tent. The lack of definite news in recent days seemed ominous . . . It was as though Shaibani Khan had vanished . . . He stretched his hands over the heat, frowning at the stiffness he still felt in moving his left wrist. The wound to his forearm was healing cleanly and well – thanks to his *hakim* – but the cut had gone deep and the flesh round it was numb. The loss of suppleness made him impatient: it was his dagger arm and he needed it.

That night, images of Shaibani Khan again stalked his mind and Babur hardly slept. As the pewtery dawn light seeped into his hide tent he was still turning restlessly when he became aware of excited shouting and raised voices coming from some way off at the perimeter of the camp. Tossing back his coverlet he leaped up and threw open the flaps to his tent.

'Find out what that noise is . . .' he ordered one of the guards on watch outside. It was probably nothing – a fight over a goat or a sheep. Yesterday he'd had five tribesmen – two Ghilzais and three Pashais – flogged for brawling. But it wasn't that. Babur could tell from the guard's surprised expression as he returned at a half-run through the lines of tents.

'Majesty, it's an ambassador . . . with a large escort.'
'From where?'
'Persia, Majesty, from the great shah himself . . .'
'Bring him to my tent.'

Hurrying inside, Babur dressed quickly. He unlocked a small, leather-covered chest on a carved wooden stand, took out a jewelled chain and hung it round his neck, then placed

Timur's heavy gold ring on his finger. His jaw was rough with stubble but there was no time to do anything about that now. Anyway, he was a warrior on campaign – the Persian ambassador must take him as he found him . . .

Five minutes later, Babur's guards ushered in the envoy and four of his attendants. Babur found himself looking at a tall, black-bearded man of about forty in cream robes. A high purple velvet cap topped by an egret's white feather secured by an amethyst pin made him seem even taller. His four attendants were in tunics of amber velvet and, like their master, also wearing high caps. One held a large purple velvet bag fastened with gold cord.

The ambassador made a graceful bow. 'I bring you greetings from the Lord of the World, the great Shah Ismail of Persia. He prays for your long life.'

Babur inclined his head. 'I am grateful, and may God grant him long life also.'

'It took us many days to find you, Majesty.'

Babur waited. What could the shah, away to the west, want with him?

'My master knows what brought you from Kabul. He, too, has been insulted by the Uzbek mongrels who have dared to encroach upon his eastern borders. In his arrogance Shaibani Khan led his army from Herat and six weeks ago attacked a rich caravan bringing goods to our city of Yazd that were destined for my master. When Shah Ismail demanded the return of his goods, the Uzbek sent him a pilgrim's staff and bowl, signifying that my master is a beggar. In return Shah Ismail sent a distaff and spindle and the message that Shaibani Khan, a sheep-rustler, would do better to spin wool than insult his betters. But, unknown to the Uzbek, my master also immediately despatched an army bearing a further message for him: "When a wild dog foaming at the mouth attacks in his madness there is only one solution. The dog must die." My master, whose magnificent armies are numberless, has

323

dealt with the mad beast and he wishes you to know it.'

'Shaibani Khan is dead?'

'Yes, Majesty. Seventeen thousand Persian cavalry ambushed his main army as it was returning towards Herat and annihilated it.'

Babur's mind was racing. If this was true . . . He searched the envoy's face, whose long, dark eyes reminded him of Ayisha's people, the Mangligh.

'Majesty,' the man bowed again but clearly had more of importance to say, 'my master has charged me to deliver this gift to you.' He took the purple velvet bag from the attendant and pulled out an oval object mounted in gold. 'It is not as richly decorated as my master would have wished but there was little time. He hopes you will find it acceptable.' He held out the object carefully in both hands.

Babur examined it curiously. It was shaped like a large, round drinking cup. The outside, smooth and gleaming, looked as though it had been dipped in liquid gold and on the bottom were four little golden prongs on which it could rest. The inside was pale grey and – Babur ran a finger over it – hard. Horn, perhaps? No, it didn't have the warmth, the mellowness of horn. It was bone . . . Babur looked again at the round shape, the size . . . Big as the crown of a man's head . . .

'Yes, Majesty. It is the skull of Shaibani Khan, boiled clean of its flesh and made into a drinking cup. The skin was also put to use. My master had it stuffed with straw and sent as a curiosity to his ally Bayazid, Sultan of Ottoman Turkey.'

Babur found it hard to believe what he was hearing. His greatest enemy was dead and he was holding his skull in his hands. Babur looked down at it but as he did so something of his exultation faded. He had wanted to kill Shaibani Khan himself, to ignite fear in the cold eyes he'd never seen at close quarters, to tell him, as he plunged his sword or his dagger into his guts, that this was for Khanzada. Instead

324

someone else, a far richer, more powerful ruler, had done it . . .

'I am grateful to Shah Ismail for his . . . gift.'

'My master has sent further gifts for you. They are outside. If you will allow me to lead you, I will show you.'

'Very well.'

Babur's guards, weapons ready in case the Persian emissary had intended harm to Babur, parted to allow them out of the tent. As they made their way through the camp some men who had not heard of the Persians' arrival were yawning, scratching and going about their morning ablutions. Several hundred yards beyond the perimeter of the camp, beneath a grove of oak trees, the rest of the ambassador's men – as well armed as they were dressed – were waiting. Their hobbled horses were grazing beneath the trees or drinking from a nearby stream. However, one horse – a stallion with a long back, powerful flanks and shining coal-black coat – was moving restlessly between two grooms, who were having difficulty controlling it as it jerked its head and snorted through dilated nostrils. It was the most magnificent beast Babur had ever seen.

'This is Sohrab, a stud stallion from the stables of my master who sends him to you – and the mares of Kabul – as a gift.'

'I thank the shah for his generosity.' Babur was puzzled. Shaibani's skull made some sort of sense but why should the shah make him a present like this? What did he want from him? Persia was not only one of the earth's most powerful nations, it was a wealthy centre of culture, its poets and painters celebrated everywhere. Both Ferghana and Samarkand had been too far from its borders for any direct contact between their rulers but now Babur was in Kabul the two lands were almost neighbours. Shah Ismail was a strong new ruler who, a few years previously, had deposed the previous dynasty and established his own. A devout man, he had also imposed the

Shia form of the Muslim faith on his subjects. Some called the Shiites heretics, since they believed – unlike the majority of Muslims, including Babur, who followed the Sunnis – that only the Prophet Muhammad's cousin and son-in-law, Ali, was his rightful heir . . . But the shah's faith seemed scarcely relevant to his gift . . . Babur pulled himself from his reverie.

The emissary was looking at him almost slyly. 'And this is also a gift from my master.' Beyond Sohrab, Babur could see a large bullock cart, drawn by a team of six creamy-coated oxen, its contents concealed by yellow hangings, bright as the yellow of Ferghana. Ferghana . . .

Babur walked slowly towards it, his breathing suddenly ragged. Though the air was cool, he was sweating. He knew what or rather who was in the cart – or hoped he did – but never in all his twenty-seven years had he felt as fearful as he did now. Reaching the cart, whose driver knelt respectfully before him, Babur paused. Slowly he put out a hand to touch the hangings, feeling for the opening. Then he paused and looked round at the group gathered close behind him – the Persians, his own men.

'Step back.' His voice was sharp. He waited till they were a good few paces away, then took the hangings, pulled them apart and peered inside. In the far corner, against the cushions, a woman was hidden by a heavy black veil. As a shaft of sunlight fell on her, a tremor seemed to run through her. 'Khanzada . . . ?' Babur's voice was a whisper.

He jumped into the cart and closed the hangings behind him. In the half-light filtering through the thin silk, he saw the woman move a little towards him. Unable to restrain himself, he reached out, took hold of the veil and pulled it from her. Khanzada's brown eyes looked into his . . .

•◆•

Fifteen minutes later, Babur climbed out again. With so many eyes upon them, even in the privacy of the cart, this was not the moment to open their hearts. Babur was not even sure he could – this had happened so suddenly, so unexpectedly he could still hardly comprehend it. He summoned the emissary to his side. 'Your master has done me a very great service,' he said simply.

'We have treated your sister with every honour due to her. Two attendants have been with her throughout the journey and will remain to serve her, if you so wish.'

Babur nodded. 'You are our honoured guests. I will order tents to be pitched for you and your people near my own in the centre of the camp.'

It was hard not to be able to be alone with Khanzada at once, but courtesy to the shah demanded that Babur play host to the Persians. As soon as he had arranged living quarters for his sister and for the Persians, he ordered a pavilion to be constructed from ten hide tents and spread with sheepskins where he could hold a feast. To sophisticated Persian eyes his hospitality would no doubt seem poor and primitive, but he could compensate for the lack of fine carpets, ornate dishes and rich hangings with roasted sheep and the barrels of strong wine his men had seized during their raids.

Two hours into the feast, Babur congratulated himself. The emissary, cheeks flushed and eyes bright, was already far gone, muttering verse couplets through his black beard. Soon, his head began to nod, his dark eyes closed and he slipped lower on his cushion.

The celebrations would go on far into the night throughout the camp. The Uzbek defeat and the death of Shaibani Khan were welcome news to all. Hatred of the Uzbeks had united even those who would otherwise be enemies but Babur was free at last. Waving away the guards who automatically formed up behind him, he ran through the camp, sidestepping drunken, singing men and ignoring their roars of invitation to join him at their fires.

Khanzada's tent had been erected in a secluded area of

the camp and she was sitting cross-legged, alone, at a low table, writing by the light of oil lamps. As soon as she saw him she rose. In the flickering light she was still the young woman he remembered from nine years ago, but as he came closer he saw lines on her face he didn't recall and a white scar running from the right corner of her mouth towards the tip of her right ear he'd not noticed earlier.

'I was writing to our mother . . . the first letter I've been able to send her for so many years. Come and sit by me . . .'

'Khanzada . . .' He was bursting with the need to tell her how sorry he was . . . how bitterly he felt all those years when she'd been a helpless prisoner, how guilty that he had been powerless to do anything . . . but somehow now he had the opportunity the words wouldn't come. Only when she reached out and gently stroked his face did his tongue free itself. 'I should have protected you better. I was young and arrogant . . . I should have used my head . . . I should never have let him take you . . .'

'There was nothing you could have done. It was the only way or he would have murdered us all, right there in front of the walls of Samarkand. My greatest fear was always that you would do something rash, something foolish . . .'

'I should have. There would have been more honour in it.'

'No – it was your duty to be prudent . . . to wait . . .'

'You sound like our grandmother.'

Khanzada's eyes filled with tears. Her first questions to him had been for news of her mother and grandmother and Babur had had to tell her the old lady was dead. 'If I am like her, I'm glad. She understood the world as it is – not as we'd like it to be – and she taught us what was expected of us.'

'Sometimes I wish we'd not been born who we are . . .'

'Of course. Yet if you could choose again, you wouldn't want it otherwise – not in your heart . . .'

As Babur stared at the floor, the red and blue flowers

on the carpet seemed to whirl before his eyes. 'But if you hadn't been a Timurid princess you wouldn't have had to endure Shaibani Khan . . .'

A tremor crossed Khanzada's face.

He reached out to touch the curve of her cheek, then the scar etched on her skin. 'What happened to you? Can you tell me . . . ?'

'He was a strange man, always unpredictable, often needlessly cruel . . . He was not . . . gentle and he made me do degrading things . . . to humble me, he said, to make me forget my Timurid blood, to remind me I was only a woman subject to his whims . . . I – I cannot speak of them but they are over now.' Her voice trembled. 'But I was only one of many in his harem and I was lucky to be one of his wives. We had a certain status – all his wives were from noble houses . . . However badly he treated us in the bedchamber we had rich clothes, jewels, good food, servants. We were symbols of his power and conquests . . . He didn't take us with him on campaign but left us where we'd be safe. If we'd been captured and dishonoured, he would have been dishonoured too. That was why the shah's men found me in Herat . . .

'His concubines – there were hundreds – were not so fortunate. When he went on expeditions, he'd select some to go with him to dance for him in the camp at night and give to his warriors who'd fought well. If they angered him he had them killed. In one of his camps a girl who stumbled as she danced was buried up to her armpits in sand and left without water under the hot sun. They say she was still alive, skin and lips blackened and peeling, when his army rode on two days later . . . Such things meant nothing to Shaibani Khan.'

Khanzada's calm, matter-of-fact tone – there was no anger, no bitterness – amazed Babur. From somewhere she had found strength to accept her situation.

'I don't understand . . .' he began, but she hushed him as

if he were still her childish small brother and put a finger to his lips.

'Just as your duty was to be patient, mine was to survive. That was what I did. I hid my thoughts and feelings. I was submissive and unresisting – dutiful, even. Sometimes I even pitied him. There was no happiness, no contentment in him, only a restless hunger for revenge against a world he thought had treated him badly . . .'

'But you must have been afraid, living in the power of a man who hated our family so much?'

'Sometimes, of course. His moods were strange, impossible to read. But as time passed, I grew less fearful that my life was at risk, at least not from him . . .'

'From who, then . . . ?'

Khanzada looked down at her clasped hands with their intricate hennaed patterning. Even as a girl she had loved to decorate her hands and feet. 'Some of the other women. Though Shaibani Khan was what he was, there was still jealousy. He was handsome, powerful. He could be generous to those who pleased him. Women vied for his attention . . . One in particular was envious of me though she had no reason . . .'

'Who?'

'The daughter of the grand vizier of Samarkand – the young woman you sent to be the wife of our cousin Mahmud Khan. After Shaibani Khan had killed him, he took her from Samarkand as a concubine. She wanted to be one of his wives and hated me because I was. But, above all, she hated me because you had her father killed. Six months after Shaibani Khan took me, she tried to stab me . . . She was aiming for my eyes but one of the harem guards saw her in time and dragged her off me, but the blade still caught the side of my face.' Khanzada put her hand to the scar.

In his mind's eye Babur saw the slender, fiery-eyed girl

begging him for the life of her despicable cur of a father. 'What happened to her?'

'Shaibani Khan had her walled up alive in an underground chamber in the Kok Saray in Samarkand. He said he was the only arbiter of who lived and died. He said he was punishing her for her presumption . . .'

As the hours of the night passed and his sister continued to speak of her ordeal, Babur began to understand how she had managed to survive and to stay sane. It was as if she had distanced herself from everything, convincing herself that the traumatic things happening around her – to her – were happening to someone else. A little like Ayisha, but with far more reason than she had ever had, she had longed to be elsewhere and, in her mind, had persuaded herself she was.

It moved him almost unbearably to see her smile but he was also filled with pride by her strength. Whatever had been done to her body she'd refused to allow her mind to be cowed and dominated. If Esan Dawlat had been a true daughter of Genghis, then so was Khanzada . . . Her experiences, horrific as they must have been, had not destroyed her. She was thirty-one years old and had spent nearly a third of her life subject to the whims of a brutal tyrant, but the girl who'd played with her pet mongoose had somehow, inexplicably, survived. Tears pricked his eyelids but he forced them back. From now on, his sister would know nothing but happiness . . .

•◆•

'The Lord of the World has a proposition that he hopes you will find acceptable.' The Persian envoy was clad even more gorgeously today in robes of bright orange and his beard was perfectly combed and perfumed. There was no sign of the aching head Babur had been sure he'd be suffering from. The man's self-possessed, rather patronising expression suggested the 'proposition' was something Babur would grab as a starving man would seize a hunk of bread.

Babur waited, eyes a little narrowed. At last he was about to find out why the shah had gone to so much trouble to please him.

'Shah Ismail has shattered the power of the Uzbek marauder. He wishes the legitimate rulers to return to their kingdoms so that the lands bordering his great empire are tranquil once more. As the last surviving prince of the House of Timur he offers you Samarkand . . .'

Babur felt his stomach contract. Samarkand, city of his dreams, Timur's capital. 'Your master is gracious,' he replied cautiously, then waited. If he had learned anything in the years since his father's death it was patience. Let others fill silences . . .

The envoy cleared his throat. Here it comes, Babur thought.

'Though Shaibani Khan has been defeated, Uzbek tribes still hold Samarkand. My lord will give you Persian troops to fight side by side with your own to drive them out.'

'And then?'

'My master admires you. He knows that the blood of conquerors runs in your veins. He believes you would make a worthy vassal.'

'A vassal?' Babur stared at the man.

The envoy seemed to read his mind. 'You need pay no tribute and you alone would govern in Samarkand. All my master asks is that you acknowledge him as your overlord.'

'And as soon as we have taken Samarkand the Persian troops will withdraw?'

'Of course.'

'And there are no other conditions?'

'No, Majesty.'

'I will consider what you have said and give you an answer when I am ready.'

The envoy bowed and withdrew. No wonder the man had

asked for a private audience. His proposition was unprecedented. No Timurid prince had ever been subject to Persia . . . yet the suggestion offered security for the shah and himself. The shah's borders would be protected by the friendly buffer of Babur's lands, and Babur would regain Samarkand. Established there, he could bide his time, build up his forces, seek opportunities for further conquests and perhaps, when the moment was right, throw off the vassalship.

He heard voices outside and one of his guards ducked into the tent. 'The quartermaster wishes to see you.'

Babur nodded. It would be good to talk this over with Baburi before he summoned his war council.

'Well, what did he want?' Baburi perched on a low wooden stool next to Babur.

'The gift of the stallion and the return of my sister were to sweeten me. The Shah of Persia has made me an offer. He will give me troops to chase the remaining Uzbeks out of Samarkand and establish my rule there on the single condition that I acknowledge him as my overlord.'

Baburi's indigo eyes flashed in surprise. 'Samarkand is not the shah's to dispose of . . . What right has he to it? And what right has he to expect you to be his vassal?'

'He is one of the most powerful rulers on earth. He disposed of Shaibani Khan . . . a task that might have taken us years . . . that we might never have accomplished . . .' Babur said slowly.

'You don't mean to accept?'

'Why not? I've always wanted Samarkand – desired it above everything else. And once I've regained it, I can retake Ferghana. With the kingdom of Kabul, I'll have the makings of an empire of my own . . . something to leave to my sons . . .'

'That primping Persian arsehole has bewitched you with his oh so soft words, his unctuous smoothness and "pwetty pwetty" promises. Is that what it's all been for? Our treks over frozen mountains, our days of hunger when a lump of mouldy meat seemed like Paradise, our shared battles . . . our mingled blood . . . our victories?'

'Isn't it time to enjoy some reward? The past years have been like living under a whirlwind. Whenever I tried to put down my roots, they were ripped out. But I am still here – unlike my cousin Mahmud Khan, whose flayed skin was stretched to make a drum, or my male kin in Herat, all slaughtered, or my murdered half-brother in Ferghana . . . I feel my time is coming at last . . .'

'Then don't be a fool by throwing everything away. Don't let understandable gratitude for your sister's return cloud your judgement. You have an army – a good one. Let the Persians stay in Persia. We're strong enough to take Samarkand on our own. Ride through the Turquoise Gate again as your own man, not as another's hireling.'

'You don't understand . . .' Babur's anger was rising. Baburi was always so obstinate.

'I do understand. Your mindless obsession with becoming another Timur is blinding you – pushing you into contemplating stupid short-cuts.'

'What would you know about that?'

'Because I come from the streets? Is that what you mean?' Baburi was on his feet now, his stool lying on its side where he'd kicked it. 'That's precisely why I can see more clearly than you – you idiot. If you take the shah's offer, it is as if I'd gone down an alley with some scumbag to suck his cock in return for a meal . . . you'll be like a brood mare to that stud stallion the shah sent you – to be mounted, dominated, and compelled to satisfy your master's every desire . . . I was never that desperate. Neither should you be . . . Once you succumb he'll be back for more . . .'

'You're being ridiculous. Leave me.' Babur got up and turned away. Why couldn't Baburi acquiesce gracefully in his schemes as others did?

Baburi didn't obey. Instead he gripped Babur's shoulder, yanking him round to face him, eyes blazing. 'What would that father of yours that you're always going on about have said? Or your old battle-axe of a grandmother? They'd have been ashamed you could be bought so easily, become any man's vassal – ready to take it up the arse whenever your master feels like it . . .'

Overwhelmed by anger that Baburi dared speak to him like this, Babur pulled himself free, stepped back and swung his fist at Baburi's sneering face with all his strength. He heard a dull crunch as his friend's nose broke and blood spurted.

For a second, Baburi's hand was on his dagger and Babur instinctively reached for his. But instead Baburi raised his right hand to cover his nose and – eyes never leaving Babur's – felt with his left hand around the waist of his now blood-soaked tunic for the end of his sash. Grabbing it, he tried to staunch the flow.

'Baburi . . .'

Pulling the sash from his face for a second, Baburi spat at Babur's feet. Then ducking through the tent flap he was gone, leaving a trail of ruby-bright droplets of blood on the sheepskins on the floor.

Babur resisted the impulse to go after him. He was a king, and Baburi should remember that. He shouldn't have hit him but Baburi had had it coming . . . He was hot headed, arrogant. When he thought about it coolly, rationally – as he would – he'd realise that the decision Babur was about to make was the right one . . . Babur would ride through the Turquoise Gate and he'd do it without shame, head high.

'Guard!' Babur shouted. A man's head poked through the entrance flap. 'Summon my war council.'

• ◆ •

Babur watched the Persian envoy and his escort ride away.

In the envoy's saddlebags was a letter from Babur pledging his allegiance to the shah. Tonight there would be more feasting in the camp. Babur would summon his commanders to announce that as soon as Persian reinforcements joined them they would ride north-east for Samarkand to purge it of its infestation of Uzbeks and claim it as their own. His men, fired by the prospect of rich booty, would roar their approval. There'd be no need to dwell on the bargain he'd made with the shah. There would be time enough, when he was master of Samarkand's blue-domed mosques and palaces, to consider how to present it to his people. And why should they care? They would again be ruled by a Timurid prince, not a barbarous ancestral foe. The Persians would depart to their distant homeland. Soon he would be able to think of further conquests.

Baburi would be nursing his wounded pride and his wounded nose somewhere. Now that his own temper had cooled, the deal had been done and the envoy was gone, Babur was anxious to see his friend and heal their rift. There was so much he had not said, so much he had said badly . . .

Still wearing the bright green tunic – chosen in tribute to Samarkand – in which he had received the Persian envoy for his farewell audience, Babur walked through the camp to Baburi's tent, pitched close to Baisanghar's.

The flaps were thrown back and he went inside. The rugs on the floor were spotted with blood and the few possessions, mostly clothes, strewn hither and thither as though someone had hastily searched through them, deciding what to take and what to leave. In one corner was what looked like splintered wood. As Babur went closer he recognised the bow and gilded quiver set with golden tiger's eyes he'd given Baburi the day he'd made him *Qor Begi*, Lord of the Bow. The bow was snapped in two, and the quiver smashed, as if someone had stamped on it – the gems had fallen from their mountings. Babur picked one up. The round little stone felt cold.

He hurried outside, almost tripping over the black leather gauntlet Baburi wore to go hawking but which now lay on the floor. Baisanghar was giving orders to two guards.

'Where's Baburi?'

'I haven't seen him since this morning, Majesty.'

'Check whether his horse is here.'

Baisanghar despatched a guard to the corral where the handsome chestnut Baburi had taken from an Uzbek chieftain should have been grazing, but Babur already knew the answer. 'He's gone . . .'

'Majesty?'

'Baburi – he's gone. Send riders to look for him and bring him back. Do it now, at once!' He realised he was shouting.

Startled, Baisanghar hurried off, and Babur went back inside Baburi's tent. He picked up the broken bow. Baisanghar's men could ride their horses into the ground but it wouldn't be any use. If Baburi wanted to disappear he would.

Chapter 19

The Kizil-Bashi

This glorious, mellow, sunlit day in the autumn of 1511 deserved a special mention in his diary, Babur thought, as he rode at the head of his army towards the Turquoise Gate where banners of bright green – not Uzbek black – again bellied in the breeze. Last time he'd entered Samarkand as its king more than a decade ago he'd been just a youth. Now he was twenty-nine, toughened and tempered by all that had happened to him since.

The city had fallen without a struggle. Babur and his army of twenty thousand, swelled by the Persian cavalry, had been too much for the occupying Uzbeks. They had fled, preferring to take refuge in their stronghold of Karshi in the northern mountains than fight a far superior force. On learning of their flight Babur had taken Shaibani Khan's skull, filled it with blood red wine and drunk deeply, before passing it round to his commanders.

My time has come, he thought exultantly, as he passed beneath the glinting gateway to the deep, echoing boom of kettle-drums. Tonight, he and Maham – travelling with the other women of the royal household in mule carts with trappings of gold and green – would make love. According to his astronomers, the planets were in perfect conjunction for the conception of a son. He would have a further heir and Maham would cease to weep because she had borne him no more children since Humayun.

As he emerged from the purple shadows beneath the gate into the city, the excited, approving cheers of his people – a human rainbow in their brightest robes – burst over him, joyously shouting his name and Timur's, as if his great ancestor were there by his side. As he rode up the broad avenue leading to the citadel and the Kok Saray he saw that the shopkeepers had draped their stalls with brilliant brocades and the ruby-red velvet for which Samarkand was celebrated. From rooftops and windows, women threw handfuls of dried rose petals that fluttered in the air like pink snowflakes.

But abruptly the happy shouting faltered. A hoarse, angry voice rose above the crowd: '*Kizil-Bashi! Kizil-Bashi!*' Redheads! Redheads! Glancing back Babur realised that the people were looking at the Persian cavalry as they came through the Turquoise Gate. The cry was now taken up by hundreds of voices. People were pointing and jeering at the Persians with their conical red caps and the long strip of scarlet cloth hanging down behind that showed they were not Sunni Muslims, like the people of Samarkand and Babur, but Shiites, like their master, the shah.

No matter, Babur told himself, staring resolutely ahead. He'd soon be rid of the Persians and his subjects would realise they had had nothing to fear from them or their differing version of Muslim faith. Yet he couldn't banish the jeers and catcalls from his mind.

This new sombre mood was still on him when, three hours later, he stood alone in his public audience chamber in the Kok Saray, contemplating the gleaming cobalt blue, turquoise, yellow and white geometrically patterned tiles on its walls and domed ceiling that had so astonished him the first time he'd seen them. He'd anticipated this moment for so long, yet the glory of his return felt diminished, tarnished.

The magnificence around him seemed to fade, to be replaced by Baburi's face. Baburi should have been here, observing him with that quiet irony in his indigo eyes. But what would he have said at this moment? That he'd been right all along, that Babur was not his own master, just another ruler's toy? As he looked into the future he had assumed would be so glorious, Babur felt truly alone . . .

'Majesty, they are waiting for you.' The lines on Baisanghar's grave face were deep. He was no longer the vigorous warrior who had ridden all those years ago to Ferghana to bring him Timur's ring. It had been right to make him grand vizier, Babur reflected. His long, loyal years of fighting and service deserved such a reward, and Maham was pleased to see her father so honoured.

Did Baisanghar ever feel the frustration that sometimes overcame himself? Did he ever long again to sweep down on a raid from the mountains on a moonlit night with a cold wind scouring his face? Or to sleep on hard ground under the stars, sword by his side, unsure what the next day would bring except that it would be hard and dangerous? Babur's hankering for action was absurd, he knew, but after only six weeks in Samarkand he was restless. He wanted to get back to Kabul to assure himself that all was well there, even though he had left it strongly garrisoned. He was also eager to recover Ferghana, which, since the Uzbek collapse, had been dismembered by petty local warlords with more fleas than real troops. He could swat them with one blow of his fist if only he were free to leave Samarkand, but he had to establish order in the city. He had summoned the leading citizens to announce how Samarkand was to be governed and now they were waiting – no doubt hoping for lucrative sinecures.

Babur entered his audience chamber and mounted his dais. At Baisanghar's command, his waiting subjects prostrated themselves on the soft, rich carpets the Uzbeks hadn't had time to loot. Mechanically acknowledging them, Babur's mind was elsewhere. The Persian troops should have departed by now. Yet, though some had left as soon as the *khutba* confirming Babur as king had been read, a thousand were still camped in the riverside meadows outside the Needlemaker's Gate. With them was the shah's own priest, Mullah Husayn. Whenever he broached the question of the Persians' departure with their commander – a cousin of Shah Ismail, haughty and cold – the answer was the same: he was awaiting orders from the shah. As soon as he received them he and his men would ride away.

Babur couldn't order them to go but he could insist that they kept off the streets of Samarkand. The populace's hostility hadn't died away. In fact, the news that he had become the shah's vassal had only fed their suspicion, instead of reassuring them that they had a powerful protector as Babur had hoped. He had received several visits from the city's mullahs, seeking assurances that the shah was not planning to interfere with their religion. An aged priest from one of the *madrasas*, his thin face nearly as pale as his white robes, had gone further, upbraiding Babur for his dealings with the heretical Persians and demanding he expel them. 'Even the Uzbeks – wicked defilers of our city though they were – are true believers . . .' he had said. 'Even the Uzbeks . . .' Babur had never thought to hear words like that. Somehow he must send the Persians on their way . . .

'Majesty,' Baisanghar interrupted his thoughts, 'your subjects are waiting to hear you.'

Babur unrolled the piece of paper on which was written the latest list of public appointments – a stout merchant in robes of peacock blue was gazing at him expectantly – but as he did so the velvet-covered, gilded throne on which he was sitting lurched sideways. Babur tried to right himself but he and the throne were flung to the floor. A rumbling, roaring, cracking sound filled the air and everything shook. A lump of masonry, bright tiles still attached, crashed down beside him.

Bitter-tasting dust clogged the air and Babur felt he was choking, but as he gasped for breath, his mouth filled with grit. He couldn't even open his eyes. Bracing himself, he covered his head with his hands, waiting for a piece of masonry to land on him. But after a few more moments the shaking stopped as abruptly as it had begun. With groans rising from all around, Babur raised his head cautiously and managed to open his streaming eyes a little. Though some stones had been dislodged, the main walls and ceilings of the Kok Saray had withstood the earthquake. Timur's builders had done a good job. But looking around he saw Baisanghar lying unconscious, his brilliant green robes of office now grey.

'Guards,' Babur yelled, not sure who would answer him. Almost at once he heard running feet. Through the drifting, stifling dust he recognised two of his bodyguards who had been on duty in the antechamber. 'Send for my *hakim* and fetch any other doctors you can find. The grand vizier is hurt – others too.' Babur got to his feet, staggered to Baisanghar and put his fingers to the side of his neck as he'd so often done to wounded comrades in battle. Yes, he was alive – he could feel the faint but rhythmic pulsing of his blood. On his forehead a huge bruise was purpling. Baisanghar's eyes flickered open and he looked up at Babur, confused.

'It was an earthquake ... The *hakim* is coming.' Babur ripped off his outer robe, rolled it up and placed it beneath Baisanghar's head. 'I must go to the women's quarters.'

All around him in the audience chamber dazed men were picking themselves and others up, but a few were lying still. Scrambling over chunks of masonry, Babur ran from the chamber, making for the broad flight of stairs leading to the top storey and the women's apartments. Hurling himself up them, he saw deep fissures in the dark stonework and that lamps and torches had tumbled from their niches – he kicked them aside – but again Timur's walls had held.

At the top, he saw that the tall double doors – resilvered and inlaid afresh with turquoises since the day when a youthful Babur and his men had battered them down – were still standing, though a crack gaped in the stone lintel above and part of the elaborately tiled ceiling had collapsed, littering the floor with shards as bright as butterfly wings. Of the attendants who should have been outside there was no sign. They would pay for their negligence, Babur thought, as he threw his weight against the doors and pushed them open.

The first face he saw was Maham's, her long hair hanging around her. She was standing in the centre of the chamber, which, apart from a few tumbled pieces of furniture, spilled food and broken clay dishes, was untouched. A sobbing Humayun was in her arms but her eyes were bright and clear.

'See, Humayun? I told you there was nothing to be afraid of . . . It was only a foolish giant stamping his feet to annoy us . . . I said your father would come.' Babur kissed her forehead and took Humayun from her, feeling the warmth of his body which, now he was three, was losing some of its puppy fat. The boy's hazel eyes – so like his mother's – looked into his own. He stopped crying and smiled.

• ◆ •

'How bad is the damage?'

'Bad enough. Many houses and granaries have been destroyed, Majesty. They were not as sturdily built as the Kok Saray. About a hundred are dead and nearly three hundred injured.' Beneath his great turban of office, Baisanghar's face was still heavily bruised though he had recovered quickly.

'The royal treasuries will pay for the rebuilding – tell the citizens so – and distribute grain from our stores to anyone in want . . . With winter approaching, my people must not starve.'

'Yes, Majesty.'

After Baisanghar had left him, Babur sat alone in the octagonal gilded room he used as his chamber of private audience. He had been lucky. Both of his wives – Maham and Gulrukh – and his two sons, Humayun and Kamran, were unharmed. Khanzada was safe in Kabul with Kutlugh Nigar. But for this to have happened so early in his reign was a bad omen. The people were already blaming the catastrophe on the presence of the Persians. The insistent, repetitive cry of the muezzin calling all to midday prayer interrupted his bleak thoughts. It was Friday and he would go to the Great Mosque to pray in public. It would please the people and he himself might find some spiritual balm, something to quell his restlessness and unease.

Twenty minutes later, regally dressed in a green brocade tunic with a tasselled dark green woollen sash, a fur-lined cloak, an enamelled gold chain around his neck, yellow deerskin boots on his feet and Alamgir hanging at his side, Babur rode out from the Kok Saray towards the soaring recessed arch, the *iwan*, that led into Timur's mosque. His guards had to use their spears to clear a path through the thronging streets but, unlike the usual babble of people hurrying to Friday prayers, the crowds today seemed sullenly silent.

On reaching the paved courtyard outside the mosque, Babur dismounted amid drifts of golden leaves that had fallen from the trees and, followed by his guards, entered. The mullah – the old man who had come to beseech him about the Persians – was in his carved marble pulpit to one side of the *mihrab*, preaching. Babur knelt in the space allotted to the king at the very centre of the mosque and bent forward to touch his forehead to the floor. The mullah was speaking

345

of the transitoriness of human life and offering consolation to those who had suffered in the earthquake. Babur, conscious of hundreds of eyes upon him, listened attentively.

Suddenly the mullah fell silent. Looking up in surprise, Babur saw that he was gazing towards the entrance. Turning he saw what the mullah had seen – the tall, stout, extravagantly bearded figure of the shah's priest, Mullah Husayn. He was wearing the pointed red cap and sweeping red robes of the Shiite. His escort of six Persian cavalrymen were also in the unmistakable insignia of the *Kizil-Bashi*. The elderly mullah in the pulpit watched as the Persian advanced towards him, ignoring the hisses rising from all around.

Husayn looked directly at Babur. 'As a guest in your city, may I have Your Majesty's permission to deliver a sermon on this the day of prayer for all believers, Shiite and Sunni.'

Concealing his anger at what could only be a deliberate act of provocation and was certainly a breach of etiquette, Babur gave a curt nod and gestured to the old mullah to step down.

Husayn took his place. 'I am grateful for the king's permission to speak. May God's manifold blessings be upon him. Several months ago, with the help of the Lord of the World, the mighty Shah Ismail of Persia, you were delivered from a great evil. Your enemies, the Uzbeks, were forced to flee and you have your king again. The shah is pleased that this is so. He is also pleased that His Majesty King Babur has acknowledged him as his overlord . . . The shah welcomes your king as his brother. But, of course, brothers should be of the same faith. The shah has asked me to receive your king as a faithful Shiite so that he may, in turn, bring all his subjects to share the light . . .'

There was a collective gasp . . .

'No!' Babur was on his feet. 'I gave the shah my allegiance but my religion is my own. I will never convert or allow

346

the forcible conversion of my people. For centuries they have been ruled by the House of Timur. They cannot be coerced. Neither can I. Tell that to your master . . .'

Husayn's dark eyes flashed and his hands clutched the edge of the pulpit. Clearly, he was unaccustomed to being gainsaid, even by kings. 'My master has been generous. Do not forget that you owe him more than a kingdom.'

Babur chose his next words with care. 'I am indebted to the shah for many things. I also know he is an honourable man who would never impose impossible conditions on a loyal friend. Clearly there has been a misunderstanding. I will send messengers immediately to Persia to resolve it. I suggest that you return there too. Your master will be missing your spiritual guidance and is doubtless anxious for your presence.'

Husayn was shaking his big, bearded head from side to side. Enough, Babur thought. Signalling to his guards he walked from the mosque. Until that moment the worshippers had been passively watching and listening, but now he could hear murmuring behind him – like an approaching swarm of hornets it was growing louder and louder. As he walked across the courtyard and mounted his horse, people spilled out of the mosque, some shouting angrily against the shah and his mullah, others, Babur realised, shouting insults against himself.

The worshippers were quickly joined by others, drawn from their houses by the disturbance and eager to know what was going on. Despite the best efforts of his guards – and despite the royal green banner of Samarkand held high by Babur's *qorchi* to command respect – as he and his men turned down the avenue that led back to the Kok Saray they were soon buffeted by the press of people making for the mosque.

This was becoming a riot. The Persians in the mosque must be protected or the shah would have every excuse to wage war against Samarkand. 'Ride to the Kok Saray for reinforcements. Hurry!' Babur ordered two of his men. Then, calling to the rest to follow, his hand on his sword hilt, he turned his horse back through the heaving mass towards the mosque. Halting before it, he addressed the angry crowds.

'You have my word on the Holy Book that not a single man, woman or child will be forced to convert!' he shouted. But no one was listening. Instead an angry roar went up. Over his shoulder, Babur saw Mullah Husayn emerging from the shadows beneath the entrance to the mosque, the Persian soldiers close behind him, swords drawn. A rotten melon flew through the air towards Husayn, who made no attempt to dodge it. It fell at his feet, spattering his robes with soft orange flesh and pips. It was followed by what looked like a fistful of dung. Then a piece of stone whirled past the mullah's left ear to hit the tiled wall of the mosque, chipping off a shard of the delicate blue glaze.

Emboldened, people began picking up whatever missiles they could find and surged forward, yelling obscenities. Their faces were ugly with hatred, lips drawn back, eyes bulging. Drawing his sword, Babur gestured to his men to form a barrier between the mob and the Persians. Then, urging his horse a few paces forward, he made a last desperate attempt to speak to his people, but it was no use. Determined to get at the Persians, they surged past him. A huge man in an orange turban grabbed the bridle of his horse. Whether he meant to push him out of the way or to attack him wasn't clear but Babur reacted instinctively and, drawing his dagger, slashed at the man's arm. Roaring with pain, he let go and stumbled forward. Babur's frightened horse reared and one of its hoofs kicked the man hard in the face. He fell like a stone.

Others were now yanking at his bridle, trying to bring down his horse. Did they even know who they were attacking? Babur slashed around him, trying to force a way through to rejoin his guards, but his assailants were determined. One was clutching what looked like a butcher's knife. Instead of trying to stab Babur, he plunged it into the throat of his horse. The beast gave a great shuddering sigh and slipped to the ground, front legs crumpling.

Tugging his feet from the stirrups Babur leaped sideways. He heard voices shouting, 'Traitor!' and 'Heretic!' then felt hands grabbing at him as he managed to wriggle away through the mass of legs until at last it seemed to be thinning. With the mob between him and his men, all he could do was get himself back to the Kok Saray. Taking a deep breath, Babur jumped to his feet and ran for it, head down, weapons in both hands.

Turning a corner, he found himself in a small square, empty and strangely silent after the mayhem he had just escaped and could still hear behind him. On two sides the houses had been badly damaged in the earthquake: their metal-bound doors hung crazily from twisted hinges and there were jagged cracks in their brickwork, a few big enough for a man to squeeze through. Their owners must have abandoned them, and others, whose houses still stood, had gone too.

In one corner, beneath the eaves of an old house that had been almost completely destroyed – each storey had collapsed neatly upon the one below – there was a well. Babur ran to it, dipped in the leather bucket and drank the brackish water. Wiping his mouth, he looked around, assessing what to do with the same deadly sense of purpose as on a raid or on the battlefield. Strange to think how he'd been hungering for action but he'd never expected his wish to be granted so soon or in this way.

He must get away. At any moment the shouting, baying mob – just a street or two away – would find him. A narrow alleyway led off the square to his right. He started towards it, only to discover that it was blocked with rubble from the earthquake.

'There he is – the bastard who would make heretics of

us.' Stepping back against the wall of the alleyway, and glancing back into the square, Babur saw some nine or ten men, clothes torn, faces blood smeared, with crude wooden implements in their hands. They'd obviously been running hard and their expressions were both crazed and exultant. Babur had seen that look many times before, on the faces of warriors who had just killed. These artisans or shopkeepers – whatever they were – had tasted blood and liked it.

But they weren't looking towards him – in fact, they hadn't noticed him. They were staring at something high up and out of Babur's sight. Cautiously, he edged back towards the square. Then he saw what had caught their attention. The 'bastard' they were after was Mullah Husayn, who was peering down from the upper storey of a tall house on one side of the square that was still intact. He'd lost his red cap and his face above the thick dark beard was pale, but as he surveyed his pursuers his eyes burned.

'All Sunnis are heretics,' he bawled. 'Not one of you will reach Paradise. Your souls will be consigned to the dungheap. Kill me if you dare. Make a martyr of me, and tonight I will dine in Paradise with my Shiite brothers . . .'

The men needed no encouragement and ran towards the wooden doors of the house, which someone – probably Husayn himself – had barred. They began to look for something to batter down the door. Much as Babur hated the mullah, he could not allow him to be murdered. Glancing up, he saw that the houses on the two sides of the square left standing were interconnected by wooden rooftop walkways, a device introduced in Timur's day to allow the ladies of the city to take the air and visit one another unseen.

Keeping close to what remained of the walls and trying not to stumble over the debris, Babur made for a plane tree growing about thirty yards to the right of the house where Husayn was still raving, thereby providing a useful distraction from his own activities. The tree's spreading branches would give him the leg-up he needed, and though it had shed most of its papery red-gold leaves, enough remained to camouflage him as he climbed. Grunting, Babur leaped into the tree and was soon on the flat roof of the house next to the one where the mullah was still holding forth.

Keeping low and praying it would take his weight, he crossed the swaying wooden slats of the little bridge connecting the two houses. Then, treading softly so that he did not alert Husayn, he raised the wooden trapdoor he found and climbed cautiously down the narrow flight of stairs into a small, white-painted attic. In one corner another broader staircase led down to where Husayn must be. Drawing his dagger, Babur crept catlike towards it and slowly descended. After a few steps he peered down. The mullah was standing at the window, declaiming angrily. Babur stepped forward and pressed the tip of his blade into the small of the man's back.

'Don't do anything to show them I'm here,' he hissed. 'Just step back from the window. Come on – now!' He would have liked to drive his dagger into the arrogant fool or throw him to the crowd below – he deserved it. But for the sake of Samarkand that mustn't happen.

Somewhat to Babur's surprise, Husayn obeyed.

'Turn round.'

As the mullah did so and saw who it was, relief flickered briefly in his eyes. Perhaps he was not as intent on martyrdom and his dinner in Paradise as he had said. Almost at once, a mighty thump, followed by a raucous cheer and shouts of encouragement, showed that the crowd were close to breaking down the door.

'Up the stairs to the roof – quickly.'

The mullah gathered his robes and half ran, half stumbled up them.

Tucking his dagger back into his sash, now he was sure that Husayn would give him no trouble, Babur followed. Up on the roof, he closed the trapdoor, then tried to decide

351

which way to go. They'd be caught if they climbed down the tree and he wasn't sure the mullah would make it anyway.

Babur ran across the roof to the opposite side and peered down. Below, a wide street was lined with what looked like workshops – the street of the armourers. As it was Friday, they were shuttered and no one was about. The distance to the paved ground was about twenty-five feet and the mud-brick walls offered little purchase. But another crash from below told him he had little time to ponder. The entrance door wouldn't hold for much longer. He made his decision. 'Take off your sash – quickly.'

Blinking, the mullah obeyed, unravelling from his waist a length of thick, heavily embroidered red silk at least nine feet long. Pulling out his dagger and sticking it into his boot, Babur unwound his own sash, a more modest seven feet of thick, strong wool. They'd still have to jump but it was the best he could think of . . . He tied the two sashes together, secured the woollen end – the stronger he guessed – to a metal pulley projecting from the roof that was used to haul grain and other supplies up there for storage. Then he threw the other end over the side.

'Go first. You're heavier – I'll take some of the strain.'

The mullah didn't hesitate. Babur turned his back to the drop and, taking the improvised rope in his left hand, passed it behind his back so that he could grip it with his right hand, then braced himself against it. At a nod from Babur, Husayn lowered himself cautiously over the edge. At once, the material seemed stretched to near breaking point and the knot between the sashes began to slip.

'Hurry!' Babur yelled, and felt the rope go slack. He peered down into the street and saw the mullah lying in a tangle of red robes, rubbing his shoulder. The sound of angry, excited voices and of the trapdoor to the roof being pushed open told him he had no more time. He tightened the knot again, gripped the rope and, trusting to fate, leaped . . . He braced his feet against the walls, bouncing off them as he descended, but suddenly his hands slipped.

His landing was softened, though not much, by a stack of wood. The mullah was still lying groaning where he had fallen, and flushed faces were looking down on them from the roof. The men were shouting obscenities. Any moment now and they'd be coming down the makeshift rope themselves. As he struggled breathlessly to heave the mullah to his feet, Babur heard the clattering of hoofs. Some of his bodyguard were galloping in single file down the street towards him, two of them already fitting arrows to their bow-strings, ready to fire at Babur's assailants on the roof who quickly melted from view.

'Majesty, we've been searching for you ever since we became separated. Quickly! There are mobs all over the city . . .'

One of his men dismounted to offer him his horse. Wearily Babur staggered to his feet and jumped up. With two of his men riding double and the mullah, still moaning, behind another guard, the little group made swiftly for the safety of the Kok Saray.

· ◆ ·

'I have withdrawn my armies westwards to protect my own borders and cannot offer you the assistance you seek. Indeed, why should I? You have spat in the face of my generosity and insulted my religion. Mullah Husayn has told me what passed in Samarkand – how he was reviled, insulted and hunted through its streets like a dog. In spurning him and the true way, you and your people have spurned me. May God the merciful forgive your crimes against him.'

Babur stared down at Shah Ismail's letter. It looked as if the mullah hadn't told him that Babur – in person – had saved his miserable neck. Slowly, deliberately, he ripped the dark red wax seal stamped with the lion – the personal emblem of the shah – from the bottom of the letter, which he tore into small pieces. Then he thrust the lot into the heart of the bright green flames of the wormwood fire, kept burning day and night in his chamber in an attempt to defeat the chill that, at the height of winter, with snow drifting against the city walls, seemed to seep from the very stones of the Kok Saray.

'It is only as we expected, Majesty . . .' Baisanghar said quietly.

'I know – but I still can't believe the shah will let the Uzbeks take the city . . . I didn't think his malice would extend that far . . .' Babur watched the wax melt and the paper flare and burn, taking with them his hopes.

'He is used to being obeyed. Once he had you in his power he expected you would yield to everything he wanted.'

'That is just as Baburi warned . . . I've been naïve. But I did not believe the shah was dishonest . . . he never said that I or my people must convert and he must know he could not have coerced them without spilling blood. As it was, it took us a month to quieten the city after Mullah Husayn's sermon.'

'At least the Persians have gone, Majesty . . .'

'Yes, but at the wrong time. I should have rid myself of them as soon as I became king. Then the people would have been less suspicious of me. Instead, I let them stay long enough to undermine me and then, just when I needed them to protect Samarkand, they left. The Uzbeks have already retaken Bokhara. As soon as the winter ends they will fall on us. Even though the system of messengers I have introduced tells me that Kabul and its territories are quiet, I cannot summon reinforcements from there or I will leave it vulnerable to attack or rebellion, just as when I first took Samarkand and unthinkingly hazarded Ferghana. I will, of course, fortify and provision the city but do I have the support of the people? I can never hold the city if I face enemies within the walls as well as outside.'

'I don't know, Majesty.'

'No, Baisangar, neither do I . . .'

· ◆ ·

What was the point of looking back? Already Samarkand's wondrous, fantastical outline was fading into the pinks, mauves and oranges of a spectacular sunset. It was as if Nature herself was celebrating his departure. Perhaps tomorrow an equally glorious dawn would unfurl to welcome the Uzbeks as they swept in from their encampment five miles north of the city.

Who would have thought that, with Shaibani Khan dead, they'd have found new leaders and organised themselves so well? The Uzbeks were like a column of ants: when some were crushed, others surged forward and their relentless advance never faltered . . .

Not only had the shah refused to help him – damning Babur as a heretic king – but he had enraged the citizens of Samarkand yet further. Almost a month ago, during the first days of spring, Persian troops had overrun an isolated Uzbek encampment west of Bokhara where many women and children, as well as warriors, had been living out the winter. Rounding up their prisoners, the Persians had quickly made clear that they were not simply punishing the Uzbeks for their past attacks on the shah and his territories, but for the divisions between Shiite and Sunni. In the mosques of Persia, at Shah Ismail's urging, the mullahs were now declaring all Sunnis enemies of God. And the Uzbeks – like Babur and the people of Samarkand – were Sunni. The Persians had offered the Uzbek men, women and children the chance to become Shiite then killed brutally and in cold blood those who did not immediately accept.

The inhabitants of Samarkand had made their feelings clear to Babur: if the Uzbeks wanted to return, let them. Better the enemies of their blood than the enemies of their faith. The brutal truth was that they trusted the Uzbeks to

355

protect them from the shah and Shiitism – they didn't trust Babur. He was fatally compromised by his previous dalliance with the shah. In vain Babur had reminded them of the horrors perpetrated by Shaibani Khan but it seemed they had short memories. Faced with near rebellion and demands from the Uzbeks, galloping down in their tens of thousands from Karshi and other strongholds in the north, to relinquish the city, Babur had issued an ultimatum to his citizens: 'Help me defend the city – our civilisation and culture – or I shall return to Kabul.' They had refused his call.

At least his hold on Kabul remained firm and his family were safe there. He had sent Maham, Gulrukh and his sons ahead with a strong escort. Now he must follow. As so often in recent weeks, he thought of Baburi. His friend had been right all along. Babur's passion for Samarkand – which had never truly belonged to him – had blinded him. Now he must pay for his folly, forget Samarkand and begin again from Kabul to seek other lands in which to satisfy his ambition for empire.

But he had one small consolation. He had returned the shah's stud stallion – gelded.

Part IV

Land of Dust and Diamonds

Chapter 20

Turkish Fire

On a day of shimmering heat in the summer of 1522, Babur's sons were in the meadows beneath the walls of the citadel of Kabul. Fourteen-year-old Humayun was galloping his horse – a chestnut mare with shining coat and white fetlocks – through the long golden grasses, firing from the saddle at a row of straw targets. He was keeping perfect balance as he drew arrow after arrow from his quiver, fitted them to his tight, double-curved bow and sent them flying through the air. Each hit its mark. Kamran, on his rough-coated pony, was watching his half-brother with respect. Babur saw him gasp as Humayun looked up into the bright blue skies and, so fast it was hard to see him do it, unleashed another arrow to bring down a bird.

Babur smiled. Even from his vantage-point high on the battlements he could sense Humayun's pleasure and his desire to show off – it was in the casual grace with which he held himself on his horse, the straightness of his back, the carriage of his handsome head. He looked every inch a warrior prince and knew it. But Kamran, just five months younger, was also growing up. Like his half-brother, he would be tall and, though not so powerfully built, was utterly fearless – a quality that had already led to several accidents.

Babur was glad his mother had lived long enough to see the two boys and to be reunited with Khanzada – something that in her heart he knew she'd despaired of. With her daughter's return to Kabul, Kutlugh Nigar had revived like a parched meadow after the rains. What Khanzada had told her of her sufferings at the hands of Shaibani Khan, Babur could only guess. Sometimes he'd seen a stricken look in his mother's eyes as she had gazed at her daughter. Khanzada must have seen it too. He had noticed how tender and cheerful Khanzada was with her, as if she was trying to reassure her that, despite everything, her inner spirit was not broken. On one matter only Khanzada had refused to gratify her mother. Kutlugh Nigar would dearly have loved to see her daughter marry again as a way of extinguishing the past but, in her gentle way, Khanzada had rebuffed any such suggestion, however good the man, however prestigious the alliance.

Kutlugh Nigar's death seven years ago had been as sudden as his grandmother's. She had been embroidering the border of a cotton robe in her apartments as Khanzada read to her and had simply slumped forward with a little sigh that proved to have been her last breath. Her spirit had passed and there had been nothing the *hakim* could do. A few hours later Babur, unable to hold back his tears, had seen her buried next to Esan Dawlat in the hillside garden he had laid out when he had first come to Kabul. He had made a vow never to forget how, through his blackest, most dangerous moments, his grandmother and mother had supported and guided him and that without them he would have had no throne at all . . . It still saddened him that neither had lived to see his youngest sons.

He turned his gaze to where six-year-old Askari appeared to be tormenting his three-year-old half-brother Hindal with a pointed stick. Their nurse was trying to take the stick away and Babur saw Askari's pointed little face screw up in a yell of defiance, which only provoked a sound cuff on the ear at which he surrendered his weapon and started to howl. Hindal – now that his nurse had intervened to protect him – was watching his brother's discomfort with huge amusement on his round, chubby face.

He was lucky to have so many healthy sons, Babur thought, and to have a rich, secure kingdom. In the ten years since he had relinquished Samarkand, he had continued to rule Kabul, quelling any opposition swiftly and winning his people's respect for his ability to stamp on the brigand tribes that infested the *kotals* – the high, narrow passes around Kabul – and preyed on the caravans. The Khugiani, Khirilji, Turi and Landar bandits had all had cause to regret their crimes. Their severed heads, cemented into high towers overlooking the passes, were a warning to others and reassured the anxious traveller that he was entering a kingdom in which the ruler ruled.

The treasuries were full, as the faithful, quietly efficient Kasim – guardian of the Royal Treasuries in place of Wali Gul, whose aged mind had finally wandered too far – proudly reported to Babur each day of the new moon. Kabul's merchants, feasting on roasted camel to celebrate every safe arrival of a caravan train, felt wealthy and secure. They might be happy but was he? Esan Dawlat – of all the women of his family the one who had understood him best – would have known instinctively the answer – that he was not.

Looking at his sons, Babur felt with renewed sharpness the unfulfilled longing that never quite left him. What would their future be? He had survived so much, learned so many lessons as a fighter and a leader of men. His experiences had taught him never to despair, never to allow setbacks to diminish his ambition. And that ambition was still for something greater than Kabul . . . something magnificent to bequeath to his sons and their sons after them . . .

361

'Majesty, we have reports of a group of riders approaching Kabul from the west.' Baisanghar's words interrupted Babur's reverie. As usual he looked anxious. When the elderly Bahlul Ayyub had died in his sleep, Babur had not hesitated to make Baisanghar grand vizier of Kabul – consolation to him for his short tenure as grand vizier of Samarkand.

'What are they? Merchants?'

'I'm not sure, Majesty. They are following the caravan route, but they've only a few pack-mules – no more than they'd need to carry their tents. Yet our informants say they have two great carts loaded with some curious metal contraptions and each pulled by thirty oxen . . .'

'How many men are there?'

'Perhaps fifty, and strangely dressed in leather tunics with high, conical hats wound about with bright orange cloth . . .'

'A group of travelling acrobats, perhaps . . .'

'I think not, Majesty.'

'I was joking, Baisanghar. Have them kept under surveillance. When will they be here?'

'In three days, perhaps four.'

'Let me know when they arrive.' All kinds of people passed through Kabul – Mongolians in embroidered brocade tunics with green leather bowcases and saddles, straggle-bearded Chinamen with their air of impenetrable superiority, swarthy-faced, thick-set merchants from Mesopotamia, as jealous as any Afghan tribesmen of their honour and as quick to pick a fight, and dark-skinned, bright-turbaned dealers in sugar and spices from deep inside Hindustan. If these new arrivals were interesting he'd summon them to the citadel . . . It might amuse Humayun and Kamran to see visitors from some far-off place.

In fact, Baisanghar's estimate was wrong. Just two days later, on a day of thin, grey drizzle, the party and its mysterious wagons were spotted approaching Kabul. They ignored the city but pressed on up the steep road to the citadel. Watching from the balcony of his private apartments, Babur could see the two wagons sliding about in the oozing mud that the rain had created from the normal layer of dust. Whatever was inside them seemed to be covered with thick felt against the weather. The bullocks were struggling, their heads low beneath the heavy wooden yoke, their shoulders straining.

The leading rider, a tall man with his face wrapped in a dark cloth against the penetrating rain, looked back at the struggling beasts. Babur saw him wave. He was no doubt shouting instructions because eight of the men at once dismounted and began pushing the carts from the back. One slipped and fell face down in the mud.

The leader seemed to lose patience. He turned his grey horse and kicked it on up the slope. Reaching the steep, paved ramp leading up to the first entrance gate to the citadel, he seemed to be urging his mount to go still faster. Only when two guards leaped in front of him did he bring it to an abrupt, slithering standstill. On his balcony, Babur couldn't hear what was being said but everything about the man suggested this was no merchant but a warrior. The angle of his head as he responded to the guards' questions was arrogant, and as he impatiently flung back his wet travelling cloak, Babur glimpsed the hilt of a sword in a strangely shaped scabbard – curved like a scimitar but narrower.

'Guards,' Babur shouted from his balcony, 'bring that man to me now.'

Five minutes later, with four guards in front of him, six behind, the man entered. His cloak had been taken from him and so had his sword – the curved steel scabbard hanging from the thin metal chain at his waist swung empty. But the cloth still concealed the lower part of the man's face and his conical hat was pulled low over his brow. The guards allowed him no closer to Babur than twenty feet.

'On your knees before the king!'

The man not only knelt but spreadeagled himself full-length on the floor in front of Babur in the full, formal Timurid salute of the *korunush*.

'You may stand.' Babur was more curious than ever. Why should a man who had demanded entry to his citadel as if of right perform such obeisance unasked? And, even more curious, why was he still face down, arms extended? Hadn't he understood what Babur had said?

One of the guards was about to jab him with the butt of his spear but Babur held up a restraining hand. Feeling for his dagger, he walked slowly towards the man until he was standing over him. 'I said you may rise.'

A quiver ran through the recumbent figure. After a moment's hesitation the man pushed himself back on to his heels but kept his head bowed. Then, slowly, he raised his face, and above the dusty, sweat-stained cloth Babur saw a pair of indigo eyes.

'Baburi!' He couldn't quite believe it, not after all these years. Stooping he grabbed Baburi's arm and pulled him upright. The face was more lined, but those high cheekbones, those intensely dark blue eyes were unmistakable.

As Babur continued to stare, Baburi pulled off his sodden headdress releasing long dark hair that was now touched with grey. 'Forgive me . . .' The words seemed to come hard to Baburi and his eyes were shining very brightly.

Babur raised a hand. 'Wait . . .' He signalled to the guards to go and waited until the double oak doors had closed behind them before turning back to his erstwhile friend. 'I don't understand . . .'

Baburi flushed. 'I've come back to ask your forgiveness. I left when I shouldn't have done. I knew it – even in the first hours – but pride wouldn't let me return . . .'

'No . . .' Babur gripped Baburi's arm tighter. 'I should ask your pardon. You were right – everything you said was right. I was the one with the pride, not you. I thought Samarkand belonged to me, that it was my destiny, that any price, even doing the shah's bidding, was worth paying. I should have listened to you . . . I couldn't hold the city for even a year. The people preferred even the barbarian Uzbeks to me . . .'

'But I was your friend . . . I knew you needed me and I failed you. All these years I've felt the shame of it . . .' Baburi's voice shook a little.

'You were the only man who was ever completely honest with me – the only one who could forget I was a king and with whom I could be myself . . . and I did need you. I searched for you . . . I never forgot you . . . I hoped you'd come back one day but then I ceased to hope . . . I feared you might even be dead.'

'How could I return unless I had some way of making amends?'

Babur let go of him. 'I never did understand you . . .'

'No. We've always seen the world differently and we always will.'

'So why come back to me now, after all this time?'

'Because at last I can give you something. For the past eight years I've been in the army of the Sultan of Turkey. I rose high and I did him a service. In a battle I saved the life of his son. He asked how he could reward me – and then I knew the time had come when I could return. Listen . . .' Baburi's eyes, so sombre a moment ago, were gleaming. 'The Turks have weapons of a type unknown in our world. With them you can do anything, conquer anybody. I've brought some to you and I've brought you Turkish mercenaries who, like me, know how to use them. Together we can train your army . . . so that you can fulfil that destiny of yours that you carry like a millstone round your neck . . .' As he said these last words, Baburi grinned and Babur saw again the street-wise companion whose sound common sense could wound like a barb but should never be ignored. 'What are these weapons?'

'Have you heard of bombards – cannon, they sometimes call them – or matchlock muskets?'

Babur shook his head.

'They are devices so powerful that eight years ago – just before I joined the Turkish sultan's army – his forces used them to defeat Shah Ismail of Persia at the battle of Chaltran, depriving him of much of Mesopotamia and fixing his borders. I talked to men who were there. They say thousand upon thousand of the shah's *Kizil-Bashi* – the Redhead cavalry – were cut down like poppies in the field. The weapons use the same black powder as we do when we lay mines beneath the walls of places we are besieging, but in Turkey they have a new name for it, "gunpowder", and a new use. You'll be amazed . . .'

But Babur wasn't really listening. It was only just beginning to sink in that the friend he had missed so much through all these years, his irreplaceable brother-in-arms, had come back. Looking at Baburi, all the burdens of kingship, the disappointments and frustrations fell away. In their place came such a riotous rush of feelings, such a wild joy that he felt he might choke. Whatever Baburi was saying didn't matter . . .

As if he had read Babur's mind, Baburi fell silent. For a moment they just stared at one another. Then, instinctively, they leaped forward to embrace, half laughing, half crying. Babur felt young again, filled with the wonder of the moment and with no thought of tomorrow.

◆

'Tell me what these years have brought you, Baburi. Do you have wives . . . sons?' Babur asked that night, as they sat alone in his private apartments. He could still hardly believe that Baburi was with him. He was half afraid that if he blinked he would find him gone.

'I told you many years ago that I had no wish for wives or children . . .'

'But don't you want sons to carry on your name? Who will remember you when you are gone?'

'Friends like you, perhaps. That would be enough . . .' Baburi paused. 'Anyway, a man would need a more settled existence than mine if he wished to marry.'

'Where did you go after you left Kabul?'

'I guessed you'd look for me so I went where you couldn't find me. I joined a caravan of merchants travelling westward to Isfahan. It was a long, difficult, sometimes dangerous journey – Uzbeks and marauding nomad tribes attacked us. By the time we finally reached Isfahan, some of the merchants had been killed and their goods plundered but my skill as a warrior had attracted notice. The caravan master asked me to travel on with a group of merchants carrying wool and silks northwards to Tabriz. There I learned you had been driven out of Samarkand and that the Shah of Persia was no longer your ally. I almost returned but somehow I couldn't . . . perhaps it was pride . . . perhaps I was uncertain of my welcome . . . I don't know . . . Then I heard that the Sultan of Turkey was recruiting mercenaries and paying them well. I joined a group of wanderers like myself, some from as far north as the borders of the Caspian Sea, and together we made our way to Istanbul.'

'To enlist in the sultan's wars . . .'

'Yes, though I'd rather have been fighting yours . . . being proved right about Samarkand and the shah gave me no pleasure. I often thought how hard it must have been for you to lose it again . . .'

'I deserved it . . .'

For a moment they bowed their heads, lost in memories. Then Baburi seemed to shake himself out of it. 'I've heard you've taken more wives and that you've two more fine healthy sons as well as Humayun and Kamran?'

'True.'

'What a family man you've become. It seems a long time since you and I rode with fire in our loins to the village whorehouses . . . do you remember Yadgar?'

367

'Of course.' Babur grinned. 'Sometimes I wonder what became of her. I hope she didn't fall prey to the Uzbeks.'

'Is Maham still a beauty?'

'She is – she's not grown fat – and Gulrukh is still plain. What did you expect . . . ? Maham is still the one I care for most, the one I most desire, but . . .' Babur hesitated '. . . she did not become the companion I had at first hoped for. Our bodies and affections meet, but not always our minds . . . I could talk to my grandmother, my mother and Khanzada about anything – appointments, campaigns – but not Maham. She really doesn't understand . . . isn't really interested . . .'

'Perhaps you expected too much. The women of your family were brought up to know about such things.'

'It's more than that.'

'What d'you mean?'

'Maham's been unhappy. After Humayun she had no more children that survived. Despite three further pregnancies, two were stillborn and the third – a son – died in my arms just minutes after my *hakim* summoned me to Maham's chamber. She was exhausted. I watched the light in her eyes fade as the new son we'd both longed for struggled for breath then went still. When I look back, it's as if something died in her, too, at that moment.'

'She has Humayun . . .'

'Yes. But she still feels she's failed . . . Even though she loves me and I care for her, it's cast a shadow between us.'

'Is that why you took more wives? For companionship? To find a soul-mate?'

'I had no such expectations. I married again for practical reasons. It's good for a king to have many heirs and it was a way to reward loyal followers and bind powerful clans to me.'

'These new wives of yours, what are they like?'

Babur thought of tall, muscular Bibi Mubarak, daughter of the powerful chieftain of the Yusufzai clan from the mountains above Kabul, and of fat little snub-nosed Dildar, whose father had fled the Uzbeks in Herat and made the long journey to Kabul to offer his allegiance. 'They're not amazingly beautiful, if that's what you mean. But they are good women . . .'

'Good in bed?'

'Good enough . . .'

'Which are the mothers of your two youngest sons?'

'Six years ago Gulrukh gave birth to a brother for Kamran, little Askari. Then three years later, Dildar also had a boy.'

'And Maham? It must have been hard for her.'

Babur's face tightened. 'It was . . . Years ago, as a new young wife with everything ahead of her, she accepted my marriage to Gulrukh without question. But her grief when I took other wives was unnatural. When rumours spread that they might be pregnant her sorrow was uncontrollable. Not even Baisanghar, her own father, or Khanzada could quieten her. One night she attempted to cut her wrists with the shards of a broken pot. My *hakim* had to sedate her with a potent mixture of wine and narcotic *kamali* . . .'

'And is she still so unhappy?'

'No . . . and there's a reason. About four years ago, while I was away on an expedition along the borders of Hindustan, Maham wrote telling me that Dildar was pregnant. Her letter ended, "Whether it is a boy or a girl, I will take my chances. Give the child to me and I will raise it as my own and be content once more."'

'What did you do?'

'It was difficult. I knew I was wronging Dildar but how could I deny Maham something that might comfort her? I wrote back that though the child was still in Dildar's womb, it was hers. As I said, it turned out to be a boy . . .'

'What's his name?'

'Hindal.'

Baburi's eyes flickered. 'Which means Conqueror of Hindustan.'

369

'I chose it in a moment of euphoria. The news of his birth came while I was still away on that expedition. Perhaps it was wishful thinking, but I took it as a sign that Hindustan, with its great wealth, its great possibilities, was where my destiny lay, if only I could find a way . . .'

'Just as we talked about all those years ago when we raided its borders. Do you remember those seemingly limitless skies, that intensely orange sun?'

'Of course – and the lake we saw filled with thousands of birds, wings as red as if they'd been dipped in blood . . . They were hard to forget.' Babur rose from the yellow brocade cushions he'd been leaning against and went over to an open casement. Torches flickered on either side of the gatehouse in the courtyard below where all was quiet, as it should be in the darkest hours of the night. 'But Hindal is three now and I'm no closer to realising my dreams of a great empire in Hindustan or anywhere else . . . I know I should be grateful for what I've got. When they look at me, my nobles and commanders – even Baisanghar, who has been with me all these years – see a king secure on his throne with little to trouble him. They don't understand the dissatisfaction and lack of fulfilment that envelop me. And why should they? I can never tell them . . .'

'What about Khanzada? Surely your sister knows you too well to be fooled.'

'She suspects my restlessness – I'm sure of it. But after all she has been through, I didn't want to load her with my gnawing ambitions and selfish preoccupations – so paltry in comparison with her sufferings . . . And I couldn't talk of it to Maham, she just wouldn't understand . . . whenever I try to speak to her of my dissatisfaction she becomes upset as if I were criticising her. If you'd been here, it might have been different. It's hard to describe to you what my life has become. I have absolute power and live in opulence but sometimes this enviable existence feels like unfulfilling drudgery with nothing to look forward to except more of the same. Often, to deaden my discontent, I hold drinking parties with my nobles where we sample the potent vintages of my kingdom – like this red wine of Ghazni that we are drinking now. We revel till dawn when my attendants carry me, head bobbing in oblivion, back to my apartments. Sometimes I take opium and *bhang* – marijuana. They take me to a bright, vibrant world where everything seems possible.'

'There's no shame in that.'

'But where's the nobility? Where's the glory my soul still hankers for? I'm scarcely four decades old but I feel as trapped as my father did in Ferghana. What's more, the old Timurid world – my world, our world – is gone. The Uzbek barbarians have shattered it for ever. What is left for me?' Babur's voice trembled. He turned to Baburi and, after a pause, added, 'I know I must seem ungrateful and conceited . . . I've never said these things to anyone and perhaps I shouldn't be saying them to you . . . you used to mock my moments of doubt . . .'

'No, not your doubt, only your self-pity. But my life these past years has taught me many things. I was so arrogant, so convinced I was right. I had far more pride than you, though you were the king, not I. Now I understand . . . I know how it feels to want something badly and be unable to find a way to it.'

'What was it you wanted so much?'

'To come back . . .'

'You'll stay?'

'Yes . . . at least, until we have another fight . . .'

• ◆ •

Baburi slapped the end of the five-foot-long bronze tube. 'This is the barrel. First linen bags filled with gunpowder and then the shot are loaded and rammed down into it. And this,' he pointed to the swelling at the bottom end of the barrel, 'is the breech. See this little aperture? They call it the touch-hole. It is where – just before firing – the gunners insert a long, sharp metal spike – the awl – to break open the bag of powder. Finally, a man applies a lighted taper to the touch-hole to create the flashing spark that sets off the main charge in the barrel.'

'How far can it throw the shot?'

'It depends on the length of the barrel and its diameter – the bore. The longer the barrel and the bigger the bore, the further the range. Many of the Turkish sultan's guns have barrels ten feet long or more and some weigh as much as twenty thousand pounds. But they're small compared with the bronze cannon they call the Great Turkish Bombard that Mehmet of Turkey used seventy years ago when he captured Istanbul. You should see it! The seventeen-foot barrel has a thirty-inch bore and it could fire a twelve-hundred-pound stone shot over a mile away. They say you could hear its blast ten miles off. But it could only fire about fifteen shots a day and needed two hundred men to operate it. It was so heavy it took seventy oxen and ten thousand men to shift it, unlike this one.'

'Show me what it can do . . .' Babur wanted to see the miracle weapon at work. The target was a ten-foot-high pile of large stones that Baburi's men had set up three hundred yards away.

Baburi shouted an order to five of his mercenaries, who were wearing round leather skull-caps, leather jerkins and breeches. One man rammed a linen bag down the barrel of the cannon into the breech with a long stick like a polo mallet, except that the top was wrapped in sheepskin. Then another two, grunting with the effort, heaved a round stone shot into the barrel and – again using the stick – sent it rumbling down into the breech. As they finished, the fourth man approached and inserted the awl to puncture the bag of powder inside and scattered a little loose powder around the touch-hole – 'Just to make sure,' Baburi explained.

'Stand back.' He waited till he was content that Babur was far enough away, then walked forward to the cannon and checked the angle of the barrel.

Satisfied, he stepped back and signalled to the fifth man to advance. He held a forked staff with a length of oil-soaked cord attached to it, the tip glowing. The man looked towards Baburi.

'Fire!'

The man pressed his smouldering taper to the touch-hole and leaped back. Seconds later, with a *boom* the missile shot out of the barrel and across the meadow to smash into the target. A cloud of dust erupted, and as it cleared, Babur saw that the tower of stones was now a pile of fragments.

'Look at that.' Baburi's voice was full of pride. 'At Chaltran, Sultan Selim used a row of cannon just like these, protected by a barrier of carts, and there was nothing the Persians could do . . . Afterwards, the Turks surged forward, and shot down any Persians who still resisted with their matchlock muskets. Look . . .'

Baburi clapped his hands and one of his men carried over a long, thin wooden box that he placed at his feet. 'You taught me a long time ago to be an archer. You made me a *Qor Begi*, a Lord of the Bow. Now I can teach you to be a marksman with one of these.' Baburi bent and took a long metal object from the box. 'It's fashioned from the finest steel.'

'It's shaped like a little cannon.'

'Exactly. It's a musket – a cannon in miniature. See, it has a long metal barrel for firing a ball. This matchlock mechanism, as it's called, is how it works. You put the gunpowder here, into the pan, then light the end of a thin piece of rope. When the flame reaches the gunpowder, it ignites it and the force fires the ball from the barrel.'

'How far?'

'More than two hundred yards but it's most accurate up to about fifty. Try it.'

As soon as one of the Turks had set up a melon on a pole as a target, Baburi poured a small amount of gunpowder into the pan and loaded the shot. 'To help take the weight as you aim, you should rest the barrel on this frame.' Baburi indicated a tall metal stick about four feet high that forked at the top to make a cradle. Thrusting the end of the stick into the ground, he showed Babur how to rest the barrel of the musket in the centre of the cradle. 'Look straight down the barrel at your target and, remember, when it fires you'll feel a kick, so brace yourself. Ready?'

Babur took the musket, placing the butt against his shoulder, closed his left eye and focused his right along the shining barrel. When he thought he had the melon in his sights, he nodded. Baburi lit the piece of rope, which began to smoulder.

'Keep it steady . . .' Baburi was still speaking as, with a sharp crack, the ball shot out and the top of the melon disintegrated in a spray of orange pulp . . . 'Good. But now let me show you what my trained musketeers can do with these . . .' He gestured to another row of targets: fifteen straw dolls lined up on a trestle table some fifty yards away. An equal number of Baburi's men lined up, primed and loaded their weapons and, one after another, fired with perfect precision, each man knocking over his target, then stepping back smartly to reload and stand to attention. Immediately the fifteenth man had reloaded, they swung round a hundred and eighty degrees, rested their muskets again in the cradles and fired at a row of clay pots set up even further away. Again, each man's aim was perfect.

'Of course, in the heat of battle, fingers fumble, targets move, but I've seen these guns shatter advancing lines of soldiers.'

Babur put his arm around Baburi's shoulders as he tried to put into words the vision that had been forming in his mind as he had watched his friend demonstrate the power of these miraculous new weapons. It was as if Canopus had risen above the enshrouding clouds to blaze brightly on him and his dynasty once more.

'You're not just my friend. You're my inspiration. You've brought me far more than weapons . . . Until now, although I've long wished to make one, a full-scale attack on Hindustan was not possible. I had neither the numbers of men nor any special advantage. The rulers there are numerous and strong. Their overlord is the proud, arrogant Sultan Ibrahim Lodi of Delhi. To win Hindustan I must defeat his huge armies and his ranks of war elephants. But with these new weapons I now see how I can do it. I may not be destined to have a great empire like Timur's in the lands of my birth but with your cannon and muskets I can surpass his raid over the Indus to Delhi. We will fulfil the dreams we had all those years ago.'

Chapter 21

Blood and Thunder

Dreams of greatness came easily. Achieving it was harder. It had taken Baburi and his Turkish mercenaries six months to create a corps of troops skilled at firing the cannon and muskets he had brought to Kabul. Meanwhile, as the citizens of Kabul had grown used to the flashes and booms around their city, Babur had despatched an embassy to the Turkish sultan, with a message from Baburi and bags of gold coin, to buy six more cannon and four hundred muskets from the foundries and gun-makers of Istanbul.

Even more satisfying to Babur had been the knowledge that his own armourers were learning to make the new weapons under the expert guidance of Ali-Quli, the grey-bearded Turkish master-gunner who had accompanied Baburi to Kabul. His ability with both cannon and musket was extraordinary – especially as five years ago, two fingers of his right hand had been blown off by an exploding matchlock with a cracked barrel.

Night after night, Babur had sat late with Baburi, questioning minutely his accounts of battles in which cannon and matchlocks had been deployed. In what circumstances were they most effective? In open battle or siege? How could you best protect your gunners and matchlock men against archers or cavalry charges? How did these weapons change the traditional methods of attack? Before he tested them in battle, he must understand everything.

Babur also sent men out into the city to linger in the large, arched caravanserais where the merchants of many lands displayed their wares on raised stone platforms in the middle of the courtyard, trading gossip as well as goods. Babur's agents listened carefully, asking the occasional discreet question. They heard much boastful talk from the Hindustani merchants about Delhi's vast palaces of carved rose-pink sandstone and the grandeur of Sultan Ibrahim's court but not the faintest rumour that he – or any other ruler of Hindustan – had acquired cannon and matchlock muskets.

But now, at last, on a cold, clear January day, Babur was leading an expedition to see for himself the effect of these weapons against an enemy unused to them. That enemy was the new Sultan of Bajaur, a dependency of Kabul, who had taken it into his foolish young head to refuse Babur the customary annual tribute in grain, sheep and oxen.

The Bajauris, living high in the mountains in dense forests of oak, olive and wormwood, noisy with rasping mynah birds, were an idolatrous, infidel people with strange beliefs. When a Bajaur woman died the men placed her corpse on a stretcher and, taking each of the four corners, raised it up. If she had lived a good life, the Bajaurs believed her spirit would cause the men holding the stretcher to shake so violently that her body would be thrown to the ground. Only then would the people don black mourning garb and begin their lament. If, on the other hand, a female corpse induced no such motion, it was considered proof of an evil life and the body was tossed unceremoniously on to a fire to be reduced to nothing.

The ruler of these singular people had provided him with a fine opportunity, Babur thought, as, with Baburi by his side, he rode out of Kabul at the head of a column that included a detachment of newly trained matchlock men and gunners, all hand-picked by Ali-Quli, and four cannon. They circled northwards up through hilly terrain towards Bajaur. In the old days, Babur and his men would have ridden fast and hard on a raid like this, taking their enemy by surprise. But the heavy cannon in their trundling bullock carts slowed their pace, providing more opportunity and time for observers to raise the alarm.

Babur brooded on this as he rode, not noticing the chill wind in his face. He was also reflecting on a passage he had come across in a chronicle shortly before leaving Kabul: 'Timur prized bold and valiant warriors by whose aid he opened the locks of terror and ripped in pieces men like lions and through them and their battles overturned the heights of mountains . . .' It also told of Timur's loathing for cowards. Any man, whatever his rank, who failed him in battle had had his head shaved and his body painted red. Then, dressed in women's clothes, he had been dragged through the camp to be beaten and reviled by his comrades before being executed. Mercy had been unknown to Timur.

Babur understood the need for ruthlessness. Just three nights ago, on a surprise tour of inspection, he had found five men asleep on picket duty and had ordered an example to be made of them. Their left ears had been sliced off and the men paraded before the rest of Babur's force, bleeding and with the severed ears on a string round their necks. But if he was to succeed, as Timur had done, in forging and holding an empire, he would have to find even greater reserves of toughness within himself, an even greater ability to sacrifice others to his ambition without the appearance of a second thought.

'Majesty.' One of Babur's scouts, well muffled in sheepskin against the cold, rode up to him. 'The sultan has fled from his capital ten miles ahead of us to a fortress on the banks of the Bajaur river in the hill country twenty miles east of here. He has taken all his army, two thousand soldiers, with him.'

'You're sure of this – it isn't a trap?'

'We saw him ride out with his troops, accompanied by many camp-followers and citizens, and tracked him all the way.'

'Tell me about the fortress.' Babur leaned forward in his saddle, green eyes glinting above his face-cloth.

'It's a large rectangular mud-brick structure, two storeys high, on the brink of a river gorge . . . Let me show you.'

The scout dismounted, cleared a patch of earth and, with the tip of his dagger, marked out a square tower with a river running through the gorge beneath its north wall. 'See, Majesty. Rising scrubland surrounds it on three sides. This single gateway in the southern wall is the only way in – or out . . .'

Baburi and Babur exchanged a glance. It couldn't be better. The sultan thought himself in a stronghold. In fact, he was in a trap.

· ◆ ·

Four days later, Babur drew on his leather gauntlets in his scarlet command tent in his camp on one of the few stretches of flat land not far from the fortress. As he had expected, the sultan had ignored his invitation the previous evening to surrender and find mercy. Now he would face the consequences. Under cover of the night men and oxen had dragged the four guns into position four hundred yards from the gateway to the fortress. As quietly as they could, Ali-Quli's men had dug mounds of earth on which to rest the guns, then concealed them with brushwood until the moment for action came.

And that moment was fast approaching. Each of Babur's commanders had had his orders. The main force was to advance openly on the fortress's southern side and immediately launch a frontal assault. Meanwhile, the matchlock men would follow them, ready to pick off defenders on the battlements. Finally, when he judged the time was right, Babur would reveal his cannon.

Under a steely grey sky, Babur gave the signal for the attack to begin. From a new vantage-point on the edge of a copse three hundred yards below the western corner of the fortress, where he and Baburi sat side by side on their horses, he watched his mounted archers charge up the stony slope to the fortress, loosing arrows as they rode. Dismounting, they began to hoist the broad wooden ladders they had dragged with them up against the fortress walls, to the left of the gateway. While they worked, Ali-Quli and his matchlock men fired at any defender rash enough to expose himself on the battlements above.

Two Bajauris fell immediately. Even from where he was, Babur sensed the defenders' consternation and dismay. More fell. As the Bajauris realised that the red-hot balls could penetrate even shields and chain-mail, they began vanishing from the battlements.

Babur's men were already swarming up the rough ladders two abreast. Keeping themselves pressed as close to the walls and ladders as possible, they held their round shields high to protect themselves against any missiles from above. Ali-Quli had already signalled the matchlock men to hold fire for fear of hitting their own side. Baba Yasaval, a courageous warrior from near Herat, was the first to reach the battlements and, fighting his way to the gatehouse, at once got to work with his men, trying to winch up the black metal grille blocking the main gateway. But now that the muskets had fallen silent, the defenders had regained their courage. Babur could see them running back on to the battlements, striking at Baba Yasaval's outnumbered men with spiked maces and battleaxes, forcing them to fall back from the gatehouse.

Babur exchanged a brief glance with Baburi who, understanding exactly what was in his mind, rode swiftly to the cannon and their teams, concealed further down the slope. Babur watched as the gunners dragged the brushwood from around the weapons and adjusted the angle of elevation of each barrel.

Next, they rammed in the bags of gunpowder and the stone shot, inserted their spiked awls into each touch-hole and quickly sprinkled a little more gunpowder around. Finally, four more men advanced to light the charges – Babur could just see the glowing tips of the lengths of oil-soaked cord. Baburi looked across at him and, seeing him circle his sword above his head, gave the order to fire. All of a sudden, above the ordinary noise of battle, booming, cracking sounds never heard before in Bajaur tore the air.

The first cannon ball smashed into the lower storey of the agreed target, the fortress's twenty-foot-high south-eastern wall to the right of the gateway. It struck about ten feet above the ground, spraying chunks of brick and dust in all directions. The second ball hit just below as did the third and fourth. When the dust and smoke cleared, a small part of the wall had collapsed and there was a large fissure in a neighbouring section. A detachment of Babur's men, held in reserve till now, were already scrambling over the piles of rubble into the fortress.

Stunned defenders were fleeing, some letting themselves down from the battlements on ropes, slipping and falling in their haste to get away before the unknown weapon that had destroyed part of the walls roared again.

While Babur's archers provided covering fire, the matchlock men moved closer, set up their forks and fired at the fugitives. Babur saw two Bajauris tumble over, one in complete silence with a musketball hole in his forehead, the other – a yellow-turbaned giant – screaming and clutching at his chest with twitching fingers that dripped blood. But so many were running, stumbling and falling down the eastward slope beneath the fortress and away from Babur's men that it was impossible for the matchlock men to deal with them all.

'Ride them down!' Babur ordered a troop of his guard. Then, sword in hand, he galloped up the incline towards the main gate where his men had now succeeded in retaking the gatehouse and raising the grille. Baburi joined him just as he reached it and they rode in together.

'Majesty.' Baba Yasaval, his face shiny with sweat from his efforts and blood running from a jagged cut above his left ear, greeted Babur as he emerged into the courtyard. 'The sultan is dead – he threw himself from the battlements into the gorge. We have taken many prisoners. What are your orders?'

'Timur opened the locks of terror and overturned the heights of mountains . . .' Those words – cruel, perhaps, but very clear – resonated in Babur's head. 'Execute the royal council. They had the opportunity to submit but rejected it. Round up the rest – women and children too – to be sent to Kabul to work as slaves for our people.'

'Well? What do you think? How did we do?' Baburi asked, as they inspected the conquered fortress and the damage inflicted by the cannon.

Babur struggled to put his feelings into words. Because of his new weapons the fortress had fallen in hours, not days, weeks or months. The possibilities seemed limitless. He gripped Baburi's shoulder. 'Today we fought in a way my ancestors never knew, that would have amazed them . . .'

'So why don't you look more cheerful?'

'Too often I've let myself be seduced by grand prospects that did not materialise. Haven't you often said so yourself? I don't want to rush into an attack against Hindustan until I'm sure we're ready.'

'But today was a beginning, wasn't it?'

• ◆ •

The weeks that followed provided further chances for Babur

to test both weapons and tactics. Leaving a conquered and subdued Bajaur, he took his men south-eastwards into the wild, mountainous country bordering Hindustan. Again, none of his opponents had any response to the crash of his cannon or the crack of his muskets.

Indeed, on learning of Babur's approach nervous chieftains fell over themselves to send gifts of sheep, grain, horses, even women, accompanied by grovelling messages. Their eagerness to placate him and preserve from destruction their villages and mud fortresses perched on hilltops provoked a wry amusement in Babur. Some even presented themselves before him with grass in their mouths – the gesture of submission Babur had seen among other wild tribes in his youth.

But his interest in subduing petty chiefs was waning. At night, when he tried to sleep, different images filled his mind. A conqueror – 'eyes like candles without the brilliance' – surveyed the great river, the Indus, that lay between him and his objective. Timur had had no difficulty is overcoming men. Neither had he let any physical barrier stand in his way – no mountain or river had stopped him. Babur must be the same. Fifteen years ago, in blistering summer heat, he and Baburi had gazed on the Indus. Waking with a start he felt a fierce desire to do so again that he could not later explain – not to Baburi or even to himself . . . But it persisted and strengthened.

Putting aside thoughts of further campaigning, Babur turned his column eastward until, on a chill March morning, a broad, swift-flowing river finally came in sight. Without waiting for any of his men, he galloped ahead over cold, hard earth. Reaching the bank, he jumped from his horse, ripped off his clothes and dived into the snow-fed waters that had flowed all the way from the distant mountains of Tibet.

The water was so cold that he gasped and swallowed a freezing mouthful that seemed to constrict his throat with ice. The strong current was already sweeping him away and cries of alarm were coming from his men on the bank. Taking another deep breath – but this time keeping his mouth well above the water – he struck out with powerful strokes, defying the elemental force that wanted to carry him off. With elation he realised he was not only holding his position but making headway. He was winning. There was a splash beside him and Baburi's head pushed up out of the water beside him.

'You idiot, what are you doing?' Baburi's face was almost blue. 'And why are you laughing?'

'Swim with me to the other side and I'll tell you.'

Together they forced themselves through the eddies and currents until they reached the far bank and, grabbing handfuls of coarse, sage-green grass, hauled themselves out. Babur flung himself on to the ground, still chuckling though he was shuddering and his chilled skin was puckering with goose-pimples.

'So what's this all about?' Baburi looked down at him, shaking his hair out of his eyes and slapping his sides to keep warm.

'Last night I was unable to sleep. The thought of the Indus so near made my blood roar in my ears like the waters of the river itself. I made a vow that if God grants me victory in Hindustan, I'll swim every river in my new empire.'

'You didn't have to start so soon . . . you're still a long way from conquering anything.'

Babur sat up. 'I had to do it. How could I look at the Indus and not cross it . . . ? Though we must return to Kabul it won't be long till we're back. And when I return, this earth will know I have already claimed it. It will welcome me . . .'

'And now I suppose we have to swim back?'

'Of course.'

• ◆ •

In the hour before dawn, eight months after his swim in the freezing Indus, Babur left Maham's chamber where, for one last time, he had lost himself in the silken folds of her body, and her long, sandalwood-scented hair, and returned to be alone in his private apartments. He listened as the war drums boomed out their sombre rhythm across the meadows beneath the citadel of Kabul. Going on to the balcony, he looked out into the soft half-light, pricked by the glow of thousands of campfires. Yesterday, on this same balcony, with Baburi close behind him, he had announced his grand design to his people.

'From the time Timur invaded Hindustan it has been the rightful property of his descendants. As chief among them I will ride tomorrow to claim what is mine from those who have usurped my birthright. Four months ago I sent a hawk to the self-proclaimed ruler of much of Hindustan – Sultan Ibrahim Lodi of Delhi – as a gift. I told him if he would acknowledge me as his overlord I would give him lands to govern as my vassal. He sent the hawk back – without its head. Now he will lose his throne for insulting the House of Timur and the ruler of Kabul.'

Babur's people had roared out their approval of his martial tone even if Sultan Ibrahim was just a name to them and they knew nothing of his palaces and fortresses in Delhi and Agra, his great treasuries and vast armies or the confederation of rulers – some Muslim like himself, others infidels – who were his vassals. Babur had smiled inwardly at their unthinking acceptance of his words. True, he had a claim to Hindustan but his greater birthright was to Samarkand. The memory of it still moved him but he knew he would never rule there again.

'Majesty, your sister wishes to speak to you.' An attendant interrupted Babur's thoughts.

'Of course. Does she wish me to go to her?'

'No, Majesty, she is here.'

Khanzada stepped out on to the balcony. As soon as she and Babur were alone she lowered her veil. The light falling on her face from a torch in a bracket on the wall softened her angular features and smoothed away the lines. Babur saw again the girl who had solemnly brought their father's sword, Alamgir, to him in the fortress of Akhsi the night he'd claimed the throne of Ferghana.

'I know that later you will return to the women's quarters to bid your wives and myself goodbye, but I wanted a moment with you alone. You and I are the only ones who remain from the happy days of our childhood in Ferghana when life seemed so secure, so full of promise. We have experienced much since then, both great highs and lows . . .' She paused. 'Our lives might have been easier and less eventful but fate made them otherwise. Now you go on this great expedition of yours into Hindustan, which will decide the place of our family in history. I pray it may bring you everything you and I desire, just as our father, mother and grandmother would have done. Victory and conquest will give a point to what we have lived through . . . but take care, my little brother.' Khanzada's raisin eyes – so like their grandmother's but darker – shone with tears.

'I will, just as when you scolded me to be careful after I fell from my first pony when I was trying to turn too tightly.' Babur put his arm round her. 'Whatever happens, you know that I'm following my destiny and trying to live up to my birth. The signs are favourable. Hasn't the court astrologer predicted that if I launch my expedition now, in late November, while the sun is in Sagittarius, I will be victorious?'

For a brief moment, Khanzada held his face in her hands and kissed his forehead. 'Goodbye, brother, till we meet again.'

'I will send for you when victory is ours.'

Then she was gone, hastening back to the women's quarters where he knew that, in the months ahead – whatever her own anxieties – she would be the strong hub, the comforter rather than the comforted. Humayun would accompany him on the campaign but he had appointed Kamran as regent in

387

Kabul. Even though he would have the wise guidance in public of Baisanghar and Kasim who would both also remain, Khanzada's astute advice would be the best guarantee of Kabul's safety and good governance in his absence. He knew also that she would prevent too many jealousies arising among his wives, listening, conciliating and consoling, just as Esan Dawlat had done.

Out of the darkness came the sound of a trumpet, a reminder that in the meadows below the citadel, more than ten thousand horsemen were stirring. Soon they would be checking their weapons and equipment and saddling their horses. The standard-bearers would be unfurling the banners that Babur had decided to stripe with yellow and green – the colours of his homeland, Ferghana, and of Timur's capital, Samarkand – and emblazon with the three circles that Timur had painted on his banners, to represent the perfect conjunction of the planets at his birth.

The gunners and matchlock men, their skills honed by rigorous, relentless training, would also be preparing. The cannons, muskets, gunpowder and shot were already loaded on to the carts. So were the huge amounts of equipment needed to set up camp – the heavy hide tents, their supporting poles and the great cooking pots needed to feed so many mouths.

As soon as the sky began to pale, the teams of oxen would be yoked. The long lines of pack-beasts – double-humped camels, donkeys, ponies – would be loaded with their burdens of grain, cured meats and other stores. The merchants who would follow Babur's army to set up the camp market would also be preparing their baggage and animal trains – a long, successful campaign offered the prospect of huge profits. With them would come the usual mass of camp-followers – labourers, scavengers, water-bearers, women with children at the breast, anxious to be near their men, other women hoping to survive by selling their bodies, the acrobats, dancers and musicians who knew soldiers would pay well for a bit of entertainment to distract them from thoughts of war. A whole city was on the move.

A few hours later, just before midday, with the winter sun shedding its silvery light over the landscape, Babur rode out from the citadel of Kabul, Timur's gold ring on his finger and Alamgir at his waist, to a glorious cacophony of trumpets. As he passed the high walls of the city a knot tightened in his stomach – apprehension, anticipation, excitement? It was all of those things and he had known them many times.

But this time it was different. He felt an awesome solemnity. Truly, fortune was extending her hand . . . if only he could grasp it, all that had gone before – his fight for his throne in Ferghana, his attempts to overcome the Uzbeks and hold Samarkand, his rule over Kabul – would prove simply stepping-stones to a greater destiny for himself and his dynasty . . .

• ◆ •

'The astrologer was right. Fortune is favouring us,' Babur told Humayun and Baburi, lounging beside him on cushions beneath leather awnings on a large raft being navigated by oarsmen down the swift-flowing Kabul river. Around them, on a string of larger craft, were the cannon and much of the heavy baggage, while the bulk of the army made its way along the banks.

'You did well, Humayun, to raise so many troops among the northern nomads.' Ten days after Babur and the main force had left Kabul, his son had joined them with more than two thousand soldiers from the wilds of Badakhshan.

'It wasn't difficult, Father – not with all the gold we had to offer.'

'They're good fighters, the Badakhshanis, though they're quick to quarrel among themselves or with others,' said Baburi, drawing his blue cloak more tightly round him against the chill air blowing off the water.

'The pace they're having to keep up should sap their surplus energy,' Babur said.

The sight of the rushing jade waters bearing him downriver towards Hindustan pushed thoughts of troublesome tribesmen from his mind and filled him with euphoria. Soon he'd call for some *bhang* mixed with opium. Once it had provided an escape from reality but now it enhanced the happiness of the present and heightened his optimism for the future. Each time he took it, even the austere, stony grey landscape they were passing through seemed drenched in a golden light and every feature – every tree, every flower, even the flocks of fat, shaggy sheep – was endowed with a fresh, startling beauty. When he closed his eyes, other images crowded his mind – of his men galloping joyously across battlefields strewn with the bodies of his enemies, their horses' hoofs scarcely touching the ground, of himself wearing a golden crown glittering with rubies and sitting on a golden throne beneath an infinite sky . . .

'What are you smiling about?' asked Baburi.

'I'm thinking about what's ahead. Where we'll be in a year from now.'

'In Delhi, I hope . . .'

'And where d'you think we'll be, Humayun?'

'I don't know, Father . . . but, God willing, we'll have slain your enemies and won an empire.'

Babur and Baburi exchanged an amused glance at his naivety but then their expressions sobered. Grandiose words, perhaps, for one so young but weren't their sentiments exactly the same?

• ◆ •

'Majesty, the scouts have returned. They have found a suitable place to cross the Indus.'

Babur's heart leaped. This was the news he had been waiting for ever since, leaving the Kabul river behind, he had marched his army safely beyond the bare, pebbly defiles of the Khyber Pass and south-eastwards towards the Indus. He and Baburi had just set out to go hunting – villagers had reported two rhinoceroses browsing beneath the interlaced branches of an oak wood five miles beyond his camp – but that would have to wait.

'Come!' Babur called to Baburi, then galloped back to where the scouts were waiting outside his scarlet campaign tent.

'Majesty, there is a place a day's march from here where, if we build rafts, we can float everything across,' the commander of the scouts reported.

'What about the currents?'

'The crossing place is just below a sharp bend in the river that reduces the strength of the current at that point – we experimented, floating three pack-mules across, and it went well. Also, there are enough trees to cut down for the rafts and there was no sign of any habitation along that stretch of the bank. We should be able to cross unmolested.'

Next day, Babur and Baburi looked for the third time in their lives on the Indus.

'You're not going to go swimming again, are you?' Baburi asked. 'Because if you are, I'm not coming in this time . . .'

'No more swimming until I have my empire. We're in luck – the level of the river is lower than when we last saw it.' Babur stooped, picked up a stick and flung it in. 'The scouts were right. That bend in the river does reduce the force of the current – the stick is floating away quite slowly . . .'

'You sound almost disappointed. Do you want some symbolic epic struggle to get across?'

'I don't want it but I expected it. We'll camp here, and as soon as our carpenters have built enough rafts, we go over.'

Constructing the rafts – felling trees, hewing wood into rough planks, securing them together with rope and covering the surface with hide cut from spare tents – took three days. On the fourth, they crossed. Although a thin veil of cold rain was falling, turning the banks to oozing mud and making the rafts slippery, getting so many men and beasts over the Indus took only from first light until midday. The advance guard went first, then the horses, camels, bullocks, and the all-important cannon and muskets. Next came the soldiers, merchants and the camp baggage, leaving the camp-followers to make their own crossing. The only losses were three camels that, badly laden and not properly tethered, had capsized a small raft and drowned.

As soon as he arrived on the other side, Babur ordered a small tent to be erected. Entering it alone he fastened the flaps. Then, he knelt, leaned forward and pressed his lips to the bare earth. 'I claimed you once and I do so again,' he whispered. 'I claim you for the House of Timur, for myself and my descendants.' Taking a small agate locket that hung on a chain round his neck, he opened it and very carefully, with the tip of his dagger, dug a few grains of earth and tipped them inside. Then closing the locket again he tucked it back inside his tunic where it rested against his heart.

• ◆ •

In the February sunset, the waters of the Sutlej river beside Babur's camp glowed amber. It was the final great waterway before the north-west plains of Hindustan and Sultan Ibrahim's great city of Delhi. They had done well to get there so quickly, Babur thought. After crossing the Indus, the winter rain had stayed with them for a while. The soft ground had slowed their pace as the horses and pack-animals had struggled, especially the beasts drawing the cannon. But at last the rain had ceased and they had advanced steadily, crossing the network of tributaries of the Indus.

So far they had faced only wild, lawless tribes. One – the Gujars – had descended on Babur's men as they negotiated a narrow pass but his rearguard had easily repulsed them. The piles of Gujari heads left in neat stacks had been an effective deterrent and no others had dared attack. Once across the Sutlej, it would be a different matter. They would be entering the lands of powerful chiefs who were vassals of Sultan Ibrahim. A few days ago, Babur had sent messengers over the river with an ultimatum to one of these – Firoz Khan – whose lands lay directly between him and Delhi: 'Your lands once belonged to Timur and I claim them as my birthright. Surrender them and pledge me your allegiance. Then you may continue to rule as my vassal and there will be no pillage or plunder.'

In reply, the chieftain had sent back the gift of a fine, mail-clad horse, the colour of pale almond blossom, with a message: 'Your claim is artificial. My allegiance is to Sultan Ibrahim in Delhi, the rightful ruler of Hindustan. After your long journey into lands that do not belong to you, your own horse will be tired and thin. May this beast carry you swiftly back to Kabul.' Babur had laughed at the man's arrogance and given the horse to Baburi.

Firoz Khan would regret his impudence, Babur thought, as he made his way back to his campaign tent. Humayun had begged to be allowed to take a small advance force of his Badakhshani nomads over the Sutlej to spy out the terrain in preparation for the advance of the main force on Firoz Khan's stronghold and Babur had agreed. Soon, God willing, he would rendezvous with his son after crossing the river and show Firoz Khan weapons he had never seen . . . In his tent, he paced up and down, restless and conscious that the success of his long-pent-up ambition would soon be decided. Towards midnight, he ordered his attendants to bring him some opium mixed with wine. It would help him relax, maybe even sleep – something he was finding it harder and harder to do.

The heady concoction did its work and Babur's mind began to wander down pleasant paths . . . he'd no idea how long had passed when suddenly the crack of thunder intruded into his dreams. The day had been hot and humid. Perhaps the rains would bring freshness to the air.

Soon heavy rain was pounding the roof of his tent. After a while, droplets started to ooze through the seams. He began to count them – one, two, three, splash . . . one, two, three, splash . . . His eyelids were drooping when suddenly he heard Baburi's voice and felt a strong hand shaking him to full consciousness. 'The river's burst its banks! The camp's being washed away.'

'What?' Dazed with the opium, he found it hard to take in Baburi's words.

'We're being flooded. The river's turning into a lake. We've got to move.'

Grabbing Alamgir in its scabbard and chaining it to his belt, Babur rushed outside and could hardly believe what he saw: the whole camp was already beneath a foot of muddy water. His commanders, struggling through it towards his tent from all directions, were looking to him for orders.

His poppy-induced languor vanished. 'Abandon the tents and the heavy baggage. Get the horses and the men to higher ground.' Through the rain – falling so heavily that it stung – he could just make out the low hills to their rear. 'Carry with you as many of the muskets and as much of the gunpowder as you can. Leave the cannon – the water cannot move them. Untether the pack-animals. They must fend for themselves, as must all in the camp . . . There is little time.'

Babur shouted through the teeming rain to his attendants to bring his horse and Baburi's. Together they rode through the rising waters, encouraging men to save what they could, but then – when the water was almost up to stirrup level – they made for the hills. Their frightened horses, half swimming, struggled at first. Bending low over their necks, Babur and Baburi whispered encouragement into their ears. Detritus from the camp floated all around them – cooking pots, riding boots, drowned chickens and sheep. When they finally reached the higher ground, Babur found many of his horsemen already gathered there. Some had managed to bring others to safety with them – women and children, sodden and miserable, were among those sheltering beneath the trees.

About dawn, the rain stopped and a few hours later the floodwaters were receding. Closing his eyes, Babur gave thanks. At least nearly all of the army seemed to have survived. As soon as the waters had subsided they would return to the camp and retrieve everything they had abandoned – the cannon, their chain-mail, armour, weapons, tents and whatever provisions were still fit to eat. Then they would round up the pack-beasts. He would take no more opium till Hindustan was his.

The whine of a mosquito landing on the back of his sunburned neck distracted Babur and he slapped it, leaving a smear of dark-red blood – his own. But it was others' blood that was about to flow. He had no need of his court astrologer to tell him that. First Firoz Khan's, and then anyone else's who opposed him on the road to Delhi. Nobody would stand in his way.

Chapter 22

Panipat

Babur's men had erected his large, scarlet command tent at the very centre of the camp they had pitched two days previously at the small village of Panipat on the plains north-west of Delhi. The tent gave little respite from the intense dry heat of an April afternoon to Babur and his military council gathered around him. When the side flaps were down the atmosphere soon grew stifling. When they were pulled back and secured with leather thongs, the omnipresent wind blew in gritty dust that clogged noses and stung eyes. The windbreaks of thick brown cloth erected some yards from the tent had improved things only a little.

Babur sat on his gilded throne with his back to the breeze, drinking a sherbet made from local limes mixed with water and some of the last of the carefully preserved ice they had brought down from the mountains. Baburi, squatting on his haunches by Babur's left side, was doing likewise, lowering the thin yellow cotton cloth he had tied over the lower part of his face to protect against the dust each time he took a sip.

Just a month after his eighteenth birthday Humayun was

seated on a stool to his father's right. He was wearing a deep green tunic woven from the thinnest cotton loosely belted over baggy trousers of the same material. Like several other commanders, he was being cooled by a great peacock feather fan wielded dextrously above his head by servants stripped to the waist but still perspiring copiously with the effort.

'What do our scouts tell us about the movement of Sultan Ibrahim's troops, Baburi?'

'They're still moving towards us but taking their time about it. They break camp only every other day and even then they only travel five or six miles before making camp again, partly because of the size of their baggage train but also, I think, because they've no great appetite for an early engagement. They'd rather leave us to eat up our supplies or – in our impatience – make an unwise attack of our own.'

'No chance of that, I hope. We must tempt them to attack us so that we can make the most of our cannon and muskets, firing from defensive positions and thus reducing the effect of their greater numbers. While we're on the subject, what are the latest estimates of their strength?' Babur put down his sherbet.

'About a hundred thousand – two thirds cavalry, the rest foot-soldiers. The latter probably with plenty of eagerness for plunder but little for battle. And then, of course, there are the war elephants. Our spies say there are around a thousand, nearly all in good condition, well trained and armoured. They're a real worry. Even if we sit on the defensive we'll need to blunt their charge before they get into our lines. Otherwise, if they do get in amongst us, we'll find it difficult to keep our men disciplined. Most have scarcely seen an elephant, never mind fought one—'

'The cannon will help,' interrupted Humayun.

'Yes, but we'll need to protect them too if they're to be reloaded and get off enough shots to make a difference. We musn't let them be overrun after firing just a couple of rounds.'

'We could position them at the centre of our formation, just as this tent is at the centre of the camp for protection,' Humayun said.

'But they'll need a clear field of fire . . .' Baburi went on.

'Let me speak.' Babur motioned both Humayun and Baburi to be silent. 'Baburi, do you remember what that old woman – Rehana – told us all those years ago, when we were not much older than Humayun is now, about Timur's strategy when he took Delhi? Last night I was thinking about our battle plan and what my great ancestor might have done when I remembered Rehana – and that I had had the good sense to have her account transcribed and still had it in the chest where I keep important royal papers and my diary . . .

'When I read it I found it provided the main elements of a battle plan against the elephants. Timur had trenches dug and used the earth to build ramparts in front of his lines. Then he ordered tethered bullocks to be roped together as a further line of protection. I thought we, too, should dig trenches and throw up earth barricades – but instead of tying bullocks together, we should link our baggage wagons by knotting their traces to each other, leaving gaps at intervals through which our cannon – placed as you suggested, Humayun, at our centre – can fire and our cavalry make sorties when necessary. We could station the musketeers and some of our best mounted archers to protect the gaps between the wagons with crossfire.'

Nods of agreement followed, but Baburi asked, 'That begs the question of how you'll make sure they actually attack us, rather than try to force us into retreat by cutting off our supplies.'

'Once we've prepared our positions, if they don't attack after a few days we'll attempt to provoke them. We'll make a flanking movement apparently aimed at their camp and its treasure or – better still – launch a limited attack and then feign retreat. We'll make them think they've bested us and that an easy victory will be theirs if only they follow through . . .'

●◆●

Over the next few days, Babur's soldiers worked from the cool hours of dawn through the hottest part of the day, when the horizon shimmered in a heat haze, and on to dusk, digging the hard, dry ground to scrape out trenches and throw up earth barricades. It was slow, exhausting work. Many collapsed from the effect of the sun, all too many falling into a delirium – eyes rolling, tongues lolling – from which they were never to rise.

To hearten the men, Babur and Humayun each took a spade and laboured with them, filling buckets with earth and carrying them two at a time suspended from wooden shoulder yokes to the top of the ramparts. After three days the barricades were of sufficient height. Behind them, the wagons had been linked together and bullocks had drawn the cannon into carefully measured positions in the gaps between them. Supplies of the heavy stone cannon balls had been piled next to each and the Turkish gunners were drilling their men in the loading process. The noise of the armourers' hammers and the clamour of numerous voices – excited and apprehensive – echoed around the camp.

As Babur rode by on his tour of inspection, Baburi at his side, the voices hushed for a moment and the soldiers stood still, bowing their heads. Baburi leaned across to Babur. 'The latest reports still show the forces of Delhi disinclined to attack although they are now only three miles off.'

'But at least – if our informers are right – there's dissent and desertion in their camp, with complaints that Ibrahim is miserly in paying his troops and even more parsimonious with promises of future reward. A divided house is easier to conquer than a united one and – equally important – easier to provoke to rash action.'

'True.'

'Ibrahim must know that waiting will sap morale and leave scope for more complaining and quarrelling, and perhaps more desertions.'

'But even we can't hold our men in check for too long, however good our discipline is and however often we explain the reasons for delay.'

'Let's plan a sortie to draw him on to us.'

'When?'

'Tomorrow. Call the military council.'

· ◆ ·

About an hour before dusk the next day Babur, on his black horse, watched as four thousand of his best men − half of them archers − mounted and then, amid the shouts of their officers and the neighing and snorting of their horses, who seemed to have absorbed some of their riders' excitement and nervous tension, formed themselves into ranks and then squadrons. As soon as they had done so, Babur led his force out of his encampment, through the barricades and trenches, and started to circle to the west of Sultan Ibrahim's position. He had decided to attack from out of the setting sun so that, with the glare combining with the dust from the horses' hoofs, his opponents would be unable to tell the number of their assailants. When they had reached a point about a mile west of Sultan Ibrahim's outposts, Babur halted his men and turned to Baburi. 'Have you chosen the men to snatch some prisoners?'

'Yes. I'll lead them myself.'

'Then let's go.'

'Keep safe for the final battle.'

With a wave of his arm, Babur gave the order to charge. Digging his heels into the glossy black flanks of his horse he rapidly outdistanced his men. Soon he was a hundred yards ahead. He realised he felt no fear, only exhilaration at the speed of his charge, and a joy that his strength remained that of his youth. Then he remembered Baburi's parting words: this was not the final battle on which his destiny depended, just a raid to bring it on. He must curb his impatience and exuberance and allow the riders following to take closer order round him. As he did so, he saw that, in front of them, Ibrahim's men were running for their weapons. Some were already mounted and the first arrows were flying towards his own troops.

Moments later, Babur's black horse had carried him in among his enemies and he was instinctively twisting and slashing to left and right with Alamgir. To him, the fight became a series of images blurring together: a Hindustani with a blue turban falling beneath his horse's hoofs, blood streaming from a slash across his face that had exposed his teeth; a brown tent suddenly appearing in front of him so that he had to drag his horse's head round to avoid becoming entangled with it; an axe whizzing through the air to embed itself in the neck of the horse beside him, followed by the thud as its slow fall pitched its rider to the ground.

Suddenly Babur saw open space before him. He was through the first line – he and his men must wheel round rather than penetrate deeper and risk being swallowed up by his opponents. Reining in his excited horse with difficulty, he gave the prearranged signal to come round and gallop back through the swirling dust that was now blanketing Ibrahim's disordered troops.

Babur knew this turn was the moment of greatest danger, when his galloping men could collide with each other and become an easy target for Sultan Ibrahim's archers. However, his cavalry were well trained and – although he saw one or two men take crashing falls as they tried to turn their mounts too tightly – most accomplished it successfully and Babur was soon back through the dust and confusion of the enemy line and riding for his own camp, pursued by a hissing shower of arrows. Just as he had ordered before the attack began, his men immediately broke formation and scattered, some throwing away their shields as if in panic.

Darkness was falling swiftly, as it always did on the plains, by the time Babur dismounted within the protection of his earth ramparts. He did not have long to wait before Baburi appeared from the gathering gloom. He had a white cloth tied tightly round the knuckles of his left hand and, from the scarlet stain, had clearly suffered a sword slash. However, he was smiling as he approached Babur.

'You've got the prisoners?'

'A fine selection – not just water-carriers but some cavalrymen including a captain who put up a great fight before we could subdue him.'

'He'll be our messenger, then. Bring him to my tent in five minutes. Make sure he and the rest stay blindfolded. We don't want them reporting on our dispositions.'

Five minutes later, Baburi led his prisoner into Babur's presence. He was a tall, muscular man with dark skin. As he approached, Babur noticed he had a bushy moustache of the type beloved by so many Hindustanis and reflected that few from his homeland – himself included – had the luxuriant hair required to produce one.

'Take off that blindfold. What is your name?'

'Asif Iqbal.'

'Well, Asif Iqbal, you are as fortunate as I am told you are brave. You're to be released to bear a message from me to Sultan Ibrahim.'

The man showed no emotion, merely bowing his head in acknowledgement that he understood.

'You will tell him that although we were repulsed in our attack today and have suffered many casualties, we defy him. We call him coward because even though he has overwhelming numbers he dare not attack us. Ask him if it is because his commanders will not obey him – you can tell him several have sent messages to me offering their allegiance for reward.

403

Or is it because he knows that God will not support him, a ruler whose army numbers far more infidels than it does followers of the true faith? Tell him, "Attack, or for ever bear the name of coward."'

After the black blindfold had been re-tied tightly round the captain's eyes and he had been led out to be released near Ibrahim's camp, Babur turned to Baburi. 'Let's hope that that and the impression of weakness we gave by our pretended flight tonight are enough to encourage Ibrahim to the attack.'

'They should be. No man likes to be called coward. Ibrahim knows that there is discontent within his army and the suggestion that some nobles are in secret contact with us should make him want to attack before his army begins to disintegrate and he loses some of his advantage in numbers.'

'I agree. Arrange for our men to be called to arms an hour before dawn. Any attack from Ibrahim will surely come before the heat of the day.'

Baburi was turning to go when suddenly he embraced Babur. 'Tomorrow will be a fateful day for us both. I feel it.'

'Sleep well. Fate will favour the rested, I'm sure.'

Without reply, Baburi walked from the tent and was swallowed up by the darkness beyond.

• ◆ •

Ever since dawn there had been great activity in Sultan Ibrahim's camp – shouting, the trumpeting of elephants and the neighing of horses. A few minutes ago Ibrahim's drummers had begun to beat out an urgent rhythm.

He really is going to attack, Babur thought. If so, this would be the most decisive day of Babur's life but he had done all he could to ensure victory. Scarcely sleeping, he had gone over his battle plan throughout the night, looking for flaws or weaknesses without finding any. There was no more he could do . . .

He called Baburi and Humayun to him for their final

orders. Humayun was to command the right wing and Baburi the left. Once battle was well joined and Ibrahim's men preoccupied with the attack on Babur's barricades of earth and wagons, they were to start an encircling movement. When, God willing, victory was theirs, they were to pursue any fleeing enemies relentlessly to prevent them regrouping.

When his son and his comrade had departed to their positions, Babur rode round the troops that would defend the barricades and addressed them in small groups. His message was usually the same: 'Yours is the position of glory. You will decide the fate of the battle. Be strong. Trust in yourself and our cause. You have seen the strength of our new weapons, the cannon and the muskets. You must defend them well from the enemy to allow them to wreak their havoc.'

Once he singled out a bunch of nervous young cavalrymen, clustered together round their mounts, checking and rechecking their equipment. 'I remember how I felt in my first battle. The waiting is the worst. I know you will fight well when the time comes. Concentrate on the enemy in front of you, trusting in your comrades to protect you from the side.'

In another part of the line he dismounted at one of the earth barricades and tested the bow-string of a leathery-skinned veteran with a pink scar high on his bald head who was at his post behind the rampart. 'How far can you send an arrow with this bow?'

'Five hundred yards, Majesty.'

'Well, I don't need to remind a seasoned soldier like you to wait until our enemies are four hundred and ninety-nine yards away before you fire. But perhaps I do need to say that you'll serve me best by aiming at the riders sitting behind the ears of those elephants I hear preparing over there. Once they are dead, the beasts are directionless and will trample their own men.'

As he rode back to his place in the centre of the barricades,

Babur made his final stop before the captain of his Turkish gunners, Ali-Quli. 'Thank you for travelling so far from your homeland to fight with me. I know that each of your weapons is worth fifty of our opponents' elephants, however daunting they may seem. Put them to flight and I'll reward you well.'

Back in his position Babur dismounted and knelt for a moment in prayer. As he finished, images of his father, his mother, his grandmother Esan Dawlat, Wazir Khan and Baisanghar came into his mind. Esan Dawlat's expression seemed the most warlike of all. Silently he promised, I will do you all honour today and prove I am worthy of you and the blood of Timur and Genghis.

'Majesty, they're definitely on the move.'

His *qorchi* broke into Babur's thoughts and he stood up, calm and confident in his destiny. His squire fitted on his steel breastplate, buckled on his father's sword and handed him his domed helmet, with its green and yellow plume, together with a long leather-sheathed dagger that Babur stuck into the top of one of his brown leather riding boots.

He could see that Ibrahim's forces were advancing swiftly now. As he'd expected, the war elephants were in the lead. Most seemed twice a man's height and the morning sun reflected off the shiny, overlapping steel plates of their armour. Curved scimitars – six feet in length – were strapped to their scarlet-painted tusks. The drivers were urging their elephants to move more quickly with blows from the large wooden sticks they held in their hands. Already archers were firing from the *howdahs* – the small castles positioned on the elephants' backs – but the arrows were falling short: they were still out of range.

Babur hoped his own men would heed his command to hold their fire until they could reach their target. But first let Ibrahim's men and beasts feel the effect of his new weapon from the west: the cannon. Babur waved Alamgir twice above his head – the prearranged signal to Ali-Quli to open fire.

He saw the first artilleryman bend to put a lighted taper to the powder in the firing hole. Then there was a flash, a roar, and white smoke emerged from the barrel as the cannon ball was propelled towards the enemy. Other flashes followed from the rest of the cannon and smoke began to drift across the barricades.

Through it Babur saw one of the leading elephants fall, dislodging its *howdah* and sending the occupants sprawling to the ground. Then the wounded beast staggered upright again, turned, trunk raised in what looked like a trumpet of pain, and crossed the path of its neighbour, bringing it down, too, before collapsing again, blood pouring from the stump of one of its front legs. As it lay, thrashing its head back and forth in agony, the scimitar on its tusk cut into an elephant following, which – frightened and in pain – bolted. But although such incidents were being repeated the length of the advancing line, Sultan Ibrahim's forces were still pressing on.

Suddenly, Babur heard the crackling discharge of muskets. More of his enemies fell. Then his archers started to fire, some riding out from behind the barricades to get closer to their targets – the drivers sitting behind the elephants' white-painted ears. Ibrahim's front line wavered. More elephants trumpeted in fright and turned to the rear, bringing a crashing halt to those behind, provoking yet more to panic and trample their own men beneath their great feet as they fled.

Babur yelled for more mounted archers to ride out and fire into the swiftly disintegrating enemy ranks. As he did so, he felt, rather than heard, a loud explosion near him and pieces of hot metal showered around him while something warm and soft stuck to his face. Dazed and partly deafened, he could not think what had happened. Then he realised one of his cannon had exploded and Ali-Quli had been blown apart. Raising his hand to his cheek he discovered it was a piece of his master-gunner's flesh that had struck him.

Ali-Quli would now receive his reward in Paradise, not on earth, but his work had been well done. More and more of Sultan Ibrahim's troops were fleeing when they could, in particular the infantry, many of whom were barefoot, wearing only a loincloth and with just a spear to defend themselves.

Pulling himself together, Babur waved his sword in a gesture for his best cavalry to follow, kicked his heels into the flanks of his black horse and led them at a gallop through the smoke and dust the half-mile into the heaving, shouting mass of fleeing, frightened men.

Some of Ibrahim's troops were made of more determined stuff and were putting up a brave fight, grouping themselves tightly into defensive formations. Babur made for a small hillock on which one such group of cavalry – about a hundred men all wearing gold turbans – were succeeding in driving off all attacks.

'It's Ibrahim's bodyguard,' one of his men yelled. Babur rode directly towards the tall officer who appeared to be commanding them. Swerving to the left at the last minute to pass him, Babur slashed with his sword in his right hand but the officer raised his shield in time to deflect the blow and, with his other hand, cut deep into the rump of Babur's black stallion with his sword. The animal reared in pain and Babur was thrown to the earth. As he struggled to regain his feet, he saw the officer urge his white horse towards him, bent on finishing him off.

Babur stood his ground until the last minute, then jumped to the side slashing wildly with Alamgir as he did so. The sword skimmed along the left side of the white horse's neck and then penetrated deep into the thigh of its rider. However, he was clearly an expert horseman and despite his wound stayed in the saddle, controlling his horse and wheeling it – bright red staining its white coat – ready to attack Babur once more.

This time, Babur ducked low as the officer swung his

sword with the aim of decapitating him, and cut with Alamgir at the back of the white horse's foreleg. He hit his target and the horse fell, trapping its rider beneath it and causing his sword to fly from his grasp. As the officer struggled to reach for it, Babur put his foot on his wrist and Alamgir to his throat. 'Surrender. You deserve to live for your bravery.' As he spoke, more of his men assembled around him, having at last killed or put to flight the rest of the gold-turbaned warriors. Seeing further resistance was useless, the officer lay still. 'I will give you my word not to renew the fight,' he said.

'Help him to his feet . . . What was it you and your fellows were struggling so bravely to protect?'

'The body of Sultan Ibrahim. It lies over there. He was mortally wounded by the sting of one of your new weapons. They have rendered bravery useless.'

'No weapon is more powerful than he who aims it.'

All the while they had been speaking, the officer's white horse had been neighing and thrashing in pain, blood running from the cut on its neck and unable to support itself on the foreleg where Babur had slashed its tendon. Now, bleeding from the mouth and speaking with increasing difficulty – probably from the effect of being crushed by his mount – the officer said, 'Allow me to have my sword to put my stallion to rest. I have ridden him in many battles. He will face death more calmly if I am the one to inflict it.'

Babur signed to one of his men to return the sword. The officer – scarcely able to walk from the wound in his own thigh as well as his shortage of breath – moved over to the horse. Taking its gold leather bridle he stroked its nose, cradled its head and whispered into its ear. His words seemed to calm it. Then he quickly drew his sharp sword across its throat severing its windpipe and artery and more red blood spurted. The horse collapsed instantly and within moments was still, its blood welling up into the dust. However, the officer was not finished. He thrust the sword into his own abdomen. 'I can no more survive crippled than can my horse.'

'May your soul rest in peace.'

'I pray so, but remember that to subdue Hindustan you'll need to subdue many men braver than I.'

As the last words bubbled scarcely audibly through the froth of blood in his throat, he too died, his body slumping across that of his stallion while his gold-turbaned head hit the bloodstained earth.

'Majesty, the battle is yours.'

The words of his *qorchi* roused Babur from contemplation of the scene before him. Looking around, he realised that the battlefield was falling silent, that the fighting was over . . . He had triumphed. 'Praise God.' He felt an enormous sense of relief. Then at the thought of what his victory meant, he punched the air in joy. He – like Timur – would enter Delhi in triumph . . .

Dragging his mind back to the present, Babur addressed the riders around him. 'We have done well. Let us hope that Humayun and Baburi succeed in capturing or thoroughly dispersing Ibrahim's retreating forces. At least with him dead they will have no leader to rally round. Bury Ibrahim – and indeed this brave officer – with due ceremony. I will return to our camp to await news of the pursuit.'

His victory had been so swift that it was not yet midday when Babur turned his horse and rode back towards his camp, past the bodies of elephants lying like great boulders amid the dust, mostly surrounded by the wreckage of their *howdahs* and the crumpled bodies of the soldiers fallen from them. In the heat, his own men had already begun to gather up their wounded, placing them on rough stretchers, binding their wounds and offering them water and what other comfort they could.

In his red tent once more, Babur paced back and forth.

Where were Humayun and Baburi? He was less worried about his friend than his inexperienced son. Although Humayun had fought in skirmishes before, and performed well, this was his first command at a big battle and the leadership of the right wing in the pursuit was a major and novel responsibility for him.

Babur distracted himself by making short visits to the wounded and to reward soldiers reported to have fought particularly bravely, as well as in hearing reports of the plunder captured from Ibrahim's camp. Already it seemed he had a vast haul of jewels and gold at his disposal.

Six hours had passed before a guard entered Babur's tent to announce, 'The pennants and flags of Prince Humayun's column have been seen approaching.'

He had barely finished speaking before a breathless Humayun entered, rushed to his father and embraced him. 'Our victory is complete. We are masters of Hindustan. We followed a large group of Ibrahim's men more than ten miles to the south-west until they made a stand in a mud fortress by a river. After an hour's fight we forced them to surrender. A little further to the west we found a group of nobles' tents that were being defended by a few guards or servants against what looked more like bandits or looters than soldiers from any army.

'When we had killed the attackers, a beautiful woman of about my mother's age emerged from a white tent with cream and gold awnings. She was wrapped in one of those garments the Hindustanis call *saris*. It was a fine silk and had many pearls and jewels sewn on to it. She asked who was in command, and on being told it was I, and that I was your son, requested to be brought before me. She told me she was the mother of the ruler of Gwalior, a wealthy kingdom to the south of Delhi. She had heard her son had been killed fighting courageously for Ibrahim.

'Instead of fleeing when she learned the news she had

411

determined to wait to receive his body and perform the proper funeral ceremonies. They're infidels who cremate the bodies of their dead on pyres. Then a fleeing soldier galloping past their camp had yelled that our forces were killing the prisoners, so many of her men, except a brave few, had abandoned her. And the brigands – dacoits, she called them – whom we defeated had seen their chance of plunder and had attacked the camp. She had feared for her life and her honour but, most of all, she had feared for her six-month-old grandson who, with his young mother, the dead ruler's favourite wife, was still in the tent.

'I told her to fear no more, that we were a cultured, civilised people, not savages like the dacoits. Tears of gratitude wetted her face and she gave me this, which I now give you as a token of our great victory.' As he spoke Humayun handed Babur a soft red leather pouch secured by a gold leather thong. Babur undid the tie and pulled out a large stone that glistened and sparkled in the gloom of the tent. 'It's a diamond, Father, from the mine at Golconda a thousand miles to the south – the biggest I've ever seen. The jeweller of the royal family of Gwalior once valued it as worth half of the daily expenditure of the whole world. It is called the Koh-i-Nur, the Mountain of Light . . .'

Babur was held by the gem's perfect purity and brilliance. Light radiated from it as if from a star – the Canopus, he thought, smiling at his fancy . . . Still, the jewel's intense brightness seemed to belong to the heavens rather than the earth whence it had been dug . . .

'Indeed, my son, you have merited your name, Fortunate. Long may it continue until—' Babur broke off in mid-sentence. Through the open entrance of the tent he had glimpsed two attendants carrying a stretcher covered with a sheet towards him. From all the shouting and bustle, it was clear that Baburi's column had now also returned. Where was he? Why hadn't he come to report and share in the joy of conquest? Then Babur saw that a hand wearing a richly chased golden ruby ring was trailing in the dust from beneath the sheet. He had given that ring to Baburi many years ago to mark the success of one of their campaigns. As the two handsome young men carrying the bier lowered it gently to the ground before Babur, he recognised them as Baburi's attendants.

Slowly Babur bent and, with a trembling hand, pulled back the bloodstained cloth and gazed at the monstrously mangled body of his brother-in-arms.

'We came upon a large body of Ibrahim's men retreating towards Delhi in good order with forty elephants in their vanguard and the same number in their rear. Our master Baburi ordered an immediate charge and we routed your enemies, who fled in all directions. But during the last moments of the fight, our master was knocked down, trampled and crushed by one of the elephants, wounded and enraged by a spear thrust deep into its mouth,' said one of the attendants.

Only Baburi's face – even paler than in life – was untouched. His intense indigo eyes still stared up at Babur and there was a half-smile on his face. Babur could not prevent himself weeping as, leaning over the bier once more, he closed Baburi's eyes and kissed him on his forehead. 'Goodbye, my brother . . .'

Chapter 23

The First Moghul

The sun's metallic glare hurt Babur's eyes. Advancing over the arid landscape where even the scrubby bushes were coated with dust, he was glad of the shade of the green and yellow brocade canopy supported on golden poles by the four riders around him. A strong wind was whipping up the dust – he had already learned that his new subjects called it *andhi* and that it meant the rains were not far off.

Immediately after Panipat, he had ordered Humayun and four of his commanders with their men to leave behind their heavy baggage and ride hard and fast to Ibrahim's capital at Agra – a hundred and twenty miles south-east of Delhi along the Jumna river – to seize the fort and the imperial treasuries there before the garrison had time to organise their defences. Now, three days later, Babur was taking the bulk of his victorious army south to Delhi. At the rear, almost obscured beneath a billowing cloud of dust, were ranks of plodding war elephants – still streaked in red paint – that his men had rounded up after the battle.

Babur should have been jubilant but grief for Baburi was blunting his triumph. In the first hours after he had learned of Baburi's death, he had shut himself away in his tent, unwilling to see anyone or to address the many tasks and decisions that awaited him as the new ruler of Hindustan. Baburi's death wasn't just the loss of a best friend – it felt like the passing of his previous life. He would never – could never – have a friend like that again – a friend who had shared his youth and his fluctuating fortunes.

When he'd first met Baburi he'd been not yet twenty, the ruler of a small part of Ferghana, more a footloose warlord than a king. Now he was a father and emperor of a large realm who must always be conscious of his dignity and keep his distance in his dealings with others of whatever rank. From now on, his closest companions would inevitably be his sons. Much as he loved them it would not be the same as with Baburi. The difference in age and experience between them, the respect, the filial obedience they owed him would always lie between them, as would his overwhelming desire to protect them, and to teach them how to live and rule. They could not challenge him, laugh at him – as well as with him – as Baburi had done . . .

So many memories, so many thoughts and feelings, kept running through Babur's mind – the first time he'd seen Baburi's sharp-featured, streetwise face and intensely indigo eyes as he'd rushed to save a child from beneath the hoofs of Babur's horse; Baburi's first tentative efforts to ride; the freedom of their youth; their wild, drunken nights together in the whorehouses of Ferghana; all those years of companionship and humour, of huddling together for warmth as cold winds buffeted their tent, of raids and battles, some victorious, some otherwise . . .

So many of those events had played out against the backdrop of the world he and Baburi had belonged to, a place of cold, tumbling, twisting rivers, of enfolding hills, sharp-sided valleys and endless plains that were sweet with clover in the summer but in winter froze hard as iron. A place of rich cities with domes and minarets of turquoise and green, ancient *madrasas* and libraries where the Timurid heritage was understood and revered. Now, without his friend, Babur was in a new land that had no understanding of him and that he, in turn, did not yet fully comprehend. Except that he already knew he didn't like the climate. Sweat was trickling down his face and the air felt almost solid, as if it had never known a breath of wind. Beneath his plumed headdress, his head throbbed.

At least they'd not encountered any hostility as they advanced. Sometimes Babur had seen small groups watching curiously from a distance as his long line of horsemen and endless baggage carts passed by. Now, shading his eyes, he could see a jumble of low, mud-built thatched houses to one side of the wide track they were following. Golden cakes of animal dung were drying in the sun. Skinny, pale-furred dogs were lying in the meagre pools of shade and a few scrawny hens were running about. Of people there was no sign, either outside the houses or in the surrounding fields where thin-legged white egrets pecked insects off the backs of water buffalo with their yellow bills.

All in all, it looked a mean little settlement. Babur turned away, but then he noticed something else just beyond the village, a large, curiously shaped sandstone edifice within a low, walled compound. Its scale seemed out of proportion with the village. As he drew nearer he saw that the front façade of the main building was a carved mass of what looked like intertwined figures, arms and legs protruding everywhere. Several times on the long road to Panipat he'd glimpsed similar buildings but had had neither the time nor the inclination to examine them.

He signalled a halt. 'Find out what this place is,' he ordered his *qorchi*.

Fifteen minutes later, the squire returned with a tiny old man, desiccated face furrowed as a walnut and eyes filmy with age, together with one of Babur's captains, Junayd Barlas.

As a youth, Junayd had learned Hindi from a Hindustani carpet dealer who had settled in Kabul. Babur had appointed him his interpreter until he could find a better one.

'This man says it is a Hindu temple, Majesty,' Junayd explained. 'I think he is one of its priests.'

'I'd like to see it.' Babur dismounted and examined the priest more closely. The man was almost entirely naked except for a loincloth which, wound around his think flanks and passing between his legs, was secured to a string around his waist. Around his left shoulder and passing under his right arm was a long loop of cotton thread. His coarse white hair and beard were long and straggling and there was what looked like a smudge of ashes on his forehead. In his right hand he carried a wooden stick, as gnarled as himself.

Slowly the priest led the way into the compound. The main building was indeed like nothing Babur had ever seen before. Its front was a seven-tiered structure perhaps thirty feet wide at the base, which tapered into a squared-off tower at the top. Carved figures of humans – men and women – with voluptuous bodies and staring, bulbous eyes, wearing clinging, seemingly semi-transparent garments, with jewels on their foreheads and around their necks and arms, covered the façade. Interspersed with these figures – some of whom seemed to be dancing and others about to copulate – were strange, fierce-looking, warlike characters – demons, perhaps, or gods. Some had the heads of animals – monkeys and elephants.

Babur stared. So much elemental life and vitality, but what did it mean? A doorway led into the building. To one side a flight of narrow dark stairs ascended to the upper storeys. There was a strong smell he didn't recognise, a scent richer, sweeter and far more pungent than sandalwood.

The priest glanced over his shoulder. Satisfied that Babur was still close behind, he walked on, his staff tapping the dusty stone slabs on the ground. Babur followed him into the building's square inner courtyard around which ran a covered gallery. The walls were carved with scenes from what he supposed must be some Hindu folktale or legend. Warriors, with the faces of monkeys, brandishing short swords appeared to be crossing a bridge to an island to do battle.

Richly carved sandstone pillars depicting more well-fleshed bodies – some with four, six or even eight arms – supported the gallery. On one side of the courtyard was a large white stone statue of a kneeling bull, a string of marigolds round its muscular neck and sticks of incense burning in a brass pot before it. Nearby, with lighted candles surrounding it, was a simple column of black stone – basalt perhaps – rounded at the top and in places worn so smooth the stone shone like marble. In front of it lay small offerings of oil, food and lotus flowers.

'What is that?' Babur asked.

Junayd Barlas consulted the priest but appeared to have difficulty in understanding the answer. At last he said, 'They call it a *lingam*, Majesty. It represents the male sexual organ and is a symbol of fertility.'

But Babur's attention had been caught by something else on the other side of the courtyard, a larger-than-life stone figure of a powerfully built man sitting cross-legged with arms raised beneath a carved canopy. Under his elaborate headdress, the face was strong, determined, forceful, the eyes staring ahead.

'That is one of their gods – they call him Shiva,' said the interpreter, after another hurried consultation with the priest. But the old man evidently had something else to say because he was continuing to mutter. Junayd Barlas bent lower to catch his words. 'The priest wishes you to know some words from one of their holy books. "Behold, I am come. I am Shiva, the destroyer . . ."'

The priest was watching him with a sly expression. What was he trying to say? That Babur was the destroyer who had

419

come amongst them – or that the Hindus and their gods would destroy him . . . ?

He turned and strode from the inner courtyard, back through the main building and swiftly out of the compound. He mounted his horse and, taking a drink of water from a cup his squire held up to him, signalled that he was ready to ride on. With his bodyguards behind him, he kicked his horse on without a backward glance at the temple and its mystifying figures.

A few yards further on, directly in their path, a cow sprawled contentedly on the ground, apparently untroubled by the cloud of black flies buzzing round its long-lashed eyes. It was a wide-horned beast and, by the standards of Babur's homeland, a scraggy creature, its bony hips and ribs clearly defined beneath its dull brown hide. One of Babur's men trotted forward and prodded it with the butt of his spear. The animal emitted a groan of protest but didn't move. The man reversed his spear, intending to give the cow something sharper to think about when, from somewhere behind Babur, came an angry cry.

Looking around, he saw the priest rush forward with more speed than he would have thought possible for such a spindly frame. The old man's face was contorted as he shouted, waving his arms and his stick. Two of Babur's bodyguards jumped off their horses and seized him before he could come too close to Babur.

Babur signalled to Junayd Barlas. 'What does he want?'

'He is cursing you, Majesty.'

'I'll have him flogged for his insolence.'

'You don't understand, Majesty, he says the Hindus consider the cow a sacred creature that must be left free to roam where it will. He feared you were about to kill it . . .'

Babur looked down at the old man. 'Let him go. And tell him I didn't understand. Tell him I meant no disrespect to his faith.'

As he listened to Junayd Barlas's translation, the old man's expression relaxed. By now the cow had become bored and rising clumsily to its feet ambled off to the shade of a tree. Babur's army was free to advance once more through his new possessions.

• ◆ •

Four days later, Babur and his army reached Delhi, whose governor offered no resistance. It was the largest and most populous city he'd ever seen. The airy grace of Samarkand or Herat was missing but some parts were not unpleasing. He inspected the large sandstone mosques, delicately arched palaces and a curiously carved two hundred and forty foot high, tapering tower – the Qutb Minar – built centuries earlier for reasons no one seemed to know. Complexes of royal tombs – domed, pillared, colonnaded – were everywhere. These smacked to Babur of conceit – clearly the Delhi sultans had wished to be as splendid in death as they had been in life. Now all they had left were these cities of the dead . . .

Babur didn't linger long – just long enough to have the *khutba* read in his name in the Friday Mosque and to inspect the contents of the imperial treasuries, filled with enough jewels, pearls and gold to justify the expedition on their own account. However, Ibrahim's nervous former chamberlain in Delhi – summoned before Babur – quickly volunteered that the main treasure was, just as Babur had thought, in Agra. He had done well to despatch Humayun there. After ordering an inventory to be made and appointing one of his commanders as the city's new governor, Babur set out south-east along the river Jumna to join Humayun in Agra.

The heat was so intense that Babur was surprised any living thing could stir. Yet as his journey continued he noticed more people than before. Soon the roads and fields seemed filled with them, staring and apparently unafraid. The tight discipline he had insisted on must be having its effect . . . His new subjects – the men half naked in their loincloths and the women in lengths of brightly coloured cloth wound round their bodies and thrown over their heads, with red marks on their foreheads and gold studs in their noses – certainly didn't seem intimidated. They pressed curiously around Babur and his army as they passed through the sun-baked villages, to which clung an ever-present sweetish aroma of drying cattle dung, spices and incense, and even brought out sacks of grain and fruit and vegetables to sell to the troops.

As the days passed, the flat, brown, dry landscape with its teeming people beneath a relentless sun began to oppress Babur. He felt leached of life and vitality. It was not much better at night when mosquitoes whined and his attendants could do little to cool his tent, designed for colder climes. He found no refreshment in looking at the sluggish Jumna. Its fetid banks of cracked mud made him long for the swift rivers and bracing air of his homeland beyond the Indus.

On the sixth evening, a messenger arrived bringing a gift from Kabul. In a metal-lined wooden cask that, at the start of its journey, must have been packed with ice, he found some melons, sent by Khanzada who knew it was his favourite fruit. Alone in his tent, as he cut into the moist flesh and tasted the sweet juice, tears pricked his eyes, so strong was his sense of exile. Khanzada had meant to give him pleasure but her gift had also brought him pain.

Reaching for pen, ink and the diary that in recent months he had too often neglected, Babur began to write:

Hindustan is a land of few charms. Its people are not handsome . . . There are no good horses or dogs, meat, grapes, fragrant melons or other excellent fruit. There is no ice, cold water or good provisions in the bazaars. There are no hot baths nor *madrasas*. Except their rivers and streams, which flow in ravines and hollows, there are no running waters in their gardens or residences . . .

He paused. What would Baburi, who had brought him the means to conquer Hindustan, have said to him? What he had just written looked bitter and carping. Baburi had detested any sign of self-pity and had always been quick to spot it. He would have told Babur to get on with it . . . that he had been given a great chance and it was his duty not to squander it. But perhaps if Baburi was still with him, he wouldn't feel like this . . .

Reaching inside his tunic, Babur drew out the soft leather pouch in which he kept the Koh-i-Nur, his Mountain of Light. Even in the gloom of the tent it shone, a potent symbol of this new land that sent renewed energy and determination flowing through him. This was no time for regret. If Hindustan was not yet the kind of land he wanted, he and his sons must make it so. They must create an empire so fabulous that, for centuries, people would speak of it with awe.

Opening a fresh page in his diary, he began again:

From the year when I first came to Kabul, I had coveted Hindustan. Now, through God's great favour, I have conquered a mighty adversary, Sultan Ibrahim, and won for my dynasty a new empire.

After a moment's further thought he added,

The best thing about Hindustan is that it is a large land with an abundance of gold and other wealth . . .

Yes, much could be done here by a man if he only had the will . . .

• ◆ •

Babur's mood lifted further as he continued his progress south-eastward. He began to notice that the land was not as bare as he had thought. Despite the dryness and the hot winds, some flowers bloomed, like the red *gudhal* with blossoms deeper in colour than those of the pomegranate, and the oleander, five-petalled like peach blossom, with a faint but exquisite scent.

With his new optimism came the thought that – if he was indeed to establish himself here – he must try to understand this new land and its customs. With the aid of Junayd Barlas as interpreter, he began to question some of those they passed on the road, farmers, merchants, peasants, about the things he saw. One day he noticed a man in a purple turban striking with a mallet a brass disc big as a tray hanging above a tank of water. He learned that this man was a *ghariyali* – a timekeeper. In Babur's homeland each day was divided into twenty-four hours and each hour into sixty minutes but he discovered that in Hindustan his new subjects apportioned day and night into sixty parts – *gharis* – of twenty-four minutes, while night and day were also each divided into four watches, *pahars*. *Ghariyalis* measured the passage of each *pahar* by submerging in water special pots with a hole in the bottom that took exactly one *ghari* to fill. At the end of the first *ghari* of their watch they struck a large, thick brass disc so that all could hear. At the end of the second *ghari* they struck it twice, and so on until their watch was over, when they struck it many times in rapid succession.

From a money-lender whom Babur observed counting coins in the marketplace, he discovered that the Hindustanis had an excellent numbering system: one hundred thousand was equal to one lakh; one hundred lakhs equalled one crore; one hundred crores equalled one arb, and on it went, even higher up the scale. In Kabul there was no need of such high numbers but here in Hindustan, where the wealth – at least

424

of its rulers — seemed almost limitless, there was. It was a pleasing thought.

Babur watched the laborious way in which the farmers irrigated their fields, using leather buckets hauled from the well by oxen, and tasted the sweet, intoxicating wine of the date palm, a plant he'd never seen before. Most of all he attempted to understand more about the Hindu religion, learning that Hindus believed in reincarnation, and that their bewildering multiplicity of gods — from many-armed women festooned with skulls to a pot-bellied elephant-man — were all manifestations of a central trio or *trimurti*: Brahma, the creator of the world, sky and stars; Vishnu, who held them all in balance and harmony; and Shiva, the destroyer. But it still seemed shadowy, confusing, even disturbing. What had Sultan Ibrahim — a Muslim like himself — made of it? Babur thought again of the temple priest's words: 'I am the destroyer . . .'

He soon discovered that he was not the only one to find Hindustan unsettling. Sitting outside his tent one night, hoping for some touch of a breeze on his face, he saw Baba Yasaval approaching.

'Majesty.' His commander touched his breast and waited respectfully.

'What is it?'

Baba Yasaval hesitated.

'Speak.'

'Majesty, my men are growing restless . . . They do not like this new land . . . these hot, incessant winds . . . Many are becoming sick . . .' He paused, torchlight falling on his mosquito-bitten face. 'We're not cowards — we never flinched in battle — but this place is alien to us . . . We want to return to Kabul. I speak not just for myself and my men but for some of the other commanders. They asked me to speak for all of us.'

'Summon them here — now.'

Baba Yasaval had spoken from the heart, saying what had been in Babur's own mind only a few days ago. But hearing those things from the lips of another made him realise how passionately he wanted to keep what he had seized. While he waited, he turned over carefully what he must say. When the commanders were gathered, some avoiding his gaze, he addressed them slowly, deliberately, his eyes never leaving their faces.

'Conquest isn't easy. For years we've struggled, overcome great obstacles, travelled great distances, subjected ourselves to hardship and danger, fought great battles. By God's grace we've overcome numerous enemies and conquered a vast new realm. How can we throw away what we have won at such great cost? How can we go back to Kabul and abandon what God has given us? What will our people say of us? That we were afraid of greatness . . .'

Babur paused to let his words sink in. 'Any man who wishes may take his share of the booty and return across the Indus. But I promise you this. When, as old men, you sit by the fire with your grandchildren and they ask you to tell them what great warriors you once were, you will have nothing to say. You will be ashamed to admit that you left your king – no, your emperor – who had given you a chance of seizing the world . . . You will stay silent and hang your heads, and your grandchildren will drift away . . .'

The commanders looked at one another uneasily and for a few moments there was silence. Then, led by Baba Yasaval, a low chant began, words that Babur had not heard for many years which took him back to his days as boy-king of Ferghana: 'Babur Mirza! Babur Mirza!' The chant grew louder and louder, vibrating through the heavy air. They were affirming their allegiance to him, their king and Timur's heir. They would not leave him. At least, not yet.

◆

Humayun was waiting in the courtyard, his commanders behind him, when, a few days later, Babur rode up the steep ramp into the mighty Agra fortress. As he dismounted, his son knelt briefly before him but Babur quickly raised and embraced him.

'Father, the treasuries are secured. In the harem we found Sultan Ibrahim's mother, Buwa, and his wives and concubines. Buwa called us barbarians – she said she despised us . . . I ignored her insults and ordered that she and the other women be well treated . . . We had no trouble from the local people – indeed, they were relieved to see order restored. When news first came that you had defeated Sultan Ibrahim, bandits – dacoits – took advantage of the chaos to plunder the villages and steal grain, animals and women. We caught some and executed them publicly, here on the parade-ground, in front of the fort where all could see.'

'You've done well. What did you find in the treasuries?'

Humayun grinned. 'I've never seen anything like it – whole vaults filled with gold and silver . . . more gems than I would have believed the mines of the world could produce. Everything has been counted, weighed and noted . . .'

'Good. I must reward my men well and I'll send money to every man, woman and child in Kabul in celebration of our success. In a few days' time, we will hold a victory feast, but now there are things I need to discuss with you and something I must ask. On the road from Delhi, I had time to reflect . . . I thought of other great warriors drawn, like us, to Hindustan – Alexander of Macedonia, who brought his army over the Indus but turned back, and Timur who raided Delhi but did not stay . . . I began to wonder whether we could prosper here . . . Some of my men, brave as they are, also began to question it . . . They don't like this place . . . We could just pile all this treasure on to the backs of our pack-beasts and go home. If we stay, we face many more difficulties and dangers.

'Panipat was a great victory but it was just the start. Only a part of this land is ours – in truth no more than a corridor a mere two hundred miles wide, even if it does extend a thousand miles down from the Khyber Pass. We've met little resistance since Panipat but only because the other rulers of Hindustan have withdrawn to their strongholds to watch and wait. They think we're mere barbarian raiders, nomads, whose rule will be as easily blown away as the morning mist. Already they will be plotting to challenge and expel us. We must ask ourselves whether we have the stomach to fight and fight again until we can call ourselves secure here. Have you that strength, that will, as I do?'

'I have, Father.' Humayun's brown eyes looked unflinchingly at Babur.

'Then we cannot fail, I'm sure of it. I've chosen a name for our new dynasty and lands. On the journey from Delhi, a messenger caught up with me bearing an impudent message from the Shah of Persia, written before he'd learned of our victory at Panipat. He said that he had heard of my enterprise – a "brigand's raid" he called it. He called me a "Moghul" – the Persian word for "Mongol" – in hopes of insulting me as a barbarian pillager. But I wrote back that I take as much pride in my descent from Genghis Khan, greatest of all the Mongols, as I do in my descent from Timur. To be called a "Moghul" is no insult. I told him I will carry that name with pride and so will our new empire which, God willing, might soon eclipse his own.'

•◆•

Preceded by two guards with drawn ceremonial swords, Babur slowly approached the gilded leather double-doors of what had been Sultan Ibrahim's private entrance to his apartments where his commanders now awaited him for the victory feast. Their men were already celebrating in the courtyards below and in tents set up along the riverbanks. No one who had helped in his victory must go unrewarded.

In the torchlight the emeralds in Babur's turban flashed. Round his neck hung a triple string of yet more emeralds intertwined with pearls and on his finger was Timur's ring. His green brocade tunic was fastened at one side with bunches of pearls and Alamgir hung from a heavy gold chain at his waist. Gazing at his reflection a few minutes earlier he had been satisfied to see a glittering image – the embodiment of power and magnificence.

To a blast of trumpets, attendants threw open the doors and Babur entered. Instantly there was silence as each of his commanders, themselves elaborately dressed, fell to the ground to perform the formal obeisance of the *korunush*. Ahead of Babur in the very centre of the room was a tiered white marble dais. On the highest tier was a golden, jewel–encrusted throne beneath a green and yellow canopy. His commanders, lined up in rows before the dais, remained prostrate while Babur, head high, back straight, ascended it, took his place and gestured to Humayun to seat himself on a blue velvet stool placed on the right side of the tier below.

'You may rise.' Babur waited until all eyes were upon him. 'God was magnanimous to us at Panipat. He gave us victory because ours was a just cause. The throne of Hindustan is our birthright. Sultan Ibrahim, who tried to oppose us, is dead. All of us – all of you, my commanders, who came through fire and water with me – are the victors. This is the beginning of a new page of our history, a new destiny for our people, now that we have made ourselves the masters of Hindustan. Still greater glories lie ahead, but tonight let us forget everything but the sweet taste of our victory . . .' Babur stood, raised his arms above his head and cried, 'To our new empire!' as a great roar of acclamation burst out around him.

Sultan Ibrahim had lived well, Babur thought a little while later as he looked critically about him. With its finely carved red sandstone columns, central cupola and rose-pink silken hangings this chamber was more magnificent than anything he had seen since Samarkand. Fragrant smoke curled from two tall golden incense burners shaped like peacocks with outspread tails of sapphires and emeralds on either side of the dais. The wall to Babur's right was a carved sandalwood purdah screen separating the room from the adjoining harem.

In the week since he and his exhausted army had arrived at Agra, the temperature had fallen a little and a breeze had at last begun to blow – perhaps this always happened in the last days before the rains or perhaps it was just good fortune. Babur watched the silk hangings stirring gently.

He and his guests were also being cooled by *punkahs*, huge rectangular pieces of flowered brocade suspended on long silk cords which ran through iron rings in the ceiling before disappearing through small apertures high in the walls to be pulled by *punkah wallahs* – concealed on the other side – so that the brocade swung slowly to and fro above the diners' heads. At low tables set up along the walls facing Babur, they were feeding on roasted mutton, stewed chickens and flat bread, the food of their homeland, but also the fruits of Hindustan: orange-fleshed mangoes oozing juice, creamy, soft papaya and dates.

Many, like him, traced their descent from the clans of Genghis Khan and Timur. All had served him well. Before the feasting had begun, he had bestowed gifts – robes of honour of scarlet silk, sable jackets faced in blue, jewelled daggers, swords and gilded saddles. Babur could see their satisfaction. Baba Yasaval was examining the emerald-studded hilt of the curved sabre he had given him.

As he ate, Babur glanced towards the purdah screen to his right. Normally during feasts the royal women would have been sitting behind it, observing what was happening through the fretwork as they feasted, too. Could Buwa in her apartments within the harem hear these sounds of celebration coming from her son's former quarters? Babur hoped not. Her grief and courage, as much as her royal blood, deserved his respect.

430

The venomous words she had spat at Humayun were no reason to punish her. Wouldn't Esan Dawlat have said exactly same if it was Babur who had been killed and his throne seized? He had decreed that Buwa could keep her jewels and servants and had granted her a pension. He hoped that in time she would be reconciled by his generosity.

Earlier that day, on the banks of the river, Babur had staged fights between trained male elephants from Sultan Ibrahim's stables with names like Mountain Destroyer and Ever Bold. Goaded by riders sitting on their necks, the enormous, painted beasts had faced one another across a specially constructed earth rampart, slashing at each other with their great tusks until one lost heart and retreated. Now it was time for something different – the Hindustani acrobats and dancers who had belonged to Ibrahim's household. Babur clapped his hands.

Two young men, their oiled bodies naked but for orange loincloths, their long black hair knotted on top of their heads, ran lightly in to where space had been cleared before Babur's dais. Between them they carried an oblong yellow box about three feet long and eighteen inches wide with a mysterious eye painted in red on each side. They put the box down and stepped away from it. Babur's men gasped as, slowly – as if of its own accord – the lid began to open. One small hand appeared, and then another, and suddenly the lid was thrown back to reveal a boy with his legs hooked back over his shoulders. It seemed incredible that any human – even one as lithe as this youth who must be double jointed – could contort himself into such a space. Unravelling himself, the boy stepped out of the box and, as the other two acrobats spun brass hoops around their foreheads, knees, hands and feet, somersaulted around the room, slim legs flashing so fast they were a blur.

Next, one of the young men jumped up on the shoulders of the other and the boy then shinned up the two of them as easily as if he were climbing an apple tree. Balancing on the head of the topmost man, he threw back his own head and a rush of flame came from his mouth. Babur's commanders yelled their approval. Quick as a flash the boy was on the floor again. Coiling up his limbs, he fitted himself back into his box and, with a farewell flourish of his hand, snapped the lid shut. The other two acrobats bowed before Babur, who threw them gold coins. Then they picked up the box and to thunderous applause bore it away.

A rhythmic stamping and jingling announced a line of eight barefoot dancing girls who entered the chamber one by one through a small servants' door. At the same time, musicians came in by another entrance. The girls formed a circle before Babur. Their thick, dark hair was plaited with sweet-smelling white flowers. Above red and purple many-layered skirts their midriffs were bare. Tight-fitting silk bodices revealed more than they concealed of their breasts, and rows of tiny bells were twined round their wrists and ankles. Six drummers in baggy white trousers and with chests naked beneath open gold-cloth waistcoats began to beat with their palms on the long, thin drums suspended from around their necks, jumping and swaying in time to the beat. The dancers' bodies began to undulate rhythmically. Soon they were whirling faster and faster, skirts flying up around them revealing their long, slender legs and hands pressed together above their thrown-back heads. As they danced they sang, their high-pitched, honey-sweet voices rising and falling.

The other musicians joined in, playing instruments Babur had never seen before – a sort of lute but with a neck over a metre long that he was told was a *tanpura*, another stringed instrument with two bowls, a *rudra-vina*, and a wind instrument like a compressed trumpet, a *shahnai*. Babur felt the whole performance with its fluid, lithe young bodies, pulsing drums, plangent strings and cascading voices was of an overwhelming, compelling sensuality unique to his new kingdom.

It was late but Babur realised that his men, pulses raised

by the dancers, were just getting started. Some were singing, in deep bass voices, the songs of the steppes and mountains they'd left behind. Others were getting up, arm in arm, to dance wild, martial dances, stamping and shouting, sharing this great moment of joy and triumph. Humayun left his stool to join them.

Babur, though, was lost in his thoughts. He was celebrating more than a victory. Tonight was the start of a new phase in his life when he would bring everything he had done, everything he had learned, to glorious fruition. But the elation was bitter-sweet. Another face should have been at the feast, sharing in it all, but wasn't – that of his truest friend and wisest commander. Babur picked up his goblet and drank a silent tribute to Baburi.

Chapter 24

Buwa

As Babur looked out one Friday evening from a covered watch-tower on the battlements of the Agra fort, the sky was piled with deep grey, almost purple, stormclouds that were releasing sheet after sheet of rain. The raindrops were bouncing off the flagstones of the courtyard and rainwater was pouring from the drainage channels out through the holes cut in the sandstone walls. On the northern and eastern sides of the fort, it fell fountain-like into the muddy waters of the river Jumna in full spate below. On the southern and western sides, it cascaded down into the already large pools that had formed on the parade-ground. Occasionally flashes of lightning lit the low, misty horizon, accompanied by the distant rumble and growl of thunder.

To the watching Babur the air felt cloyingly warm and humid, so different from the intense dry summer heat at this time of year in Central Asia. Here in Hindustan, the rains the native people called the monsoon had already lasted three months. Damp got into everything, mildewing furnishings and clothes if given a chance. He had even had to have his precious diaries dried before a fire to get rid of

435

the moisture that had penetrated the metal casket in which he kept them.

Still, he reflected, shortly he was to dine quietly in his apartments with Humayun which was good – he wasn't in the mood for wider company. He had commanded his chief cook to make one of his favourite dishes: a stew of tender young rabbit cooked slowly in a sauce of cumin and raisins into which curd was stirred just before serving. He had also asked that the four chefs he had retained from Sultan Ibrahim's household to introduce him to the tastes of his new kingdom should produce some of their heavily spiced, garlicky dishes of which he was becoming increasingly fond. The thought of the food awaiting him banished the incipient headache which the monsoon so often produced in him. Turning, he made his way down from the tower to his own apartments.

Humayun was already sitting cross-legged at a large, low table covered with a turquoise linen cloth and set with silver plates. In the middle, a large platter was piled with buttered rice into which pistachios, almonds and other nuts had been stirred. As Babur entered, Humayun rose to embrace him. A little taller than his father, he was broad and muscled – the expedition to Hindustan had brought him to manhood. Babur smiled and motioned to his son to sit. Then, with a clap of his hands, he indicated to the two attendants, both dressed entirely in white, that they should bring in the rest of the food. Within minutes they were back, accompanied by four others, all carrying large metal dishes covered with cloths. As they removed them, a delicious smell of spices filled the room.

'Majesty, this is one of the Hindustani chefs' dishes – chicken simmered in a rich stock with crushed mustard and coriander seeds, ginger, cardamom and cinnamon. This is lamb cooked with butter, bright yellow turmeric, onions and lentils. Then there is another dish of chicken, with spinach – *saag* as the people here call it – garlic and fenugreek seeds baked in a pot over a fire to give it a smoky flavour. Then there are vegetable stews with okra and aubergine – each excellent tasting.'

'All very well and very good, I am sure, but where is my rabbit with raisins?'

'Your steward is bringing it.' As the attendant spoke, the steward – a tall, grey-haired man – brought in the dish and removing the lid showed it to Babur.

'It looks as good as ever, Ahmed.'

'Thank you, Majesty.'

'Let my son try some of the Hindustani dishes so he can advise me on which to taste, but first give me some rabbit.'

The two men began to eat. 'Tell me what arrangements you've made for the embassy to the Sultan of Gujarat.' Babur spoke through a mouthful of rabbit stew.

'I've asked that it be ready to leave as soon as the roads are passable following the rains. They tell me this should be early October. Is that soon enough?'

'I'm sorry – repeat the last bit. I had a sudden cramp in my stomach which took my mind entirely away from Gujarat.'

'Father – are you all right?'

Babur was not. His face was covered with a cold, clammy sweat and he felt another cramp convulse his stomach like a red-hot iron hand had squeezed it. He doubled up in pain, motioning to Humayun and an attendant to help him to his feet. As they did so, yet another cramp seized him and sour vomit rose into his mouth. He tried to swallow it back once, then again, as his gullet heaved once more. He had not gone more than three paces from the table when he vomited, retching from the pit of his stomach. Undigested rabbit mixed with the red wine and sweetmeats he had eaten earlier splashed on to the exquisite rich pink and purple carpet.

Babur retched again as yet another spasm gripped him. This time, mucus and bile were mixed with the food as well as what looked like flecks of blood. He clutched his stomach in agony. 'Forgive me. I don't know what's the matter. I am never sick – not even when I've taken too much wine. Lay me over there on that divan.'

Humayun and the attendant eased Babur on to the cushions and Humayun ordered the *hakim* to be sent for. 'Drink this water, Father.' Babur obediently sipped from the goblet Humayun held out but as soon as the water contacted his stomach, it convulsed again and Babur vomited in a projectile stream.

'Take me to the latrines – my bowels are about to give way too.' Babur tried to rise. Humayun half carried, half supported his father to the latrines where he voided his bowels liquidly, noisily and noisomely.

As he emerged after five painful minutes, Babur was standing slightly more upright than he had been before but his face was still pale and sweating. 'Humayun – do not let them dispose of the vomit – I suspect I've been poisoned – have the vomit scraped from the carpet and given to one of the dogs. Have some of the remains of the rabbit stew given to another. Keep the cook, the tasters and the other servants under guard. I must lie down. I feel very weak.'

•◆•

Early next morning, Humayun was at his father's bedside. Babur was still pale and there were purple bags beneath his eyes but he looked in less pain.

'He can take some liquid without vomiting,' said the brown-robed *hakim*, Abdul-Malik, a sturdy, grey-eyed man who had come with Babur from Kabul and had treated him and his family for many years.

'We followed your directions, Father. We gave the vomit to one dog and some rabbit stew to another and watched them throughout the night. The first was sick, and had violent diarrhoea – just as you did – then slowly recovered. The second lay motionless and whimpering for hours, its stomach

438

distended. Even when we provoked it by throwing stones we could not induce it to move or even bark. But then – an hour ago – it too vomited and is now moving again. The learned *hakims* spent all night consulting their volumes. They confirm that your symptoms and those of the two dogs are indeed those of poison.'

'I thought as much.'

'How can you have been poisoned? You have food tasters and the cooks are not left unsupervised . . .'

'Money will often overcome loyalty. We must find out who is responsible and punish them hard – so hard, so harsh must be the punishments that this will never happen again. Question the chefs, then the tasters. Put any who seem even a little evasive to the torture. Ask Ahmed first whom he suspects. Start with them and don't stop until you have the answers. I've suffered enough pain. Let them suffer too.'

Two hours later Humayun returned, his face grave. 'You were right . . . you were poisoned . . . the culprits have confessed and revealed their backer.'

'Tell me.'

'Ahmed suggested that we start first with one of the Hindustani cooks – a small stringy fellow who served Ibrahim for ten years and had been seeking permission to visit his relations in the next few days. Even the sight of the red-hot irons was too much for him. He blubbed and blurted out what he knew. Roshanna, an old serving woman of Ibrahim's mother, Buwa, had come to him. She told him Buwa wanted revenge against the "barbarians", as she called us, for the death of her son – the cook's old master. To poison you would be an act of merit and of profit and she offered him two gold pieces. He accepted and she gave him the poison in a little paper packet.

'He is a crafty man. He bided his time and ingratiated himself with one of your tasters – one of our own people who was so anxious to return home that he was prepared to be bribed not to taste your rabbit stew . . . the cook cunningly preferred to poison the stew rather than one of the Hindustani dishes to avert suspicion. Then, at the last minute, the cook was disturbed just as he was sprinkling his poison into the stew. He only managed to tip half of it in and threw the rest into a cooking fire.

'We questioned the taster and the old woman. The taster was soon begging for mercy but Roshanna is of sterner stuff. Eventually she broke under the hot iron so far as to confess her own part – but we had to hold her head under water for minutes to make her reveal her mistress's involvement.'

'You have done well.'

'What shall we do with the traitors?'

'They must die publicly and painfully.'

'Buwa too?'

'No, she is of a royal line. For the present confine her to a room in one of the watch-towers from which she can witness the executions.'

'How should the others die?'

'Hack the cook limb from limb. Let the taster, whose breach of trust was the greatest, being one of our own people, be whipped to death. And let the old woman be pressed beneath the elephants' feet in the Hindustani way. Do it at midday – and be sure that a good crowd, including all the kitchen staff, is assembled to see the example made. You must take charge. I am still too weak.'

It was no longer raining but the sky was still grey and lowering as Humayun sat beneath a red canopy on a dais hastily erected among the puddles of the parade-ground to watch the executions. The cook had died quickly, and his bloody and dismembered limbs had been carried off to be impaled separately over the fort gates. The taster's high-pitched cries as the whips fell on him – spread eagled and naked –

440

had been almost animal. They had lasted a long time but he had at last grown silent and his mangled body was being dragged away by the heels through the muddy puddles to be exhibited on the battlements. Now it was Roshanna's turn.

Four guards led the old woman out of a small gate at the foot of one of the fort's towers. She was dressed in a simple white tunic. With her grey hair and calm demeanour she looked – as she probably was – a kind grandmother. Ignoring the crowd, some of whom spat at her and shouted insults as she passed, she looked straight ahead and walked steadily to a slightly raised stone slab ten yards in front of Humayun on which her execution was to take place. Before any of the guards could push her, she had lain on it, face up. Guards bound her hands and feet to the four iron rings set into the slab for the purpose. At the sound of a trumpet, a red-painted elephant began making its way slowly from the stables on the opposite side of the parade-ground, and guards cleared a path for it through the large crowd.

The elephant – a particularly large male – had been specially trained to act as executioner. Such punishments had been commonplace under Ibrahim. At a command from his driver, sitting as usual behind his ears, he lifted his massive right front foot and placed it above the old woman's body. Still she made no sound. Then, at another command, the elephant obediently brought the foot and its full weight down on Roshanna. Humayun heard no scream, just a soft squelch followed by a crunch as the elephant's foot ruptured Roshanna's stomach, spilled her intestines and crunched her spine and pelvis. Then as she lay squashed and lifeless, her white linen shift stained with her bodily fluids, the driver gave the beast the order to turn and begin to make its way back through the now silent onlookers to the stable. It did so deliberately, raising its gory foot from the body.

Before it had taken more than five steps, Humayun heard

a disturbance on the battlements behind him. Turning, he saw a woman run along them, her dark garments billowing around her in the rising breeze, which carried her words to him: 'Rest in Paradise, my son Ibrahim, my faithful Roshanna. I come to join you, crying curses on the upstart Babur and his four sons. May Hindustan slip from his grasp. May his sons quarrel and destroy each other. May they all fall to the dust.'

Buwa, Humayun realised. As he watched, she evaded the guards pursuing her and, reaching a position above the Jumna, plunged headlong into the river and was carried away, long black hair streaming around her in the frothing waters, still screaming defiance. Just as the waters engulfed her, a flash of lightning, followed immediately by a crash of thunder directly overhead, heralded the breaking of the long threatened storm. The rain began to beat down, splashing into the parade-ground's muddy puddles, as Humayun hastily retreated into the shelter of the fort.

That night, images of Buwa flinging herself from the battlements coalesced in Humayun's dreams with the stories Babur had told him of his grandfather's fall from the walls of Akhsi among his fluttering doves.

'I am much better,' Babur told Humayun three days later. 'The opium Abdul-Malik gave me mixed in milk has quieted my cramps. For the first time I really felt death's hand upon me . . . There have been many, many occasions when I might easily have died but afterwards I didn't give them a thought. This time I'm just so glad to be alive. Even the smallest things give me pleasure – the sight of a flower, the sound of birdsong through the stone casement. I was just writing my thoughts in my diary – listen . . .

'"I have come to value each day God grants me. I didn't understand fully before that life was so sweet a thing. Whoever approaches the gates of death learns the value of life. I pray merciful God to allow me long to enjoy my life and my sons."'

Chapter 25

Jihad

'The water channels will intersect there, in a pool at the centre, which will have fountains and water lilies. I intend to plant apple, pear and quince trees in the garden to remind me of our homeland. The gardeners say they will need to be watered every day in this climate but labourers are plentiful and cheap.'

Babur and Humayun were standing on the north bank of the Jumna river, about a mile downstream from where its brown waters took a sharp, right-angled turn by the Agra fort. Babur was showing his son the progress the workers had made on the first garden he had commissioned in Agra.

'What else will you have planted?'

'I want lots of sweet-smelling plants that will produce scent during the evening – one of my favourite times for sitting in the garden. The chief gardener tells me that there are many kinds of stocks and also the creamy, white, night-flowering champa flower that will suit my purpose. He is a good man and works well to my instructions, even though he was once one of Sultan Ibrahim's gardeners.' Babur paused. 'I only wish more people, both inside and outside our borders, were as ready to accept us as the new masters of Hindustan. I understand – even if I don't accept – the hostility of those who had close ties to Sultan Ibrahim. I can hardly blame his mother for what she did – it was a kind of display of loyalty, I suppose. Nor am I too worried about the Shah of Persia at the moment, even though he is always craftily probing our north-western borders in Afghanistan, trying to buy supporters around Kandahar and Quetta. We have enough money from the miserly Ibrahim's brimming treasuries to outbribe the shah – at least for now.'

'Who is it then that concerns you most?'

'The Rajputs, to the west of us here in Agra. From their strong citadels and mountain fortresses they used to maintain a kind of armed neutrality with Ibrahim, even sometimes hiring him soldiers to fight in his distant campaigns. They are brave, brave soldiers – a warrior people with a heroic code of honour, never retreating and never surrendering.'

Babur paused again. 'Reports have kept reaching me over the past few weeks of the boasting of Rana Sanga, the ruler of Mewar, the strongest and most wealthy of the Rajput kingdoms, that he will rid Hindustan of us, the upstart invaders, and put a true Hindu – himself, of course – on the throne for the first time in three hundred years.'

'Will the rest of the Rajput kingdoms support him?'

'Probably not. They're a jealous, independent lot, as touchy of their honour, as suspicious of each other and as quick to pick a fight as some of our own Afghan chiefs. The other Rajput rulers won't want to see him even more powerful.'

'How much trouble could he make on his own?'

'Plenty. He has a large, loyal and well-trained army. Even though he's ageing, he's still a good tactician and a great warrior, who prides himself on always leading the charge himself. He also makes a virtue of the number of times he's been wounded and lost parts of his body. I hear that his court poet brags on his behalf that he is "a mere fragment

446

of a man but what a fragment". He lost one eye in a fight with his brother, his arm in a battle against Sultan Ibrahim, and he limps from a severe leg wound. He has eighty wounds scattered across what remains of his scrawny body and his poet claims the randy old goat has fathered a son for each of them.'

'I'd heard that too. He must have plenty of wives – and clearly at least one part of his anatomy remains intact. How long can we leave him to posture without confronting him?'

'That's the very question I've been turning over in my mind. It's only nine months since we defeated Ibrahim. Our grip on our conquest is not yet secure and the future of our dynasty here in Hindustan hangs in the balance. I would like to think that you, your brothers and your children will enjoy these gardens. Only this morning I learned that Rana Sanga has made another incursion into our territory on the pretext of chasing rebels. Admittedly it lasted only a week but he penetrated deeper than before . . .'

'We can't let him ride into our domains whenever he wishes. If we let him continue to treat them pretty much as his own it will be seen as weakness – and rightly so. He needs teaching respect now.'

'I'm losing your youthful ardour for war, but you are right. We're going to have to fight him some time and better to do it sooner than later to safeguard our martial reputation and, more importantly, while we're still the only people in Hindustan with cannons and muskets. At least another campaign will curb any restlessness among our own young bloods. The prospect of battle and plunder will give them something to think about. I will call a military council for tomorrow to begin our preparations . . .'

• ◆ •

Babur turned in his saddle. Humayun was quite close behind

but his bodyguard was strung out some way further back. He was hot and sweating, and dust had stuck to every inch of his exposed flesh, crusting around his eyes, but he was delighted that at forty-four he had ridden a hundred and fifty miles in two and a half days and had still been able to out-gallop his men to this hilltop vantage-point.

The rocky outcrop gave a fine view over the dry deserts of Rajasthan, but there was little enough else to be pleased about. He had ridden the hundred and fifty miles in pursuit of Rana Sanga but he and his men had not even come in sight of the rana's main army, not even a glimpse of their dust on the horizon. He had been on campaign for the last six weeks but during that time had been unable to bring his enemy into a pitched battle in which his muskets and cannon – including one he had had newly cast which could throw a ball over three quarters of a mile – could be deployed to good effect.

The wily rana had wisely preferred a war of movement, using his more mobile forces to make hit-and-run raids on Babur's forts and supply caravans, just as Babur had once done from the hills above Ferghana against his half-brother Jahangir's men. The raids had weakened the morale of Babur's battalions, leaving them edgy and always on the lookout for attack. The raids had also forced Babur to detach more and more of his best troops from his main force to guard the baggage train.

Humayun was at his side now. 'I can still outride you just as I could when you had the little white pony ten years ago . . .'

'You have the best horse and there'd be a different result if we were on foot,' responded Humayun, provoked almost despite himself into adolescent competition with his father and an adolescent touchiness about any perceived failure.

'I was only joking. Anyway, neither of us seems able to catch the rana and he's older than both of us and crippled.

448

The plain out there is deserted. We need to think again. Let's dine alone so that we can talk frankly.'

· ➤ ·

The two servants dressed in white tunics and baggy trousers disappeared through the tent flaps carrying the remains of the last course of the dinner – oranges, nuts and sticky sweetmeats. Babur and Humayun lay back from the low table against the large purple cushions embroidered with elephants and peacocks that had once graced Ibrahim's palace in Delhi. Each had a gold goblet of red wine, newly arrived from the vineyards of Ghazni, south of Kabul.

'I've been thinking how we can entice Rana Sanga into conflict.' Humayun put his goblet down. 'We both know that, for the Rajputs, honour – their personal honour, their family honour – is everything. We should occupy a place of particular importance to the rana so that he will believe his honour has been impaired if he doesn't re-capture it quickly.'

'A good idea in principle but have you actually got anywhere in mind?'

'I asked some of the native chiefs we number among our allies. They tell me that Sanga's mother was born in a small village called Khanua at the edge of his territories twenty miles north-west of Agra – about seventy-five miles south-west of here. He built a shrine there to one of his gods in her honour and still worships there once a year.'

'You've certainly done some thinking. I'll send scouts first thing in the morning to check the terrain between Khanua and here and also to see whether the place itself looks a good one for us to fight. If all goes well, I should be able to order our forces to concentrate there within a few days. But you're not the only one who's been thinking. I've been worrying about how to hearten those of our men unsettled by Sanga's success in his hit-and-run raids.'

'Where have your thoughts led you?'

'Perhaps in a strange direction. All of my previous campaigns have been against armies that included at least some men who shared our faith. This time our opponents are all Hindus – that is to say, infidels. We will declare holy war – *jihad*.'

'But now we're in Hindustan, some of our allies among the local rulers are Hindus, too.'

'We'll make sure we detach them from the main army for this battle. In any case, I've been worried about the loyalty – or, at least, the effectiveness – of some of them for a while now. They can garrison rear areas or some such.'

'It may work.'

'It will work . . . I've even thought of how to symbolise this change. This fine red wine of Ghazni I've drunk tonight will be the last alcohol I shall taste. I'll pour the remainder of the shipment away in front of our men when I tell them of the *jihad*.'

'But you've drunk all my life . . .'

'Yes and I've enjoyed spirits, *bhang* and the fruit of the opium poppy, I know. We people of Timur's blood – and of Genghis's – have taken strong drink since long before the mullahs brought the true religion to us. Fermented mare's milk – *kvass* – was, after all, what kept Genghis's people alive in the winter cold on the high steppes. All but the strictest mullahs realised it would be impossible to change people completely and at once. They lauded abstinence as the ideal and helped the pious and ascetic to achieve it but tolerated drinking among men of the world. They encouraged us to forswear it for short periods – such as during our holy month of Ramadan and as we became older and could sooner expect to be called to account by our creator.'

Babur took another sip. 'Yes, wine is good and I'm known to enjoy it. That's why my renouncing it will have a big impact on morale. That's why I'm expecting you to renounce it too.'

Humayun grimaced.

'You must – at least for a while ... I'll make the announcement to our troops in a couple of days or so when I've had a chance to tell the mullahs and detach our Hindu allies to other tasks.'

• ◆ •

Babur's army was drawn up in a hollow square at the centre of which was a raised wooden dais, covered with gold cloth, on which their emperor stood in his green robes. His belt was of intertwined pearls and round his neck he wore a gorget of uncut rubies and emeralds. His gold crown was on his head and his sword, Alamgir, was at his side. Next to him, Humayun was similarly royally attired, and they were surrounded by their senior mullahs, all in black and each with the Holy Book in his right hand.

Babur began to speak: 'Men, we march tomorrow for what I intend to be our climactic confrontation with this upstart Rana of Mewar, who dares invade our territories. He is not a man of our religion. He does not follow the one true God but worships many. He mistakenly believes he will be reincarnated on earth many times. That may be what makes him so reckless. We must show him the superiority of our religion and of our courage. We are not afraid to lose our one life because we are certain of Paradise if we fall martyrs in our battle against the infidel. I have consulted our mullahs, these wise and holy men you see around me. They have agreed that because we fight against infidels, to demonstrate the superiority of our divinely inspired courage, we should declare this a *jihad*, a holy war. We fight for our God, for our beliefs. We will conquer in their name. *Allah akbar!* God is great!'

A loud cry of approval went up from the army's front ranks, spreading and growing in volume and fervour as it was relayed to the outermost. Soldiers raised their swords and banged their shields.

After a few minutes, Babur lowered his hands repeatedly, palms down, to signify he wanted silence once more. As the crowd hushed he spoke again: 'You know me as a man who has not always succeeded in following all of God's teaching. Weak, as we all are, I have indulged my senses. You know I have enjoyed alcohol. You may have heard of the wine of Ghazni – the finest of the year's crop – that I had shipped down the Khyber Pass only a week ago to indulge myself. To show my passion for our holy war I now renounce alcohol and so does my son, Humayun. To symbolise this, we will pour away the fine Ghazni wine I imported into Hindustan with such effort.'

As he spoke, he and Humayun both raised axes above their heads and brought them crashing down on the wooden barrels of wine that had been placed before the dais, smashing them open so that the ruby-red wine flowed out to soak into the dust. The roar that followed was even greater than the first. Babur's nobles and generals, as well as many of the common soldiers, vied with each other to shout that they, too, wished to reform and renounce intoxicants ... that, purified and renewed, they would conquer ...

• ◆ •

Babur stood at the top of a low hill overlooking the red sand of the Rajasthan desert at Khanua. Behind him was the village itself, mainly mud-brick houses but, at its centre, the intricately carved sandstone Hindu temple raised by Rana Sanga in memory of his mother. Babur had made the shaven-headed, white-robed priests watch while his men defaced or chiselled out all references to the rana or his mother on the temple. Then he had expelled the priests from the village, knowing they would take the news to the rana.

Predictably, Rana Sanga's Rajput honour had been unable to stomach the insult and he was now encamped about three miles away on the plain below. Although his camp was shrouded in early-morning mist, only a few minutes ago scouts despatched before dawn had reported back to Babur that they had heard and seen the unmistakable sights and sounds of preparation for battle – cooking fires doused, swords sharpened, horses saddled and orders shouted.

Babur's own deployments had been agreed a few days previously – immediately after the arrival of his army at Khanua – in the familiar surroundings of his scarlet tent.

'I believe we should follow basically the same battle plan as at Panipat,' he had begun, 'but we should use the hill to strengthen our position further. Let us place the cannon on the hilltop and dig trenches and build ramparts around the hill to protect them.'

Then one of Babur's longest serving commanders, the usually taciturn Hassan Hizari, a Tajik from Badakhshan who had been with him for more than twenty years, had spoken. 'That is well, Majesty, but Sanga has fewer than two hundred elephants and relies mainly on his cavalry. Our perimeter will be longer than at Panipat. Horses are much nimbler than the lumbering elephants, if less frightening. Even if the Rajputs lose some of their cavalry to cannon shot, it won't deter them. Many will simply jump the ditches and barricades. We must be ready for at least some to penetrate our perimeter.'

'You're right, of course. We'll need to station archers and musketeers as a further line of defence halfway up the hill.'

'We will need cavalry up there, too, to rush to any breach,' Humayun had added. 'Let me take charge of them.' Babur had not had the heart to deny him.

Over the past few days Babur's troops had put the plans into practice, digging earthworks and positioning cannon with the help of oxen. They had even made some of the wagons into a kind of movable barricade by encasing their sides and wheels in thick planks.

When Humayun had reviewed the dispositions with Babur

only a few minutes earlier they had found need for only the most minor adjustments. After embracing his father, Humayun had departed to take up his position with his cavalry detachments a little further down the hill. Left alone on the hilltop Babur prayed for Humayun's safety in the coming battle. Despite his son's protests, he had ensured that the young man had a strong bodyguard – forty men from Hassan Hizari's Tajiks. He could do no more but still he was anxious – the memory of Baburi's hand trailing in the dust after Panipat remained vivid . . .

By now the mist was beginning to lift and Babur could see that the Rajputs were deploying fully. There were rank after rank of horsemen. Babur's spies had estimated that the rana's forces outnumbered his own by at least four to one.

Suddenly a tall Rajput galloped towards Babur's lines. He was dressed all in orange, his saddle and bridle ornamented with tassels of the same colour. His white horse's head was protected by a steel headguard that glinted in the morning light. He wheeled his horse within just a hundred yards of Babur's defences to shout what sounded like a herald's challenge. Babur's response was to send an order to his matchlock men to shoot the herald down. They obeyed. The man fell from his horse, but his foot caught in the stirrup and the animal bolted back towards the Rajput lines dragging its rider along, his orange-turbaned head quickly reduced to bloody pulp as it banged along the rocky ground.

Just as Babur had intended, his contempt for the traditional challenge goaded the Rajputs into a headlong, undisciplined charge. Their horsemen soon outdistanced the hundred or so armoured elephants Rana Sanga had deployed. Babur lowered his sword as a sign to his artillerymen, musketeers and archers to fire as soon as their enemy was in range. From his position on the hill, the Rajputs seemed like a great wave rushing forward to engulf his perimeter. Often a man or a horse fell. Sometimes a cannon ball stopped an elephant in its seemingly ambling but actually speedy run. But nothing stopped the onward charge, until it crashed around the trenches and barricades from behind which Babur's archers were firing as fast as they could draw arrows from their quivers.

Babur could see the flashes as the musketeers discharged their weapons further up the hill and, nearer still, acrid white smoke billowing from the cannons' mouths. Around the western side of his perimeter, Babur saw the wave of Rajput horsemen break and dissipate their force and after swirling around in front of the barricades pull back to regroup. However, to the east, a number of Rajputs who had jumped the earth ramparts and kicked their horses on up the hill were scattering a group of musketeers and archers. Babur saw several slashed down by the Rajputs who then turned their mounts towards the cannon.

Immediately, Babur signalled to Humayun that his cavalry must charge. Humayun, his Tajik bodyguard around him, led them pell-mell down the hill to crash into the Rajputs. Several Rajputs fell, their horses knocked over by the sheer weight and speed of Humayun's charge. Others were still fighting and more were joining them by jumping the barricades from which the defenders had retreated. Humayun seemed to be fighting well but through the drifting smoke Babur saw that the Rajputs were pressing round him. Then the smoke enveloped him and his bodyguards completely.

To Babur it seemed an age before the smoke cleared again. But it was in fact only a short time before he could make out that the Rajputs were now turning back down the hill and the few survivors were retreating back beyond the barricades. Five minutes later Humayun rode up.

'There was so much smoke I couldn't see what happened properly.'

'Our first charge knocked them back a little but they regrouped and, seeing I was the leader, tried to cut me out from the rest.'

'That much I saw.'

'Well, my brave bodyguard held them off and I decided to repay the Rajputs in kind. We broke out of the heaving mêlée and charged one of their officers – a great black-bearded man with peacock feathers in his turban. I got in the first and only blow, slashing him across the face and neck, and down he went, backwards out of the saddle on to the rocky ground, to lie motionless. His men seemed to lose heart and we pushed them back, helped by the surviving musketeers who had taken up new positions on the flanks. Soon our perimeter was secure again and the front-line barricades were remanned.'

'You did well.'

'Shouldn't we follow up and attack them?'

'Not yet. Neither their strength nor their will is exhausted. See? They're massing for another attack. Tell the bearers to get water-bottles and new supplies of arrows to our men. The fight is not yet over.'

Babur was proved right. The Rajputs continued to make periodic attacks throughout the heat of the day. Each time they were repulsed without breaking the perimeter, leaving wounded or dying men and horses piled around the barricades. Babur saw one wounded Rajput half walking, half crawling back towards the Rajput lines. Slowly and agonisingly, he made about seven hundred yards when a new Rajput cavalry charge rode over him and his body was crushed and spreadeagled in the stony desert dust. His turban, half-unwound and occasionally caught by a breeze, was the only movement from the corpse.

The sun was low in the sky when Humayun, at his father's side, pointed towards yet another regrouping. 'They seem to be massing again. There are elephants and cavalry as before, but in the middle there's a large number of men on foot. Something we've not seen before – and there seem more of them than ever. It's as if their camp-followers and servants have joined the front line.'

456

'They probably have. I've heard that even the humblest water-carrier prefers to sacrifice his life in one last charge than to return home in defeat. They call these charges *jauhur*. Beforehand they pray and sacrifice to their gods to stiffen their resolve.'

'One of our Hindustani allies told me they also chew opium pellets to deaden the fear as well as the pain of any wounds . . .'

'No doubt. Here they come again . . .'

The blare of trumpets, the mesmeric tattoo of drums and the clash of cymbals grew louder as the Rajputs advanced, moving more slowly this time because so many were on foot.

'Tell my groom to ready my horse,' Babur shouted to Humayun. 'I will lead the charge when the time comes.'

'I'll be with you.'

'But first pass the word to our drummers to out-sound the Rajputs, and tell our officers that each time the Rajputs give their war-cry, our men should reply, "*Allah akbar*" – it will hearten them.'

On came the ragged line of Rajputs. Babur's artillery despatched cannon balls into them, knocking men over. Musketeers and archers emptied saddles. Sometimes an elephant would lurch and fall or – wounded and in panic – turn to the rear, scattering those around it. Still the Rajput drummers kept up their hypnotic beat. Gaps in the lines of men were filled. To Babur, the noise of drums and trumpets and the mingled cries of 'Mewar' and '*Allah akbar*', resounding in his head, seemed to drown the cannon shot and the screams of the wounded.

When they were about two hundred yards away from the barricades, the Rajput cavalry jabbed their horses into action, riding over the bodies of the dead and wounded from previous attacks. The infantry used their fallen comrades as soft stepping stones across the trenches and aids to climb the barricades.

All along the perimeter the fighting was hand to hand, personal and determined. But the greatest crush was directly downhill from Babur and Humayun.

'That is where we aim our charge.' Drawing Alamgir, Babur ordered his cavalry to attack once more, then led them at a gallop down the hill through the remaining barricades and into the fray. Again, the shock of their downhill charge hurled the Rajputs back, their horses rearing and trampling foot-soldiers. As he rode on, Babur saw a Rajput archer aim at him, and before he could reach him to cut him down, the arrow had thudded into the leather pommel of his saddle. Babur slashed at the archer's unprotected body – few Rajputs deigned to wear chain-mail even if they could afford it – and he fell beneath Babur's horse.

Once through the mass of Rajputs, Babur wheeled his horse and waited while his men and Humayun, who to Babur's consternation had lost his helmet, re-formed around him. Then they charged into the Rajputs again, this time from the rear. Although they fought bravely, the orange-clad Rajputs were soon surrounded, separated into isolated groups and beginning to be overwhelmed. When one band of five men was given the chance to surrender, they embraced then plunged their swords into each other. But everywhere the clamour of battle was lessening. Babur realised victory was his.

Then he noticed that, a hundred yards to his right, Humayun was on the ground and three of his bodyguards were cutting his garments from his lower body. Paternal anxiety overwhelmed the joy of victory as he rode over. With intense relief he saw that Humayun was conscious, though grimacing in pain. 'It's just an arrow in the thigh – a lucky shot from way over there as the Rajputs were retreating.'

The arrow still protruded from his son's leg and blood was seeping from around the metal head, only half of which had embedded itself in Humayun. 'It seems not to have penetrated too far. All the same it needs to come out at once

458

– I know from years of battle. I will hold my son's shoulders,' Babur said to the bodyguards. 'One of you hold his ankles. The strongest of you draw it out. It's very important you pull straight – no twisting. Humayun, keep still!'

Babur gripped his son's shoulders. Instantly, one of his bodyguards grabbed Humayun's feet and another stooped, gripped the arrow shaft in both hands and, in a single movement, pulled it out. Blood spurted but soon subsided.

'Bind a pad of cloth tightly over it. Praise God, he will live to share in our victory. Prepare a litter to carry him to his tent.'

'No, Father. I will ride with you to review our troops once I am bandaged and dressed in clean clothes.'

Half an hour later, Babur and Humayun rode around the battlefield in the dusk. By the light of flaring torches, Babur's stretcher-bearers were bending over the bodies of his men, separating the living from the dead. Camp-followers and scavengers scuttled around the field under cover of the gloom to pick over the Rajput dead for objects of value, roughly pulling aside bodies and brawling over the richest-looking corpses. They disappeared into the darkness as Babur, Humayun and their entourage approached closer.

Father and son were quiet as they reached the tents to which their wounded were being brought. Some men were lying still and quiet, some trying to drive away the black flies crawling across their bodies and clustering on their wounds, some screaming out in pain, others biting the backs of their hands to prevent themselves from doing so and yet others begging for help.

'So it's true, Father, as you once said, that the badly wounded cry either for their mothers or for God.'

'Their mothers have been their greatest and most unquestioning comfort in this world, and God is their greatest hope for the next.' Babur paused, then continued, 'We must give thanks that the bravery and sacrifice of these men have made us undisputed masters of Hindustan. We must repay them by seeing that the families of the fallen are cared for and those who survive compensated. Above all, we owe it to them and to ourselves not to squander the results of their sacrifice. Nevertheless, we should not dwell on sacrifice and death. Both – whether of the rulers or the ruled – are essential to all empires. To become overly concerned about them is to grow weak and indecisive. Tonight we should rejoice in our victory. We have vanquished our greatest enemy. When they hear of his utter defeat, other rulers will not dare to attack us. We have secured a bright future for our dynasty.'

• ◆ •

In the late afternoon of the next day as shadows were lengthening, Babur once more addressed his troops, assembled around him. Many were bandaged and some supported themselves on crutches.

'Men, let us rejoice and give thanks to God for the great victory you have won by your courage and belief in our righteous cause. We have shown ourselves once more worthy successors to the noble Timur and history will remember us as such. We celebrated last night and when we are back in Agra, which lies scarcely four days' march away, I will again break open my treasuries and reward each and every one of you.

'Last night I learned from a prisoner that late in the battle Rana Sanga – our insolent opponent who dared set his power against ours – was wounded in the abdomen so badly that he had to be carried from the field in a litter slung between four horses. Today, scouts checking that the Rajputs were not regrouping came in sight of a great funeral pyre being built ten miles west of here. A peasant working in the fields told them it was for Rana Sanga, who had died nearby, and that those building it were the surviving members of his bodyguard. Our scouts hid in tall crops nearby until they saw it was indeed his body that was placed on the pyre. They rode away only after they had witnessed the torch applied to the base of the brushwood. Looking back, they saw orange flames flare to the sky. The rana did not live to boast of his eighty-first wound. The flames consumed not only him but Rajput ambitions to deprive us of our new lands.

'To ensure any surviving rebels or others who wish ill to our empire understand the futility of opposing us, we will again follow the custom of Timur. I have ordered the corpses of our enemies to be decapitated and the heads collected to be piled in towers at every crossroad from here to Agra. Let the hopes of our enemies rot with them.'

• ◆ •

That evening Humayun made his way to the part of his father's vast scarlet campaign tent that contained his private quarters. His mind was buzzing with images of battle and his ambitions for his own place in the new empire. He must be his father's heir. After all, he was his eldest son – even though under the traditions of Timur and his descendants the eldest did not succeed by right – and also the son of Babur's favourite wife. Now he had proved himself in battle too. Perhaps he should broach the subject of succession with his father now. Or, at least, seek a new command in which he could impress further.

Pushing aside the heavy gold curtains which shielded his father's quarters, he saw Babur stretched out on a low divan covered with gold-embroidered cream and purple cushions, a silver pipe at his side. He seemed neither to see nor hear Humayun enter but continued to gaze into the middle distance. Coming closer, Humayun saw that his father's expression was of a benign content and that the pupils of his green eyes were dilated. He put out a hand and shook Babur gently by the shoulder. His eyelids fluttered briefly and his eyes began to focus. 'Humayun, when did you come in?'

'Only a minute or two ago.'

'After dinner, I took a pipe of *bhang* and opium, which seemed to transport me away from this brown-baked land with its multitudes of people and all the cares of conquest. I was back on the hillsides of Ferghana. The emerald grass was waving, dotted with the scarlet of tulips and the blue of irises. I watched the waters of the cascading rivulets sparkle and glisten – each drop holding a world within itself. The sound of the soft breezes and the tinkling of water filled my ears. I felt the lightness, the carelessness of a young man. Peace washed over me and took away my worries and responsibilities.' Babur smiled a tranquil, slightly dazed smile. 'What do you say? Should we call for some of those excellent rosewater-flavoured sweetmeats?'

Humayun realised it was no time to talk of his ambitions. His father was relaxing into some of his old distractions. Perhaps he should, too. The red wines of Ghazni were good. It wouldn't be long before he at least would be drinking them again. 'I only came in to tell you that the preparations are well under way for the beginning of our march back to Agra tomorrow and, of course, to say good night.'

As he made his way back to his own tent, Humayun looked up into a night sky pricked by stars. As he watched, more appeared, patterning the heavens. Suddenly he felt impatient with the clamour of the camp, noisy with men and animals, and the crackling of fires whose flames seemed crude compared with the celestial light above. He called for his horse, mounted and rode out into the darkness to be alone with his thoughts beneath the silent stars.

Chapter 26

The Bondage of Kingship

The waters of the Ganges were warm and Babur swam the thirty-three strokes it took to cross the river with pleasure. It felt good to fulfil the final part of his vow, made six years ago when, with Baburi, he had plunged into the icy Indus and sworn to swim every major river of his new empire. Shaking droplets of water from his hair and eyes, Babur hauled himself out on to the bank and lay down in the sun. On the opposite bank, the bodyguards and huntsmen who had ridden with him from his nearby camp at Kanauj, a hundred and fifty miles east of Agra, waited with the horses in the pool of green shade beneath a leafy neem tree. Tonight, when it was dark, he and his men would go fishing, holding candles just above the surface of the water. For some reason the shimmering light was irresistible to fish, luring them to the surface where their silvery bodies were easily grabbed.

Babur closed his eyes and contemplated the river. According to the scholars he had ordered to draw him maps of Hindustan, the Ganges flowed eastward, passing through Bengal to spill into a great blue ocean. One day, Babur promised himself, he would see the great shining expanse of water he found so hard to visualise . . . How did it look, the horizon where the water met the sky?

He was still finding Hindustan a bewildering, surprising place. Compared to his homelands it was indeed another world. Its mountains, rivers, forests and wildernesses, its villages and provinces, its animals and plants, people and languages, even its rains and winds were altogether different . . . But whereas when he had first crossed the Indus he had thought Hindustan alien, even oppressive, now he was starting to appreciate it. Since defeating Rana Sanga he had spent much of his time on the move, setting up vast encampments, cities in miniature, with his own red tent at the heart − just as Timur had once made tours of inspection from Samarkand. His journey had given Babur the opportunity to show himself to his new subjects but also to learn.

At night, he took increasing pleasure in writing his diary, documenting everything from how the peasants tended their fields to the teams of *deotis* who, with their gourds of oil and thick wicks embedded in metal tripods, lit the streets of the towns and villages. He tried to describe creatures new to him, like the playful, leaping river dolphins with bodies shaped like waterskins, and the lizard-like, sharp-toothed crocodiles.

Soon he'd return to Agra, where the gardens he had planted were flourishing and had recently yielded the first grapes and melons grown by the gardeners he had summoned from Kabul. In addition, seven hundred Hindustani stonemasons were at work on the mosque he had commissioned in Agra to celebrate his crushing of Rana Sanga. With its high recessed arches − *iwans* − elegantly tapering minarets and relief carvings of his favourite flowers − the Hindu craftsmen could fashion tulips and irises so lifelike they seemed to toss their fragile heads in the breeze − it would be a fine structure. He had also established a post system to link Agra with Kabul, with staging points every eighteen miles. Teams of post horses and riders were kept in constant readiness so that messages could be swiftly carried between Babur's capital in Hindustan and his lands beyond the Khyber Pass.

Having achieved so much, it was satisfying to reread some of the early passages of his diary, especially his despairing laments about his hopeless, throneless state and his yearnings for Samarkand. How ironic that he had not managed to hold Timur's city long enough to create anything lasting whereas here, in Hindustan, he was building something permanent. When, eventually, he was called to Paradise, he would, God willing, leave his sons a rich and stable empire.

Babur sat up and watched the river flow past. A bird's wing flashed emerald in the sunlight as a green woodpecker swooped among the reeds. What about his sons? With Maham, Gulrukh and Khanzada, their aunt, Kamran, Askari and Hindal had made the long journey south-east to Agra as soon as Babur had thought it safe to send for them. He had marked their arrival with a grand ceremony, awarding his two elder sons robes of honour, yak-tail standards, drums, fine horses, ten elephants apiece and strings of camels and mules.

He was proud of them. Khanzada had told him that Kamran – now twenty-one and sprouting a black beard – had heeded her advice and Baisanghar's and had done well as regent in Kabul, a position since filled by Baisanghar. Thirteen-year-old Askari was also showing himself able and ambitious. And why not? Babur had been King of Ferghana at that age. Since their arrival he'd found plenty of employment for them, sending them on tours of inspection and occasional small campaigns to quash sporadic resistance.

They should be content, but something in their manner towards Humayun – especially Kamran's – occasionally troubled Babur. They seemed resentful, even jealous. But it was healthy, he tried to tell himself. After all, Humayun had been at Babur's side throughout the conquest of Hindustan. It was inevitable that he and Humayun should have grown close and equally inevitable that Kamran, so near in age to Humayun, should feel excluded. Babur had talked it over with Khanzada, whose wise advice had been that he should ask Humayun to be a little more tactful towards his brothers.

Maham, too, had noticed the friction but she blamed Kamran and Askari's mother, Gulrukh, for stirring up her sons against her own, Humayun. Maham's pleas that he formally declare Humayun his heir were growing more persistent, but that was a decision only he could take – and only when he was ready. The king's right to choose his heir from among his sons was a good one – indeed, in the old days, sons had been expected to compete with one another . . . Only the strongest deserved to rule because only the strongest could protect the clans. Humayun was undoubtedly a good warrior but now, in addition to fighting skills, a king needed other talents to win loyalty and make alliances. Babur must be absolutely sure before making any final decision.

At least ten-year-old Hindal did not seem part of this sibling rivalry. Maham still kept him close to her, although Babur must appoint a tutor for him. Hindal's birth-mother, Dildar, had not come to Agra. She had been ill and had remained in Kabul with Hindal's sister Gulbadan. When she was recovered Babur would send for them and his entire family would be with him, which was as it should be.

Babur stood up, dived in again and cut powerfully through the water of the Ganges – only thirty strokes this time – to where his men waited patiently.

◆

'I want you to have this.' Babur held out a copy of his diaries bound within carved ivory covers. 'It is the account of my life that I have kept for many years and will continue to keep. I ordered my scribe to copy what I have written so far . . .'

Humayun took it, his brown eyes – so like Maham's – widening in surprise. 'It is a great honour, Father.'

'More than that, I hope. I want you to learn from it. You have known campaigns and battles but never what I went through . . . I became a king at not much more than half your age. I survived only because of the loyalty of a few of my men, the determination of my mother and grandmother and my own wits. There were times when I had nothing and a bowl of soup brought me tears of happiness . . . They were bleak days but they toughened me, fitting me to rule an empire and hardening my determination that I would win one . . . You have grown up with greater security, with a father to protect you, with brothers to share your youth . . . You should value that . . .'

'I do, Father.' Humayun seemed puzzled.

Babur looked away. This was hard. He was proud of his tall, muscular, athletic son, who had shown so much bravery and resourcefulness.

'You behave arrogantly to your brothers. Kamran is only a few months younger than you. It was not his fault that he took no part in the conquest of Hindustan. He had a task to fulfil in Kabul and he acquitted himself well – yet you lord it over him. You treat Askari as the child he no longer is and he resents it. A little rivalry between you is only natural but you should be more sensitive to your brothers . . .'

Humayun said nothing.

'Our strength in this new land must be our unity or we will fail. Spend more time with your brothers, teach them some of the things that you have learned . . . You pass too much time alone. Many evenings when I ask for you, I am told you've ridden out alone . . . Some of our commanders have commented to me that they've found the same when they've sought you out for orders or to make reports. Why this need for solitude?'

'I need time to think free from distraction . . . to understand

467

myself and the world about me, what it all means and how it works . . . I particularly like to contemplate the heavens. That's why I go out in the evenings and at night.'

'And what do you learn from your star-gazing?'

'That under God the stars shape our lives, our destinies. Haven't you often told me about the time you saw the Canopus star shining on the high, snowy mountains and knew it was a sign . . . ?'

'I do believe there are signs in the stars of the will of God, but I also believe that men have the power to shape their own destinies. The heavens indicate things but the choices, the decisions, are for us to make . . .' Babur's tone was sharper than he had intended because Humayun's expression told him he wasn't getting through.

'Father, I've never told you this, but the night before we fought at Panipat, my astrologer told me that if, next day, when the midday sun was at its height over the battlefield, three eagles appeared, we would win a great victory. In the dust and press of the battle, I raised my eyes to the skies, hot and clear above the smoke of cannon and musket, and I saw three eagles circling high above us. That's not all. Now my astrologer is predicting a great destiny for the Moghuls in Hindustan . . . That is why I spend so much time trying to discern from the stars what will happen next.'

Babur allowed himself a brief smile. 'Your belief in our destiny pleases me greatly. I would not wish it otherwise. But the heavens do not foreshadow everything. Did they predict that Buwa would try to poison me? Above all, we need resilience and application to hold on to our new possessions. Leadership and dedication count even more than the stars . . . listen to this passage from my diary . . .' Babur took the ivory-bound volume back from his son and quickly found the place:'"A ruler must at all times be vigilant, listening to what his courtiers are saying and ready to pounce on any sign of disloyalty."

'Remember, Humayun, that there is no bondage like the bondage of kingship. Remember that – as my son – eyes are constantly upon you. Spending so much time alone will be seen as a flaw. Let us be frank. I know what is in your heart and in your mind because I see it in your face all the time. You want to know whether I will name you my heir. My answer is I am not certain enough to do so . . . not yet. I don't doubt your bravery but show me you have also the mental strength, the leadership, the focus, dedication and application . . . Prove to me the blood of Timur and Genghis flows with as much fire and purpose through your veins as it does through mine . . .'

• ◆ •

'Majesty, the first heat of the riding contest is about to begin.'

From the battlements of the Agra fort Babur could see the yellow and green banners driven into the riverbank marking where the race would start. Six rows of stakes – ten feet apart and extending four hundred yards – marked the course. The riders would gallop their horses in and out of them until they reached the far end where each would try to spear one of the six sheep's heads placed on the ground eight feet beyond the final stake before turning sharply and zigzagging back through the posts. The turns were tight and to be the swiftest would take skill and nerve.

The race was part of three days of celebrations to mark the fourth anniversary of Babur's arrival in Hindustan. Later there would be wrestling matches, then a contest between his three eldest sons: the first to shoot a pottery jar off a post using an improved design of musket that Babur had recently purchased for his bodyguard would win an emerald ring. The gem was engraved with the three circles representing the felicitous conjunction of the heavens at Timur's birth, the design Babur had adopted as the symbol of his new empire.

Humayun, Kamran and Askari gathered around Babur to

watch with him. If any of them had been competing they might well have won, but this race was reserved for Babur's commanders. It was their chance to display their skill to their emperor. The prize was a white stallion with a gilded saddle and a bridle mounted with solid gold.

Baba Yasaval, recently appointed Babur's master-of-horse, was standing by the starting post, almost obscured by the mass of spectators lining each side of the course, pushing and shoving to get the best view. As he raised his spear, the six riders in the first heat trotted up to the start. After a glance at Babur, who signalled he was ready, Baba Yasaval lowered his spear. The riders shot away, ducking and weaving through the posts, so low in the saddle they were almost horizontal with their horses' necks. It reminded Babur of his days of playing polo with sheep's heads and he felt a spasm of nostalgic excitement.

The riders were reaching the end of the stakes and lowering their spears. The foremost horseman – the grey-bearded Tajik, Hassan Hizari – caught the sheep's head expertly on the tip of his spear and wheeled round neatly. The rider just behind him was not so skilful. His spear tip missed the sheep's head and caught instead in the mud, lifting him out of the saddle and sending him into a spiralling somersault to land on his backside to roars of laughter. The other four were safely round, all but one having speared the target.

It was nearly an hour before the five remaining heats were completed, the winners had raced each other and one man had emerged the victor – not Hassan Hizari, as Babur had hoped, but a younger warrior from Kabul who had made his bay mare move like lightning. Tonight at the feast Babur would award him his prize. Now the stakes were being pulled up and Babur's men were hurrying into the fortress to watch the wrestling contest that would shortly begin in the main courtyard where layers of thick carpet had already been laid over the stone slabs.

'Father, I'd like to wrestle.' Humayun was an excellent wrestler and knew it. Babur nodded and Humayun left to prepare. Descending to the courtyard with Kamran and Askari, Babur seated himself on the chair placed on a specially erected wooden platform.

As soon as it had become known that the emperor's son wished to compete, Humayun had been placed in the first bout. He and his opponent Saqi Muhsin, a broad, sinewy warrior from Herat, whose habitual boast was that he could wrestle four or five men at a time, approached the dais and made their obeisance. Both were barefoot, stripped to the waist and wearing close-fitting, striped breeches that fastened just below the knee. Saqi Muhsin's much scarred, solidly muscled body looked impressive but Humayun's even more so. He was at least four inches taller than his opponent; the taut, perfectly defined muscles in his arms, back, shoulders and torso – gleaming with oil – had the beauty and grace of a thoroughbred horse. His long dark hair was bound back with a scarlet cloth.

At Babur's nod, the bout commenced. The two men circled one another, Humayun swaying on the balls of his feet, eyes fixed on his opponent's face. Suddenly, Saqi Muhsin tried to rush him. Humayun stepped quickly aside, hooked his leg around the other man's knee and brought him crashing to the ground. At once, Humayun was straddling his adversary's back, one arm round his throat, forcing his head back while, with the other, he grabbed his right arm and twisted it till it was almost touching his shoulder-blade. Sweat was pouring off Saqi Muhsin and his face was contorted with pain. 'I yield . . .' he gasped.

Humayun won the next three bouts which meant, under the rules, that he could retire from the contest with the title Unvanquished. Babur watched several more bouts but a headache, sharp and persistent, behind his eyes, was troubling him. He decided to return to his apartments to rest for a while. Kamran and Askari accompanied him to the door of the chamber, promising to return for him in three hours' time so he could witness their shooting contest with Humayun.

Babur ordered his attendants to bring him some opium

mixed with milk. He swallowed the pale, sweetish liquid and lay down. As the pain in his head eased, he slipped into sleep. His dreams were vivid and jumbled but pleasing, of Humayun's strong but graceful body as he hurled assailant after assailant to the ground, of himself, young again, careering through the green and yellow posts to win the riding contest, of Maham as she was when he first saw her, of Khanzada running on bare hennaed feet along the dark passages of the fortress of Akhsi in pursuit of her pet mongoose, of Wazir Khan teaching him patiently how to string a bow, and of Baburi in the meadows below the citadel of Kabul, revealing the mysteries of cannon and matchlock.

When Babur awoke, sunlight was still slanting through the marble fretwork of the windows. The shooting contest wasn't due to take place until early evening so he still had plenty of time. Stretching, he got up and splashed his face with rosewater from the jade bowl his attendants replenished four times a day. The cool water felt and smelled good and his headache had cleared.

He caught a low murmuring from the small anteroom beyond the brocade hangings that separated it from his bedchamber. It must be his attendants, keeping their voices down so as not to disturb him. Approaching the hangings, he was about to draw them back but stopped. Surely that was Kamran? Even though he was whispering, his deep, emphatic voice was unmistakable.

'Saqi Muhsin's an idiot. I've told him a hundred times that if he wants to out-wrestle Humayun there's no point in rushing at him like a mindless bull – Humayun is too quick. He should have waited for Humayun to make the first move. Then we might have had some fun. I'd have given a lot to see Humayun knocked flat on his arse . . . or, better still, to hear a rib crack . . .'

'What about the shooting match?' Askari's voice, higher-pitched than his brother's and a little sibilant, sounded anxious.

'Will he win or does one of us have a chance?'

'It's already taken care of, little brother.'

'What d'you mean?'

'One of my men is responsible for loading the muskets. I've told him to adulterate the powder for Humayun's gun so that it doesn't flash or discharge properly. Even if it doesn't wound him, at least he'll miss the target. The emerald ring will be one thing of Father's at least that Humayun won't get his hands on . . .'

Babur backed away. For a moment he had hoped he was dreaming but what he had heard had been real enough. Deliberately he dashed the jade bowl with its rosewater to the floor. The sound carried as he had intended. Kamran and Askari drew back the hangings and entered. 'We didn't want to disturb you, Father, so we sent away your attendants and have been waiting for you to wake. It's nearly time for our shooting competition. The target has been set up and the muskets are ready. Humayun is already in the courtyard.'

'There will be no contest, Kamran. I've changed my mind.'

'But why, Father . . . ?'

'Do you dare to question me?'

'Of course not, Father.'

'Leave me, both of you, and send my attendants to me. I will see you later at the feast.'

As his servants dressed him for the evening's festivities, Babur barely noticed the dark blue, gold-edged tunic they were fastening at his right shoulder with turquoise catches or the gold brocade trousers that tucked into high kid boots. Mechanically he went through the motions of choosing the necklaces and turban ornaments he would wear. Timur's heavy gold ring, which never left his finger, gleamed. Usually the sight pleased him, but not tonight.

He had been in Hindustan for four years. Tonight he and his men would eat and drink. Later, the sky above the Jumna would explode with stars as the magicians he had brought

473

to his court from far away Kashgar let off the devices they called fireworks. He'd already had a private demonstration and the glittering sprays shooting across the velvet depths of the night sky had made him catch his breath.

But now everything seemed tainted, tarnished. It was less what his sons had said – immature, spiteful and stupid – but the venom in their voices. What he had taken for normal sibling rivalry was something more and it was his fault. Preoccupied with his new possessions he hadn't paid enough attention to what was happening around him.

A ruler must at all times be vigilant.

Wasn't that what he himself had written in his diary and what he had propounded to Humayun? And all the time he'd been failing to take his own advice.

Babur's jaw tightened. Immediately after the celebrations he would appoint Askari and Kamran governors of provinces in Hindustan. He would find plenty of tasks to keep them busy and he would have them watched. As for Humayun, he would make him governor of the province around Agra where he would keep a close eye on him. He would discourage those tiresome mystical and solitary tendencies and involve him more in the business of government. If Humayun proved up to it, he would declare him his successor before all the court. Kamran and Askari would have to accept the appointment and with it the futility of feuding with their brother. Hindustan offered many opportunities. Much was still unconquered and they could carve their own place in it – even if that meant being Humayun's vassals.

It was lucky, Babur thought, examining his appearance in a mirror of burnished bronze, that he was still relatively young. *Inshallah*, God willing, he would have plenty of time to correct the faults in all of his sons and to find ways to satisfy their competing ambitions.

Chapter 27

The Dying of the Light

Babur's head was throbbing with the persistent ache that dogged him during the monsoon. The warm rain had been falling for three days now but the still, heavy air held no promise of relief. The rains would go on for weeks, even months. Lying back against silken bolsters in his bedchamber in the Agra fort, he tried to imagine the chill, thin rains of Ferghana blowing in over the jagged summit of Mount Beshtor and failed. The *punkah* above his head hardly disturbed the air. It was hard even to remember what it was like not to feel hot. There was little pleasure just now even in visiting his garden – the sodden flowers, soggy ground and overflowing water channels only depressed him.

Babur got up and tried to concentrate on writing an entry in his diary but the words wouldn't come and he pushed his jewel-studded inkwell impatiently aside. Maybe he would go to the women's apartments. He could ask Maham to sing. Sometimes she accompanied herself on the round-bellied, slender-necked lute that had once belonged to Esan Dawlat. Maham lacked his grandmother's gift but the lute still made a sweet sound in her hands.

Or he might play a game of chess with Humayun. His son had a shrewd, subtle mind – but so, he prided himself, did he and he could usually beat him. It amused him to see Humayun's startled look as he clamed victory with the traditional cry *shah mat* – 'check-mate', 'the king is at a loss'. Later, they would discuss Babur's plans to launch a campaign when the rains eased against the rulers of Bengal. In their steamy jungles in the Ganges delta, they thought they could defy Moghul authority and deny Babur's overlordship.

'Send for my son Humayun and fetch my chessmen,' Babur ordered a servant. Trying to shake off his lethargy he got up and went to a casement projecting over the riverbank to watch the swollen, muddy waters of the Jumna rushing by. A farmer was leading his bony bullocks along the oozing bank.

Hearing footsteps Babur turned, expecting to see his son, but it was only the white-tunicked servant.

'Majesty, your son begs your forgiveness but he is unwell and cannot leave his chamber.'

'What is the matter with him?'

'I do not know, Majesty.'

Humayun was never ill. Perhaps he, too, was suffering from the torpor that came with the monsoon, sapping the energy and spirit of even the most vigorous.

'I will go to him.' Babur wrapped a yellow silk robe round himself and thrust his feet into pointed kidskin slippers. Then he hurried from his apartments to Humayun's on the opposite side of a galleried courtyard, where water was not shooting, as it should, in sparkling arcs from the lotus-shaped marble basins of the fountains but pouring over the inundated rims.

Humayun was lying on his bed, arms thrown back, eyes closed, forehead beaded with sweat, shivering. When he heard his father's voice he opened his eyes but they were bloodshot, the pupils dilated. Babur could hear his heavy wheezing breathing. Every scratchy intake of air seemed an effort which hurt him.

'When did this illness begin?'

'Early this morning, Father.'

'Why wasn't I told?' Babur looked angrily at his son's attendants. 'Send for my *hakim* immediately!' Then he dipped his own silk handkerchief into some water and wiped Humayun's brow. The sweat returned at once – in fact, it was almost running down his face and he seemed to be shivering even more violently now and his teeth had begun to chatter.

'Majesty, the *hakim* is here.'

Abdul-Malik went immediately to Humayun's bedside, laid a hand on his forehead, pulled back his eyelids and felt his pulse. Then, with increasing concern, he pulled open Humayun's robe and, bending, turned his neatly turbaned head to listen to Humayun's heart.

'What is wrong with him?'

Abdul-Malik paused. 'It is hard to say, Majesty. I need to examine him further.'

'Whatever you require you only have to say . . .'

'I will send for my assistants. If I may be frank, it would be best if you were to leave the chamber, Majesty. I will report to you when I have examined the prince thoroughly – but it looks serious, perhaps even grave. His pulse and heartbeat are weak and rapid.' Without waiting for Babur's reply, Abdul-Malik turned back to his patient. Babur hesitated and, after a glance at his son's waxen trembling face, left the room. As attendants closed the doors behind him he found that he, too, was trembling.

A chill closed round his heart. So many times he had feared for Humayun. At Panipat he could have fallen beneath the feet of one of Sultan Ibrahim's war elephants. At Khanua he might have been felled by the slash of a Rajput sword. But he had never thought that Humayun – so healthy and strong – might succumb to sickness. How could he face life without his beloved eldest son? Hindustan and all its riches would be worthless if Humayun died. He would never have come to this sweltering, festering land with its endless hot rains and whining, blood-sucking mosquitoes if he had known this would be the price.

Babur spent the next half-hour pacing round the dripping courtyard and resisting the desire to send at once to the *hakim* to demand news. But at last Abdul-Malik appeared. Babur tried unsuccessfully to read his face.

'The prince has a very high fever and is becoming delirious . . .'

'What is it? Not poison?'

'No, Majesty, there has been no vomiting. I cannot say what the cause is. We can only try to sweat the infection out. I have ordered fires to be lit in his room and I will prepare a cordial of spices to heat his blood . . .'

'Is there nothing else to be done? Nothing I can send for?'

'No, Majesty. We must wait. God alone will decide his fate as he does for us all.'

All through the night, Abdul-Malik and his assistants tended Humayun. In the almost suffocating heat of the room, Babur sat close by the bed as his son heaved and tossed, struggling to throw off the thick wool blankets that the *hakim* had ordered to be piled on him. All the time Humayun was muttering, sometimes shouting. The words were incomprehensible to Babur.

In the hour before dawn, as a pale yellow sliver of light appeared on the eastern horizon, Humayun's delirium worsened. He began to shriek as if in terrible pain and to shake so convulsively that had the *hakim*'s assistants not held him down he would have fallen from the bed. His eyes were bulging and his tongue – furry and yellow – protruded through dry lips.

Suddenly unable to bear the sights and sounds of his son's suffering, Babur turned and left the chamber. In the courtyard, he bent and immersed his head in the lotus basin of one of the fountains. As the cool water filled his nose and ears, it was as if – just for a moment – he could insulate himself from the pain and anxieties of the world. Reluctantly he straightened and wiped the water from his eyes.

'Forgive me, Majesty . . .'

Babur glanced round. The diminutive figure of Humayun's astrologer, in the rust-coloured robes that always looked too large for him, was standing beside him. Babur brushed his wet hair off his face. 'What is it?'

'I have been looking into the heavens, Majesty, trying to discern what is written there about God's plans for my master. There is something I must tell you. Your son's life lies in your hands. If you wish him to live you must make a great sacrifice . . .'

'I would do anything to save him.' Without realising it, Babur had seized the astrologer's wrist.

'You must offer up the most precious thing you possess . . .'

'What is that?'

'Only you can know, Majesty.'

Babur turned and, half running, half stumbling, made for the fort mosque. Flinging himself down on the stone floor before the ornately carved plaster niche of the *mihrab* he began to pray, rocking back and forth, eyes tight shut, pouring every ounce of himself into the promise he was making to God: 'Let me be the sacrifice. Let me take on the burden of my son's pain. Let me, not him, be the one to die . . . Take my life . . .'

•◆•

For three long days and nights, Babur had been sitting alone in his chambers, barely eating and drinking and postponing all official business. He knew he should go to Maham but the thought of her anxiety for her son – her only child –

on top of his own overwhelmed him. Neither could he write to Kamran and Askari in their distant provinces. What would he say to them? That Humayun had fallen ill and that the *hakim* held out little hope? Even if he did write, they could never reach Agra in time. And at the back of Babur's mind was a suspicion he could hardly bring himself to contemplate: that Kamran and Askari might not be sorry to learn that their older half-brother was dying.

Why hadn't God accepted his sacrifice? Why was he still breathing whilst Humayun's life ebbed . . . ? Babur had never known quite such depths of despair as the hours dragged by. Whichever path he tried to turn his mind down, it ended in the blackest darkness. Though the loss of Baburi had felt like the death of part of himself, that had been a personal grief. If Humayun died it would also be an overwhelming personal loss – he had become closer to Humayun than to any of his other sons – but it would be something more too. It would be God's way of saying that everything Babur had striven for, everything he had achieved, had been for nothing . . . that he would never found an empire or a dynasty to prosper in Hindustan . . . that he should never have come – or, at the very least, not tried to outdo Timur by staying on. He should have been less proud, less blown up with vanity, and contented himself with his mountainous lands beyond the Khyber Pass.

Babur glanced at his diary, lying open on a low table. What a piece of conceit it had been to think it worth giving to Humayun to guide him one day in ruling, never thinking his son might not live long enough to rule. He was tempted to throw it on to the fire, burning so bright and hot in Humayun's sick chamber . . . But he could no longer bring himself to go there and witness Humayun's shrieking, agonised delirium.

'Majesty . . .'

Babur turned. One of the *hakim*'s assistants was before

him. The man looked worn out, the skin beneath his eyes so shadowed it looked bruised. 'My master asks that you should come . . .'

Babur ran to Humayun's chamber.

Abdul-Malik was waiting for him at the entrance, hands folded across his stomach. 'Majesty . . . your son gave a great groan . . . and I thought – I truly believed – his end had come . . . Then his eyes opened and he looked at me and knew me . . . He is very weak but the fever has left him even more suddenly than it came . . .' The *hakim* shook his head, as much puzzled as he was joyful. 'I have never seen a case like it, Majesty . . . It is a miracle.'

◆

Humayun was cantering along the sunlit riverbank below the Agra fort, his black hawk in its tufted red leather hood on his gauntleted wrist. Later he would join him, Babur decided. It had been a long time since he'd gone hawking. First, though, he'd visit his gardens over the Jumna where he wished to discuss the planting of apricots with his gardeners. Reluctantly he drew his eyes from the sight of Humayun, so vigorous and strong again just four months after his miraculous recovery from his illness.

Babur made for the carved sandstone staircase that descended to a little gate at the base of the fortress wall. A few feet beyond it, further steps – narrow and mottled with lichen – led to the jetty where his gilded barge was waiting to carry him along the river. Suddenly he felt a searing pain in his stomach so severe that he gasped and put out a hand to clutch the balustrade. As the pain started to ease and he began to breathe more deeply, it came again, spreading to engulf his whole body. He swayed dizzily . . . 'Help me . . .'

Strong hands took hold of him under his armpits, raising him. Who was it? He looked up gratefully but saw nothing except an enfolding darkness.

'His bowels have not moved . . . he passes no urine . . . he doesn't eat. He's taken nothing but a little water for thirty-six hours now . . . Whether this is a delayed consequence of Buwa's poison I cannot say . . .'

Babur could hear voices, low, strained, anxious. Who were they talking about? His mouth and tongue were so dry . . . A few drops of water flowed between his parched lips. He tried to swallow but it was so hard . . . His eyes flickered briefly open. The figures hovering over him were shadowy and indistinct. He tasted more water – someone was gently pushing a metal spoon into his mouth . . . Now he knew who it was and where he was . . . He was lying ill in a cave tucked in a fold in the mountains where his enemies couldn't find him. Wazir Khan was on his knees beside him, dripping water into his mouth. As soon as he was well they would ride together for Ferghana . . .

'Wazir Khan . . . ?' He managed only a croaking rasp. 'Wazir Khan . . .' He tried again. That was better, his voice sounded louder this time.

'No, Father. It's me, Humayun.'

Humayun? Babur struggled to make sense of this and failed.

'Your son.'

This time it registered. With a tremendous effort Babur brought himself back to the present, opened his green eyes and saw his son's stricken face. 'What . . . what is happening to me . . . ?'

'You're ill, Father. You've been drifting in and out of consciousness . . . You've had another attack – that makes four in all since you were first taken ill, each worse than the last, I'm afraid . . . But don't worry . . . Abdul-Malik is hopeful. He is doing what he can.'

After drinking a little more water – it was still all he could do to swallow – Babur lay back again, eyes closed, exhausted by the effort but feeling his faculties return. He must be seriously ill . . . perhaps so ill he was going to die . . . The prospect sent an involuntary shudder through him. Could it really be? Not when he still had so much to do in his fledgling empire . . . so much of life to enjoy. He wanted to see his sons mature and guide them as they did so. Surely God would not deny him that . . .

But then another thought washed through his mind. Perhaps God had decided to call in his promise to give his own life for Humayun's. Perhaps he had been right when, in his euphoria and relief at Humayun's miraculous recovery, he had believed God had listened to his despairing prayer . . . If so, the greatest achievement of his life had been to save his son because it was Humayun whom God intended to secure the future of the empire. Maybe there was a pattern, a meaning to his life after all. That would be a pleasant, comforting thought. Babur lay back, defiance yielding to acceptance, even to a sense of triumph, in his hazy mind. What did his death matter so long as he had laid the foundations for his dynasty?

Then a new thought pierced him with a sudden and absolute clarity. If he really were going to die, either in fulfilment of his vow or by random fate, he must make Humayun's position secure. Otherwise, the fledgling Moghul empire would disintegrate, just as Timur's had done, into conflict between his sons and rebellion by his vassals. He must name Humayun his sole heir . . . bind his commanders and nobles to him . . . give him what guidance he could in the short time he had left . . .

Babur was beginning to sweat. His pulse was racing and the pains were returning. It needed all his resolve . . . more than in any battle . . . for his mind to master his body but – he told himself – he had never lacked courage. He pulled himself into a sitting position. 'Summon my council. I must speak to them . . . Have a scribe present to record my words.

But first let me speak to my sister alone ... Bring her quickly.'

While he waited, he tried silently to rehearse his words but his mind kept drifting.

'Babur ...' Khanzada's voice roused him.

'Sister, it is many years ago that you first looked down on me in my crib ... Since then we have endured much and achieved much. Like most brothers, I've never told you how much I've loved you ... appreciated you ... I do so now ... now that I feel I am dying. Try not to grieve ... I don't fear death, only what will happen to our dynasty when I am gone. I wish Humayun to succeed me but I worry his brothers will not accept it ... that they may rebel against him. You are the only blood kin common to all my sons. They respect you ... and what you have suffered for the family, so they will listen to you ... Watch over them as you once watched over me ... Remind them of their heritage and their duty to it ... and do not let their mothers incite their rivalries ...'

Babur paused, exhausted.

'I promise, little brother.' Khanzada's lips brushed his forehead and he felt moisture – her tears not his – on his cheek.

'We've travelled a long road, have we not, sister?' he whispered. 'A long and sometimes painful road, but one that has brought our family to a glorious destination ... Now call my attendants to put on my ceremonial robes. I must speak to my council and my time is ebbing ...'

A quarter of an hour later, when the council was ushered in, Babur was sitting in his green robes on one of his gilded thrones, cushions supporting his body. As they entered, Babur closed his eyes again but willed himself not to drift away. He must keep his mind clear. He heard a murmuring all around him.

'Father, they are here.'

Opening his eyes, Babur found he could no longer focus fully . . . No matter. What mattered was that they should all hear his words. He took a deep breath of air into his congested lungs and began: 'As you can see I am unwell . . . My life is in God's hands. Should I die, our great destiny must not die with me, evaporate in the heat and dust . . . It is up to you all to fulfil it, united as you are now, undistracted by internal strife. To achieve that you must know my wish for my successor.'

Babur paused to take more strength. 'I have for some time thought of Humayun as my heir because of his virtues and bravery . . . but seduced by my vigour, my desire, into assuming I might live long, I have failed to tell you. I do so now. I appoint Humayun my heir. I commend him to you. Swear to me you will follow him as loyally and bravely as you have followed me. Swear to him your allegiance.'

There was silence for a moment, then a united chorus: 'Majesty, we so swear.'

'Humayun, take Timur's ring from my finger. It is yours. Wear it with pride and never forget the duties it imposes on you to your dynasty and to your loyal people. Have you all heard my words?'

'Yes, Majesty.'

'Then leave me, all of you, except Humayun. I wish to be alone with my son . . .'

Babur shut his eyes and waited. He heard feet shuffling away over thick carpets but then a door closed and all was quiet. 'Are they gone?'

'Yes, Father.'

'Listen to me. I have some other things to say to you. First, take care to know yourself, to understand yourself, and how to master any weaknesses . . . but, above all, preserve the unity of our dynasty. I am not so foolish as to think jealousies will not arise between you and your half-brothers. Do nothing against them, however much you think they might deserve it. Reconcile them, love them. Remember the principle established by our ancestor Timur that the lives of princes are sacred . . . Promise me, Humayun . . . promise me you understand my commands and will fulfil them.'

Babur began to feel dizzy. He could hear nothing from Humayun. 'Why don't you answer me?'

'Do not distress yourself, Father. I promise.'

Babur slumped against the cushions, his face and body relaxing, but then he spoke once more. 'There is one last thing. Do not bury me here in Hindustan. This will become your homeland and the homeland of your children, but it is not mine. Take my body back to Kabul . . . I have written my wishes in my diary . . .'

Humayun was starting to sob.

'Don't be sad for me. It's what I prayed for when you were ill. Your astrologer told me what I must do – that I must offer up what was most precious to me. I offered God my life for yours and I did it gladly. God has been good. He gave us some time together before gathering in the debt . . .'

Humayun looked down at his father's wasted face. How could he tell him that that hadn't been what the astrologer had meant? The man had told him of the conversation. He had been asking Babur to give up some of his treasure, perhaps the Koh-i-Nur, his Mountain of Light, not his own life . . .

But a smile was curving his father's dry lips and he was trying to speak again. 'Don't grieve. It means God listened to me . . . I go gladly . . . knowing that you will continue what I have begun. They are all waiting for me, all those I loved who have gone before me to Paradise . . . my father, my mother and grandmother, Wazir Khan and my friend Baburi . . . even Timur with his eyes like candles without brilliance . . . I can see him and I will tell him what we did . . . how we, like him, crossed the Indus and won a great victory . . . how we . . .'

Babur felt a warm peace envelop him. He was falling, floating, his consciousness diminishing. Whatever he had been going to say next, Humayun would never know. With a long, low sigh his father breathed his last and his head slumped forward.

Humayun lowered his own head and began to pray: 'Speed my father to Paradise. Give me the strength to continue what he began so that, looking down on me, he will be proud . . . Give me the strength . . .'

Rising at last, Humayun took one last look at his father, then turned away. Tears filled his eyes again and he struggled to steady his voice. 'Abdul-Malik,' he called, 'the emperor is dead . . . Send for the embalmers . . .'

• ◆ •

Two days later, Humayun watched as six officers laid Babur's body, washed in camphor, wrapped in a soft, woollen shroud and enclosed in a silver coffin packed with spices, on a gilded cart drawn by twelve black oxen. Then, to the slow beating of drums, the funeral cortège began the long, slow journey that would take it north-west over the bleached plains of Hindustan, across the Indus and up through the winding, dun-grey hills of the Khyber Pass to Kabul. Humayun knew it was right that in death his father should return to the mountainous lands he had loved.

As Babur had asked, when his body reached Kabul it would be laid in the earth in the hillside garden Babur himself had created beneath a simple marble slab close to Baburi's grave and those of his mother and grandmother. As Babur had also wished, nothing would be constructed over it, no great edifice. The grave of the first Moghul emperor would lie exposed to the winds and soft rain beneath the infinite canopy of the sky.

Humayun glanced at Kamran, Askari and Hindal close beside him. Their sombre faces told him they shared his grief and that for the moment, they were united. But how long would that last? Might they come to resent his father having given him supreme power rather than dividing his realm between them? Ambition – the relentless hunger for fresh conquest and the power it would bring that he had long felt stir within himself – would undoubtedly rise in them, especially Kamran, so close to him in age . . . Would he not feel resentment in Kamran's place? Or Askari's? Even little Hindal might soon consider the world with a cool, ambitious, speculative eye. All sons of an emperor, it was in the blood of each of them to desire to be the one to lead their dynasty to new heights. How long before Babur's memory faded and brotherly feeling waned? Might they become like snapping dogs circling the same piece of meat? Before he realised what he was doing, Humayun stepped away from his half-brothers, whose eyes were still on the cortège as, with its escort, it slowly disappeared round a bend in the road through the city of Agra, leaving a pall of orange dust hanging in its wake.

'Do nothing against your half-brothers . . . love them . . . reconcile them . . .' Babur's words, the last instructions of a loved and loving father, resounded inside Humayun's head. He had made a promise to Babur and he would keep it. Doing so would not be easy and might demand all his self-restraint. Babur's words had in part been a warning . . . For generations the House of Timur had ripped itself apart. Brother had turned on brother, cousin on cousin, and their feuding had irredeemably weakened them, making them easy prey to external enemies like the Uzbeks. He, the new Moghul emperor, must not let that happen in Hindustan. It was his sacred duty.

Humayun looked down at Timur's heavy gold ring, an unaccustomed weight on his right hand, with the spitting, flat-eared tiger carved deep into the metal. It had seen so many conflicts, so many conquests . . . where would it travel with him? What glories, what disasters might it see while on his hand? That was not yet for him to know but, whatever happened, he would never bring dishonour on his dynasty or on his father's memory. Raising the ring to his lips he kissed it and made a silent vow: 'I will be a worthy successor to my father, and all the world will have cause to remember me.'

Historical Note

Babur's life was a whirlwind of battles, blood feuds and epic challenges so numerous that even he did not document everything in his disarmingly frank memoirs, the *Baburnama* – the first autobiography in Islamic literature. In fact, he left numerous gaps, some covering considerable periods of years. Despite these omissions, the main events of his life, such as his three captures of Samarkand, his conflict with the Uzbeks and, of course, his establishment of the Moghul Empire in north-western India – Hindustan, as it was then known – are clear from the *Baburnama* and other sources. I have described the principal events in their historical sequence, though condensing, combining or omitting some incidents and compressing some timescales.

Babur's grandmother Esan Dawlat – whose advice, he says in the *Baburnama*, he relied on in his youth – his mother Kutlugh Nigar and his sister Khanzada all existed, as did his traitorous half-brother Jahangir. Babur's father indeed fell to his death from his dovecote at Akhsi when the battlements collapsed beneath him. Similarly, Babur's main enemies – Shah Ismail of Persia, Sultan Ibrahim of Delhi and the Uzbek warlord Shaibani Khan, who really did carry off Khanzada, are also historical. However, I have used the liberties afforded to historical novelists to flesh out some of the other characters or to create new ones based on a combination of real people important in Babur's life. Wazir Khan and Baisanghar fall into these categories, as indeed does Baburi – though in his memoirs Babur writes fondly of a market boy of that name.

The social and military contexts are described as accurately as possible. For example, though he was a Sunni Muslim, Babur describes with relish his mammoth drinking binges and frequent consumption of *bhang* (cannabis) and opium. His acquisition from Ottoman Turkey of gunpowder weapons and his skilful deployment of them are also based on fact and were indeed the turning point in his fortunes.

At one time or other, I've visited nearly all the places important to Babur's story. His ancestral kingdom of Ferghana – in modern-day Uzbekistan and Kyrgyzstan – is still a place of apple, almond and apricot orchards, with beds of juicy melons the size of footballs. In late summer, men and women still thresh the grain by hand, using flails, sending clouds of golden chaff into the air, and herds of sheep, goats and shaggy yaks browse the high pastures, guarded by mounted herdsmen and their vigilant dogs. I've slept in their conical felt tents, eaten their root vegetables, mutton and buttered rice, which would have been so familiar to Babur, and drunk the fermented mare's milk that warmed him. In late September, I've felt the air turn suddenly chilly and watched the first snowflakes start to fall in the high passes. In spring, I've seen the rivers and streams swollen with meltwater. I've followed Babur over the rolling hills and golden grasslands to Samarkand, to Kabul where his simple grave – recently restored with funds from Unesco – still sits on the hillside above the city, down through the Khyber Pass to the plains of northern India, to Delhi, Agra and Rajasthan.

492

Everything I saw on those travels, everything I experienced, added to my admiration of and affection for Babur not only as warrior, adventurer, survivor and founder of the Moghul Empire but also as writer, gardener and lover of poetry and architecture.

Babur, of course, would have used the Muslim lunar calendar but I have converted dates into the conventional solar, Christian calendar we use in the west.

Specific Notes

p.3   Timur, a chieftain of the nomadic Barlas Turks, is better known in the west as Tamburlaine, a corruption of 'Timur the Lame'. Christopher Marlowe's play portrays him as 'The Scourge of God'.

p.30   The reading of the sermon, the *khutba*, in the mosque was the usual formal means of proclaiming sovereignty in Islamic countries.

p.59   Timur's fortress in Samarkand, the Kok Saray, was in later times destroyed by the Persians. A square now covers the site.

p.98   Registan Square: today two sides of the square are formed by *madrasas* built after Babur's time on the sites of earlier pilgrims' hostels and caravanserais. However, Ulugh Beg's exquisite *madrasa*, decorated with bright blue stars, survives from the early fifteenth century.

p.100   A Russian archaeologist in the early 1940s obtained permission to open Timur's tomb. He entered the crypt on 22 June 1941, at night to avoid offending local sensitivities. Around three a.m. he opened the coffin. Almost immediately his assistant rushed in with the news of the invasion by Hitler of Russia. His examination of Timur's remains took more than eighteen months and confirmed that Timur was lame through an injury to his right leg. Within days of the skeleton being reinterred, the Germans surrendered at Stalingrad.

p.104   The visionary Ulugh Beg's observatory on Kohak Hill outside Samarkand is thought to have been a three-storey circular tower with a diameter of some forty-six metres. The remains of the half of his giant sextant that was set into the ground can still be seen.

p.105   In the courtyard of the Bibi Khanym mosque, amid mulberry and quince trees, there is a giant marble stand on which the Osman Koran, said to be the second in history and captured by Timur from the Turks, once rested. It is now in Tashkent. Bibi Khanym's tomb lies opposite the mosque.

p.221 The story of Borte, Genghis Khan's wife, is true.

p.298 Humayun was born to Maham in 1508.

p.308 As Kamran was born to Gulrukh during a period not covered in the Baburnama, the precise date is unknown but he was clearly very close to Humayun in age.

p.324 Shah Ismail's forces killed Shaibani Khan in 1510. The Shah had a gold-mounted cup fashioned from his skull and sent the straw-stuffed skin of his head as a present to the Ottoman Turks.

p.340 The Safawid dynasty had made the Shia practice of Islam the state religion of Persia in 1501. The distinction between Shia and Sunni derived from the first century of Islam and originally related to who was Muhammad's legitimate successor and whether the office should be an elected one or restricted, as the Shias claimed, to the descendants of the Prophet through his cousin and son-in-law, Ali. 'Shia' means 'party' and comes from the phrase 'the party of Ali'. 'Sunni' means 'those who follow the custom, "Sunna", of Muhammad'. By the sixteenth century further differences had grown between the two sects, such as the nature of required daily prayer.

p.360 Askari was born to Gulrukh in 1516. Hindal was born to Dildar three years later, in 1519.

p.369 Maham did beg Babur – even before Hindal was born – to let her adopt Dildar's child and he agreed.

p.372 The sultan had several 'Great Bombards', one of which is today in the Fort Nelson Museum in Portsmouth, UK.

p.397 The battle of Panipat was fought on 20 April 1526.

p.435 In his memoirs Babur recorded meticulously, and in detail, the dreadful effects on his digestive system of the meal poisoned on Buwa's orders.

p.445 Babur's garden in Agra was sited across the Jumna from the spot where his direct descendant, Shah Jahan, built the Taj

Mahal as the mausoleum for his dead wife, Mumtaz Mahal. Shah Jahan modified Babur's garden to make it into a scented moonlight garden from which he could view his lost wife's tomb across the Jumna.

p.452   The battle of Khanua was fought on 17 March 1527.

p.487   Babur died on 26 December 1530, eight months after Humayun had fallen ill.

p.487   Babur's grave in his gardens above Kabul fell into dilapidation and was subsequently damaged during the recent troubles in Afghanistan. It and the gardens have been restored under the auspices of UNESCO and the Aga Khan's Foundation.

If you enjoyed

RAIDERS FROM THE NORTH

please read on for an exclusive extract
from Alex Rutherford's next novel in the thrilling
Empire of the Moghul series:

BROTHERS
AT WAR

coming soon from Headline.

Part I

Brotherly Love

Chapter 1

Riding the Tiger

The wind was chill. If Humayun closed his eyes he could almost imagine himself back among the pastures and mountains of the Kabul of his boyhood, rather than here on the battlements of Agra. But the short winter was ending. In a few weeks the plains of Hindustan would burn with heat and dust.

Drawing his fur-lined scarlet cloak more tightly around him, Humayun walked slowly along the walls. He had ordered his bodyguards to leave him because he wanted to be alone with his thoughts. Raising his head, he gazed up into clear skies that were splashed with stars. Their intense, jewel-like brightness never failed to fascinate him. It often seemed that everything was written there, if only you knew where to look and how to interpret the messages.

A firm, light footstep from somewhere behind him disturbed him. Humayun turned, wondering which courtier or guard had been rash enough to disobey their emperor's expressed wish for solitude. His angry gaze fell on a slight, tall figure in purple robes, a thin gauze veil pulled over the lower face, with above it the raisin eyes of his aunt, Khanzada. Humayun's face relaxed into a smile.

'We are waiting for you in the women's quarters. You said you would eat with us tonight. Your mother complains you spend too much time alone, and I agree with her.'

Khanzada dropped her veil. The tawny light from a torch burning in a sconce fell on a fine-boned face no longer as

501

beautiful as in her youth, but one that Humayun had loved and trusted for as many of his twenty-three years as he could remember. As she stepped a little closer he caught the soft fragrance of the sandalwood that burned constantly in jewelled golden saucers in the women's apartments.

'I have much to reflect on. I still find it difficult to accept that my father is dead.'

'I understand, Humayun. I loved him too. Babur was your father but don't forget he was also my little brother. He and I went through much together and I never thought to lose him so soon . . . but it was God's will . . .'

Humayun looked away, unwilling for even Khanzada to see the tears gleaming in his eyes at the thought that he would never see his father, the first Moghul emperor, again. It seemed incredible that this strong, seasoned warrior, who had led his nomadic horsemen down through the mountain passes from Kabul and across the Indus to found an empire, was dead. Even less real was the thought that only three months ago, with his father's eagle-hilted sword Alamgir at his waist and the ring of his ancestor Timur on his finger, he himself had been proclaimed Moghul emperor.

'It's so strange . . . like a fantasy from which I keep expecting to wake.'

'It's the real world and you must accept it. Everything Babur wanted, everything he fought for, had one purpose only – to win an empire and found a dynasty. You know that as well as I – weren't you fighting at your father's side when he crushed Sultan Ibrahim Lodi at Panipat to claim Hindustan for the Moghuls?'

Humayun said nothing. Instead he looked up once more at the sky. As he did so, a shooting star sped across the heavens and vanished, leaving not even a trace of its fiery tail. Glancing at Khanzada, he saw that she had seen it too.

'Perhaps the shooting star was an omen . . . perhaps it means my reign will fizzle out ingloriously, that no one will remember me . . .'

502

'Such self-doubt and hesitancy would anger your father if he were here now. Instead he would have you embrace your destiny. He could have chosen one of your three half-brothers as his heir but he selected you. Not just because you are the eldest – that has never been the way of our people – but because he thought you were the most worthy, the most able. Our hold on Hindustan is precarious – we have been here only five years and dangers press in from every side. Babur picked you because he trusted not just in your courage, which you had already demonstrated on the battlefield, but also in your inner strength and your self-belief, your sense of our family's right to rule, which our dynasty must have to survive and prosper here in this new land.' Khanzada paused.

When Humayun did not reply, she raised her face to the light of the torch and ran her finger down a thin white scar running from her right eyebrow almost to her chin. 'Do not forget how I got this scar, how when I was young and your father had to abandon Samarkand to the Uzbeks, I was seized by their chieftain Shaibani Khan and forced to submit to him. He hated all who, like us, have the blood of Timur. It gave him pleasure to humiliate and degrade a princess of our house. I give thanks that I never despaired all the time I was a captive in his *haram* . . . never forgot who I was or that it was my duty to survive. Remember that when another woman attacked me and stole some of my beauty, I wore this scar as a badge of honour – to show that I was still alive and that one day I would be free. After ten long years that day came. I re-joined my brother and rejoiced to see him drink to my return from a vessel made from the skull of Shaibani Khan. You must have the same self-belief, the same strength of character, Humayun, as I had.'

'Such courage as yours is hard to emulate but I will not fail my father or our house.'

'What is it, then? You are young, ambitious . . . you were eager for the throne long before your father fell ill. Babur knew; he spoke to me of it.'

'His death was so sudden when it came. I left so much unsaid.

503

I didn't feel ready to be emperor . . . at least not so soon, nor in such a way.'

Humayun let his head drop. It was true. His father's final moments still haunted him. Summoning the last of his strength Babur had ordered his attendants to dress him in his royal robes, seat him on his throne and call his nobles to him. Before the entire court, voice weak, but firm in his resolve, Babur had ordered Humayun to take Timur's heavy gold ring engraved with the head of a snarling tiger from his finger, saying 'Wear it with pride . . . never forget the duties to our dynasty it imposes on you.' But Babur had been just forty-seven, still in his prime and far too young to hand on his fledgling empire.

'No man, not even an emperor, can know when he will be called to paradise and in what manner. None of us can predict or control fully the course of our lives. Learning to live with the great uncertainty of mortality, as well as the other vicissitudes of fortune, is part of growing to adulthood.'

'Yes. But I often think there is more we can do to understand the underlying patterns behind our lives. Events that appear random may not be. For example, Aunt, you said just now that my father's death was God's will, but you're wrong. It was my father's will. He deliberately sacrificed himself for me.'

Khanzada stared. 'What do you mean?'

'I've never revealed to anyone my father's last words to me. Just before he died, he whispered that when I was sick with fever a few months earlier, my astrologer, Sharaf, had told him that he'd read in the stars that if he wished me to live he must offer up what was most precious to him. So he went to the mosque and falling on his face offered God his life for mine.'

'Then it was indeed God's will – God accepted the sacrifice.'

'No! Sharaf told me that all he intended was that my father should offer up the Koh-i-Nur diamond – not his life. But my father misinterpreted him . . . It seems overwhelming that my father loved me so much, saw me as so important to the future of our dynasty, that he offered his own life. How can I live up to such faith in me? I feel that I don't deserve the throne I once so hungered for. I fear that a reign that began in such a way will be tainted . . .'

'Such thoughts are absurd. You search too hard for patterns of cause and consequence. Many a reign begins in loss and uncertainty. It is up to you to make sure by your own actions that yours doesn't end so. Any sacrifice Babur made was done through love for you and trust in you. Remember also he did not die immediately – you recovered and he lived eight more months. His death at that time might well have been pure coincidence.' Khanzada paused. 'Did he say anything else to you in his last moments?'

'He told me not to grieve . . . he was happy . . . his life had been good. He also made me promise to do nothing against my half-brothers, however much they might deserve it.'

Khanzada's face tautened. For a moment Humayun thought she was about to say something about his brothers but instead, with a toss of her small, elegant head, she seemed to think better of it.

'Come. That's about enough of these musings. The cloth is spread in the *haram*. You must not keep your mother and the other ladies waiting. But Humayun . . . one last thought. Don't forget that your name means "fortunate". Fortune will be yours if you will be strong in mind as well as in body and seize it. Banish these foolish self-doubts of yours. Introspection may become a poet or a mystic but it has no place in the life of an emperor. Grasp with both hands what fate – and your father – have bequeathed you.'

With a last look up at the sky that showed him that the moon was now obscured by cloud, Humayun slowly followed his aunt towards the stone staircase that led down to the women's apartments.

◆

Prostrating himself before Humayun in the emperor's private chambers some weeks later, Baba Yasaval, his usually blunt, ebullient master of horse, looked strangely nervous. As the man rose again and looked up at him, Humayun noticed that his skin seemed stretched unnaturally tight over his wide cheekbones and a pulse throbbed at his temple.

'Majesty, if I might speak to you alone?' Baba Yasaval glanced at the guards positioned on either side of Humayun's low silver chair. It was an unusual request. Security dictated that the emperor was seldom on his own – even when he was in the *haram* guards were always near at hand, ready to turn an assassin's blade. But Baba Yasaval, who had fought loyally for Humayun's father, could be trusted.

Humayun dismissed his guards from the chamber and beckoned Baba Yasaval closer. The man approached but hesitated to speak, scratching his stubbly skull which, to remind him of the old ways of his clan since arriving in Hindustan, he had taken to shaving, except for a single lock of coarse, greying hair that swung like a tassel.

'Baba Yasaval, speak. What is it you wish to tell me?'

'Bad news . . . terrible news, Majesty . . .' A sigh that was almost a groan escaped Baba Yasaval's lips. 'There is a plot against you.'

'A plot?' Humayun's hand instinctively reached for the jewelled dagger tucked into his yellow sash, and before he knew it he had risen to his feet. 'Who would dare . . .?'

Baba Yasaval bowed his head. 'Your half-brothers, Majesty.'

'My brothers . . .?' Only two months ago he and they had stood side by side in the courtyard of the Agra fort as the gilded cart drawn by twelve black oxen and bearing their father's silver coffin departed on the long journey to Kabul, where Babur had asked to be buried. His half-brothers' faces had been as marked by grief as his own and in those moments he had felt a rush of affection for them and a confidence that they would help him complete the task their father had left unfinished: making the Moghuls' hold on Hindustan unassailable.

Baba Yasaval read the incredulity and shock on Humayun's face. 'Majesty, I speak the truth, though I wish for all our sakes that I did not . . .' Now that he had started, Baba Yasaval seemed to take courage, becoming again the tough warrior who had fought for the Moghuls at Panipat. His head was no longer bowed and he looked unflinching into Humayun's eyes. 'You will not doubt me when I tell you that I have this information from my youngest son . . . he is one of the conspirators. He came to me just an hour ago and confessed everything.'

'Why should he do that?' Humayun's eyes narrowed.

'Because he fears for his life . . . because he realises he has been foolish . . . because he knows his actions will bring ruin and disgrace on our clan.' As he spoke these last words, Baba Yasaval's face creased as he struggled to contain his emotions.

'You have done well to approach me. Tell me everything.'

'Scarcely a fortnight after His Majesty your father's coffin left for Kabul, the princes Kamran, Askari and Hindal met in a fort two days' ride from here. My son, as you know, serves Kamran, who offered him great rewards to join the plot. Hot-headed young fool that he is, he agreed, and so heard and saw everything.'

'What are my brothers planning?'

'To take you prisoner, force you to break up the empire and yield some of your territories to them. They wish to return to the old traditions, Majesty, when every son was entitled to a share of his father's lands.'

Humayun managed a mirthless smile. 'And then what? Would they be content? Of course not. How long before they were at each other's throats and our enemies began to circle?'

'You are right, Majesty. Even now, they can't agree amongst themselves. Kamran is the real instigator. The plot was his idea and he persuaded the others to join him, but then he and Askari came almost to blows over which of them was to have the richest provinces. Their men had to pull them apart.'

Humayun sat down again. Baba Yasaval's words rang true. His half-brother Kamran, just five months his junior, had made no secret of his resentment that while he had been left behind to govern as regent in Kabul, Humayun had accompanied their father on his invasion of Hindustan. Fifteen-year-old Askari,

Kamran's full brother, would not have been hard to persuade to join in. He had always followed worshipfully where Kamran led despite being both bullied and patronised by him. But if Baba Yasaval's account was accurate, now that he was almost a man, Askari wasn't afraid to challenge his older brother. Perhaps their strong-willed mother Gulrukh had encouraged them both.

But what about his youngest half-brother? Why had Hindal become involved? He was just twelve years old and Humayun's own mother, Maham, had brought him up. Years ago, distressed at her inability to bear any more children after Humayun, she had begged Babur to give her the child of another of his wives, Dildar. Though Hindal had still been in the womb, Babur − unable to deny his favourite wife − had made Maham a gift of the child. But perhaps he should not be so surprised at Hindal's treachery. Babur himself had been just twelve when he had first become a king. Ambition could flare in even the youngest prince.

'Majesty.' Baba Yasaval's earnest voice brought Humayun back to the present. 'My son believed the plot had been abandoned because the princes could not agree. But last night they met again, here in the Agra fort. They decided to bury their differences until they had you in their power. They plan to take advantage of what they call your "unkingly desire for solitude" and attack you when you next go riding alone. Kamran even spoke of killing you and making it appear like an accident. It was then that my son came to his senses. Realising the danger to Your Majesty, he told me what he should have confessed weeks ago.'

'I am grateful to you, Baba Yasaval, for your loyalty and bravery in coming to me like this. You are right. It is a terrible thing that my half-brothers should plot against me and so soon after our father's death. Have you mentioned this to anyone else?'

'No one, Majesty.'

'Good. Make sure you keep it to yourself. Leave me now. I need to consider what to do.'

Baba Yasaval hesitated then, instead of departing, threw himself on the ground before Humayun. He looked up with tears in his eyes. 'Majesty, my son, my foolish son . . . spare him . . . he sincerely repents his errors. He knows – and I know – how much he deserves your wrath and punishment, but I beg you, show him mercy . . .'

'Baba Yasaval. To show my gratitude to you not only for this information but for all your past services I will not punish your son. His actions were the indiscretions of a simple youth. But keep him close confined till all this is over.'

A tremor seemed to pass through Baba Yasaval and for a moment he closed his eyes. Then he rose and, shaven head bowed, backed slowly away.

As soon as he was alone, Humayun leaped to his feet and seizing a jewelled cup flung it across the chamber. The fools! The idiots! If his brothers had their way, the Moghuls would quickly return to a nomadic life of petty tribal rivalries and lose their hard-won empire. Where was their sense of destiny, their sense of what they owed their father?

Just five years ago Humayun had ridden by Babur's side as they swept down through the Khyber Pass to glory. His pulses still quickened at the memory of the roar and blood of battle, the odour of his stallion's acrid sweat filling his nostrils, the trumpeting of Sultan Ibrahim's war elephants, the boom of Moghul cannon and the crack of Moghul muskets as these new weapons cut down rank after rank of the enemy. He could still recall the ecstatic joy of victory when – bloodstained sword in hand – he had surveyed the dusty plains of Panipat and realised that Hindustan was Moghul. Now all that was being put at risk.

I'll not have it – this *taktya, takhta*, 'throne or coffin' as our people called it when we ruled in Central Asia. We're in a new land and must adopt new ways or we'll lose everything, Humayun thought. Reaching inside his robe for the key he wore round his neck on a slender gold chain, he rose and went to a domed casket in a corner of the chamber. He unlocked it, pushed back the lid and quickly found what he was seeking – a flowered silk bag secured with a twist of gold cord. He opened the bag slowly, almost reverently, and drew out the contents – a large diamond whose translucent brilliance made him catch his breath each time he saw it. 'My Koh-i-Nur, my Mountain of Light,' he whispered, running his fingers over the shining facets. Presented to him by an Indian princess whose family he had protected in the chaos after the battle of Panipat, its flawless beauty always seemed to him the embodiment of everything the Moghuls had come to India to find – glory and magnificence to outshine even the Shah of Persia.

Still holding the gem, Humayun returned to his chair to think. He sat brooding and alone until the sound of the court timekeeper – the *ghariyali*, striking his brass disc in the courtyard below to signal the end of his *pahar* – his watch – reminded Humayun that night was falling.

This was his first major test, he realised, and he would rise to it. Whatever his personal feelings – at this moment he'd like to take each of his half-brothers by the neck in turn and throttle the life from them – he must do nothing rash, nothing to show that the plot had been betrayed. Baba Yasaval's request for a private audience would have been noticed. If only his grandfather Baisanghar, or Kasim, who had been one of his father's most trusted advisers, were here. But the two older men had accompanied Babur's funeral cortège to Kabul to oversee his burial there. They would not return for some months. His father had once spoken to him of the burden of kingship, the loneliness it brought. For the first time, Humayun was beginning to understand what Babur had meant. He knew that he and he alone must decide what to do, and until then he must keep his own counsel.

Feeling the need to calm himself, Humayun decided to pass the night with his favourite among his concubines – a pliant, full-mouthed young woman with grey eyes, from the mountains north of Kabul. With her silken skin and breasts like young pomegranates, Salima knew how to transport his body and patently enjoyed doing so. Perhaps her caresses would also help clear his mind and order his thoughts and thus lighten the road ahead, which seemed suddenly and ominously dark.

· ◆ ·

Three hours later, Humayun lay back naked against a silk-covered bolster in Salima's room in the *haram*. His muscular body, scarred as befitted a tested warrior, gleamed with the almond oil she had teasingly massaged into his skin until, unable to wait a moment longer, he had pulled her to him. Her robe of transparent yellow muslin – a product of Humayun's new lands where weavers spun cloth of such delicacy they gave it names like 'breath of wind' or 'dawn dew' – lay discarded on the flower-patterned carpet. Though the pleasure Salima had given him and her response to him had been as intense as ever and Humayun had relaxed, his mind kept drifting back to Baba Yasaval's revelations, re-igniting his anger and frustration.

'Bring me some rosewater to drink, Salima please.' She returned moments later with a silver cup inlaid with roundels of rose quartz. The water – chilled by ice carried down in huge slabs from the northern mountains by camel trains – smelled good. From a small wooden box beside the bed, Humayun extracted some opium pellets and dropped them into the cup where they dissolved in a milky swirl.

'Drink.' He raised the cup to Salima's lips and watched her swallow. He wished her to share his pleasure but somewhat to his shame he also had another purpose in doing so. His father had nearly died when Buwa – mother of his defeated enemy Sultan Ibrahim – had tried to poison him in revenge for the death of her son. Since then, Humayun had been wary of anything untasted by others . . .

'Here, Majesty.' Salima, lips lusciously moist with rosewater, kissed him, then handed him the cup. He drank deeply, willing the opium that in recent weeks had helped blunt his grief and lessen his anxieties to do its work, uncoiling softly through his mind and carrying him to pleasurable oblivion.

But maybe tonight he had taken too much or was expecting too much of its soothing powers. As he lay back, portentous images began forming in his mind. The gleaming blue domes and slender minarets of an exquisite city rose before him. Though he'd been too young to remember his brief time there, he knew

511

it was Samarkand, capital of his great ancestor Timur and the city his father had captured, lost and yearned for all his life. From Babur's vivid accounts, Humayun knew he was standing in the Registan Square in the centre of the city. A crouching orange tiger on the soaring gateway before him was coming alive as he watched, ears flattened, lips drawn back over pointed teeth ready to spit defiance. Its eyes were as green as Kamran's.

Suddenly Humayun felt himself on the tiger's back, wrestling it with all his strength, feeling its sinewy body twist beneath him. He gripped hard with his thighs, smelling its hot breath as, arcing its body and swinging its head from side to side, it fought to dislodge him. Humayun locked his legs yet tighter around the animal and felt its flanks writhe and plunge anew. He would not be thrown off. He leaned forward, sliding his hands beneath its body. His fingers encountered flesh that was soft and smooth and within it a warm, rhythmic pulse, the source of its life force. As he began to grip harder, to press and to thrust, the beast's breath came in jerky, rasping gasps.

'Majesty . . . please . . .'

Another, weaker voice was trying to reach him. It, too, was gasping for breath. Opening his eyes and looking down through his dilated pupils, Humayun saw not a wild tiger but Salima. Her body, like his, was running with sweat as if the moment of climax were approaching. But though he was indeed possessing her, his hands were gripping her breasts, grasping the soft flesh as if Salima was the ravaging beast he was fighting to subdue. He relaxed his grip but continued to thrust harder and harder until finally they both climaxed and collapsed.

'Salima, I'm sorry. I should not have used you in such a way. I felt thoughts of conquest mingling with my desire for you.'

'No need for sorrow, your love-making filled me with pleasure. You were in another world and I was willingly serving you in that world as I do in this. I know you would never intentionally hurt me. Now make love to me again, this time more softly.'

Humayun gladly complied. Later, as he lay back exhausted and still dazed by opium, *haram* attendants came to sponge his body with cool scented water. Finally, wrapped in Salima's arms, he found sleep. This time he dreamed of nothing at all, waking only when the soft light began shafting through the latticed window of the room. As he watched the strengthening rays play over the carved sandstone ceiling above him, he knew what he must do. His battle of wills with the tiger had told him. He was the ruler. He should not always be gentle. Respect came with knowing when to be strong too.

•◆•

'Majesty. Your orders have been carried out.'

From his throne on its marble dais in the audience chamber – the *durbar* hall – with his courtiers and commanders positioned around him in strict order of precedence, Humayun looked down at the captain of his bodyguard. He already knew what had happened – the officer had come to him soon after midnight – but it was important that all the court should hear it and witness the scene about to take place.

'You have done well. Tell the court what occurred.'

'As Your Majesty instructed, I and a detachment of guards arrested your half-brothers last night while they were feasting in Prince Kamran's apartments.'

As a collective gasp went up around him, Humayun smiled inwardly. He had chosen his time well. Since Baba Yasaval's warning he had kept safely within the fort. Then, a week ago, a consignment of red wine from Ghazni, the finest the kingdom of Kabul could produce, heady and rich, had arrived by mule train – a timely gift from his maternal grandfather, Baisanghar. Knowing Kamran's love of wine, Humayun had presented some to him. As he had guessed, Kamran's invitation to all his brothers to join him in drinking it had not been long in coming. Humayun himself had declined it graciously but Askari and even young Hindal, not yet of an age to enjoy drinking but doubtless flattered to be in company with those who did, had hurried eagerly to the party. With all three together and off their guard, the opportunity for Humayun to act decisively had been perfect.

513

'Did my brothers resist?'

'Prince Kamran drew his dagger and wounded one of my men, slicing off part of his ear, but he was soon overcome. The others did not try to fight.'

Humayun's gaze swept the faces before him. 'Some days ago, I received word of a plot. My half-brothers intended to kidnap me and force me to relinquish some of my lands – perhaps even kill me.' His courtiers looked suitably shocked. How many were play-acting, Humayun wondered. Some, at least, must have known of the plot, even tacitly acquiesced in it. A number of the tribal chieftains who had accompanied Babur on his conquest of Hindustan had never adjusted to their new home. They disliked this new land with its featureless, seemingly endless plains, hot, gritty winds and drenching monsoon rains. In their hearts, they longed for the snow-dusted mountains and cool rivers of their homelands over the Khyber Pass and beyond. Quite a few would have welcomed an opportunity to collude with the conspirators that would enable them to return home richly rewarded. Well, let them sweat a bit now . . .

'Fetch my brothers before me so that I can question them as to their associates.'

The silence was absolute as Humayun and his courtiers waited. At last, the sound of metal chains scraping the stone slabs of the courtyard beyond the audience chamber broke the silence. Looking up, Humayun saw his brothers enter in a stumbling line, half dragged along by the guards. Kamran was first, his hawk-nosed, thin-lipped face showing nothing but disdain. He might have shackles on his legs but the proud carriage of his head showed he had no intention of pleading. Askari, shorter and slighter, was another matter. His unshaven face was creased with anxiety and his small eyes looked beseechingly at Humayun from beneath his dark brows. Hindal, at first half hidden behind his two elder half-brothers, was gazing about him, his young face beneath his tangle of hair blank rather than fearful, as if what was happening were beyond him.

As the guards stepped back from them, Askari and Hindal,

though hampered by their chains, prostrated themselves full length on the ground before Humayun in the traditional obeisance of the *korunush*. After several moments' hesitation, and with a contemptuous half-smile, Kamran did the same.

'On your feet.'

Humayun waited until all three had struggled to stand. Now that he could study them more closely he saw that Kamran had a dark bruise on the side of his face.

'What have you to say for yourselves? You are my half-brothers. Why did you scheme against me?'

'We didn't . . . it's not true . . .' Askari's tone, shrill and nervous, was unconvincing.

'You're lying. It's written on your face. If you do so again, I'll have you put to the torture. Kamran, as the eldest, answer my question. Why did you seek to betray me?'

Kamran's eyes – green as their father Babur's had been – were slits as he looked up at Humayun on his glittering throne. 'The plot was my idea – punish me, not them. It was the only way to redress the wrong done to us. As you yourself said, we are all Babur's sons. Doesn't the blood of Timur flow through all our veins? And through our grandmother, Kutlugh Nigar, the blood of Genghis Khan as well? Yet we have been left with nothing except to be your lackeys, to be sent hither and thither according to your whim. You treat us as slaves, not princes.'

'And you behave – all of you, not just you, Kamran – like common criminals, not brothers. Where is your sense of loyalty to our dynasty, if not to me?' Glancing up at an intricately carved wooden grille set high in the wall to the right of his throne, Humayun caught the flash of a dark eye. Doubtless Khanzada and probably his mother Maham, were observing him from the little gallery behind it where the royal women, unseen, could watch and listen to the business of the court. Perhaps Gulrukh and Dildar were also there, waiting in trembling anticipation for the sentence he was about to pronounce on their sons.

But now that the moment had come, Humayun felt strangely

515

reluctant. Even half an hour ago he had been certain what he would do – ruthless as Timur, he would order Kamran's and Askari's immediate execution and send Hindal to perpetual imprisonment in some far-off fortress. Yet looking down at the three of them – Kamran so arrogant and defiant, Askari and young Hindal plainly terrified – Humayun felt his anger ebbing. Their father had been dead only a few months; how could he ignore Babur's dying words? *Do nothing against your brothers, however much they might deserve it.* Just as in love-making, there was a time to be rigorous and a time to be gentle.

Stepping down from his throne, Humayun walked slowly over to his brothers and, starting with Kamran, embraced them. The trio stood before him, swaying slightly, expressions confused as they searched his face for the meaning of his actions. 'It is not fitting that we brothers should quarrel. I do not wish to spill the blood of our house into the earth of this new land of ours – it would be a bad omen for our dynasty. Swear your loyalty to me and you shall live. Then I will give you provinces to govern which, though part of the empire, you shall rule as your own, subject only to me.'

Around him, Humayun caught sounds first of astonishment and then of approval rising from his courtiers and commanders, and pride flooded through him. This was real greatness. This was truly how an emperor should act – crushing dissent but then showing magnanimity. As he embraced his brothers a second time, grateful tears shimmered in Askari's and Hindal's eyes. Kamran's green ones remained dry. His expression was bleak and unfathomable.